PENGUIN

If You Didn

Annie Taylor is a writer and freelance copywriter. She has a BA in American Studies from the University of Birmingham and a Masters in English and American Studies from Oxford. Her previous published works include *Forget Me Not* and *Innocent or Guilty*, under the name A. M. Taylor, and *The Truth About Her*.

By the same author

The Truth About Her

If You Didn't Kill Her

ANNIE TAYLOR

PENGUIN BOOKS

PENGUIN BOOKS

UK | USA | Canada | Ireland | Australia
India | New Zealand | South Africa

Penguin Books, Penguin Random House UK,
One Embassy Gardens, 8 Viaduct Gardens, London SW11 7BW

penguin.co.uk
global.penguinrandomhouse.com

First published 2024
001

Set in 12.5/14.75pt Garamond MT Std
Typeset by Jouve (UK), Milton Keynes
Printed and bound in Great Britain by Clays Ltd, Elcograf S.p.A.

The authorized representative in the EEA is Penguin Random House Ireland,
Morrison Chambers, 32 Nassau Street, Dublin D02 YH68

A CIP catalogue record for this book is available from the British Library

ISBN: 978-1-405-95460-0

www.greenpenguin.co.uk

For the lodge.
And also for Soph and Cojo.

*Transcript of interview with Chelsea Keough on 28 October 2007
conducted by Detective Inspector Rob Bailey and Detective
Constable Natalie Ajala at Birmingham Central Police Station*

Detective Inspector Rob Bailey: What is your relationship
with the deceased, Isabella Dunwoody?

Chelsea Keough: She's … she's my friend. And housemate.
Was, sorry. She was my housemate.

RB: How long have you been housemates?

CK: Since September.

RB: September of this year? So just for a month or so?

CK: Yes.

RB: And how long have you known her?

CK: Um …

RB: That's a fairly simple question, isn't it?

CK: Not really. We went to school together, but we weren't
friends until uni. Until last year.

RB: Okay, so you went to school together. Do you mean
secondary school?

CK: Yes.

RB: So, you've known each other since you were eleven,
twelve?

CK: Well no. Not really. She was in the year above, so I knew
of her. I knew her by sight. But we weren't friends. I'm not
sure we'd ever even spoken until Freshers'.

RB: Freshers' Week? Was that September last year?

CK: September, yeah.

RB: Okay, so last September. But you weren't living together
last year?

CK: No. We were in the same halls, but we didn't live together. We weren't in the same flat.

RB: And when did you decide to move in together?

CK: Um, just before Christmas. That's when you start having to find accommodation for second year.

RB: Okay, let's fast-forward a bit here. When did you last see Isabella alive?

CK [quietly]: Izzy.

RB: Sorry?

CK: Izzy. No one calls her Isabella. *Called* her Isabella. God, I'm sorry, I can't … I can't get used to that.

RB: That's okay, Chelsea, you can take your time with these answers. So, when did you last see Izzy alive?

[long pause]

CK [sniffling]: I'm sorry, can I have a tissue? And some water?

[pause]

RB [sigh]: Sure. Constable, could you see to that?

[sound of chair scraping floor]

For the recording, Detective Constable Natalie Ajala has left the room.

[sound of crying]

[sound of door opening and closing]

RB [coughs]: For the recording, DC Ajala has returned to the room.

Detective Constable Natalie Ajala [quietly]: Here you go. Chelsea, are you okay? I'm sorry we have to do this, we just need to establish a timeline of events.

CK [through tears]: I know …

[sound of nose blowing]

NA: Chelsea, are you okay to continue?

CK: [unintelligible]

RB: Chelsea? We need audible replies for the recording.

CK: Yes, I'm okay.

RB: When did you last see Izzy alive?

CK [deep breath]: Last night. I think ... I think it was probably about one o'clock.

RB: One o'clock this morning? The morning of Sunday, October the twenty-eighth, to be clear.

CK: Yes.

RB: Was this at your residence, 257 Tiverton Road?

CK: No, we were out. It was at the Factory.

RB: That's in Digbeth?

CK: Yes.

RB: Do you know if she left alone?

CK: I think so.

RB: This was at one o'clock?

CK: Maybe ... it might have been a bit before, I can't remember the exact time, but I remember thinking it was early.

RB: One o'clock is early? Here I was thinking that was pretty late.

CK: We didn't get there until almost eleven. It was early. But she just didn't seem to be in the mood.

RB: For a party?

CK: Yeah.

RB: How did she seem? Was she drunk?

CK [sniffles]: She was pretty drunk, yeah.

RB: Even though she wasn't in the mood to party?

CK: She was ...

[sound of sniffles, blowing nose]

Sorry, this is hard.

RB: It's okay, take your time. Why don't you have some water?

CK: Thanks.

[pause, sound of water being sipped]

She was drunk, but it was … I don't know, she was sad drunk, I suppose. I felt bad not going home with her, but she said I should stay.

NA: Why was she sad, Chelsea?

CK: Her dad died last month. It was sudden. This was the first time she'd come out like that, to a club.

RB: That's very sad. Had they been close?

CK: Yes, very. I shouldn't have made her come … it was so stupid, but I really thought it would make her feel better.

NA: You can't have known, Chelsea.

CK [crying]: But if I'd just been a better friend …

[pause as CK cries]

RB: Chelsea, I'm very sorry, but if we can just go back to last night again. You didn't see anyone else leave with her?

CK: No. She texted to tell me she was going home.

RB: So, you didn't actually see her leave?

CK: No, I guess not.

RB: Do you know how she got home?

CK: She would have got a cab. A minicab.

RB: And what time did you get home?

CK: I'm not completely sure, but maybe about four. No, a bit before four, maybe?

RB: Four o'clock on the morning of Sunday, October twenty-eighth?

CK: Yes. But I'm not completely sure, I can't remember. Maybe more like three thirty.

RB: But you didn't see Izzy?

CK: No, I was trying to be quiet. I didn't want to wake her up.

4

RB: And did you go straight to bed?

CK: Yeah, I think so. I can't remember exactly, but I probably went to the bathroom and then went straight to bed.

RB: What time did you wake up this morning?

CK: I think about eleven, eleven thirty.

RB: Eleven thirty?

CK: I think, but I just went to the loo, got some food and went straight back to bed. I fell asleep again, but I don't know what time it was.

RB: And at this point you hadn't seen Izzy, hadn't said hello or good morning to her, hadn't checked if she was okay?

CK [quietly]: No.

RB: And this was at about eleven thirty, we think? Shall we say eleven thirty?

CK: Probably. I don't know for sure. Look … should I … do I need a solicitor?

RB: No, no, like we said, we need your help with establishing a timeline, this is just a helpful chat. You're an invaluable witness, Chelsea. So, to go back: you called the police at … three seventeen p.m.

CK: Yeah … yes.

RB: That's almost four hours, Chelsea.

CK [swallows]: I know … I really think'… I think I should talk to someone? I'd like to talk to someone.

RB: Four hours is quite a long time. You didn't check on her in all that time?

CK: No, I … I fell back to sleep for a bit, like I said, and then I woke up and I thought she'd be up by then too, but she wasn't so that's when I … went into the room. That's when I found her.

In the end it's her aunt who picks her up. Her aunt on the other side of that gate, waiting to welcome her back into the world.

It should have been her mother, of course. For the first thirteen years of her sentence, it was always her mother who Chelsea saw standing there on the day she was finally released. But then her mother died. A massive heart attack at the age of fifty-seven, gone in sixty seconds, never to see her daughter again. Alternatively: never to be seen by her daughter again.

So, it's Nikki waiting for her.

They don't hug. Nikki just gives Chelsea a tight smile and nods her head in the direction of the car. 'Sorry love, nothing personal, I just absolutely reek. Long drive.'

'Don't worry about it,' Chelsea says. 'I wouldn't want to get my prison stink all over you anyway.'

Nikki cuts her eyes at her, a sliding, slicing glance. 'Okay.'

Her mother would have hugged her, of course, but Chelsea has to stop this thought from fully forming. If she dwells too long on the ways in which Louise and Nikki are similar yet different, she might not be able to get through the next few hours, the next few days.

There may have been eight years between them, but Chelsea can hear her mother every time Nikki speaks.

Their London accents with a blink-and-you'll-miss-it Irish lilt.

The car is moving now, moving away from Foston Hall, moving away from the last sixteen years of her life.

Nikki changes gears efficiently, speeding up. She glances at Chelsea, sees her flinch. 'Don't worry, love, it'll be disappearing from the rear-view mirror before you know it.'

Chelsea nods, her jaw giving an involuntary twitch. She doesn't look back.

They've been driving for just over two and a half hours when Nikki stops for a break, smoothly curving her way into a parking space and bringing the car to a stop. Chelsea watches as her aunt cracks her neck and rolls down her shoulders.

'Coming?' Nikki says, once the engine is off and she's undone her seatbelt. 'I know you must be desperate for a wee by now. Plus, I don't want to toot my own horn or anything, but I have purposefully stopped at what has been voted the nicest service station in the country several years in a row.'

'Wow,' Chelsea says, 'quite the accolade.'

Nikki shakes a finger in her direction, 'Just you wait until you see it, Chelsea Keough. You're going to eat that sarcasm.'

But Chelsea still doesn't make a move. She is desperate for the toilet, her aunt is right. And she wants to stretch her legs. But the whole time she imagined this part of her release, she hadn't imagined coming face-to-face with the public so soon. She'd failed to take into account the fact that Nikki lives in Scotland now, and that, on a long drive, you tend to have to take breaks.

8

'What's going on? You look like you've seen a ghost,' Nikki says.

'Do you think anyone will recognize me?' Chelsea finally says.

Nikki looks taken aback at first, but then understanding clears her face. 'No, I don't think so, love,' she says slowly.

'But what about the papers? Has it been reported? My release?'

'No, it hasn't been picked up by the media yet, the fact that you've been released early.' Chelsea nods, chewing at the inside of her bottom lip. The early release was a surprise, due to years of good behaviour and an overcrowded prison system, and although she knows it wouldn't have been publicly announced, she also knows that people – and specifically the media – have a way of getting hold of this information anyway. 'Besides,' Nikki continues, 'maybe you'll be pleasantly surprised, and people will have moved on.'

People will have moved on. The words shouldn't hit her the way they do – of course people have moved on. She wants them to, to forget all about her. But *she* hasn't. Hasn't been able to, hasn't been allowed to. She's been stuck, quite literally, staring at the four walls her life was reduced to, for something she didn't do. Not just something. The worst thing. Murder. The thought burns through her and she worries at her lip so hard she starts to taste pennies and the look of concern on her face turns to a grimace. 'Come on,' Nikki says, slapping her palm down on Chelsea's thigh and giving it a shake, her faux cheer unconvincing. 'I don't think anyone's going to recognize you. And if it looks like they might, I'll cover for you.' This isn't all that reassuring. How exactly would Nikki be able to 'cover' for her? But Chelsea does need to use the toilet, and to make matters worse, her stomach has begun to rumble. So, she unbuckles her seatbelt and gets out of the car, looking towards the bright lights of the service station. It's surprising how familiar it is, that sight, the years of normal memories temporarily outweighing the past sixteen years of static, but then a family charges past them, one of the kids blaring an unknown song from their mobile and another with their head bent over their own phone, and Chelsea feels unmoored again, lost in what should be a totally innocent scene. Nikki has hurried on ahead, and Chelsea has to jog to catch up, a feeling, she realizes, she may never be able to shake.

The small car is stuffed. Three suitcases, a rucksack, one of those giant blue IKEA bags brimming with pots and pans, bedding, a bedside lamp – the shopping spree an early birthday present her mum treated her to last week. Everything else is second-hand and in boxes she borrowed and begged from the local corner shop.

The car is so laden, they're actually going at the speed limit – a once-in-a-lifetime thing for her mum, who may be a paralegal but has the soul of a boy racer once she gets inside a car. They're travelling the inside lane for once, hugging the edge of the M40. London is behind them, somewhere in the rear-view mirror, the choked-up traffic a thing of the past as they make their way up the motorway in the after-work dark. Her mum couldn't get the time off work, and Chelsea couldn't change her move-in date to a weekend, so here they are, at seven o'clock on a Thursday evening, moving her across country into halls. Louise will settle her in and then turn right back around and drive home to London. Or so she says. Because Chelsea knows she'll probably end up staying, forcing her to spend her first night of university sleeping on the floor, so that her mum can get a few hours of sleep before driving back to London to get to the office on time.

This is how they work together; Louise comes up with a plan, and Chelsea anticipates the ways in which that plan will necessarily change. She is almost always right.

'You're quiet,' Louise says, glancing at her. There's one of their favourite mix tapes playing. Louise gave Chelsea licence to pick and choose the tunes for the drive, 'Nothing maudlin, though,' she'd stipulated. 'There's a time and a place for that stuff, Chels. Let's have something upbeat, yeah? Get me through this drive.' So, Chelsea chose a party mix, one she'd made for Louise's fortieth birthday a few years ago. A weird mix of Cher and ABBA, Prince, and Bloc Party and the Libertines. A weird mix that worked.

'Chels?' Louise says again. 'You're a million miles away. You're not nervous, are you?'

Chelsea shrugs, 'Shouldn't I be?'

'Yeah, I suppose that's normal. You're going to be fine though. What is it you're most nervous about?'

Chelsea sighs. Her mum would ask this question. She knows her answer, of course, but she's too chicken to say. Would Louise even understand? Her mum who is so outgoing and confident, and magnetic and inviting she could make friends with a lamppost? 'Hmm?' Louise says now, casting another sidelong glance her way. 'Let me work this out for you. It won't be the work because you're too good at that. It's not going to be getting around a new city because you have a photographic memory when it comes to map-reading and seemed to know Rome like the back of your hand even when we'd only been there for twenty-four hours.'

Chelsea lets out a laugh at this and her mum smiles. 'It's called being able to read a map,' Chelsea points out, shaking the Ordnance Survey that's open on her lap.

'Yeah, yeah, show-off. So, as we've established, you'll

be fine getting around, and it's definitely not going to be living on your own because A, you'll have five flatmates, and B, you have basically been the head of our household for ten years . . .'

Louise waits for another laugh but when it doesn't come, she blithely continues, 'So, it must be the friends thing. Meeting new people.'

'How did you guess?' Chelsea says as drily as possible. Louise smiles at the road in front of her, and reaches across to her only daughter, giving her knee a squeeze.

'You're gonna be fine, babe. This is your time. I've always known you were a university girl. Just you wait and see, you'll find your people, you'll find your place.'

Chelsea nods in response, but there is still an annoyingly and embarrassingly large lump in her throat, one that makes her too nervous to say anything, lest she burst into tears. She's not meant to cry, going off to university – shouldn't that be her mum? But all that new-ness, all that unknown, all that's still to come, has her brain in overdrive, her heart heavy and loud. She didn't have a lot of friends at school, hell she didn't really have any. Just people she shared notes with, spent lunchtime with, people she left behind at the school gates. But at least she'd known what every day looked like, at least she'd known what she was doing. Now, she has to start all over again. Louise looks over at her and smiles, her fingers reaching to turn up the volume on 'Super Trouper' as she starts to sing loudly along and, despite her worry and her fears, the lump in her throat, it only takes a second or two before Chelsea joins in.

* * *

It's five a.m. when the alarm her mum set goes off. Chelsea had predicted the course of events correctly, and Louise had ended up staying the night, and Chelsea had ended up sleeping on the floor.

Louise groans now, reaches for the bedside alarm clock Chelsea has had since she was eleven years old and turns it off, shuffling her way out of bed as quietly as possible. Chelsea doesn't move. She's hardly comfortable, on the sofa cushions from the shared common room next door, but she is warm, her limbs heavy with exhaustion, so she keeps her eyes closed as she listens to her mum getting ready to leave. Somehow, Chelsea has ended up in student halls with an en-suite bathroom; Louise had let out a whistle when she'd first seen it. Now, Chelsea can hear her taking a quick shower, before brushing her teeth with Chelsea's toothbrush.

Twenty-five minutes later, Louise is washed, dressed and ready to go. Chelsea yawns as she gets up from the bedroom floor. In the morning half-light of her strange new bedroom, Louise looks both young and old at the same time and Chelsea realizes that this it: everything is about to change. Staying the night had delayed the inevitable, had stopped the future from happening just one night longer, but now it is staring them both starkly in the face. Louise is leaving and Chelsea is staying, and in a matter of minutes, they will no longer live together.

'Don't you want any breakfast?' she asks her mum, whispering to avoid waking up her new flatmates.

'No, I'm fine, babe. I better get on the road. I'll stop at that McDonald's drive-thru we saw on the way here.'

'You haven't even had a cup of tea.'

'I'm fine, Chels, you go back to bed.'

But Chelsea walks her out. They go down the outside stairs in silence, the dark surrounding them, their dual tread on the concrete steps the only sound they hear. They say goodbye next to the Clio and Chelsea holds on longer than she thought she would; she can feel Louise holding back tears, swallowing them down as they hug. Chelsea is taller than her mum, has been since she was twelve or thirteen, and for the first time in a long time, she thinks back to when she was smaller, when Louise could envelop her in love. Now, she is always the comforter, even as they comfort each other.

'All right, love,' Louise says as she pulls free, 'I'll see you in a couple of months, eh? Remember, this is all the beginning of something amazing. Your life's about to start.'

Chelsea nods, suddenly unable to speak. 'But you can still call whenever you want,' her mother adds, seeing her daughter's stricken face in the smudgy pre-dawn light.

As Louise exits the car park, another car pulls in. The early hour keeps Chelsea there, watching; surely, someone can't be moving into halls at this time of the day? But it's a minicab, she realizes, the licence in the rear window giving it away. As she stands there, one of the back doors opens and a girl half-slinks, half-stumbles out, slurring a thank you to the driver. The girl is in high heels, and she totters to a standing position, pulling down a short, sequinned skirt as she does so before lurching towards the building perpendicular to Chelsea's. It's only when she turns to walk up the stairs and Chelsea sees her face that recognition shoots through her. Unbidden, she takes half a step forward, her mouth open to shout the other girl's name, but something stops her.

What does she have to say to Isabella Dunwoody anyway?

It's dark by the time they roll through the small Highlands town Chelsea's aunt has chosen to live in. Not even *in* – Nikki keeps driving through, pointing out the Spar shop and the pub, and towards the edge of town, the veterinary clinic where she's a nurse, and then still on they continue, driving through the dark. Chelsea looks through the window, stunned by all the space; the width and depth and breadth of it. Tucked into the small car, the only head-lights on the road, it feels safe, enclosed, familiar, but what the hell is out there? In all that black?

'Wait until you see it in the morning, love,' her aunt says. 'You'll be blown away.'

'What made you move up here?' Nikki had still been in London when Chelsea went to university, but sometime in the intervening sixteen years she'd made the five-hundred-mile move north, from the shove and bustle of the city to the whistling quiet of all of this.

'Ah, just needed a change after the divorce. And it's a lot cheaper than London.'

Nikki's divorce had happened two years into Chelsea's sentence and she'd moved almost a year later. Prior to that, she'd visited Chelsea pretty regularly at Foston Hall, often accompanying Louise whenever she came up. But the drive to and from Scotland is long, as Chelsea can now attest to, and her visits were far less frequent once she'd moved. This was the excuse she always gave anyway, whenever they spoke on the phone, and it wasn't that Chelsea didn't believe her or didn't appreciate the logic in it, but she also knew it wasn't the only reason. Because the longer she was in there, the further away she became from those she loved. The easier she was to forget. 'So, it wasn't anything to do with . . . me? The newspaper coverage?'

'No, no. Nothing like that. That was tough, of course, I'm not going to lie. But it was much worse for your mum.' Nikki glances over at Chelsea as she says this, but then turns her attention quickly back to the road, flicking on her indicator even though there's no one else for miles, and turning into a driveway that Chelsea would've missed in the dark if she'd been on her own. Ahead of them, a small, squat house glows in welcome, and Chelsea watches as the front door swings open and a black silhouette appears against the yellow square of light.

For a second, Chelsea sees the figure of her mum and feels sick with relief; it's fine, she's here, it was all just a bad dream. But then Nikki says, 'There's Saoirse. She wanted to be here to welcome you home,' and the short spell is broken.

Nikki pulls the car slowly up to a stop outside the house, but Chelsea still can't bring herself to move. If you'd asked her a week ago what she was most looking forward to on her release, the answer would have been simple, one word: freedom. Maybe two: freedom, space. Maybe three: freedom, space, privacy. But now she's here and those things are in front of her, and she has no idea how to feel. In fact, she thinks what she feels is nothing, and that's scaring her.

'Saoirse?' she says now. 'She lives here too?'

'No,' Nikki says, unbuckling her seatbelt, grabbing up her phone and handbag. 'She's in Edinburgh these days, but she wanted to say hi.'

Saoirse must be twenty-six or twenty-seven by now, was still at primary school when Chelsea was arrested and then sent to prison, has only ever really known her cousin as someone behind bars, someone with the word 'murderer' attached to her, someone to deny being related to. She had come to visit Chelsea a few times, with her own mum, of course, but now Chelsea's thinking about it, she can't remember when the last time was; her only news of Saoirse has been through Nikki and she wonders, is she only here now at her mum's behest? Or worse, is she only here so she can report back to her friends what it's like to have your killer cousin released from prison? Standing in front of her, Chelsea suddenly feels a lurching anxiety and looking at the other girl, she can tell she feels weird too. Saoirse steps back as Chelsea moves towards her, and while it could be taken for a welcome, Chelsea can see a scrim of wariness in her cousin's eyes as she steps through into the warm light of the cottage. They don't hug. Instead, they both stand, staring at each other with arms hanging at their sides as Nikki bustles into the house and the shouting bark of a dog welcomes her into the kitchen, sending a shockwave through Chelsea, making her jump.

Saoirse laughs, awkwardness dissolving, and says, 'That's just Shandy. Completely harmless, completely obsessed with Mum, absolutely huge.'

Chelsea raises her eyebrows. 'Right.'

'Come on, I made Mum's famous beef stew, but it'll probably be inedible knowing me.'

'I've become pretty good at eating inedible food.'

'Right. Of course,' Saoirse says, her fair cheeks colouring. And then, 'It'll probably taste great to you, then.'

Chelsea lets out a weak laugh, 'Probably.'

And she follows her cousin through to the kitchen, where Nikki is feeding two dogs, one comically large, the other comically small, both ravenously hungry.

'The little one's Guinness,' Saoirse explains, 'but everyone calls him Guin, or Guinea.'

'Okay.'

'Sorry, you don't need like, a complete inventory of all our dogs right now,' Saoirse says.

'No, it's fine. It's . . . it's ages since I've been around pets. I forgot you'd got dogs,' Chelsea says to her aunt. Chelsea and her mum had had a cat, Penny, but she'd been almost ten when Chelsea went off to university and she'd died several years before her mother did. Thinking about the little swirl of a tabby cat now, Chelsea takes a deep breath, remembering the way she'd wake up with Penny draped across her head on winter mornings. As if sensing this memory, the way only animals can, Shandy trots over to where Chelsea has taken a seat at the kitchen table and lays her muzzle in Chelsea's lap. Swallowing hard, Chelsea feels Nikki's hand rest just briefly on her head as she strokes back the dog's fur. She can barely believe how soft it is.

'D'you want a shower or to get changed before dinner, love?' Nikki asks. 'Saoirse's bought you some clothes.'

'Oh,' Chelsea says, looking up startled. 'Wow, that's so nice. You didn't have to do that.'

Saoirse shrugs, 'Don't worry about it, it was fun.'

'So?' Nikki says. 'Do you want a shower first?'

'Actually, I'd love a bath. If you have one?'

The air in the bathroom is cold, the small window above the bath completely black as Chelsea turns the taps on. Nikki told her that, in the daytime, you can see the mountain rising in the distance from the window, but there's nothing to see now as the bath begins to fill with water and the room starts to fill with steam. Nikki lit some candles for her, pointed out the bath salts and bubble bath, told her she was free to use anything, but despite all this help, this warm welcome, she is relieved to be in the room on her own now. As long as the day has been, as slow as the drive up here felt, she still feels like she's playing catch-up, her brain in constant overdrive as she tries to take everything in, tries to figure out her place in all of this. It's nice of her aunt to have her, of course, but Chelsea can't help but feel that Nikki is doing it for her mother rather than for her – for the memory of Louise – knowing that this is what she would want her to do for her only daughter. And she's grateful, of course she is. There's no one else who would take her in like this, but she also didn't expect to get out of prison feeling so much like a guest in her own life. The bath is full now and she begins to strip, the water a blinding shock against her cold skin when she gets in. Her feet go almost immediately red with the heat, but she relishes it, this kind-of pain. It reminds her that this is real, that as surreal as it all is, as much as she might feel like this is all happening to someone else, it is in fact happening to her. But then that also means everything that's happened in the past sixteen years is also real. She sinks into the water and leans back, closing her eyes against the flickering, dim light of the candles. Maybe that's why all this feels so strange, so insubstantial. Because she should have been going home to her mum, and she's not. A loud laugh comes from downstairs, and she sits up suddenly, water skimming over the edge of the bath and on to the tiles, skittering across her skin. Was that Nikki or Saoirse? Either way, it sounded just like Louise, and as Chelsea leans back against the bathtub, she closes her eyes again, hot tears leaking out against her lashes.

* * *

After, Chelsea re-joins her aunt and cousin downstairs. The windows in the kitchen have steamed up from the stew warming on the stove and the dogs have quietened down, curled up in their respective beds while Nikki and Saoirse sit and chat quietly together. Chelsea is caught at the bottom of the stairs, looking in on this scene, feeling as though her heart might stop at any moment, when the tableau shifts and she realizes that her aunt and cousin aren't simply chatting in low voices, but having a whispered argument. She wants to walk into the room even less now, but she pushes on the already half-open door noisily, announcing her arrival, watching as Saoirse's back stiffens at the sound. She doesn't turn to greet Chelsea, but instead gets up quickly, her chair scraping loudly at the flagstone floor, waking one of the dogs, the smaller one, who looks up and barks twice before settling back down again.

'Oh, there you are,' Nikki says, smiling, but Chelsea can see it's forced. 'Good bath?'

'Yeah, great.'

'The water's never hot enough here,' Saoirse offers.

'Felt hot enough to me.'

'You missed a call while you were in there,' Nikki says, smiling over at her.

'I did?' How could she miss a call when she didn't have a phone? Not to mention, no one to call her on it.

'Ayesha. I let her know about your new release date, and I guess she just wanted to check in, see how you were doing.'

Chelsea hadn't told anyone except for her aunt that was she was being released four months early. The news had come as a shock, but she'd been glad for the ano-nymity it had allowed her – there'd been no cameras or reporters when her aunt picked her up, and no one knew she was here except her family and her parole officer. And now Ayesha. She trusts Ayesha, of course. Aside from Nikki, she is just about the only person she does trust, and it will be good to hear her voice – whenever she calls back – but still, she can't help the spill of anxiety she feels when she thinks about the world outside this room, this cottage. It's what she's been missing for well over a decade, what had been ripped from her one cold October morning in 2007, and yet now that it's there, outside the front door, she's not so sure that she's really ready for it.

'I didn't know you were in touch with Ayesha.'

Nikki raises her eyes from the cutlery she's placing around the old farmhouse-style table. 'Oh yeah, we've been in contact for a while. She came to your mum's funeral, did she never tell you that?'

Chelsea swallows, grips tightly at the back of the chair she was about to pull out in order to sit down. 'Yeah, yeah, she did mention it.'

'They text all the time,' Saoirse says, placing a bowl of stew in front of her mother.

'She's a good friend,' Nikki says simply.

'Yeah, it's amazing she never . . . I mean, did she *ever* think you might be guilty?' Saoirse asks.

Nikki's spoon stops halfway to her mouth as she looks at her daughter, and Chelsea feels her heart catch, her voice trapped in her throat, heat rise to her cheeks.

'No, of course she didn't,' Nikki says, brow furrowing as she addresses Saoirse. 'She knows Chelsea too well for that.'

Chelsea has been staring at her cousin, but when Saoirse turns to her, she immediately dips her gaze to her bowl of stew, not wanting to look her in the eye. There are very few people who have never questioned Chelsea's innocence – despite the guilty verdict. Saoirse will have read and seen so much in the intervening years, so maybe she shouldn't be surprised by this, maybe it shouldn't hurt so much. But it does; hearing a question like that from her cousin still manages to land like a gut punch.

'Sorry, Chelsea, I didn't mean to imply anything. I'm just saying. That's a good friend.'

Chelsea nods, head still down, 'I know. I do still have one or two left.' Although really, it's just one – Ayesha – and whenever she thinks of Ayesha, she can't help but think of Izzy, and whenever she thinks of Izzy, she can't help but think of everything else she has lost. She scoops up an overflowing spoonful of the homemade stew, the aroma rich and savoury, and even though her mouth is watering at the smell, nausea rises unbidden through her, and she barely tastes it as she chews, the meat turning to sawdust in her mouth.

Chelsea spots Isabella Dunwoody again a few times over the next few days. The first time at the freshers' BBQ and again at a club night in the city centre. She's even a couple of people ahead of her in line at a cashpoint on campus, but Chelsea says and does nothing. They weren't friends at school, so why would they be friends here? Izzy had been in the year above Chelsea, too distant to get to know and not just because of the one-year age difference; she was one of those glossy girls, always with the right shoes and bags, always with the perfect hair and make-up, always surrounded by as many people as possible. Considering they attended the same school, they couldn't have been further apart, really. Chelsea isn't even sure Izzy would recognize her, but then, there she is at their history induction lecture and Chelsea realizes they're not just at the same university – they're taking the same course.

They're waiting for the lecture-room doors to open – their head of department ran off just moments earlier, shaking her head at the lack of organization as she realized their booked room wasn't even ready for them. Chelsea is surprised to spot Isabella in the crowd, even more surprised to see her leaning against the wall not talking to anyone. She's sucking on the straw of her iced coffee from the only Starbucks on campus when she catches Chelsea's eye and pushes herself off the wall.

'Hey,' she says, as she comes towards Chelsea, teeth still chewing on the straw, 'I know you.'

'Izzy Dunwoody.'

'That's *my* name, dummy,' Izzy says with a smile. 'I can't remember yours though, I'm so sorry. Weren't we on the netball team together?'

'No,' says Chelsea, who hated netball, 'I'm Chelsea. I was the year below you.'

'That's right. You're one of the scholarship girls. Always on stage at the start- and end-of-year assemblies.' Izzy says this with a smile still, but Chelsea can't help but shift a little uncomfortably where she's standing. Izzy tilts her head towards the locked lecture-room door and says, 'What a cock-up, eh? I was meant to be enrolled in History and History of Art, but apparently they never got the "of Art" part of the message, so I'm just doing single honours for now. I've been at the department office trying to sort it out for hours. On a raging hangover, of course.'

'Oh, shit, sorry,' Chelsea says.

'Not your problem. What about you? You just doing history?'

'And sociology.'

'Nice. All my flatmates are medical students, can you believe it? They've been absolutely wasted all week which has been massively fun, but you know I'm going to be the odd one out all year. Me with my silly little history degree while they're out there saving lives.'

'I think the saving lives part might come a bit further down the line.'

'True, but I can already tell one or two are going to be so

26

self-righteous about it. Like, "look at me, I've got a calling, oohee".'

Chelsea laughs and watches as Izzy smiles at this reaction. 'Doctors can be so sanctimonious,' Chelsea says in agreement, even though she hasn't seen a doctor in years.

'What about you? Are any of your flatmates here?' Izzy says, looking around as if one of Chelsea's flatmates might be standing right next to them.

'No, I've got two English, one geography, a lawyer and a dentist.'

'Oh, nice. Impressive range. When did you get –' but Izzy is interrupted by the return of their lecturer, and she grabs at the sleeve of Chelsea's jacket, pulling her along in her wake as they all pile into the lecture hall, and Izzy finds them seats right in the middle of the auditorium.

After the lecture, which Izzy faux-yawned through, mugging falling asleep half the time and leaning over Chelsea's shoulder as she dutifully took notes throughout, Izzy convinces Chelsea to bypass the library tour and go to the pub instead.

'You haven't been to Gunnies yet?' she asks, astounded.

'It's all the way the other side of campus from my halls,' Chelsea says.

'So? You're young, you've got legs. Plus, it's where all the second and third years hang out.'

'But we're first years,' Chelsea points out.

Izzy rolls her eyes, 'Yeah, but no one has to know that. Besides, I took a gap year, didn't I?'

Chelsea doesn't say anything. It's pouring with rain, as it has been all week, and neither of them is particularly appropriately attired. Izzy is in ballet flats and Chelsea in ancient Converse high-tops, feet squelching through puddles, soaked through to their toes, and only Chelsea has an umbrella which they both huddle beneath as they cross the campus.

'My dad made me work at his company for six months before I could go travelling,' Izzy says, continuing as though Chelsea had asked her a question. 'God, it was so boring.'

'What's his company?' Chelsea asks. She knows Izzy and her family are rich – they live in one of the biggest houses in Dulwich Village – but she has no idea how or why. Almost all the girls she went to school with were rich, but their parents seemed to have got there in a variety of different ways.

'Pennington's,' Izzy says, naming one of the most famous gin brands in the world.

'Oh,' Chelsea says, 'I would've thought working for an alcohol company would be pretty fun.'

'Yeah, I suppose it could've been worse,' Izzy says with a sigh. 'What about you? What do your parents do?'

'My mum's a legal clerk – a paralegal. I have no idea what my dad does.'

'Oh,' Izzy says, turning her face towards Chelsea's. Under the cover of her umbrella, both of their faces have taken on a strange, greenish hue and Chelsea can tell Izzy is about to say something but thinks better of it, exclaiming instead, 'Look, here we are! Not so far after all, hey?'

Gunnies is just a regular pub, but the pints are £2, all meals are 2 for 1, and at just after two o'clock on a Wednesday afternoon, it's absolutely packed even though term hasn't officially started yet. As they're standing at the bar, waiting to be served, Chelsea's mobile phone beep-beeps with a new text message. 'It's Ayesha and Hannah, two of my flatmates. They're the ones doing English. They just got out of an introductory lecture, d'you mind if I invite them along?'

'No, do, do!' Izzy says, looking elated at the interruption. 'Ooh, yes, this means we should get a pitcher.'

'What, are you saying we don't get discounts on Pennington's gin?' Chelsea asks, giving Izzy a nudge.

'God, no. Dad's way too tight for that.'

Pitcher of beer in hand, Chelsea follows Izzy through the busy pub as they search for an empty table. The other girl's blonde head twists and turns, craning to see a spot, her hair swishing back and forth, and Chelsea almost laughs at being here with her. How has this happened? But then, Izzy's hand reaches back, grabbing Chelsea's arm, making her almost spill the beer, and Izzy practically shouts, 'Over there, look, get it, get it!'

Chelsea really can't help laughing now, Izzy's irrepressible energy infecting her as she sets off at an almost-run to make sure another group of students don't get to the table before them. When she sits down, breathless, Izzy says, 'Nice work,' and gives her a wink, making Chelsea smirk as she pours them both a pint. Sitting back and taking a sip, surveying the scene surrounding them, she feels on the verge of something while also feeling right at the centre of it. She wouldn't have come here without Izzy, and when she looks over at her, Izzy is doing the same thing as her, looking around, taking it all in. She meets Chelsea's eye over the rim of her glass and raises it in cheers before taking a sip and sitting back with a satisfied sigh, and suddenly Chelsea can't wait for Ayesha and Hannah to arrive, to introduce all of them to one another, to get this part of her life truly started.

It's silent when Chelsea wakes up the next morning. Or, if not actually silent, then a level and kind of silence she isn't used to and hasn't heard in almost two decades. Kicking a leg out, she stretches across the bed on a diagonal. It's soft and warm in a way she had forgotten about, or had become something she only dreamt about, a level of comfort that had become simply a memory. She can't think too much about all the nights she has spent in a bed so decidedly not like this one, doesn't want to be dragged back there, especially on this, her first morning of freedom, so instead she sits up and opens the curtains.

There's condensation rising up the windowpane, and a wintry mist outside. Seen through this veil, the scene looks otherworldly, sun just gilding the edges, trying to break through. Like a painting she's seen in a long-ago art gallery, or something from a film. It doesn't look real. At least, not to Chelsea. Getting up, she pulls on a jumper over her pyjamas and slips her feet into a pair of sheepskin slippers. All these clothes, as nice and new as they are, feel borrowed. A borrowed life. She's grateful to Saoirse for getting them, of course, and there's nothing wrong with them, but wearing them feels like putting on someone else's clothes. Someone else's life. When will all that stop? The sensation of having stepped into someone else's shoes, just for a while.

There's low talking coming from somewhere in the

house when she steps out on to the landing, but ignoring it, Chelsea heads straight downstairs to the front door and out into the morning. The cold is monumental, hits her in the chest and the face, chilling her instantly, and yet she stays there, taking it all in, wrapping her arms around herself, savouring it. She realizes suddenly that this is her first time in Scotland. It is bigger and barer than she'd imagined. There are one or two other houses within sight, but otherwise the land stretches out, bracken-layered moorland studded with trees pointing straight up into the hazy sky like evergreen arrows. The ground is frosted, glazed like something baked and delicious, and where the weak sunshine hits it, it sparkles and dances.

Was this what she thought of when she thought of the outside world? No, this wasn't within her reach. She'd dreamed only of London and occasionally Birmingham, and hot Mallorcan beaches, rocky and dusty beneath her feet.

'Hey!' comes Nikki's voice, cracking through the misty morning, breaking her frozen reverie. 'You must be freezing out there.'

Back inside the cottage, the fire in the woodburning stove is already lit, the two dogs soppy and stretched out in front of it.

'We've already been out for our morning walk,' Nikki explains. 'Shandy's the world's best natural alarm clock.'

'I didn't even hear her, or you, this morning.'

'You must've been out like a light last night. Big day.'

'Yeah,' Chelsea says as she reaches for the kettle and fills it with water. 'It actually took me a while to get to sleep though. It was so quiet; I'm not used to it.'

Nikki doesn't say anything, but Chelsea watches as her aunt puts two crumpets into the toaster and presses the lever down. 'These still your favourite?' she asks, turning back to look at her niece.

'Yeah,' Chelsea says, nodding, although in truth she has no idea. No idea what any of her favourites are now. For fifteen years, she's just eaten what she's been given and made no complaints, formed few opinions. She can still taste the deep savouriness of Saoirse's stew last night. Once she'd got over the awkwardness between her and her cousin, she'd managed to enjoy the food, letting the flavour melt on her tongue, so rich and heavy it had felt overwhelming in the moment. She'd forgotten how good food could taste.

'So,' Nikki says, brushing invisible crumbs from her hands, sounding all business. 'Saoirse left an old phone of hers for you, it's there on the table with a new SIM. Just pay as you go for now, as that seemed the simplest thing.'

Chelsea is making tea, and has to look behind her to where Nikki is gesturing at the phone. It's smaller than Nikki's, with a white, shiny, plastic back. An iPhone. 'It's pretty old and shit,' Nikki continues, 'but it should do for now.'

Sitting down with her mug of tea, Chelsea picks up the phone, turning it over a few times in her hands. There were phones in prison, of course. The ones you were allowed to use, stuck to the wall, and the less legal ones that some inmates carried around in their bras, hid underneath mattresses. But those still looked like the kind of phone Chelsea had used before being arrested, small enough to cup in a hand, buttons you could actually press.

'It's not going to hurt you,' Nikki says, laughing.

Chelsea raises her eyebrows and shrugs, 'Really?'

'You'll get used to it soon enough. They're easier than they look. Even Mum has one.'

'How is Gran?' Chelsea asks, putting the phone down carefully on the table again.

'She's all right, although she can't get around much any more. The arthritis is too bad.'

Chelsea nods; she knows all this already, really. Her gran had moved back to Ireland years ago when Chelsea was still at school, and Chelsea had spoken to her religiously once a month throughout her sentence, even though her gran had never been able to make the trip over to visit her in prison.

The crumpets have popped up out of the toaster, and Nikki starts to butter them both. 'So, we've got a few things we need to get to today, but how do you feel about starting work tomorrow?'

'Tomorrow?'

'I spoke to David, he's the head vet and owner of the practice, and Shelley our practice manager, and they both agreed to let you try out on reception for a couple of days a week.'

'Oh.' Chelsea gulps at her tea and stares at her aunt's back as Nikki layers Marmite on top of the butter. She had no idea Nikki had gone to such efforts for her, and she's grateful, of course, but she already feels like she is walking tilted against the wind, and this surprise has been another buffet.

'Well, it's important for your probation. To get you into work as quickly as possible. It won't be the most challenging, but I'll be able to help show you the ropes and they're all lovely people.' Nikki sits down at the table, putting the plate of crumpets down in front of Chelsea. 'D'you want cheese, love?'

'Yes please,' Chelsea answers dully. 'Don't they mind though? That . . . that it's me they're giving a job to?'

Nikki places a block of Cheddar and a knife on the table. 'Well, I've talked it all over with them, and they're willing to give you the benefit of the doubt.'

'But why?'

'Because they trust my judgment.'

Chelsea pulls the cheese closer to her so she can cut a slice off, and wonders how much her aunt is protecting her from the actual reason, how much she's bending the truth. Surely, there has to be something else her colleagues are gaining from hiring someone straight out of prison. A tax incentive, probably.

'There are other people who'll be willing to do the same, you know.'

'What?' Chelsea looks up sharply, from the table.

'Give you the benefit of the doubt.'

Chelsea grunts, neither agreeing nor disagreeing as she clumsily cuts the cheese. The knife slips and for the barest moment, she thinks she's about to lose her grip on it, before she regains control. She can feel Nikki watching her, but she can't quite meet her eye. She wants to believe that what her aunt is saying is true. That people will trust her, believe her. That they won't assume the worst. But it's been over fifteen years of people assuming the worst and she is beyond sceptical. But if this is going to work, this new life out in the world, she's going to have to put her trust in it.

The question is, how can she trust something that has already betrayed her?

'Trust me, trust me!' Izzy squeals at the top of her lungs, 'you are going to *love* it.'

'Baileys and lime? That sounds disgusting,' Chelsea says.

'But I thought you were *Irish*!' Izzy says through a raucous laugh. They've been at Gunnies for hours and they've already gone through pitchers of beer, Jägerbombs, and several vodka and cranberries.

'My mum's Irish. Sort of.'

Izzy shrugs and hiccups before saying, 'Whatever, it's called a cement mixer.'

'What's that got to do with being Irish?' asks Hannah.

'The Baileys, Han,' Ayesha says.

The shots are already on the table and Izzy is looking at the other three girls, wide-eyed and expectant. Chelsea makes a disgusted face but grabs a glass nonetheless, Hannah and Ayesha quickly following suit. 'Yessss,' Izzy says, picking up her own glass and making a 'bottoms up' gesture before all four of them down their disgusting shots in one.

'Urghhh,' Hannah says, shuddering theatrically as she slams the empty shot glass back down on the table.

'Gross,' Chelsea says.

'Well, that was exactly as disgusting as we predicted it would be,' Ayesha says as she wipes residual Baileys from her top lip.

Izzy just laughs and drinks from her pint glass, washing away the taste of her cement mixer. 'Man, that was worse than I was expecting it to be.'

'What? I thought you loved them? What was all that "trust me, trust me" about?' Chelsea says.

'I've just always wanted to try one but didn't want to do it on my own.' Chelsea rolls her eyes while Hannah gives Izzy a betrayed look. Ayesha doesn't look surprised. 'Oh, come on, it was fun,' Izzy continues, nudging Ayesha with her elbow. 'We're only young once, right? Speaking of, what are you guys up to tonight?'

'There's something on at the union, but we were talking about having a night off. Just staying in and watching some films or crap TV,' Ayesha says.

'God, no, we can't go to the union. I've been there enough already and it's only the first week,' Izzy says. 'Let's go into town. I wanna go to some clubs when it's not a Freshers' night, you know? See what people really get up to.'

'They'll all be full of Freshers too, though,' Ayesha says with a shrug, 'it's *Freshers'* Week. Clue's in the name.'

'I know, I know, but there must be at least one that's not. Where all the other normal people go.'

'You sound like Ariel,' Chelsea says.

'What?'

'*I wanna be where the people are!*' Hannah sings at the top of her lungs, garnering them all several looks from nearby tables.

Izzy laughs and Hannah blushes a little. 'You're so cute,' Izzy says to her, a little condescendingly for Chelsea's liking, but Hannah's blush deepens. 'Don't tell me; we're going to be watching you in a play before this term is out.'

36

'Well, I was thinking of trying out for something, yeah.'

'That's great!' Izzy says. 'We'll all come and see you, won't we guys?'

Chelsea catches Ayesha's eye as Izzy says this. Chelsea, Ayesha and Hannah have only known each other for five days at this point, but it already went unsaid that of course they would see Hannah in whatever play or musical she was cast in. Hannah sporadically burst into song at least once a day, so Chelsea's money is on it being a musical, and while she isn't the biggest fan of musicals, she's already willing to put that aside in order to support her. Chelsea is surprised by how close to these girls she already feels. She gets on fine with their other flatmates, but Hannah and Ayesha already feel like friends she has known for years, not days. This first week – this Freshers' Week – has been full of short days and long nights that have flown by and yet it also feels like she's been here for ever. Like she's known these people for ever. She sinks back into her chair and takes a long sip from her pint glass, finally washing away the disgusting taste of the cement mixer. 'We could go to Snobs,' she suggests.

Izzy's nose wrinkles, 'Snobs? No, what about Mechu?'

'We went there Monday night,' Ayesha says, 'it was okay.'

'Only okay? I've heard it's great on a Wednesday. Plus, that was a special Freshers' night, it'll be different tonight. Less students.'

'Fewer,' Ayesha says under her breath, but Izzy either doesn't hear or pretends not to.

'But we're students,' Chelsea points out with a laugh.

'Yeah, but y'know,' Izzy shrugs, 'we don't have to like, constantly shout it from the rooftops, do we?'

'Why not? I love being a student,' Ayesha counters, picking up her pint glass to continue, 'drinks in the pub at three p.m. and no work so far to speak of? What's not to like?'

'Hear, hear!' Izzy says, looking as though she has had her mind changed. Leaning forward, she lifts her glass in a cheers. 'And here's to the first week of the rest of our lives.'

The town is tiny, population two thousand people or maybe even less, but Chelsea feels every eye on her as she walks next to her aunt. This is what she was scared of, coming here to somewhere so small. In London, she would've been able to disappear, to slip down those streets, hide out among anonymous crowds. Here, everyone knows Nikki, and that means everyone knows Chelsea, or at least it feels that way. Not everyone they've seen so far has stopped to say hello to her aunt, but when they have, they've looked at Chelsea with sidelong glances, their eyes sweeping her from head to toe as Chelsea pretends not to notice, not to care.

'Right, so the two most important things we've got to do today are speak to your solicitor and meet with your parole officer.' Nikki's voice is smooth, unruffled, as if she hasn't noticed the looks and stares, the pointed 'hellos'. As if she doesn't feel the throb of interest and gossip lining these granite streets. Maybe she hasn't noticed because it's not there at all, and it's all in Chelsea's mind. Maybe.

'My solicitor?'

'Yes, I've been executor of your mum's will in your stead, but it passes to you, now that you're out of prison.'

'Oh.'

Chelsea hasn't thought about any of this. Prison walls have shielded her from the bureaucracy of death, or at the very least her aunt has, but now here it is, rising up to

39

remind her that her mother is gone. Tears swell behind her eyes and she has to stop to take a breath. It's more than bureaucracy and paperwork those walls hid her from; in there she could pretend her mum was still out here, but out here there's nowhere else for her mother to be but underground.

Nikki is up ahead, already several strides ahead of her even though Chelsea only stopped for a second. She takes another long breath, the exhale hitching on a hidden sob, and scurries to catch up. 'We need to get you signed up at the doctor and dentist's too,' she's saying as Chelsea falls in step beside her once more.

'Where is the solicitor? Are we going to meet them now?'

'No, oh sorry, didn't mean to confuse you there. We can Zoom with them for now, but they're down in London. We have to go in person to see your parole officer, though, and that's in Aberdeen.'

'So, what are we doing here, now?' Chelsea asks. There's a rise in her voice and a tell-tale scratch as it catches on the tears she's been holding back.

Nikki stops and squints at her, her hand on Chelsea's right arm. 'I just thought you might like a wander around the town, see the sights, grab a coffee.' At this last option she nods behind Chelsea, towards a café painted sea-foam green.

'Oh,' Chelsea says again, taking a deep breath, 'Okay.'

'Are you sure you're okay?'

Is she okay? How can she be okay? But how can she not be okay? This is meant to be the first day of the rest of her life. A day she has been counting down to since the very start of her sentence, the days marked off in her mind one by one, one by one, one by one. Interminable, incessant. A sentence written word by word; a house demolished brick by brick. But she's back at the start line again, and instead of a long ribbon of a road stretching out ahead of her, freedom written on the white lines, fresh air and cool breezes, she's at the bottom of a dark, dark well. No way out. How is she supposed to crawl out of it without even a ladder, a torch? But that would be too easy. And she never thought this was going to be easy. Because being out here, it's more than just paperwork and bureaucracy, getting used to new things, and avoiding the prying eyes of new people. Trying to find her place in a world she hasn't lived in for fifteen years. No, she's got work to do. Not that she can breathe a word of any of it to Nikki – she can already tell that her aunt wouldn't approve – but honestly, as much as she loves and appreciates her, her opinion is neither here nor there, because Chelsea needs to do this, needs to find out who really killed Izzy, and who should really have been living out her sentence for all these years. Because it's been eating away at her, has whittled down to her very core, until sometimes she thinks that it's all that's left of her. Maybe that's the real reason why she hasn't been able to grieve her mother yet, or Izzy for that matter. It's not only that the prison walls have hidden her from the real world, but this question, this one burning question, has taken over everything: if Chelsea didn't kill Izzy, then who did?

'Come on, their banana bread is out of this world and they have the best coffee in town,' Nikki says, pushing open the café door, leading the way. She turns back, 'Wait, do you even like coffee? I can't remember.'

Chelsea shrugs. All these questions, and even the simplest one can trip her up. 'Yeah, coffee sounds good,' she says, for lack of a more definitive answer, unable to say what she's really thinking, and follows her aunt into the café.

Inside it's quiet. Bleached blonde wood and more soothing blues. But that doesn't stop the few customers who are there from looking up when the bell above the door chimes. Is she imagining it, or do they all shift slightly, eyes widening as they spot her? Nikki says she'll order and points to a table in the window, and even though she'd rather hide in the back, far from view, safely ensconced, Chelsea takes a seat there, where she can watch the whole world go by and the whole world can watch her.

'Am I imagining it?' she asks her aunt when she joins her.

'Imagining what, love?' Nikki says. She's distracted, balancing two plates of banana bread, looking over her shoulder to where their coffees are being made.

'Is everyone staring? Does everyone know who I am?' Chelsea had meant to whisper, but it comes out as a hiss instead, questioning her aunt through gritted teeth.

'Oh,' Nikki says, looking her in the eye now, 'you're not okay, are you?' She spreads her gaze around the café, taking in the room. She probably thinks she looks subtle, but she doesn't, and Chelsea bows her head, eyes lowered to the banana bread in front of her.

'I don't think anyone's watching us, Chels. It might feel like it, but I honestly don't think anyone except my colleagues and a few others even know who you are or why you're here.'

'But they could've told anyone.'

'They could've done, yes, but I don't think they would. I think you're just anxious, which is totally understandable.'

Chelsea cuts into her banana bread hard, causing the plate to upend and crash back on to the table. She doesn't look up, cheeks beginning to burn. If no one was looking before, they surely are now.

'Two flat whites?' a friendly voice asks.

Chelsea sits ups, shuffling on her chair, and guardedly gazes around the room from beneath her eyelashes, trying to figure out who is watching. But no one is. She looks up into the face of their waitress, who is smiling blithely down at both her and Nikki, simply doing her job.

'That's lovely, thanks, Leah,' Nikki says.

Chelsea murmurs her thanks before taking a sip of her coffee. 'Nice,' she pronounces after a couple more sips.

'These weren't really a thing before, were they?' Nikki says. Chelsea shakes her head. 'Lots to get used to.'

'Well. Coffee's pretty much the least of it, really.'

'Yeah. Listen, I'm sorry if it feels like I'm throwing a lot at you. I just really want to get this right, Chels. For the authorities, I mean. With the early release and everything . . . I feel like I'm ticking these boxes, but I don't want you to feel like you're a box being ticked.'

'Right.' Chelsea drinks more coffee, looks out of the window. Feels the eyes of her aunt on her.

'It's just hitting you now, isn't it? I didn't even really think . . . it's been so long, I've got used to her being gone, and honestly, I didn't even think about how different it would be for you, processing it all in there.'

'*Not* processing it all,' Chelsea says, still looking through the window, seeing nothing. 'It feels like day one.'

43

'It is day one, love. In a lot of ways. That's totally okay.'

'What's the deal with the solicitor?' Chelsea turns, meets Nikki's eye. She wants the subject changed.

'We can put that off for a bit if it's too much. It doesn't have to be dealt with right away, I don't think.'

'But what is it? Mum's will?'

Nikki nods, 'And her estate.'

'Her estate?' Chelsea repeats, the 'Ts' coming out through her teeth.

'That's just the terminology. Makes it sound grander than it is, but she left you the house and obviously any money she had, so it's all in trust for you.'

'Right,' Chelsea says again, even though everything is anything but.

'You'll have to think about whether or not you want to sell it.'

'Sell it?'

'The house. I didn't want to make that decision for you. I know you said . . . to do whatever I thought was best, when Louise died, but that didn't feel like my decision to make. I wasn't sure if you'd want to live there eventually.'

'Could I?'

'If you wanted to, of course.'

'I . . . I don't know, right now.'

'No, I know. It's a lot. And it's good for you to be here for now, I think. With some support.'

'Yeah,' Chelsea says, taking another sip of coffee. What would it be like, to move back to London, into her old home? Like stepping back in time, perhaps. Her hand grips the small cup and the heat of the ceramic burns her fingers, but she doesn't put it down. She doesn't want to go back, not even to the good times. Because between the here and now and the good times there is so much bad time to wade through, and she's not sure she has the strength to make it through all that again. London could be easier in a way, so many more places to hide in a big city where barely anyone looks in your direction, rather than here, where she sticks out like a sore thumb. There's the familiarity of it too, that ineffable, undefinable sense of home, but would it even feel that way now, after all this time, after where she's been, what she's been through? And then there's the people. Yes, she's more noticeable here, but she can't help thinking that in London she'd be more likely to run into someone who knew exactly who she was. Someone could be listening to that damn podcast they made at the very moment Chelsea walks on to the tube and they could recognize her as 'Killer Keough'.

'A lot to think about,' Nikki says, but her voice is a long way away and it's all Chelsea can do to give her a small nod in response.

'Hiiiii!' Izzy calls over the balustrade, watching Chelsea, Ayesha and Hannah trudge up the staircase. 'Sorry it's such a trek. The price you pay for high-rise living, eh?' She says this with a laugh, because really, they're only five floors up, but still, it is a bit of a climb.

'Well, welcome to my humble abode,' she says with a flourish and a dainty curtsey as she pushes the front door open and ushers them all inside. The flat has the exact same layout as Chelsea, Ayesha and Hannah's shared flat but is its mirror image, although that is where the similarities end.

'Oh, God,' Ayesha says, stopping in the doorway to the open-plan kitchen and living room. There are shoes, socks and other discarded clothing items all over the floor and sofas; dead beer and vodka bottles line the windowsill and skirting boards; dirty plates, saucepans and dishes are piled in the sink and all over the countertops. 'Did you guys have a party last night or something?' Ayesha asks, turning back to Izzy.

'Nope, this is just a regular Tuesday in flat 34B,' she says, rolling her eyes. 'I try to avoid going in there as much as possible, to be honest. Come on, let's go to my room.'

Izzy's room is at the end of the corridor, as far from the kitchen as it's possible to get, and looking at her face, Chelsea gets the impression she is more than a little bit relieved by this. 'Med students are pigs, it turns out,' she says as her bedroom door crashes closed behind them all and she flounces on to her bed, 'or at least, my ones are.'

Her room couldn't be more different from the shared living space. She has framed pictures on the wall where most students would have posters stuck up with Blu Tack, and has replaced the standard issue mirror with an ornate, gilt-framed one that Chelsea suspects is probably an actual antique. Her bed is piled high with a duvet that looks like it could double as a cloud, and plenty of extra cushions and pillows. In the corner, where in her room Chelsea has stuffed her empty suitcases, Izzy has set up a reading nook with a pretty standing lamp and an armchair.

'Oh my God, this is so nice,' Hannah says, looking round with wide eyes. 'How'd you make it look so much nicer than everyone else's? It's not fair,' she says with a pout which Izzy laughs at.

'Come on, come in properly, guys, sit down,' Izzy says, unscrewing the top of a wine bottle as she shuffles backwards on the bed, making space for Hannah and Chelsea. Ayesha sits on the armchair, leaning back and closing her eyes with a contented smile. 'Did you bring glasses?' Izzy adds to Chelsea.

Chelsea pulls them out of her tote bag, passing them out to everyone, 'Yeah, I didn't get why you asked at first, but seeing your kitchen . . .'

'I didn't want to accidentally poison you with any of my bacteria-ridden glassware,' Izzy says. 'Ironic really. All these med students and they're going to end up dying of never-doing-the-washing-up.'

'I thought you got on with them?' Hannah says.

Izzy pulls a face, splashing wine into their proffered glasses, 'Week one Izzy got on with them, week three Izzy is pissed off and trying to switch halls.'

'Really? Where would you go?' Chelsea asks.

'Anywhere. I'd prefer to stay on the Vale near you guys, but honestly, who cares at this point. I've put in for Stapleton, although I doubt I'll get it. I thought I wanted non-catered but I haven't used that kitchen since last Monday, so I may as well move into a catered halls.'

'Have you tried talking to them about it?' Ayesha asks. 'You guys could set up a cleaning rota?'

'Is that what you lot have done?' Izzy asks archly.

'No, we're all really nice and just tidy up after ourselves,' Hannah says without a hint of malice or judgment in her voice.

'God, that sounds heavenly,' Izzy says dramatically, leaning her head on Hannah's shoulder. 'I wouldn't know how to talk to them about it, to be honest. There's so many of them I'd feel way outnumbered and I basically never see them anyway.'

'Leave a note?' Hannah says hopefully.

'It would probably get eaten by rats before they even read it.'

'You haven't actually seen any, have you?' Ayesha asks, sitting forward in the armchair, eyes scanning the corners of the room.

'No,' Izzy says with a laugh. 'Not yet, anyway.'

'I'd feel so bad if I was forcing my squalor on someone else,' Hannah says.

'Yeah, me too,' Chelsea says.

'Well, anyway,' Izzy shrugs, staring down into her glass

of wine, 'it is what it is. My mum's coming up this weekend and I'm planning to spend the whole time lounging in her spotlessly clean hotel room, pretending I don't live with a bunch of animals.'

'Why's your mum coming up?' Chelsea asks.

'It's my birthday.'

'What?' Hannah exclaims, sitting up so suddenly that she splashes wine all over the duvet. 'Shit, sorry,' she says, patting ineffectually at where the wine landed. 'I'm sorry? It's your birthday and we're only just hearing about it now? Is it actually this weekend or next week? What are we going to do for it? Can we get dressed up?'

Izzy laughs, 'It's not a big deal. It's only my twentieth.'

'Only your twentieth?!' Hannah roars.

'Twenty is a nice round number,' Ayesha says.

'What do you think, Chelsea? Should we go big for my twentieth? Mum's coming up on Saturday so we could do something Friday night.'

'Is your birthday Friday or Saturday?'

'Saturday. Why?'

'So's mine.'

'Oh my God, birthday twins!' Hannah squeals. 'That's so cute, we can do a joint party, right? We have to.'

'That's so weird. How did we not know that?' Izzy says, gazing at Chelsea.

'Well, it literally only just came up,' Chelsea points out.

'I know,' Izzy says, with a roll of her eyes, 'but we went to the same school. Feels like the kind of thing we should've already known.'

Chelsea just shrugs at her, as Ayesha says, 'Were you planning on going home, Chels? To see your mum?'

'Nope.'

'Are birthdays not a big thing in your family?' Hannah asks.

Chelsea smiles at Hannah, who is from a family of six – two boys, two girls, two parents – and shakes her head, thinking of her family of two. Three if you count Penny. 'I guess it depends on your concept of a "big thing". Mum always makes a fuss, but we're so close to the start of term, I told her we could do something if I go back for reading week or whatever.'

'Part-y. Part-y. Part-y!' Hannah chants as the rest of them laugh.

'I know,' Izzy says, sitting up a little straighter from the bed, 'we can do a twenty–nineteen party.'

'Twenty–nineteen?' Ayesha squints at her.

'Twenty,' Izzy points at herself, 'nineteen,' she says pointing at Chelsea. 'You are turning nineteen, right?'

Chelsea nods. 'Cool, we can all dress up like it's 2019. The future,' she says, eyes widening in mock horror.

'And you can come to dinner with me and Mum on Saturday, Chels. She's booked somewhere super fancy. I mean, I assume.'

'Really . . . ? I don't want to –'

'Yeah, of course. We're birthday twins, right? We've gotta stick together.'

After the quiet of the café, Nikki drives them to Aberdeen and the nondescript building where Chelsea's assigned parole officer works. Nikki can't come in with her, and after hours in the car yesterday, tells Chelsea she'll take herself for a walk to blow out the cobwebs. Inside, Chelsea is expected. Kate McClure welcomes her with a handshake, leading her from the small waiting room into her office. There's no window, and everything seems to be brown, and yellow, and grey, with a bookcase full of criminology and psychology textbooks, and huge lever-arch files Chelsea will never know the contents of.

'Take a seat,' Kate says coolly, sitting down in her own chair and taking a sip of water. 'How're you feeling, Chelsea?'

'Strange,' Chelsea says eventually, unsure and unwilling to articulate that she currently feels like she's living someone else's life.

'That makes sense. Most offenders experience a level of uncertainty upon release, even those who are happy to return to their friends and family.' Chelsea straightens up in her seat at the word 'offender'. She knows that that is how Kate views her, how so much of the world views her, but it doesn't stop her hating it. Because 'offender' is just another word for criminal, and although she may have been labelled as such since she was just twenty years old,

Chelsea is not a criminal. She wants so much to be free of that word, and, even worse, of the word 'murderer', but she knows she never will be, not unless she does something about it. 'I understand you lost your mother during your sentence. That must be hard to return to?' Kate continues, bringing Chelsea back to the here and now, to the dingy office she wants nothing to do with.

'Yes.' There is so much she could say here and Kate nods encouragingly at her, willing her to open up, but even as Chelsea opens her mouth to continue, she feels her throat close over, choking on her words.

'Okay, well, you've got a lot to get used to. You're living with your aunt, is that correct?'

Chelsea nods, and as they go over Kate's list of questions for her, her muscles loosen incrementally. This isn't the interrogation she was expecting. Kate is clear about the rules Chelsea has to follow, but there's compassion there too. She wonders what kind of offenders she normally deals with. Is it mostly drugs? Domestic violence offenders? It's hard to age her, but she seems competent enough so Chelsea assumes she's been doing this for a while. Still, is Chelsea the first convicted murderer she's been assigned? Maybe not. But is she the first female murderer? Chelsea breathes in sharply, and Kate looks up, eyes bright and aware, from the paper she's been reading.

'It says here you completed a degree in sociology from the Open University during your sentence.' Once again, Chelsea nods. 'And you worked in the library?'

'Yeah.'

'That's good. Are you planning to use that experience upon your release? As has probably been explained to you, getting you into steady employment is a key part of your rehabilitation.'

'My aunt's helped me get a receptionist's job at her veterinary surgery for now.'

'Okay, great,' Kate says, although by the way her eyebrows pull together, her face doesn't seem to be agreeing with her words. 'I'll have to contact them, to ensure any and all drug paraphernalia is inaccessible to you.'

Chelsea stiffens, shifting in her seat. 'I don't have any drug offences,' she says.

'I know, Chelsea, it's just procedure, really. But you do understand that drug testing can be made a part of your licence conditions, if deemed necessary?'

'Um, yes. I don't do drugs.'

'So, that's fine then. And you understand that our meetings are set to take place weekly?'

'Yeah.'

'And I'll have to come and visit you at home within the next ten days.'

'The next ten days?'

'Yes. Are you planning on going anywhere?'

'No, uh, of course not. I just didn't realize.'

'Okay, back to the job. Will you be happy to stay at the surgery, do you think?'

'I haven't even started it yet,' Chelsea says slowly. 'It's a relief, though. I was dreading having to apply for jobs where anyone could just look me up, know everything about me.'

'I can see that being a worry. But, by being in Scotland, you're some distance from where it all took place, at least. And people's memories are short, you'll be surprised.'

Chelsea doesn't believe this. She knows people's memories are long, because hers is long, and she's sure Kate knows this too. As if to prove this, Kate asks, 'You've heard about the podcasts and documentary, I expect?'

'My aunt told me. And I got some interview requests when I was inside. But I declined them.'

Kate nods. She's had a pen in her hand this whole time, and now, she starts twirling it around, a nervous tic, maybe? 'That was probably for the best. I'm not going to sugar-coat it for you, Chelsea, obviously that kind of attention will make life a little more difficult for you. Than the average offender, I mean. All that to say, that I think it's good you're staying with your aunt, somewhere quiet.'

'Right,' Chelsea says, even though she didn't have much choice in the matter. She's grateful, of course, but as difficult as it is to tell how she would've felt, if she'd gone back to London instead, she can't help but feel like her homecoming would feel a lot more like coming home, if she were actually at home. But the fact is, her home doesn't exist any more. Not as it did before she went to prison, before her mother died. And so, here she is, in a strange town, in a new part of the country, trying to restart a life that had barely got started in the first place, trying to wrap her head around the loss of people who have already been lost for years. Kate's office seems to be getting smaller by the second, and she's glad when the other woman stands up, to let her know they're done for this session. Chelsea looks at the clock hanging by the door as she passes through it. Just thirty minutes have gone by, but she feels like she was sitting in that chair for a lifetime.

In the car on the way back to the cottage, Nikki doesn't

badger her with questions, for which Chelsea is grateful. All she asks is how it went, and when Chelsea tells her, she remarks that it sounds almost more like a counselling session. Sitting in the car, as Scotland thunders by, Chelsea supposes that it was a bit, although that doesn't make her resent it any less. It's not that any of this is a surprise – she'd been told exactly what to expect upon her release – but she hadn't realized it would chafe so much. She can't help thinking about who should really be attending these meetings, who should have served out her sentence, who should have had their life and opportunities and loved ones taken away from them. She'd grown so used to the everyday routines of prison life that she hadn't realized how much this small taste of freedom would affect her. And now she wants more. But she's sure, as measured and empathetic as Kate McClure seemed to be, she wouldn't hesitate to lay down the law should Chelsea ever step out of line. Something about the set of her jaw, the sharp glint in her grey eyes. Warm and welcoming, perhaps, but also not a woman you'd want to cross. Still, Chelsea is going to have to, if she wants to find out who really killed Izzy.

2006

On Saturday evening, Chelsea gets the train into the city centre and then walks through town to meet Izzy at her mum's hotel. Izzy was picked up earlier in the day, shepherded to the hotel in her mother's car and has been hanging out there ever since, pinging off texts to Chelsea every few minutes, the beep-beep of them coming through and interrupting Chelsea's hangover. As she walks, she receives another one, this time from her mum.

> Enjoy tonight, love! And hope ur in full recovery from last night by
> now . . . remember, ur only 19 so no complaints about hangovers.
> They're only going to get worse ha. Love u loads and wish I was
> there. So weird not seeing you today. Kiss kiss Mum

And then:

PS REMEMBER TO SAY THANK U TO IZZIE'S MUM!!!!!

Chelsea smiles and puts her phone back in her pocket, digging out the map of the city centre Ayesha printed out for her before she left the flat. She's pretty sure she knows where she's going, but Ayesha insisted on putting the directions into Google and then printing them off for her – proclaiming herself to feel like Chelsea's dad while doing so. Hannah had been flopped down on Ayesha's bed while this happened, and the three of them realized it would be the first time they spent an evening apart since moving into their halls of residence.

'Wait, do we spend way too much time together?' Ayesha had joked, eyes wide.

'No, but good for us for getting some space. We wouldn't want to become too cliquey now, would we?' Chelsea had said with a raised eyebrow.

As she looks at the map – Ayesha has gone as far as to draw her route in pencil – watermarks appear as it starts to rain, and Chelsea picks up her pace. It may not have stopped raining since she arrived in Birmingham but she realizes, too late, that she's forgotten her umbrella. Hunching her shoulders as a form of protection, she walks with her head down, ignoring everyone else on the street. It's a weird time of day and there's a mix of straggling shoppers, weighed down with bloated bags, and early revellers who spill out on to the streets outside pubs and bars already, puffing on cigarettes, pints in hand. The building she's looking for is one she's previously overlooked, one of those shiny skyscrapers, shrink-wrapped in endless windows, that in earlier visits to the city centre she's dismissed as having nothing to do with her or her student life. At the revolving door she tries to shake raindrops from her faux-leather jacket, like a dog emerging from a pond. Izzy has told her to go straight up, but as soon as she's in the sleek, anonymous lobby she feels eyes on her, so she heads over to reception and tells them she's there to meet the Dunwoodies. The receptionist nods precisely, her eyes never leaving Chelsea's face as she picks up the phone on her desk to call up to their room.

'They're in the Presidential Suite. You can go on up,' she says upon putting down the phone.

Chelsea nods back at her and walks over to the bank of lifts, wishing she'd worn something different. Getting dressed, she'd thought she was doing okay, but in the light of this hotel lobby, her black skinny jeans look grey with all the times they've been washed, and her white Converse are rain-pocked and muddy. In the lift, she bangs the button for the top floor, breathing with relief when the doors finally ding closed.

'Happy birthday!' Izzy sings out as she opens the door to Chelsea. She has a glass of champagne in one hand, drops of it spilling to the carpet below as she throws her arms wide in welcome.

'Happy birthday to you too,' Chelsea says, laughing at the other girl's enthusiasm. They hug as the door closes behind them, as if they haven't seen each other in days when really it's only been a few hours.

'God, I feel pretty wretched, don't you? Wish I'd gone to bed earlier, but what can you do.'

'It was our birthday party, we had to be the ones to close it down,' Chelsea points out.

'So true.'

Izzy pours Chelsea a glass of champagne without even asking, and Chelsea takes the opportunity to look around her at the suite. The floor-to-ceiling windows would probably prompt vertigo if she were standing any closer, but from here she can admire the view across the city as it comes alive in the twilight grey, without feeling as though she's about to fall through the air. Through the mist and rain of the autumn evening, it looks almost futuristic, neons and reds and greens lighting up the city below, while inside everything is dark wood and grey and brown, with the occasional pop of cherry red.

'Not the most inspiring of penthouse suites, but Mum and I spent the whole afternoon at the spa and it was diviiiine,' Izzy says, dropping into one of the armchairs.

'Where is your mum?' Chelsea asks, annoyed at how nervous she sounds.

Izzy points to a chair, indicating Chelsea should sit in it, 'She's showering. She'll be out soon and we can head to the restaurant.'

'She's out now,' a voice says from behind them, and Chelsea turns to see an older, slightly smaller version of Izzy. Her voice is low and smooth and only slightly accented. If she didn't already know she was French, Chelsea may not have been able to detect it. She stands up now, quickly, and Izzy laughs as Chelsea hits her shin on the edge of one of the strangely boxy and unwelcoming armchairs in her hurry to shake the older woman's hand.

'Hi, Mrs Dunwoody, I'm Chelsea, thank you so much for inviting me tonight.'

'Of course, but you must call me Camille,' she says, her voice still smooth and unruffled even though she looks like she wants to laugh along with her daughter. 'It's a pleasure to meet you, Chelsea. Although – have we met before? I hear you were at the same school as Isabella?'

'We haven't met before,' Chelsea reassures her.

'She was in the year below, Mama,' Izzy says, sounding as if this might not be the first time she's explained the situation, 'we didn't know each other.'

'Of course, that's right. But oh! Happy birthday! How could I forget, the reason we are all here?' Here, she winks at Chelsea before picking up the bottle of champagne to top up the girls' glasses and pour herself one. 'Isabella has been texting me all week, telling me how excited she is to be celebrating her birthday with you. "Birthday twins", I think that's what she called it?'

'Yeah, although I think it was Hannah who said that first.'

'Ah, Hannah, yes, I'm just trying to wrap my head around all of Isabella's new friends. Is she the singer?'

'She's pretty into musicals, yeah.'

'And the other one. Alisha?'

'Ayesha, Mama.'

'Ayesha. That's right. I'm just so glad you all seem to be getting on well and having such a good time. I was worried at first, Isabella coming here without knowing anyone. It's normal for a mother to be worried, of course, but there was that mess with your friends at school, and I know you were nervous too, *mon coeur*.'

Chelsea looks over at Izzy, sipping on her champagne, leaning back in a giant armchair. Nervous? She hadn't seemed it, and what does Camille mean by 'mess with your friends at school'? Izzy hasn't mentioned any kind of falling-out, but she is determinedly avoiding Chelsea's gaze, so perhaps there was one. One she'd rather forget about.

'Those weren't nerves, Mama, that was excitement.'

'If you say so, but there is a fine line between nerves and excitement, I always think. Regardless, I hear you had quite the party last night, Chelsea. Are you still paying for it, like Isabella, or have you fully recovered?'

'The champagne's got me fully recovered, Mama, don't worry.'

'Ah yes, a little hair of the dog,' Camille says with raised eyebrows. 'In French, we like to say we're killing the worm.'

'Savage,' Izzy says, over the top of her champagne glass, smiling at her mother.

'Don't you mean "*sauvage*", *mon coeur*?'

'I didn't know you could speak French, Iz.'

'Oh, she can understand it, but she refuses to speak it. I tried and tried when she was growing up, always only speaking French to her, but she always responded in English. Little did she know she was breaking her poor mother's heart.'

'I can get by,' Izzy pouts.

'What about you, Chelsea? *Parlez-vous français?*'

'No, I did Spanish instead of French for GCSE.'

'No language A-levels?' Camille asks.

'No.'

'Well, I hate to say it, but you will regret that.'

Chelsea watches as Camille laughs and drains her champagne glass.

'Mum, God.'

'What?' Camille says with a shrug. 'Chelsea, I didn't mean to be rude, only that it's always our adult selves who pay for our childish mistakes and oversights.'

Chelsea feels her cheeks redden as Camille speaks and takes a big swig of champagne to hide her embarrassment.

'Yeah, yeah, and hindsight is twenty–twenty,' Izzy says with a roll of her eyes.

'Wasn't that the theme of your party last night?'

'Actually, it was twenty–nineteen.'

'And how exactly did you dress up as twenty–nineteen?' Izzy is about to launch into an explanation of their fancy dress, but Camille checks her watch and exclaims, 'Oh, girls, we really should leave! I told them to order us a taxi for now, it's probably waiting downstairs. Are you ready, Isabella?'

'Yep, all good. Chels, you ready to go?'

Chelsea nods, chugging down the rest of her champagne while Camille and Izzy are busy gathering up their coats and handbags.

'If you're really lucky, Mum will tell you the story of my birth in the cab on the way over,' Izzy says to Chelsea as they leave the suite, the door banging swiftly and decisively shut behind them, making Chelsea jump.

* * *

'Come on, it'll be fun. A cute little slumber party tonight, room-service breakfast tomorrow. What's not to love?'

Chelsea looks between Izzy, who is sitting next to her in the back seat of the taxi, and Camille, who has taken the front passenger seat, staring resolutely through the rain-sluiced window as the windscreen wipers do their best to sweep it all away. In the dark, mother and daughter look so similar, Izzy could be a carbon cut-out, but in their demeanour, they could not be more different. Where Izzy wears her heart on her sleeve, fizzing energy and a ready laugh, Camille is contained, controlled, her sphinx-like smile a badge of honour she only bestows sparingly. Chelsea wants to know if she really is welcome to stay the night, or would she be interrupting family time, overstaying her welcome, but Camille makes no indication either for or against. In fact, it is almost impossible to tell whether or not she has heard the two girls in the back.

'How else can I sweeten the deal?' Izzy muses. 'Okay, here's something — you won't have to put up with with Hannah's over-enthusiastic morning singing.'

Chelsea groans and laughs. She shares a wall with Hannah and has been woken by a pitch-perfect but nevertheless annoying rendition of 'Unwritten' by Natasha Bedingfield almost every morning since the beginning of term. Which, as much as she loves Hannah, has begun to wear thin. 'All right, you've convinced me.'

'Yay!' Izzy claps, and Chelsea thinks she can see Camille smile in the gloom of the passenger seat. Or maybe it's just the flashing of the lights, as the city passes by.

It's a two-bedroom suite and Camille bids them a '*bonne nuit*' as she escapes to her own space, while Izzy makes them gin and tonics from the minibar and insists they change into the fluffy white hotel robes hanging in the bathroom before getting into bed. King-sized, the bed could easily fit two more of them, but Izzy piles up the space in between them with chocolate and sweets as Chelsea flicks through the TV channels.

'So, is it everything you imagined it to be?' Izzy asks, snuggling down into the bed, her face almost disappearing amid the bank of pillows and vast, billowing duvet.

'What, the suite?'

'No, uni. The collegiate life.'

'I guess so,' Chelsea says, turning her attention from the TV to Izzy. 'What about you?'

'I asked you first.'

'I mean, yes. I think so. It's everything I *hoped* it would be. I was pretty nervous, to be honest.'

'Really? You hid that well. You're so . . .' Izzy makes a gesture, brushing her shoulders off with just the tips of her fingers and Chelsea laughs. 'What? You are. Like water off a duck's back.'

'I guess I just hide it well, maybe. That's not how I felt. The water was very much on this duck's back.'

'Oooh, so you're a faker? You're admitting to faking it?'

'Fake it 'til you make it, baby. Just like MTV taught us.'

Izzy lets out a half-hearted 'ha', as she opens a packet of Minstrels. She pops a couple in her mouth, talking around them as she says, 'Do you think it's weird we weren't friends at school?'

'Not really,' Chelsea says, turning her attention back to the TV channels. 'We weren't in the same year, we didn't really know each other.'

'Yeah, but I feel like I've known you for ever now, and it's only been three weeks.'

'That's uni, though, isn't it? It's the same with Han and Ayesha, I can't imagine not knowing them now.'

Izzy is quiet and Chelsea stares at the other girl's profile as she gazes intently at the TV screen. Chelsea has stopped at Film4 and they're showing a movie she knows she's seen before but can't remember the title of. It's there, at the back of her mind, on the tip of her tongue, but she can't quite reach it yet.

'It makes me feel bad,' Izzy says, still watching the TV.

'What does?'

'That we didn't know each other. Like I was ignoring you or something.'

Chelsea shrugs. 'It really doesn't matter, Iz. Not to me, at least. We weren't friends then, we are now. That's all that really matters.'

'Really?'

'Yeah, you didn't know me well enough to ignore me back then. Don't worry about it. Now, if you ignored me now . . .'

'I'd have something to worry about?'

'Absolutely.'

Izzy laughs, but it sounds half-hearted as she picks at another packet of sweets, seems to think better of it, and peels back the lid of the fancy gold box of Godiva chocolates. But instead of choosing a chocolate, or offering Chelsea one, she flips the lid up and down, up and down, before picking up her phone and immediately putting it back down again. Chelsea snuggles down into the bed and watches her friend.

'What about your friends from school?' Chelsea asks eventually. 'Where have they all ended up?' She'd been surprised by Camille's comment earlier that evening, about the 'mess' Izzy had found herself in with her school friends. She hadn't heard any kind of gossip about a falling-out, which, as out of the loop as she was at that school, still strikes her as strange.

'Umm, all over really,' Izzy says, finally picking out a chocolate and popping it into her mouth. 'Victoria's at Oxford, of course, Emma's gone to Bristol, Ridgely – Sophie Ridgely, remember her? – she's at Leeds, Poppy's at St Andrew's. Like I said, all over.'

Izzy is staring determinedly at the TV still, not looking Chelsea's way. Chelsea can see a pulse at her jaw where she is clenching and unclenching. As Izzy reels off these names, Chelsea can visualize them perfectly, even though it's over a year since she saw any of them in person. Victoria was head girl and Chelsea can still see her pin-straight honey-brown hair swishing down her back as she'd head up on to the stage every assembly to read the morning bulletins. Sophie Ridgely was one of those sports girls, so popular with pupils and teachers alike that she got away with wearing trainers with her school uniform, a move no one else would ever even dare make. Poppy and Emma, both blonde and pretty, practically interchangeable although Chelsea's sure she'd be able to pick them out of a line-up if pushed. Those five girls – Victoria, Emma, Sophie, Poppy and, of course, Izzy – ruled the school, the tightest of tight-knit groups, impermeable, unpunishable, unreachable to a girl like her in the year below.

'Are you still in touch?'

'Ummm,' Izzy says, and Chelsea swears she can hear a tremble in that long, drawn-out sound. There's a big sniff and shit, yes, Izzy is crying.

'Iz? What the fuck? What's wrong?'

'Nothing, nothing,' she says, shaking her head, looking down at her lap and not meeting Chelsea's eye. Chelsea reaches over to the bedside table and pulls a tissue from the box there, passing it wordlessly to her friend.

'What's going on?' Chelsea asks after Izzy has blown her nose.

'Nothing, it's fine. It's just … they haven't texted or called about my birthday, at all. It's petty. I'm being stupid.' She's ripping up part of the tissue now, tearing it into smaller and smaller pieces. Chelsea can't help but think of that snotty tissue getting all over the bed they're going to be sleeping in but says nothing. 'They're just busy. It's uni, we're all in new places, and Victoria and Sophie didn't do a gap year so they're like, busy being second years. It shouldn't bother me so much.'

'Does this have anything to do with what your mum mentioned? About a big mess with your friends?'

Izzy loudly blows her nose again. 'Oh, it was nothing, she was over-exaggerating. We just had a bit of a falling-out during my gap year. Everything's fine now.'

'Really?' Izzy nods, still not looking at her. 'Then they should at least have texted to say happy birthday.'

Izzy shrugs. 'Oh, it's fine. I'm being stupid. It's only my birthday, right?'

But Izzy isn't an 'only my birthday' kind of girl. Chelsea has only known her properly for three weeks, and she already knows that much about her. In fact, she would've guessed that even before they got to know each other. So, for her best friends not to text her on her birthday – not even one of them – well, that does make her think there's something more going on. But maybe now is not the time to get to the bottom of it.

'Hey, speaking of, we've only got . . . six minutes of our birthday left. What should we do with it?'

Izzy turns to her, eyes wide if a little watery still, 'Go out on to the balcony and scream our lungs out?!'

Chelsea laughs, 'Won't we wake your mum up?'

'Oh, she always wears ear plugs, she won't hear a thing.'

The door to the balcony soundlessly slides open and suddenly the city is below and all around them. Streams of cars, illuminated like green and red insects, swarm the traffic-choked roads even at this time of night, while the rest of the city appears in greyscale, rain-soaked and autumn-smoky. Chelsea doesn't want to get close to the edge, not really, but Izzy grabs her hand and pulls her closer to the balcony's balustrade, Chelsea's pulse ratcheting up, nausea sweeping through her, as she tries to avoid looking down. They're both in the hotel robes, beacons of white fluffy luxury in the otherwise dull night, the towelling material getting slowly pockmarked by raindrops.

'Come on,' Izzy says, giving one last tug on Chelsea's hand, until she's standing right next to her at the balcony's edge. Chelsea watches as Izzy bends forward, bracing against the balustrade, and with a deep breath, opens her mouth to scream. The sound tears at the night, ripping a hole in it, clawing at the city air, but even as Chelsea opens her mouth to join Izzy in her primal yell, she knows that, down below on the rain-soaked streets, no one will hear a thing.

'That wasn't so bad, was it?' Nikki says, buckling herself in before turning over the key in the ignition. It's dark already, and they're only just leaving the vet surgery after Chelsea's first day on the job. As she looks out of the passenger window, her gaze snags on the crescent moon hanging in the black sky, and for some reason, she can't take her eyes off it.

'Chelsea?' Nikki prompts. 'That was all okay, right?'

'Yeah, yeah, sorry. I'm just a bit dazed.'

Everyone had been as welcoming as Nikki had promised they'd be, but behind their warm smiles and solicitous words, Chelsea knew there was something else, a wariness, yes, but also a hunger to know more about her, to ask questions her aunt had probably prepped them not to ask. She already dreads going back, getting more comfortable there, sharing lunches with her new colleagues, who, sometime from now, will feel confident enough to actually ask those questions. It's good that they know who she really is. It would be worse, she thinks, if they didn't, and she was forced to reveal it in the future, a big twist for them to gasp and recoil at. But just because they know, doesn't stop them from wanting to know more. It never does. She can't say this to Nikki though. For one thing, it would make her feel bad, and Chelsea doesn't want that, so she just says, 'They were all really nice. And I loved being around all those animals all day.'

'Did you? Oh, I'm glad.'

'Horrible seeing the really sick ones though – don't you find it hard?'

'Yeah, of course, but we're helping them get better in most cases, so that's what keeps me going.'

'I just hate that they don't know what's going on, and you can't explain it to them.'

They've reached the turning for Nikki's cottage now, and Nikki looks over at Chelsea briefly, her face illuminated by the light of the dashboard, 'Me too, love. Me too.'

Once inside the cottage, Nikki says she'll start work on dinner after she's showered and changed. 'Why don't you take a look at some of those boxes in your room?' she says, as she disappears upstairs. Chelsea had seen the boxes as soon as she entered the bedroom on her first night, of course, but hasn't touched them, hasn't really been able to look at them. They're unlabelled, but she knows some of them are from her room in Birmingham – packed up and put away by her mum once the police allowed her to. Others are from their house in London, these ones packed up by Nikki after Louise died. Nikki has already asked her to go through them, to see what she wants to keep and wants to give or throw away. Her aunt didn't feel able to make those decisions when she sorted through Louise's home, which Chelsea appreciates, but the thought of going through a stack of memories, each one as mundane as it is painful, makes her stomach coil up. She's already started to think of them as her 'Izzy' boxes, and her 'Mum' boxes, and as she makes a cup of tea and takes it upstairs she wonders which will be the less painful of the two, which loss she should start with.

'Oh good,' Nikki says, popping her head round the door to Chelsea's room about twenty minutes later, 'you're getting started . . . Chels, are you all right?'

Chelsea nods, unable to reply. There is something stuck in her throat, something she can't talk around, it's been there ever since she first opened one of her 'Izzy' boxes. Some – most, in fact – of it is as mundane as she'd imagined, so mundane she let out a laugh when she first took out the almost-ancient bottle of Tigi surf spray, its nozzle crusted over with chemical residue. Her mum must have just swept everything up that she was allowed to take, because the boxes aren't organized in any way, everything jumbled together so that a perfume bottle has been leaking its too-sweet scent into the cardboard all these years, sending up a rose-scented smoke signal as soon as she lifted the lid. Chelsea had completely forgotten she used to wear that particular perfume, but the smell takes her right back, first to their halls of residence and then to that house in Selly Oak, to all those nights out. But then, underneath all those everyday things, she'd found more significant things – tickets and postcards and wristbands, yes, all totally normal, and yet also memorials, tokens to a life she had once lived and a time and a place that no longer existed.

As Nikki stands over her now, she flips through a pile of postcards she'd bought during Freshers' Week and taped up over her desk. There are some moody black and white shots – she turns one over and sees the name Henri Cartier-Bresson – but there are also bright, Art Nouveau

71

illustrations, their twists and turns and curlicues, women's faces half turned away from the viewer, coy, mysterious and yet frank, full on. She doesn't remember each individual image, despite how long she'd had them up on her walls first in halls, and later in Selly Oak, but she remembers being at the card stand in the campus Waterstones, picking these out between their introductory classes. Izzy had been there too, sucking on the straw of a Starbucks drink, as she always seemed to be doing in those days. And then, tucked into the stack of cards, there are the photos.

'Ah,' Nikki says softly above her, and Chelsea feels rather than sees her aunt sit down at the edge of her bed. 'Must be nice to see those again, I bet.'

Chelsea's eyes are swimming as she leafs through them. She knows her aunt means well, but 'nice' isn't the word she'd use. It's a specific kind of torture, a rosy-hued nostalgia sliced all the way through with razor wire, people and a place she can never go back to, people and a place that led her into a hell she's only just beginning to work her way out of, fifteen years later. 'Nice' doesn't come close, doesn't even begin to cover it. But maybe it is good to see all their faces again, the way they were. To remember what all of this has been about: a girl, a young woman taken from them too soon. In so many of the photos, Izzy stares out at her, blonde hair shining, white teeth grinning. Her face is softer than Chelsea remembers it being, that bounce of youth that Chelsea will never get back and Izzy will now never lose. Who did this to her, really? Who saw that girl and decided she didn't get to live in the world any more? The question claws at Chelsea now, just as it has clawed at her for the past fifteen years, and she has to take a deep breath to steady herself. The photos are mostly from nights out, taken on disposable cameras and out of focus or dark and grainy, but she can see them all so clearly in her mind's eye, hear and smell them all getting ready, perfume and that particular scent of cheap make-up, vodka and cranberry juice and hair burning on hair straighteners, 'Chelsea Dagger' pumping tinnily out of Ayesha's laptop. She would always play that as they got ready, elated at being able to scream Chelsea's name at the top of her lungs along to music. Towards the end there's a picture from much later, all four of them sombre in black, with their arms around one another standing in a South London cemetery. Izzy hadn't wanted to be in the photo, hadn't wanted the photo to be taken, and Chelsea could hardly blame her, but someone – Camille? A distant relative? – had insisted, claimed that one day, she'd be ready for the memory, grateful for memorializing the moment. And Chelsea, who always had a disposable camera on her back then, had provided the means to do so. She can't remember getting it developed, or looking at it at the time, but she must've done, the evidence of her doing so held in her hands right now. She passes it to Nikki. 'Izzy's dad's funeral,' she says.

'Oh, of course. God, it all happened so close together, didn't it? That poor family.'

'Is that where she is?'

'Sorry?'

'The cemetery? Is that where Izzy is buried?'

'I don't know, love. But probably, if that's where her dad is.' Chelsea doesn't say anything, she can't. Again,

73

made mute by memory, trying to hold back a feeling she's already been holding back for fifteen years. Nikki pats her thigh. 'I'll give you a call when dinner's ready,' she practically whispers, and Chelsea nods in response, staring down at the photo in her lap. She picks it up, brings it closer to her face. They all look so young, so much future ahead of them despite the sad circumstances; how could any of them have known that less than six weeks later, Izzy would be dead? The photo starts to shake in her hand, wavering in front of her face, and she leans forward, drops it back in the box. The only other things in here are stuff from her desk. She imagines her mum simply taking her arm and sweeping everything off her dressing table and desk into this box, shutting it up and never looking at it again. *Did* she ever look in here again? It doesn't look like it. She rifles through a couple of notebooks, before coming across the course guide for the year 2007/2008, and she lets out a bark of laughter; those dates seem so far away now. And yet they've remained so present, the year her life completely changed.

She sighs, paging through the course catalogue, and then stops dead, her breath pulled from her body. The face staring up at her from a page detailing the options available for history students is so immediately familiar. In fact, it's a face she hasn't been able to stop thinking about for the past fifteen years. The face of the person she thinks might really have killed Izzy: Jamie Sinclair.

'Ugh, God,' Izzy says, looking at her phone and then throwing it carelessly into the open mouth of her gaping bag.

'What?' Chelsea asks.

They're in the Mason Lounge, buying tea and crisps and chocolate to see them through their final lecture of the day, which starts in twenty minutes. Chelsea stirs her tea, pressing the teabag against the side of the cardboard cup before throwing it in the bin, shoving a plastic lid on top of it and grabbing her pack of salt and vinegar crisps.

'Brother Charles,' Izzy says in a glum, ominous voice and Chelsea has to stare back to look at her face, downturned and lined with an uncharacteristic frown. They find a seat and settle down, placing overflowing bags at their feet, folders on the table, cups and crisps. Izzy hasn't told Chelsea much about her brother, only that he is older and from her dad's first marriage, but usually she refers to him simply as 'Charlie', so things must not be good.

'What does he want?' Chelsea asks.

'Oh, it's just . . . boring company stuff. He keeps sending things over for me to read, and then when I don't get back to him about it, he cc's Dad in whenever he's reminding me just so dear Dad knows I'm not on top of things. He was just texting to ever so politely remind me to respond to the email he sent this morning.'

'So, this is all stuff to do with your dad's company?' Chelsea says.

'Yeah,' Izzy says with a sigh. She reaches for her tea and gives Chelsea a sidelong glance before continuing. 'I became a shareholder when I turned twenty, so now I'm on the board.'

'Oh. The board . . . like, the board –'

'Of directors.'

'You're a director? But you're . . .'

'Practically a child still? At university? Have better things to do? Yeah, I know. Weirdly, this is the one thing Charlie and I agree on, but we have very different ways of convincing Dad that I shouldn't be included yet. *He* wants to make me look stupid and incompetent, while *I* just want to have fun. For now, at least. And I'm not a director, not really. Just a shareholder and . . .' she waves her hand, trying to take in a world Chelsea can barely understand, 'I don't know, I get to vote and stuff. Who cares.'

'Your dad clearly cares if he wants you on the board.'

'Yeah, but it's just tradition.' Izzy takes a sip of tea, makes a face when she realizes it's still too hot, and rips into her chocolate bar instead. 'He's just made me do it a little earlier than usual. Charlie got to wait until he was twenty-five, but yay me, I get to start going to these meetings and reading all these minutes a whole five years early. I don't know why, it's not like I even want to go into the business, you know?'

'Does he know that?'

'Who?'

'Your dad, Iz.'

'Yeah, he knows. This is his way of keeping all of us close, regardless of what we decide to do in life.'

'What about Charlie?'

'Oh, Charlie works for him,' she says, rolling her eyes. 'Charlie is like, waiting for the throne to become vacant, not that he'd ever admit to that. It's like, I just wish it wasn't assumed I wanted to work for the company, I wish I was given the option to do whatever I want, you know?'

'Oh, come on, you can do whatever you want. I bet your dad would be fine with it if you just told him how you felt,' Chelsea says, her voice tight.

Izzy looks at Chelsea, and there's a beat of silence before she finally says, 'Hmm, yeah, you're probably right.' Chelsea nods and leans forward to grab her cup of tea again as Izzy says a bright, 'Hey!' to someone standing over their table.

'Oh, hey Joe,' Chelsea says, looking up at the person who has just appeared in front of them. Joe is one of the few students on their course that Chelsea and Izzy have spent any time with. From that first lecture when they sat together, right in the middle of the auditorium, they have come as a pair, always sitting in the same place, arriving together, leaving together, not really talking to anyone else. But a few weeks into term, Joe had taken the seat one removed from Chelsea, and proceeded to sit there every time, until they were told they had to form groups to create a presentation and he turned to them and finally spoke, asking to be part of theirs. So, now he doesn't leave a space between their seats and the three of them tend to arrive and leave together.

'Hey, guys. Are you heading into the lecture soon?'

Joe hovers over them and Chelsea pulls an empty chair

closer to them, motions at it for him to sit down, 'Yeah, we're just fuelling up. How did you get on with this week's reading?'

'Oh my God, what a yawn-fest. I could barely make my way through it,' Izzy says.

'It was a little tough,' Joe concedes.

'I want to learn about history-history, not like, the *concept* of history,' Izzy says.

'We have to do both though; history-history only exists as we know it because whoever tells it to us has been allowed to tell it.'

'History's not exactly made up though, Chels,' Izzy says, frowning at her. 'It's history.'

'It kind of is made up though. Or at least, there's plenty that's left out of the main narrative. Whoever is doing the telling is always missing something, whether on purpose or because of perspective. There are always things that fall through the cracks.'

'You two should really save this for seminar,' Joe says, looking between the two girls.

'Yeah, Chelsea, stop making me think for myself outside of seminar,' Izzy says with a pout and a laugh.

Joe laughs. 'Did you hear about Robertson? He's not teaching any more classes this term; apparently, we're getting a new guy today.'

'What?' Izzy says. 'Who do we have instead? How did we not hear about this?'

'Maybe we need to make more friends on our course,' Chelsea posits.

'Take that back immediately,' Izzy says, before turning to Joe. 'Do you know who the new lecturer is?'

'Yeah, we got an email about it this morning. Didn't either of you see it? It's some guy called James Sinclair.'

'James Sinclair,' Izzy says slowly, taking a sip of her tea, before standing up suddenly and launching herself at one of the spare computers that sit in the middle of the room. After a few seconds she waves both of them over. 'There he is. Ooh, he's young, look, Chels. Doesn't he look . . . kinda hot?'

Chelsea is staring at the photo Izzy has directed them both towards and laughs, 'I'm going to reserve judgment until we see him in the flesh.'

'You think he's hot?' Joe says and Chelsea flicks her gaze to him, noticing that the skin on his neck has started to turn a little pink.

'Yeah, he looks like . . . oh, come on, Chels, help me out here, you remember everything.'

'I can't read your mind though. He doesn't look like anyone to me.'

'Yes, yes, he does. The guy in *The Notebook*, but not the main guy. The one she doesn't end up with?'

'What? No. You're crazy.'

'No, I'm telling you, just imagine that guy with a beard like this guy.'

'I think you need glasses.'

Izzy turns away from the computer screen to look up at Chelsea, a smile on her face that Chelsea hasn't seen before. 'Ooh, this is going to be fun. I can't wait to debate the meaning of history now. Come on, we're going to be late.'

Izzy rushes up to grab her stuff but as Chelsea makes to follow her, she realizes that Joe is hanging back, still staring at the computer that Izzy hasn't bothered to log out of. 'Come on,' she says, tilting her head towards the exit, 'we are a bit late now.'

'You really think he's hot?'

'*I* don't, Izzy does.'

Joe nods. 'Right, right.'

But as they leave the Mason Lounge, Izzy already ten steps ahead of them, Chelsea's sure something's not quite right.

Jamie Sinclair. It's the name that has rung, like a bell, in her mind for fifteen-plus years. As incessant and predictable as the hourly marking of a grandfather clock, there hasn't been a day that's gone by without Chelsea thinking about him. When she was first arrested, it was like a clamour, a ringing that wouldn't stop. She'd mentioned him to the police when she was first being questioned, but they seemed to just shrug off her suspicions, not caring at all that Chelsea knew – she *knew* – something had happened between him and Izzy. She'd had no proof, of course, and even thinking about it now, her chest starts to constrict with the same anxiety she felt when the detectives started to home in on her, when she began to realize they weren't planning on looking elsewhere, looking at anybody else. She presses her hand to her chest now, that same anxiety making it hard to breathe, her heart straining at her ribcage, at the injustice of it all. Back then, it had felt like she was in the passenger seat of a car about to be driven off a cliff, no control, no way of making it all slow down, making it all stop, no one else in the car to help her. She'd been forced to slow down in prison, forced to grind to a halt even. That hadn't halted her suspicions, but the constant ringing in her ears had quietened over the years. If it hadn't, she would've been driven mad.

But now she can actually do something about it. Now,

she can heed the warning of the bell only she can hear. She takes a deep breath, and it rattles around in her chest, sounds enormously loud in the quiet of the room. Dropping to the floor, she quickly searches the rest of her boxes, looking for the heaviest one, the one that might hold her now ancient laptop. And then she remembers, the realization slamming into her chest – how could she possibly forget? The police took it as evidence.

* * *

Nikki lends Chelsea her own laptop after dinner and she takes it back to her room, the prospectus still there, reminding her of what she wants to do. She lies on her bed, computer resting in her lap, and turns it on. It's not particularly new – Nikki says she doesn't use it much – and it feels unbalanced and weighty on her legs, but still, it's a hell of a lot newer than the computers at Foston, booting up in half the time it used to take them. She wants to check the university website first, see if Jamie is still working there, but when she scrolls though the History Department website, she can see he's no longer part of it. There are still a few familiar faces – professors who seemed ancient even back in 2006, but are somehow still working, plus one or two she remembers with an element of fondness, despite everything that happened. She chews the inside of her cheek, knowing where she needs to go next, not wanting to, dreading it in fact.

Facebook.

She knows Jamie was on it back then, probably still is, but she has steered clear of social media, both old and new, ever since she was arrested and has no intention of joining or re-joining any of the platforms now. She doesn't need that kind of visibility – in fact, would prefer to avoid it at all costs – but this might be the only way she can get an idea of where Jamie is, what he's doing and how to get hold of him. She's barely let that idea unfurl itself inside her brain, but it's there, nascent, nagging. Because there's only so much a Facebook profile will tell her after all. And what she really needs is the opportunity to ask Sinclair all the questions that have been burning a hole in her brain since 2007. Fingers sweaty with nerves, she opens up the internet browser and goes to Facebook, hoping that, after all this time, she'll still be able to access her long dormant account. She can remember the password easily enough – it was the only one she ever used – and yes, there it is, the still familiar platform with its blue banner blinking back at her.

She searches his name and he comes up easily enough, Facebook knowing in that way it does, that they have a shared history. But when she clicks on his thumbnail she sees that he has set his profile to private now, and she can go no further. She's not an idiot, she's not about to add him as a friend, so she bites down on her bottom lip, wondering where to go and what to do next. Shoving the laptop off her knees, she gets up and sits down again amongst her boxes, amid the detritus of her life. She picks up the old hair-product bottle, sticky with age. It doesn't make her smile this time, her heart swelling up, pushing at her breastbone, knocking at her chest, tears pricking at her eyes. How can this be all she has? It's more than she had a week ago, back in Foston Hall, sure, but how can her life be reduced to such few, seemingly worthless possessions? How can this be all that's left of her mum? Of

Izzy? She puts the bottle down again, picking up the small stack of photos instead, flicking through them like a flip book; smiles and laughter, smiles and laughter, the occasional pout from Izzy or Hannah. She lets go of a deeply held breath and it's as if something breaks inside her; a dam that's she kept built up for the past fifteen years, letting loose a vast well of anger and pain. She picks up the Tigi bottle, throws it across the room, the clatter it makes as it hits the skirting board and rolls backwards from the wall an anti-climax. She's felt this brewing, this breaking dam or eruption, or whatever you want to call it, ever since she got to Scotland, but she's so aware of the narrow road she's meant to be walking right now, overlooked, not just by her parole officer but by Nikki too. If she makes one detour, steps off the path for even a moment, not only could she find herself on the wrong side of both Kate McClure and the parole board, but she could lose the support of Nikki. Maybe even find herself back in prison.

How is she supposed to do this? It's harder than she'd anticipated, this freedom that's not quite freedom. She would never willingly go back, of course, but inside, at least the walls were there to keep her imagination in check, to keep her theories at bay, to keep her anger from spreading too far, too wide. She was contained. Here, now, she sees where she might be able to roam freely, but that ability hasn't been gifted to her yet. Is she supposed to simply wait? Wait until she's worked free of the system, and her parole? She'd thought she might be able to do that – what's a couple more years after all, when she's already done fourteen? – but now she's not so sure. Now she wants to hunt down the answers to all those questions that have been burning a hole in her brain for fifteen years. Now she wants to know what happened to Izzy all those years ago, and who she took the fall for. Now she wants to show them what fifteen years of waiting can do to a person.

Transcript of interview with Chelsea Keough on 28 October 2007
conducted by Detective Inspector Rob Bailey and Detective
Constable Natalie Ajala at Birmingham Central Police Station

Detective Inspector Rob Bailey: Talk us through when you got home on Saturday night, Sunday morning, Chelsea. How did that go?

Chelsea Keough: What do you mean? I've already told you I can't remember exactly what time it was.

Detective Constable Natalie Ajala: That's fine, Chelsea, but how did you get home, for example?

CK: I got a minicab.

RB: From Digbeth?

CK: Yes. You can pick them up from the main road by the Factory. There's normally loads.

RB: And when you got home, can you remember anything being out of place? Was the front door shut and properly locked?

CK: Yes. It wasn't double locked, but I wasn't expecting it to be because I knew Izzy was home.

NA: So your door needs a double lock?

CK: When we leave the house we have to double lock it, yeah.

NA: But it locks when you pull it shut? You don't have to use your keys for it to be locked?

CK: Yeah, yeah, exactly.

RB: And the door to Izzy's room, was that closed the whole time?

87

CK: Um ... I don't think I noticed when I got home ... like I said, I was pretty drunk, but I expect it was. And it was definitely shut the whole morning, so I guess so.

RB: Okay. So, the doors were closed as they should've been.

CK: Yeah, but ...

[pause]

NA: But what, Chelsea?

CK: In the morning ... I noticed there was stuff out of place in the living room.

NA: Like what?

CK: Um, the coffee table.

RB: There were items missing from the coffee table?

NA: We didn't log a coffee table in the living room.

CK: Yeah, exactly. It was missing.

RB: An entire coffee table was missing?

NA: Why didn't you mention this earlier, Chelsea?

CK: Um, I don't know, sorry. I only just thought about it, I'm really sorry.

NA: Why do you think it would be missing?

CK: I don't know ... it's just ... just a coffee table.

NA: What did you think when you noticed it was missing last night? Or did you notice? Maybe you didn't realize until this morning?

CK: I can't remember if I noticed it last night ... probably not. I definitely noticed it this morning. I just thought it was weird? I assumed Izzy must've done something to it.

RB: Like what?

CK: I don't know, damaged it somehow or taken it into her room for some reason. It was hers anyway.

NA: What sort of coffee table was it, Chelsea?

CK: Um, I don't know. A nice one? It was an antique. It had a marble top.

NA: Was it round?

CK: No, square.

NA: Okay, that's good to know. Thanks for alerting us to that.

CK: Yeah. Sorry I didn't mention it earlier.

RB: That's fine, it can be hard to know what is and isn't important. That's why we want you to take us through everything. Did you notice anything else missing?

CK: I don't think so. I don't know. It's hard . ... hard to remember.

RB: What about her mobile phone?

CK: Her phone?

NA: We haven't been able to find it, Chelsea. It wasn't in her room or anywhere else in the house.

CK: Oh. That's ... she definitely had it with her at the Factory. She was texting me while she was still there.

NA: Do you think we could see those messages, Chelsea?

CK: Sure. Okay.

[sound of movement, something landing on the table]

Look, she texted me at ... 12:43.

RB: That's very helpful, thank you.

[short pause]

CK: She didn't text to say she got home though. I should've ... should've realized ... oh God.

NA: It's okay, it's not your fault, Chelsea.

CK: But ... but maybe this means she left the phone in the minicab?

RB: That's a thought. You know the make and model of the mobile?

CK: Yeah, um, it's a Motorola RAZR. You know, those really flat ones? It's bright pink.

NA: Okay, that's really helpful, thank you Chelsea. We'll come back to this later. Moving on: is there anyone Izzy has had any issues with at uni?

CK: What? No.

NA: Nothing? No break-ups, or big fights with anyone?

CK: No, I don't think so.

NA: You'd know though, wouldn't you? You're very close friends?

CK: Yes.

[pause]

NA: Chelsea? I can see you thinking. Anything could be relevant at this point, so it's important you let us know about anything you think could have led to this.

CK: Well, I don't know about ... *this*, but Izzy did have this thing for one of our lecturers.

RB: Who?

CK: James Sinclair. Jamie. We had him for two different modules last year.

NA: So, he's in the History Department?

CK: Yes, and actually he was assigned as Izzy's personal tutor this year.

RB: And what does that mean, being a personal tutor?

CK: It just means if you have any issues you need extra help with, that's the person you're meant to go to first.

NA: Pastoral care.

CK: Yeah, right.

RB: Izzy lost her dad at the beginning of this academic year – do you think that meant she would have been more in touch with him than usual?

CK: Yeah. I know they were, actually. Jamie had asked me to help out with getting Iz back up to speed with everything, otherwise he was worried she'd have to repeat this term at some point.

RB: Okay, and you say Izzy had a 'thing' for him, this Jamie? What exactly do you mean by that?

CK: She had a crush. She fancied him.

RB: Okay.

NA: Do you know if anything ever happened between them, Chelsea?

[pause]

Chelsea? Like I said before, anything could be relevant at this point.

CK: Well ... I ... I did see them together once.

2006

'Oh my gosh, I'm so glad you're here,' Hannah says in a rush.

'Of course we're here, Han,' Ayesha says.

'Yeah, you told us you'd kill us in our sleep if we didn't turn up, remember?' Chelsea says.

'I know, I know, we were all just so scared the auditorium was going to be completely empty, and I really wanted my parents to come but it turns out they couldn't make it.'

'Calm down, Han,' Izzy says with a laugh, 'you need to save your breath for the performance. And tell everyone they can bloody relax, because it looks like a full house in there.'

'Really?'

'Yeah, I've already been in to save us seats. I was just coming back to help with the wine.'

'Oh, good! Yay! Phew. Don't get too drunk though, please?'

'We won't embarrass you,' Ayesha says, 'don't worry.'

'It's not that, it's just . . . oh, never mind. God, I'm so nervous, I feel like I've taken something.'

'*Have* you?' Chelsea asks, because Hannah does seem even more worked up than usual, her bright eyes gleaming with nervous energy.

'No!' she cries, outraged at Chelsea's accusation before

grabbing on to her arm and practically whispering, 'Oh God, I don't know if I can do this.'

'Hannah, come on, this is what you were born to do,' Chelsea says. 'I didn't spend all term waking up to you singing for nothing, did I?'

Hannah grimaces, and Ayesha says, 'Yeah, and I didn't run lines with you for three whole weeks for you to back out now, so you better get backstage right now or I'm revoking our friendship.'

Hannah's eyes widen in horror, as if she really thinks Ayesha might stop being her friend if she doesn't perform onstage tonight, but it seems to do the trick, and the three of them watch as she scurries off just in time for a student with a loudspeaker to alert them that it's time to take their seats.

* * *

They're leaving the auditorium in the scrum of the audience, high on the performance and Hannah's talent despite all three of them admitting that they're not normally fans of a musical, when someone touches Chelsea just above the elbow and says her name.

'Joe, hey, I didn't see you earlier!' They don't see Joe much outside of their lectures, seminars and the Mason Lounge in between classes, so it's a little weird seeing him here, now, out of context. Chelsea certainly wouldn't have thought he'd be much of a theatre-goer – she's sure she's spotted him through the crowds at Snobs and other indie nights in the city, although they've never actually bumped into each other at any of them.

'Hey Chelsea, Izzy.'

'Hi Joe,' Izzy says, her eyes slicing towards him before grabbing Ayesha by the arm and starting to discuss where they should go for a drink. Chelsea isn't sure if Izzy meant this to seem like a rebuff to Joe or not, but it certainly comes off that way, and she turns to him to give him a smile, trying to silently communicate that, sometimes, that's just Izzy's way. But Joe doesn't seem too bothered, smiling back and sort of rolling his eyes, so it feels like they're in cahoots.

'What did you think?' Chelsea asks.

'Good, yeah. Not normally my kind of thing. My flatmate's in the chorus so I thought I should show support on opening night.'

'Oh, us too,' Izzy says now, 'we were literally just saying we're not musicals people, but Han was so good.'

'Han?' Joe says.

'Hannah Grant,' Chelsea says, 'our flatmate. She was Cinderella.'

'Shit, yeah, she was great,' Joe says.

'Thank you!' Izzy says, interested again, now that there's a compliment to accept, despite it being meant for someone else.

Joe gives a startled laugh before saying, 'Are you heading to Gunnies? The whole cast and crew are going there after, apparently, and then on to the director's house for a party.'

'Oh perfect, we didn't know there was a plan. Han was all over the place when we saw her earlier,' Izzy says. She links arms with Ayesha, and the two of them set off at a rapid pace, expertly weaving through the now dispersing crowd. Chelsea follows more slowly, Joe at her side, as he introduces her to his own flatmates and they all start to chat about the show.

'We've seen you around, right? At all the indie nights?' his friend, Gareth, asks her.

Chelsea nods and, from the corner of her eye, thinks she can see Joe's face turning red. Interesting. If you'd asked her last week, or even just five minutes ago, she would've guessed Joe fancied Izzy, but maybe that was just Chelsea's assumption that everyone was always more interested in Izzy than her, leading her astray. Away from the theatre, campus is much quieter, the crowd having disappeared into the black night, but despite that Joe is still walking close to her, his arm brushing hers every now and again, the swish-swish of his jacket sleeve touching hers a constant reminder that he's there. Illuminated only by the orangey glow of the campus streetlamps, Chelsea does her best to look over at him as subtly as possible while he chats animatedly with Gareth – they're comparing notes on the city's various indie clubs, debating which is the best, when suddenly Joe grabs her hand, saying, 'Oh shit, I was going to mention it on Monday – we got tickets to Mystery Jets and Foals in Manchester. Do you want to come? Bit of a mission, but they're not playing in Birmingham.'

'Yeah,' Chelsea says, 'yeah, of course, that sounds amazing.' Gunnies is looming in front of them now and she's completely lost sight of Izzy and Ayesha, who must've already gone in, intent on getting drinks. By the time she, Joe and his flatmates are in the pub, Ayesha and Izzy are already at the front of the bar, made easily visible by the distinctive thread of blue that runs through Ayesha's braids. Instead of joining them, Chelsea goes with the boys to the area that's been reserved by the drama club, and is almost immediately accosted by Hannah.

'How was I, Chels? Was I good?' she asks breathlessly, throwing her arms around Chelsea's neck.

'Well, you were a lot more sober, that's for sure,' Chelsea says with a laugh, extricating herself from the other girl's grip.

'We did shots backstage,' Hannah explains, although really, Chelsea could've guessed that.

'At least you waited until after the show, I guess.'

'Oh, I'd never drink *before* a show, Chelsea,' Hannah says with a hiccup, 'that would be very unprofessional.' Chelsea laughs, and she realizes that Joe is still standing next to her, laughing along too, so she introduces him to Hannah, whose eyes goes wide. 'What did *you* think? Did you love it?'

'Don't say anything, Joe, she's just looking for someone to feed her ego.'

'No, I thought you were great. Really.'

'Really?' Hannah asks, her eyes still wide.

'Yeah, you played the witch, right?' he says and Chelsea laughs at Hannah's explosive response. 'Calm down, calm down,' Joe continues, 'I know you were Cinderella. And you really were great. Didn't I say that already, Chelsea?'

'He did actually. Unprompted.'

'Hmm,' Hannah says, 'gonna have to keep an eye on you, Joe. Bit mean.' But then Izzy and Ayesha arrive with drinks and Hannah is absorbed into their exuberant slipstream, leaving Joe and Chelsea standing alone in the crowd together.

For a second they both watch Hannah, Ayesha and Izzy

97

chatting and laughing together, but then Joe turns to Chelsea and asks, his voice low, 'Can I ask you a question?'

'Sure.'

'Is it true that Izzy's dad is the Pennington's gin guy?'

'Oh.' Something dips in Chelsea's chest, but she ignores it, focuses her eyes on Izzy, whose crown of bright blonde hair bobs and waves in the crowd, glossy and gleaming even in the glare of bad pub lighting. 'Yeah, yeah. That's true.'

'Man,' Joe says, 'that's mental. Someone on our course told me, but I thought they were just making shit up. She must be loaded.'

'Mmm.' Is she disappointed? Maybe. But then again, maybe Joe's just making conversation. She tries to imagine how she would view Izzy if they hadn't started talking on the first day of term, if she didn't know her – or at least, know of her – from school, and she can see how a story, rumours, maybe even a myth, might develop around her. Even though she's just a girl, just a student, like all of them, there is undeniably something about Izzy, that effortless gloss, that social ease that can't be acquired, can only be inherited. Chelsea's gut twists in an uncomfortable way, and she wishes she had a drink in her hand, something to distract her, something to do, but her gaze stays on her friend, watching how her halo of hair glitters, how everyone turns to look when she throws back her head in laughter. Strange, how even though it's Hannah who put on a performance tonight, it's still Izzy receiving all the adulation.

Chelsea takes the train to London. She never learned to drive and couldn't bring herself to ask Nikki to make that journey for her, while flying, with its requisite ID, is out of the question, what with both her passport and provisional driving licence being so long out of date. But she's glad she's on the train. Here, she can at least claim anonymity among the tourists and commuters who sit, just like her, staring wordlessly out of the window, or at phones and tablets, TV shows racing across their tiny screens, hunched over laptops, typing while mumbling under their breath or simply sleep, foreheads against the window, choosing rest while the train rumbles on, racing down the country towards the capital. So, no one is interested in her, no one gives her a second glance, but she's still glad of the baseball cap she stole off her aunt that morning, shoving it over her head and immediately relaxing into the cover it provided. Because her early release date may not have been publicized in the press yet, but it is the anniversary of Izzy's death soon, in fact it's just days away, and surely this means public interest is going to have one of its peaks soon, and it's only a matter of time before her face, along with Izzy's, is back in the papers or all over social media again. She used to think all those *Heat* magazine paparazzi shots of celebs in baseball caps were so stupid, but sinking down into her seat, she gets it now. It may not provide full anonymity, but at least it offers some level – however small – of control.

They're racing through the countryside now, the train's top speed eating up fields and villages, soaring through small towns and bypassing cities. With each mile, the tight band around Chelsea's chest releases slightly, making it easier and easier to breathe. By the time they reach the London suburbs, she has slept and reawakened, the sight of the identical houses and bare-limbed trees making her feel like a new person. At last, she is home. King's Cross is different though, lighter, airier, cleaner. Weak, late afternoon sunshine suffuses the once grungy station and everything looks glossy, manicured. She follows the signs to the underground, feeling like a tourist, a new visitor in her hometown, and of course she hates it. How can this be home if she doesn't even recognize it? Maybe she should've anticipated this, all the ways that London would've changed in her absence, not just this station, but its very streets, its contours, even its skyline. It's not a city that stands still. It's old, yes, ancient even in some places, but it's not trapped in amber the way some cities are; the new always pushes through, causing teething problems at first before everyone stops complaining, wonders what all the fuss was about in the first place.

She wasn't sure about making this trip, and Nikki was even less sure. Because while arriving in London feels like a homecoming, there's also a lot to lose by coming here. She's terrified of being spotted and having her identity exposed, splashed across a tabloid somewhere or on someone's phone screen, and she's not really meant to be away from her registered address for too long, or to veer off from her new routine of working at the vet surgery and spending every evening at home in Nikki's cottage. She'd had to ask permission from her parole officer too, informing her that she'd be away from Nikki's, and letting her know the address she'd be staying at instead. Chelsea had seen Kate's hesitation immediately, her face tightening, her whole body going still as she assessed the situation. But she'd agreed — as long as it was for no more than two nights — and on the proviso that Chelsea would do a call with her that evening. Her aunt had reservations too, when she first brought the topic up, but when she started to explain her reasoning, Nikki's attitude softened and she agreed it was a good idea for Chelsea to see her solicitor in person, and get started with putting her mum's house on the market.

She's still not sure she really wants to sell it, the memories alone make it priceless to her, but the last couple of weeks have made her realize that whatever happens in the next few months or even years, she may not ever find herself living back in London. At least not for a while. She's chafing under the constant scrutiny of Nikki and Kate, but for now their supervision is the price she must pay for this semblance of freedom. So, what's the point of hanging on to a house that's no longer her home? And besides all that, she wants to go to the cemetery and finally see where her friend was laid to rest. With the anniversary coming up, Nikki seemed to understand her need to say goodbye the way she would've done, if everything that happened, hadn't happened.

Underground, the tube is packed and she has to work hard to keep her head down, her eyes lowered as she squeezes into the carriage of a Northern Line train. But when she does look up, she realizes that almost everyone is doing as she's doing, avoiding eye contact, bending their heads over a free newspaper, a book, their phones. She tries to even out her breath, which feels unsteady and erratic; she's barely even admitted to herself how nervous she is about this part of the journey. Because once she gets off this tube at Balham, she's going to see Ayesha. She joins the stream of people leaving the station and takes a second to get her bearings, re-reading the text Ayesha sent her with directions. Amid this gaggle of commuters, it's almost as if she's just another one of them, heading home after a long day, and for a second she soaks in this sense of the everyday, the utterly normal. But then someone jostles her, their elbow sharp against her arm as they push past, and she stops dead, heart banging. But it's nothing to do with her – just someone rushing home or to the pub – and she takes a deep breath and carries on. Unlike in Nikki's small Scottish town, she doesn't feel any eyes on her here; just as she suspected, it's so much easier to disappear when there's a crowd to disappear into, and even when she turns off the main road and there are far fewer pedestrians on the pavement, she still feels blessedly anonymous, as if she could be anyone. Ayesha lives in a maisonette about a fifteen-minute walk from the station and as Chelsea approaches it, she starts to feel nervous again. They've spoken on the phone since she was released, and Ayesha is the only person, aside from first her mother and later Nikki, who stayed in regular contact with her throughout the past fifteen years. She visited at least twice a year, and made sure to call frequently. At first it was twice a month, and then once a month. As Chelsea's sentence stretched out, those calls did admittedly become less frequent, but Ayesha always assured her that it was more about her having too much on her plate, than not wanting to talk to Chelsea, and Chelsea, left with one friend in all the world, had to take her word for it. Because she didn't have to do any of that: Ayesha could have turned her back on her, just as almost everyone else did, just as Hannah did. And as Chelsea walks down the dusk-filled road to Ayesha's flat, all she can be is grateful that her friend believed her, that there was someone in the world, who wasn't related to her, who knew her well enough to know that she couldn't kill anyone. That she wasn't a murderer.

Now, as she presses the bell to Ayesha's flat, a series of images flash across her mind, a zoetrope of memories, and she tries to focus on the good ones, the moments that are worth remembering, rather than those she's spent half her life wishing she could forget. Ayesha's smile greets her first as she opens the door, wide and bright, and the other woman half laughs as she sets eyes on Chelsea, and then pulls her across the threshold and into a tight hug. Chelsea can't speak as she does this; there's a tightness in her throat, in her chest that she just can't move around.

Letting her go, and standing back as if to get a good look at her, Ayesha says, 'I used to worry this day would never come.'

'Me too.'

'You look –'

'Like shit?'

'No, no, not that, it's just so surreal. It's like the ghost of Christmas past standing on my doorstep. I know I've seen you at the prison, but it's so different, seeing you here, in front of me, in my own home.'

'Are you sure it's okay that I stay?' Chelsea can't help but ask this question. She's been worrying about it all the way from Scotland, because as loyal as Ayesha has been, as good a friend as she has proved to be, there's a big difference between biannual visits and frequent phone calls, and having Chelsea to stay in her home. But when Chelsea had called to ask if it would be okay if she stayed with her whilst she was in London, there wasn't even one moment of hesitation in Ayesha's voice as she said 'yes', and the relief of that had almost brought her to tears. She hadn't wanted to stay in an anonymous hotel or hostel in the city centre. Not least because she was so worried about what would happen if someone saw her name on a reservation, but also because she is desperate to pick Ayesha's brain. She's always been one of Chelsea's most trusted sounding boards, even back when they were still at uni, before all this happened, and all Chelsea needed to ask her opinion on was what to wear on a night out, or how best to wrap up a particularly testing essay. She knows that, just like her, Ayesha will have thoughts and theories on who really did this to Izzy. She'd tried to bring it up before, after the trial, when the worst had happened, and she was in prison, but Ayesha hadn't wanted to, had told Chelsea she should focus on getting through her sentence – it was Ayesha, in fact, who'd first suggested she try finishing up her degree inside. She didn't think it was healthy for Chelsea to dwell on other outcomes. Her mum had been the same. But she's hoping that now she's out, her friend might be more willing to help her think through possibilities, help work out what really happened that night. Help her clear her name and, just as importantly, find out who really killed Izzy.

And so now here she is, following her old friend down her narrow hallway, trying to take everything in. It's painted a deep, burnt coral colour and everywhere Chelsea looks, she sees evidence of how full and well-lived Ayesha's life is. There are photos lining the walls, mostly of Ayesha's family who Chelsea vaguely recognizes even as, in many, they have grown so much older, but also of people she doesn't know at all. There are prints and post-cards, posters from exhibitions Ayesha's been to, of films she loves, places she's been. Chelsea knows it was hard for her friend. Ayesha had dropped out of uni after Izzy's death and Chelsea's arrest, moving back in with her family in Leeds before choosing to pick her degree back up at Newcastle instead. But here was the evidence of not just Ayesha's survival, but her ability to thrive and grow. Chelsea is proud of her, there's no doubt about that, but she also has to push down that bitter taste of jealousy, the 'what if' questions that fill her mind as she notices all the little details of Ayesha's home and life and wonders what could have been, if her own course hadn't been so drastically derailed. Is this what Chelsea's world could have looked like for the past fifteen years, is this the kind of home she might have built for herself if given the time and opportunity like Ayesha has been? It couldn't be more different to what she's had to live with; it couldn't be more different to where she finds herself now, a guest in someone else's home, living in someone else's bed, wearing clothes bought for her by someone other than herself. Ayesha's right; she's like a ghost on her friend's doorstep, without the substance and heft of a whole person. She feels so flimsy, so vulnerable and insubstantial that she could walk through walls, but if that was true, she would have escaped prison long ago.

In the kitchen, there's music playing at a low volume and the combination of the yellow-painted walls and the warm light of a table lamp makes the whole room glow. There's also a recipe book lying open on the kitchen counter next to a chopping board loaded with already chopped up vegetables. 'I was just getting some prep in before you got here,' Ayesha explains. 'Do you want a drink? Tea? Wine? G & T?'

Chelsea nods, feeling like a character in a play, and says, 'Yeah, gin and tonic, I guess. Thanks.'

She takes a seat at Ayesha's small kitchen table. It's pushed up against one of the walls, with a cabinet hovering above it, and as she sits down she wonders how many people have hit their heads on the cabinet's edges. 'How long have you lived here?' she asks.

'About two years,' Ayesha says, slicing into a lime. Chelsea is taken aback by the fresh, zingy scent that seems to zip through the room – have limes always smelt so good? 'First time living on my own and I absolutely love it. Mum and Dad helped me, of course – I couldn't have afforded to buy anything without them.'

Chelsea nods. Ayesha's parents are – or were, she has no idea whether they have retired yet or not – both doctors, so she's not all that surprised by this revelation. And she may have been in prison for fourteen years, but *Location,*

Location, Location was a sort of masochistic favourite in there, so she's well aware of London house prices. Ayesha brings two full glasses over to the table, ice cubes tinkling tantalizingly together. She sits and passes Chelsea a glass, but before she can take a sip, Ayesha raises hers in a cheers and says, 'To you. To being on the other side.'

Chelsea clinks her glass, but she has to stop herself from grimacing. She doesn't feel like she's on the other side of anything. She feels like she's deep in the thick of it still, wading through tall grass with no map and no idea of the way out or through. 'How do you feel?' Ayesha asks, once they've both taken a sip.

'Honestly, I have no idea. Surreal, like you said. Like I'm not really here.'

Ayesha raises her eyebrows, 'You don't feel even a tiny bit better? Now that you're out, I mean.'

Chelsea shrugs, suddenly exhausted. She puts down her glass. Is there even any point trying to explain this feeling to someone who couldn't possibly understand? But then she looks at Ayesha, who has welcomed her into her home, has made her a drink, is about to cook her dinner, who is still here, still her friend, and is waiting to hear her answer and she knows it would be a disservice to her, not to at least attempt to put it into words. 'It feels like I'm walking around in someone else's life, but it's barely even a life, you know? I know I should be happy to be out – and I am – but the place I've come back out to doesn't really exist any more ... not just because Mum's gone, but because the person I was doesn't exist any more either. I'm a murderer. At least, that's what the world thinks of me, that's what everyone sees first. Even though it's not true, and I just ... I'm not sure I can live with that ... It was almost easier to forget, or not to forget but to live with, inside, because everyone's in the same boat, in the same position. But now, here ...' She trails off, her voice about to give out.

Ayesha is staring at her, a pained look in her eyes. 'I'm sorry, Chels, I hadn't even thought ... all I could think about was how great it must be to be out. To be free.'

'I'm not free. Constant check-ins, pages of rules to follow, just so much ... constraint, you know?'

'Constraint?'

'Like my life is being so constrained, so contained. I'm not free to live it anyway I might want to.'

'Right. But that's just ... that's the system, right? They have to keep tabs on you –'

'Because I'm a murderer?'

'Well. Because they think you are.'

'I know the logic behind it, Ayesha, that's not the problem.' Ayesha shifts in her chair, takes a sip of her drink and Chelsea realizes she may be making her uncomfortable. 'Sorry. Didn't mean to bite your head off. It's just so frustrating. I mean, I'm even going to have to call Kate in a minute, just to reassure her I'm not doing anything stupid.'

'Kate?'

'My parole officer.'

'Right,' Ayesha says, nodding as though she understands, although Chelsea doesn't see how she possibly could.

Sitting here, with her, Chelsea is only just beginning to realize how far their lives have diverged, how different their experiences have been. It should have been obvious in prison, of course, but she's actually more aware of it now, now that she can see for herself, everything she's missed out on. There's an ache in her chest, that may never go away. A nostalgia for something she never even had. 'Do you . . . do you ever think about who actually killed her? Izzy?'

Ayesha's eyes widen just a fraction, but then she nods. Chelsea takes another sip of her G & T, the bubbles in the tonic knocking around in her mouth as though they were alive. And then she says, 'Do you know what happened to him? Jamie Sinclair?'

'You still think it was him, that he had something to do with it?' Ayesha asks.

Chelsea nods. 'It was always so obvious to me, that it must've been him.'

'But . . . I mean, they must have questioned him, right?'

'I don't know. You'd think so, but then look, they got the wrong guy in the end, so how can we really know? Anyway, I looked him up the other day. He's not at Birmingham any more.'

'Where is he?'

'I don't know. I looked him up on Facebook after that, but his profile is set to private.'

'Hmm.' Ayesha picks up her phone from the table, and starts typing and scrolling across the screen. Within what feels like mere seconds, she says, 'He's at Aberystwyth.'

'University?'

'Yeah. In Wales.'

'I know where Aberystwyth is, Ayesha.'

'Just checking.' Ayesha puts the phone down, picks up her glass and raises her eyebrows at Chelsea over the rim. Without her saying anything, Chelsea knows she's asking her what she's planning to do with this information. She pulls her own glass towards her but doesn't pick it up, tapping at the side instead, an insistent drumming to mirror the pattern of thoughts in her mind. She wants to say that it's not fair. Not fair that she has spent fourteen years in prison, that Izzy is no longer with them, and Jamie Sinclair has simply moved a couple of hundred miles away and continued to live his life as normal. Still a lecturer. Still teaching. Still meeting thousands of new students a year. But 'not fair' is a refrain for children. It's something you say when someone else gets more sweets than you. It's not big enough or deep enough to cover how Chelsea really feels, to encapsulate the burst of frustration, frustration that really is anger, when she thinks of this man, sitting in his office, sheltered by the walls of a university, protected by his profession.

'We're coming up to the anniversary, aren't we?' Ayesha says now, her voice lower.

There's a pause while Chelsea tries to adjust to the shift in the room, to think of Izzy, instead of Sinclair. 'Yes, on Thursday.'

'Sometimes I can't actually believe how long it's been.'

Chelsea, who has experienced every one of those fourteen years as though each one were a decade, can believe it, but at the same time knows what Ayesha means. Now that she's out, sitting here with her old friend, those years seem to have collapsed in on themselves, as though they were a black hole, and everything that happened when Izzy died feels ever more pertinent, even more present, in some ways, even more real than what is happening now, right in front of her. She has never had to live out in this world without Izzy. She has never had to live out in this world without her mum. And now she has to face up to the fact that this reality, the one she's been waiting well over a decade to return to, isn't one she particularly wants. 'Have you ever been to visit her?' Ayesha blinks, confused. 'Her grave, I mean.'

'Oh. Yes. A few times. It's not far from here, just a couple of stops on the train. You could probably go tomorrow – you said you wanted to visit it, right?'

Chelsea nods. There's so much she needs to do, now that she's out, but this is something she can't skip. It's time to finally say goodbye to Izzy.

'I can't believe this is it,' Hannah says, looking sadly around at the rest of them. 'Our last meal.'

'You are so sentimental,' Chelsea says with a laugh, only feeling bad when the other girl pouts her disapproval.

'I'm not going to apologize for caring, Chelsea!' her voice is a little shrill and Chelsea sits up a little straighter in response.

'Okay, okay, I'm sorry – I care too, Han. Calm down.'

'And we are seeing each other again in a month. It's not that long,' Ayesha points out.

It's their last meal of term together before they all go home for Christmas, and despite making fun of Hannah's sentimental stance, Chelsea has to admit that it's strange to think she won't be waking up in the same flat as Ayesha and Hannah for the next month. All four of them – Izzy, acting as their honorary housemate – are arrayed over the living room sofas, eating a chicken Hannah roasted for them along with all the traditional Christmas side dishes you'd expect, plus a few extras. Chelsea has to get up and finish her last sociology essay of the term after this, a mad dash before handing it in tomorrow, but for now, with her friends all around her and a belly full of food, she is content.

'I know,' Hannah says, and Chelsea thinks she can see tears forming in her friend's eyes, 'but we're never going to have this term again, are we? It's all felt so special and now it's over.'

'God, Han, do you have to be so maudlin?' Izzy says, licking cranberry sauce off her fork. 'It's not over, we've barely begun. And it's all going to get so much better, because next year you're living with *me*.'

'Well, I know *that's* exciting, obviously I can't wait until we're officially housemates, but I still can't help feeling a teensy bit sad.'

'I think you might be the most prematurely nostalgic person I've ever met,' Ayesha says.

'Ah stop, we're ruining her fun,' Izzy says. 'We can't let our little Han feel like we're ganging up on her.'

'Thank you, Izzy,' Hannah says with a pout in Ayesha's direction.

'I'm just glad we found somewhere in the end,' Izzy says. 'Can you believe what dumps some of those places were?'

All four of them have spent the last week trawling houses in Selly Oak, the neighbourhood right by campus that most second years and onwards live in, but with every other first year doing the same thing, and with only a certain number of houses available – let alone those that meet Izzy's high standards and specific criteria – the search had been hard. At least there was never any question about who they were going to live with. Izzy was obviously always going to join them – not only does she spend every waking moment with them all anyway, but she's become more and more estranged from her own flatmates but was never able to switch accommodation. Meanwhile, Chelsea, Ayesha and Hannah are happy enough to be leaving their three other flatmates – one of whom rarely leaves their bedroom – behind. But they finally found a house yesterday, and signed the contracts this morning, Chelsea relieved to realize her rent was going to be dramatically cheaper next year thanks to moving out of university-owned accommodation, and Izzy anticipating a tearful goodbye with her en-suite bathroom.

Hannah's sentimentality may feel slightly premature, but Chelsea does understand where she's coming from. Things are changing already, even while other things are being set and settled. Chelsea keeps waiting for something to rock the stable foundations of their friendship, not because she wants it to, but because it just seems too good to be true. Who walks into university and immediately meets their three best friends? But it hasn't happened yet, and if it hasn't after a full term of partying, and drinking, and late nights and early mornings, last-minute essays, and hungover lectures, maybe it won't ever happen, maybe they really are that lucky. Maybe this is really how the next three years of her life will be.

Hannah prods her with a socked foot, and Chelsea realizes she's been saying something but Chelsea hasn't been listening.

'What? Sorry, zoned out there.'

'I was saying it's all right for you and Iz, you'll be able to meet up all the time over Christmas.' Is there an edge of jealousy to her voice, as Hannah says this? Maybe, Chelsea's not sure. Hannah's relationship to Izzy is one that can sometimes descend into puppyish devotion and it's something both she and Ayesha have brought up with her already, especially at times when Izzy has started to treat Hannah more as a lackey than as a friend. She regularly texts Hannah with requests to pick up a Starbucks, for instance, and whereas both Chelsea and Ayesha would respond to this with a roll of the eyes and a firm 'no', Hannah always does so dutifully. It's a little weird, and makes Chelsea want to shake Hannah out of it, or maybe shake Izzy into not exploiting Hannah's feelings the way she sometimes does.

'Yeah, it'll be nice to see each other during the holidays,' Chelsea says as lightly as possible, not wanting to make Hannah's jealousy any worse. She lives somewhere in the rural heart of Norfolk, miles away from anything or anyone, apparently, and has already said she probably won't leave her parents' village until they come back to uni.

'Well, yeah, you only live like, five minutes away from each other, don't you?' Hannah says. 'You'll be round each other's houses all the time.'

'Yeah, I guess so,' Chelsea says, glancing over at Izzy, who is stretched out under a blanket on the other sofa. She has her mobile phone flipped open, texting someone rapidly, and Chelsea gets the distinct feeling she's ignoring her.

And then suddenly, despite the warm fuzzies she was feeling mere moments ago, Chelsea wonders just how stable their friendship is, what the last three months really mean to Izzy and whether their Birmingham-based relationship will translate to London, where Izzy will be surrounded by her family and old friends and everything that goes along with that. Has she got this all wrong? Where does she, Chelsea, fit in with all that? It was one thing to meet her mum here, and be taken to dinner by them, but once they're home, will Chelsea and Izzy even still be friends? Because their houses may be five minutes apart geographically speaking, but Chelsea can't imagine two homes further apart in many of the ways that matter. She's never once stepped foot in Izzy's home and as she looks at her now, she wonders suddenly if she ever will. But Izzy is still intent on her mobile, and Chelsea gets the feeling that the other girl is feigning concentration on her phone, listening intently as her attention flickers for just a nanosecond over to Hannah and Chelsea, and then back to her texting again.

Chelsea sits up suddenly, giving herself a coughing fit in the process. 'You okay, Chels?' Ayesha asks, passing her a glass of water.

Chelsea tries to nod and swallow some water at the same time, but it only prompts more coughing and it feels like a full minute has passed before she gets herself under control, although surely it must be less. 'Fuck. Yeah, thanks for that.'

'No worries, just try not to die on us.'

'I better go finish my essay though, guys. If I don't now, I probably never will.'

Hannah makes a sound of distress and Ayesha issues a hearty 'good luck', but Izzy stays silent. When Chelsea glances back as she's leaving the room, she is still staring intently at her phone as though transfixed, but Chelsea wonders if there is anything on the screen at all, or if Izzy is just looking for an excuse not to meet her eye.

* * *

116

Chelsea turns her essay in the next day, and gets the train back to London in the evening. Izzy isn't with her. She'd been picked up earlier in the day – she hadn't specified whether it was by her parents or a driver, but she'd told Chelsea they couldn't wait until after she'd handed her essay in as she had to get back in time for lunch with her grandmother. As Chelsea sits on her slow-moving train – she'd bought the cheapest ticket available, of course – she wonders if she'll hear from Izzy at all over the holiday. She knows the other girl is going skiing in the New Year, but until then they will be around the corner from one another while, what, acting like strangers? There are times when Chelsea feels closer to Izzy than even Ayesha; maybe it's coming from the same place, the connection of having been to the same school even though they were never friends there, but whatever it is, it's allowed for an unspoken bond to develop that she simply doesn't feel with the others. But at moments like this, and even last night, when Izzy seemed so unwilling to meet her eye, Chelsea wonders if they're as close as she thought they were – whether they're even really friends at all, or if they just happen to be in the same place, at the same time. A relationship of convenience. Would Izzy abandon her if it wasn't so convenient to be her friend? Sitting on the train, with the countryside rolling by, rain running down the darkened windows, Chelsea realizes that she may be about to find out.

Chelsea has an appointment with an estate agent at eleven, so once Ayesha has given her a spare set of keys and left for work, Chelsea showers and gets dressed before going to the cemetery. She wishes Ayesha was with her, but she's drawn a terrible map of the cemetery with arrows pointing in the direction of the Dunwoody mausoleum, where Izzy's ashes are held alongside her father's and the remains of her relatives and ancestors. As she leaned over the kitchen table, pencil in hand, Chelsea had recalled the time Ayesha printed out a map for her when she was going to meet Izzy and her mum in Birmingham city centre, and despite everything, they'd both laughed at the memory, revelling, for just a second, in how some things never change and how, sometimes, that can be a good thing. It's only two stops on the train, and before she knows it, Chelsea is walking through the gates of West Norwood cemetery, a peace descending almost instantly. She draws Ayesha's handmade map from her jacket pocket and checks the movement of the arrows, taking the path that veers off to the right, the sound of the busy roads just beyond the walls getting quieter and further away as the tweeting, fluttering sounds of birds and falling leaves take over from the incessant hustle of traffic and pedestrians.

It takes a little longer than she expected to find the right spot. She thought she'd have some memory of it, from Ian

Dunwoody's funeral, but even with Ayesha's map all the paths look the same; overgrown and wild, crooked gravestones jumbled and jagged in the uneven earth, and the quiet, while tranquil, is also deeply discomfiting, making her jump every time she comes across another person, or a fox crosses her path. Finally, she thinks she sees it, the distinctive terracotta walls of the mausoleum, its tiles decorated in leafy motifs. As she nears it, there's a movement, and for a second she thinks it's nothing, just another fox or maybe a neighbourhood cat, but then the sense of movement solidifies and she realizes that it's the outline of a person, going from kneeling or crouching, to standing up, their back slowly unfurling as they turn their face up to the mausoleum. Every step Chelsea takes now is leaden, weighted, and yet she herself feels dizzy, lightheaded, as she realizes that the person standing in front of the mausoleum, the person standing in front of her, is Izzy's mother. Camille.

Chelsea hasn't seen Camille since the day of her sentencing just over fourteen years ago, and the other woman doesn't make a move as Chelsea walks towards her, even though she must hear her tread. She is utterly still, as cast in stone as the many weeping angels Chelsea has seen adorning the Victorian headstones. If you'd asked her to guess, Chelsea would have said Camille wasn't even breathing, that she was completely lost in her grief, in her own opaque way, but once Chelsea is alongside her, the other woman says her name quietly but clearly, as though it were a curse. Chelsea doesn't say anything, she cannot speak; she opens her mouth, but nothing comes out.

'I shouldn't be shocked by you,' Camille says, in her

cool, distinctive voice, 'but I am. To have the audacity to come here, of all places. It's quite something.'

'It's the anniversary on Thursday,' Chelsea says, her mouth dry, her blood panting at her wrists and neck.

'I know. Do you think I do not know the anniversary of my own child's death?'

'I – I . . . I'm sorry. I'll leave if you want me to.'

Camille blinks at her, and suddenly Chelsea sees how small she is now – she was always smaller than her daughter, but now, fourteen years later, she looks so diminished, so much older, albeit still perfect. Perfectly preserved. 'I thought you had gone to Scotland.'

Chelsea wonders how she knows this. Are victims' relatives informed of the perpetrator's whereabouts upon release? It doesn't seem fair, to be on such uneven footing with Camille, but for all her marble coolness, for all her money and beauty, Camille has also been dealt a pretty shitty hand, and Chelsea isn't cold-hearted enough not to recognize this. 'I had some meetings in London,' Chelsea explains, 'and I wanted to see . . . to see Izzy. To pay my respects.'

'Meetings,' Camille says with raised eyebrows, managing to make the word sound completely ridiculous. Chelsea doesn't say anything to this, and Camille is quiet too, the space filled by the sound of scrabbling birds in the tree branches overhead, and the loud squawk of a parakeet, the flash of its acid-green feathers so bright against the browns and reds of the leaves. 'She is not in there, you know,' Camille says quietly, once the parakeet has left them alone. Chelsea thinks this remark is metaphysical, rather than literal, but then Camille continues, 'I scattered her ashes at

Mirador.' Mirador. The Dunwoody home in Mallorca, where they had stood above the waves that first and last summer all together, and Izzy had proclaimed, *Here, just leave me here*, arms thrown open, stance wide and stable, laughing hysterically as Ayesha pretended to push her to her death. Chelsea can remember the conversation vividly, a clear summer night, the sky a deep navy blue, and yes, they were drinking, but they'd just found out about Izzy's dad's diagnosis the night before. Sat on the rocks above the crashing waves in Mallorca, the very idea that someone could be so profoundly ill, could in fact, die, had seemed impossible, news from another world, a different timeline. How could they, limbs bare and tanned, muscles strong and toned, defying gravity above the cracked shoreline, one day *die*? They couldn't. They wouldn't. They were immortal, they knew it.

No, but really guys, she'd stated more seriously, sitting down, that intense, bleary-eyed sincerity of the very drunk, *scatter my ashes here. My happy place.*

Chelsea is relieved to hear this, that Izzy's drunken wishes have been honoured. The surroundings of the cemetery may be peaceful, lovely even, but knowing that her friend isn't actually in there, inside that ancient mausoleum, sends a rush of relief through her. That Izzy's name may adorn the tomb's walls, but that her body has become ash and been thrown to the wind and the waves, gives her just a tiny moment of peace. It would be too much to think of her entombed, for ever, in this terracotta box that, despite all its pomp and circumstance, still manages to feel faintly clinical and cold. Camille moves closer to its walls, her fingertips grazing its sides, and starts to whisper a few words to her daughter, and maybe her husband – she's talking too quietly for Chelsea to hear, but she thinks she can see tears tracking down her face, making streaks in her otherwise flawless foundation. Chelsea doesn't cry. She wants to, she wants to be able to let go and unburden herself of this grief that has lived, coiled up so tightly inside her for the past fifteen years, but she's too used to holding on to it for dear life. Or maybe a part of her knows she shouldn't cry in front of Camille, shouldn't cry in front of this woman who thinks Chelsea killed her daughter. But then, suddenly, tears do prick her eyes, tears of sorrow yes, but also tears of frustration, and she has to take a deep breath to stop them falling.

A loud cheep-cheep pierces their silence, and both Chelsea and Camille raise her heads to see those parakeets flying against the grey sky again. Camille turns her face to Chelsea and says, very quietly, almost too quietly for Chelsea to hear, 'We should go.'

Chelsea wants to demur, to tell her no, she's going to stay here, thank you, going to say goodbye and mark the anniversary alone, but she just can't. You don't say no to Camille Dunwoody, especially not with tears running down her face. So, the two of them set off together, the most unlikely duo winding their way through the cemetery's toy-town streets – they even have names, Chelsea realizes. She wants to say something, but has no idea what, or how, so they both remain silent. Camille walks slightly ahead of her, and despite the tears, she is as serene as she is unreadable. She's had many visits here, Chelsea reminds herself, was given the gift of grieving that Chelsea was so cruelly denied; she'll be used to this route, this path, the walk back from her daughter's grave. Although, maybe, Chelsea concedes, you never get used to that. All of a sudden, they're nearing the entrance, a quiet, overgrown path spitting them out on to the main concourse, the sound of the street beyond suddenly louder, more present, London making itself known again, even in this genteel, urban wilderness. Camille turns to her slightly, she's reaching into her handbag for a pair of sunglasses, despite the overcast day, and as she slips them on her face she says, 'I will leave you here, Chelsea. We shouldn't be spotted together, if possible, and my car is waiting.'

Chelsea nods, still rendered mute, is unprepared entirely, for what comes next, 'I would like you to join me at my hotel tomorrow, though.'

'What – why?' Chelsea says, practically spluttering, the question coming out ruder than she would have liked, the shock written all over her face.

'I think we have some things to discuss. Don't you agree?'

'Uh . . .'

'I'm at the Hotel Café Royal, do you know where that is?' and then, not waiting for Chelsea's response, assuming she couldn't possibly know it, 'Piccadilly.'

Chelsea just nods, her throat constricted in surprise, and then nods again when Camille tells her what time to turn up. She watches the other woman walk away, a prickle of unease starting at the back of her neck, working its way down her spine. She knows what it's like to be watched, to be looked at, and that is exactly what this feels like. There's a scuff of something and she whips around, sure to find someone standing there, but there's nothing, just a loud clatter as two crows take off from one of the nearby bare branches. She takes a deep breath, telling herself it's just paranoia, and starts to walk in the direction Camille went, looking over her shoulder whenever she hears a noise she doesn't like, certain, somehow, that despite appearances, she's not alone. Reaching the main gates, she spots Camille's distinctive figure, all perfect posture and a straightened spine, waiting as someone holds the door to a sleek black car open for her. Chelsea's eyes barely glance at the mute man standing over her, but then, something deep, instinctual and reflexive tells her to look again and she realizes the man towering over Camille isn't her driver, but her stepson, Charlie. She inhales sharply, the breath catching in her throat, almost making her choke as she quickly steps out of sight, hiding behind the ivy that trails over the iron gates. But in doing so, she's able to see into the car, see that there's another person sitting on the back seat, waiting for Izzy's mum, and her eyes go wide, she swears her heart almost stops as she realizes the person sitting in there is heartbreakingly familiar.

Hannah.

It can't be. She takes a step, inching closer to the car, but still being careful to remain hidden behind the ivy-clad gate, and yes, she's sure. That's her. Hannah Grant. She swallows down something between a laugh and a sob, her eyes beginning to mist up with the tears she didn't allow herself to shed by the mausoleum. How can Hannah be here? What is she doing here with Camille and Charlie Dunwoody? Within seconds, the car has slunk away, smoothly blending in with the rest of the north-bound traffic, but Chelsea stays, her back against the iron gate, a strand of ivy tickling at her face. She pushes it away, trying to make everything line up, trying to unravel this to make any kind of sense. It's possible, as one of Izzy's closest friends, that Hannah has simply stayed close with the family since her death, and accompanied Camille here to the cemetery, to pay her respects, just as Chelsea is doing. But something, that same prickly feeling that came over her minutes ago while standing among the tombstones, tells her it's not just that. There was something about the set of her shoulders, the way the weak autumn light hit her blonde hair through the car window. Chelsea shivers, draws her jacket closer around her. She has to get to North Dulwich to meet with the estate agent, and she's already taken too long here, so she walks quickly back to the station, keeping her head down the whole way, determined to keep her face hidden from any prying eyes.

2006

Chelsea wouldn't have known about the party if she hadn't joined Facebook just before Christmas. It was Izzy who convinced them all to do it – she'd been home during reading week and almost everyone she knew was already on the site, posting photos, updating their relationship statuses, writing on walls, so she'd joined immediately and eventually Hannah, Ayesha, and Chelsea had all followed suit. Chelsea has seen Izzy a few times since getting home from uni, but she hadn't ever mentioned a party, so when Chelsea logs in to see photo after photo from a Christmas party at Izzy's house the night before, she doesn't know what to think.

At first, she wonders if it might have been an oversight on her part. Had Izzy mentioned anything the last time they saw each other or spoke? She even flips open her mobile to check their text messages, but there's nothing from Izzy about a party, even though she texted Chelsea yesterday about some reading for history they both have to do before the start of term. It could've been a last-minute thing, of course. The party. Although the sheer number of people present tells her this probably isn't the case, as does the fact that one album Izzy is tagged in has been titled THE BIG DUNWOODY CHRISTMAS BASH, while Izzy's own album is rather more inventively called FIZZY IZZY'S FESTIVE TIZZY.

Chelsea sighs and shuts the lid of her laptop. She doesn't

need to obsess over this. It's fine. So, Izzy didn't invite her to a party – so what? She doesn't have to be invited to everything, she doesn't have to go to every party.

'That's a bit shit though, isn't it love?' Louise says. They're having dinner and Chelsea has just told her about the party. 'I know you weren't friends at school but you are now. She should've invited you.'

Chelsea shrugs, 'Maybe I would've just felt weird and out of place though? Maybe it's better I wasn't there.'

'You don't know that. And she certainly doesn't know that. She should've at least let you know, given you the option of going.'

Chelsea is quiet as she twirls her fork through the strands of her spaghetti. 'Yeah, maybe.'

'Maybe? Chels, the pair of you are good friends, you spent your birthdays together, you met her mum. She should be behaving better than this.'

'What can I do about it, though? What's done is done. The party's over, so what's the point?'

'The point is to let your friend know if she's hurt your feelings.'

'Ugh . . .'

'Don't make that sound, you know I'm right. Why have friends if you're not going to be honest with them?'

'But I don't know if I even care that much.'

'You do care, Chels. Otherwise you wouldn't have told me about it.'

Her mum's words echo in her mind as she walks through the gate and up the impressive gravel driveway to Izzy's impressively large house. It's the day after Boxing Day, and Izzy has finally invited her round, although Chelsea is fairly sure it's only because Izzy is off skiing in France tomorrow and hasn't yet packed, so doesn't have to time to get a drink in the Crown and Greyhound as they'd initially planned. This suspicion is confirmed when someone other than Izzy answers the door to her. Dressed in a steam-pressed, crisp-cornered black shirt, trousers and nondescript black shoes, her grey hair tied back in a low bun, Chelsea realizes almost immediately that this must be the housekeeper.

'Chelsea?' the woman asks.

'Yes.'

'I'm Helen, Isabella told me to expect you. She's up in her bedroom.'

Not knowing where Izzy's room is, Chelsea is relieved when Helen turns on her heel and leads the way up the staircase and along the house's airy corridors to her friend's bedroom, watching as the housekeeper raps neatly at the door, before pushing it open and ushering Chelsea inside. The room is so big that Chelsea doesn't even see Izzy at first. She takes in the enormous canopied bed, the huge bookshelves that fill two corners of the room, the piles of clothes that litter the floor, and then, finally, she spots Izzy among them, holding a dress up to the light and squinting.

'Do you think this would look good with Moonboots?'

'What are Moonboots?'

Izzy points to a pair of larger-than-life silver boots, that do indeed look like they might be able to traverse the surface of the moon. The dress she's holding is pink satin – possibly even silk, what does Chelsea know? – with a blue lace trim. It looks like underwear, but Chelsea doesn't mention this.

'Won't you get a bit cold in that up a mountain?'

'Duh, it's for après ski. But I'm not sure about it. Anyway,' she scrunches the dress up into a ball and throws it into a pile some distance from her. 'How are you? How was Christmas?'

'Good. Nice. We went to my aunt and uncle's. How was yours?'

'Pretty awful. Dad and Charlie got into a huge fight and Charlie's mum Rose decided she wanted to come after all, so she and Mum just ignored each other all day. Like, they literally didn't look at each other or say a word to each other all day. Mad. Oh, and then my grandma thought she was having a heart attack but it turned out to be indigestion, but by then she was already in hospital and being absolutely horrible to everyone.' Izzy takes a deep breath and finally meets Chelsea's eye. 'So, yeah. Merry Christmas, I guess?'

'What were they fighting about? Your dad and brother?'

'Who knows?' Izzy says, rolling her eyes. 'Something, something, you don't appreciate me or my ideas, blah blah blah, you'd be nowhere without me – that's Dad – I could take my experience anywhere, anyone would love to have me – blah, blah, blah – who are you kidding, no one takes you seriously except as my son – something, something, make me CEO now or I storm out like a whiny little baby.'

'Jesus. Did he storm out?'

'Yup, got right on his silly little motorbike and rode off into the sunset. As if Dad's gonna make him CEO after a performance like that.'

'Isn't your dad CEO anyway?'

'Yeah, exactly. That's the stupid part. Charlie's just mad

he has to wait – it's not like it's not ever going to happen, Dad's just not ready to retire yet. Charlie's only making things worse for himself.' She looks up from her position on the floor, eyes alight, 'Hey what do you think James Sinclair did for Christmas?'

Chelsea laughs, she can't help herself. Izzy's crush on Sinclair hasn't abated over the term, but Chelsea's pretty sure her friend plays it up, just to get a laugh out of her. Chelsea finds the whole situation absurd. 'Um, probably spent it with his family?'

'Hmm, he doesn't wear a wedding ring.'

'He still has family, though, Iz. I mean, I assume.'

'I'm so excited we're getting a seminar with him next term.'

'God, I'm not. You're going to be insufferable. Did Charlie come back, though, after the fight? Have you seen him since?'

'No,' Izzy sighs. 'He might've called Dad, but I don't know. God, I'm just glad he's not coming skiing. He's such a drag.'

'Is it just you and your mum going?'

Izzy nods as she folds up a cashmere jumper and adds it to one of the neater piles of clothing. Chelsea assumes this pile is to go in her suitcase. 'And Dad. Hey, you want to meet him? I just realized you've never met. He's in his study.'

'Oh, well . . .'

'Oh my God, do not be scared. He'll bite when prodded with a large stick, but he's a teddy bear. Seriously. Besides, I want a drink, so we need to go downstairs anyway.'

So, they go downstairs, Chelsea having to restrain

herself from peering into every open doorway or checking the bottom corner of every painting for the signature of some unbelievably well-known artist. She thinks she spots a Matisse, but she can't be sure – Izzy is moving too quickly in her Ugg slippers and soon enough they're in the kitchen with its cathedral-like dimensions and view on to the rambling garden. It currently looks as bare and barren as Chelsea's own garden, except you could probably fit fifteen of her garden into this one, not to mention the statues and sculptures that draw the eye with their uplights.

'G and T?' Izzy asks. 'Or there's beer, wine, sherry, brandy, whisky, sake, whatever the heart desires.'

'Not sure I'd dare to meet your dad with anything other than gin in my glass,' Chelsea says.

'Ha! Honestly, I don't think he'd notice, but yes, we do have an unlimited supply of the stuff.'

Their drinks made, Izzy knocks on her father's study door and opens it before Chelsea hears him say anything.

'Hi, Piz,' Ian Dunwoody says without looking up from his desk, and then, when he does, 'Oh, hello, didn't realize we had visitors, sorry.'

'Dad, this is Chelsea. From Birmingham.'

'Hi, Mr Dunwoody. Nice to meet you.'

'You don't sound like you're from Birmingham.'

'I meant from uni, Dad,' Chelsea says, with a roll of her eyes.

'I'm from London, actually. Around the corner, to be more specific.'

'Oh, right. What a coincidence. Lovely to meet you, Chelsea. You two have been looking out for one another up there then, have you?'

'Yep, we've been keeping each other out of trouble,' Izzy says.

'That doesn't sound much like you, Piz. Chelsea, what are you studying?'

'History and sociology.'

'Interesting,' he says with a lift of his eyebrows. But before he can continue, the mobile phone on his desk begins to ring and he picks it up with a grim look in his eye. 'Ah. Girls, I must take this. See you again soon, Chelsea. Piz. Time to pack, yes?'

They leave the room quietly, neither of them saying anything until they reach the bottom of the stairs, and Chelsea turns to Izzy and says, 'Piz?' both of them collapsing into laughter, without any real reason why. As Chelsea follows Izzy back up the stairs, she thinks she made the right decision not to mention the party. It's easier this way, just to slip back into their dynamic without the bother of friction. And it really is so easy being with her, especially when Izzy's like this, flitting from thing to thing, being the consummate host, brimming with unspent energy. Chelsea doesn't want to upset that, doesn't want to upset their balance, so she says nothing, just laughs along as Izzy explains where her dad's nickname for her came from, warmth spreading through her chest and limbs. From the gin, yes, but also from being drawn in by Izzy, being let in on this family joke, being surrounded by her family home. Yes, she made the right decision.

2022

Chelsea is unprepared for how much seeing her old house affects her. Or rather, she has tried to prepare for it and failed. She gets off the train at North Dulwich station, memories roaring in her ears as she sees the end of Izzy's road and then makes her way past their old school. Just as with everything, it looks the same and yet a little bit different, with new additions here and there, gleaming signage, a lick of paint – or probably several in the many intervening years. She walks on autopilot, her body and brain so used to this familiar pathway that her feet are making the turning to Deventer Crescent before she even realizes how close she's got. Here, despite being alongside the railway track, it feels as though you're tucked away from the world, a secluded pocket just seconds from the busy main road, as if all the traffic has been put on mute. As peaceful as it is, her heart beats as though she's approaching something much more frightening, and she's sweaty and clammy despite the chill of the day. The houses on the small estate are all identical, until you know what you're looking for, and she'd know her own home anywhere at any time, day or night, but today it's distinguished by the suited estate agent studying his phone. As she nears, he looks up, and tidily slips the phone into his jacket pocket, pushes himself off the wall with ease and puts his hand out for a shake.

'You must be Chelsea,' he says, and if he knows exactly

who she is, other than her name, he doesn't give himself away. 'I'm Stephen, from Franklin and Watts.'

'Nice to meet you,' Chelsea says, trying not to think how clammy her hand must feel to him as she shakes his.

Stephen smiles, showing his teeth, before turning sharply on his heels towards the house, heading up the concrete pathway towards the front door. 'Right, as you know, we've been managing the letting of the place, but the tenants are out at the moment so we can have a good look around, see what needs to be done before putting it on the market. As you can probably imagine, tenanted homes often develop a bit of wear and tear over the years and this house has been rented for quite some time, so we may have quite a bit of work on our hands.'

He's unlocked the door and as it swings open, Chelsea follows him inside into the cool of the hallway. She shivers, and Stephen notices this, turning to look at the thermostat. 'I imagine they leave the heating off while they're out, and they probably left for work hours ago,' he explains, almost apologetically and completely unnecessarily. Chelsea would've shivered even if the radiators had been on full blast, pumping out their artificial heat, but she nods anyway and he nods back, smiling again.

'How long have they lived here?' she asks.

'Ooh, about three years now, I think. I can check the exact dates for you, but I think that's about right. They're a nice couple, very easy to deal with. One kid.'

'Right. They must be annoyed we're putting it on the market.'

Stephen shrugs, leading the way into the lounge, 'These things happen. It's your house, after all.'

But it's not Chelsea's house, it's her mum's. Or was her mum's, because now it's someone else's completely. The walls are painted an inoffensive off-white, almost beige colour, the living room furniture is completely unrecognizable to Chelsea, and the photos, of course, are all of strangers. The TV is massive, much bigger than any TV she and her mum ever had, and there are video game remote controls in a tangled heap just in front of it. On the dining table is the detritus of another family's daily life: letters, a closed laptop, a box of tissues, a vase of flowers, drooping and spewing fallen petals. The sliding doors are at least the same, and the garden looks fairly unchanged, the too-long grass indicating that whoever lives here now has as lax an attitude to lawn-mowing as Chelsea's mum did. Standing in the middle of the room, Chelsea's heart drops at how little of a connection she feels to the house. She was expecting to be overwhelmed by memories, nostalgia, loss, and that's all there – of course it is – but this building is just a shell of the home she shared with her mum, there is so little of either one of them left here. Stephen walks through the archway to the small kitchen and Chelsea is surprised to see that even this is different. She didn't realize how much work had been done. Instead of their pine cabinets, they're now white and glossy with a faux-wood countertop, and bright red tiles on the splashback. The red and white are not what she would've chosen, and she feels a pang as she thinks of the square, rustic-look tiles they'd had here once, every fifth one or so adorned with a raised bunch of grapes, as if they were in an Italian trattoria, rather than a 1960s two-up, two-down in North Dulwich.

'Kitchen's looking good,' Stephen says, interrupting Chelsea's reverie, 'not too much to do in here, although I think all the rooms could do with a lick of paint. The bathroom's where some real attention is needed, and there's a few bits of modernization here and there I think we could do, to make it really marketable.'

Chelsea nods, hearing but not really listening to Stephen as he continues to talk about how much houses in the area have been going for recently. 'D'you mind if I go upstairs on my own?' Chelsea asks, once the estate agent's spiel has come to an end.

''Course, like I said, it's your house. Let me know if you have any thoughts about the bathroom. It'll be a bit of an initial outlay but will really help the resale value.'

Chelsea nods again, feeling like one of those dogs people used to put on the dashboards of their cars, and proceeds to head up the stairs alone. She ignores the bathroom though – she has no doubt it needs work as Stephen has already warned her in an email that it hasn't been updated since she and her mum lived there – and heads straight for her bedroom. The bedrooms are almost identical, with one ever so slightly bigger than the other, which was, of course, her mother's, both with large windows that look out over the garden and on to the back of the identical house beyond the wall. This is the kid's bedroom now, a single bed pushed up against the wall with the window, the dark blue duvet dotted with planets and rockets, taking off into space. Pushed against another wall is a large pine desk and Chelsea walks over to it, touching the varnished sheen of the tabletop. Is it? Yes, this was hers, maybe the only thing left in the house from her and her mum's life here. She sits down at it and wonders what the young boy who now calls this room his does here. He can't be more than eight judging from the photos – does he really need a desk? She pulls the top drawer out and sees an array of coloured felt-tip pens, some sticker sheaths. Normal stuff. She sighs and stares out of the window, the view so familiar she could probably sketch it from memory, if she had any artistic talent.

She hasn't been back here since Izzy died. When she was arrested, she was taken straight into custody where she was forced to await her trial, having been judged too much of a threat to society to be released. She thinks now of all the times she'd thought of and imagined this house back then, how she'd longed for it, the shelter of home, the comfort of her own bed, the protection of her mother. But she's glad now, almost, that she never came back. It's untainted by that time, free from the fear and grief, the guilt and unwavering anxiety, finally the submission to what was happening. Here, she and her mum live on for ever, chatting over dinner, silently, sleepily watching TV together, laughing and dancing in the kitchen, arguing over chores, her mum run ragged from work and the responsibility of single motherhood, begging Chelsea to pay more attention to when the bins needed to go out, when the dishwasher needed emptying, harried but happy, making it all work, just the two of them. Chelsea has started to cry without realizing it, and she gets up to grab some toilet paper from the bathroom, suddenly desperate to be gone. She'd thought they weren't here, she and her mum, that this house was no longer theirs, just a building they'd both once lived in, both once shared. But here they are, their ghosts still roaming the hallways, their lives and life still echoing in its rooms. Standing in the cold bathroom, damp clinging to its poorly ventilated corners, she wipes at her nose and splashes cold water on her face, shivering as it hits her skin. She's been lost without her mum, such a childish realization to have. But no matter how old she is, no matter how long her mum's been gone, she's still her daughter. Still Louise's only child. Grief grips at her throat and suddenly she is gasping for breath, sobbing uncontrollably. She's been so weighted down with the injustice of what happened to her, while she was inside, that she didn't realize she'd lost her anchor in life. It's only now, now that she's out in the world, trying to live in it, that she can feel how unmoored she is, how little she has to hold on to. No. How little she has to hold on to her. Even when she went to prison, Louise had stayed, gripping on to her so tightly, letting her know that she was still there for Chelsea, no matter what. Chelsea thinks about her mum's last few years in this house, what they must've been like; reporters and photographers right on her doorstep, at least in the early days, shedding friends and acquaintances when they realized who her daughter was, making the trek up and down to Foston whenever she could. Living here. Alone. In the beginning, with all her legal knowledge as a clerk, Louise had been able to help Chelsea with navigating the appeals system, but with every failed attempt, her mum lost more and more of herself. Lost weight, lost hair, lost that thing that made her *her*. And eventually, Chelsea knows, it had killed her. There was no other explanation, for an otherwise healthy 57-year-old going into cardiac arrest. Is she really expected to let go of her last remaining link to her mother? Does she actually have to sell this house? She looks around herself again, wiping away at tears, looking properly this time. Maybe she should keep it. So, she might not be moving down soon, but she will want to move back *one* day, after all; she isn't planning on staying in Scotland with Nikki for ever. But then she hears her aunt's voice, the mention of the mortgage that is, of course, being covered for now by renters. She couldn't pay for that on the wages of a receptionist, not on top of everything it takes just to survive in London. She takes a deep breath, lets it out slowly and hopes the estate agent hasn't been able to hear her break down. Leaving the bathroom, she shuts the door behind her and makes her way downstairs, where the house feels less like her own and more like what it really is: someone else's home. So, she'll leave them both here, her and her mother, unchanged by the tragedy that took place over a hundred miles away, all those years ago. She'll leave them here, happy and whole, waiting for a future that never comes.

* * *

'Hannah? Are you sure?' Ayesha says. She'd been about to start cooking them dinner, but sits down abruptly at the kitchen table, joining Chelsea.

'I'm pretty sure.'

'But you were far away, right? You weren't looking right at her, she was in the car? You might be mistaken?'

Chelsea takes a sip from her glass of wine, meeting Ayesha's gaze over the rim. What does Ayesha want her to say here? 'I mean, I could be, obviously. I might be wrong. But I could've sworn it was her.'

'Hannah.'

'Yeah,' Chelsea says. 'You guys haven't kept in touch at all, then?'

'No,' Ayesha says, glancing at her, then looking away. She shakes her head, but in a way that lets Chelsea know she's answering an internal question, not Chelsea's. She sighs loudly, and then says, 'I did hear something about them being together, but I guess I just didn't really believe it.'

'What? Who?'

'Hannah and Charlie.'

'Hannah and Charlie? Charlie Dunwoody?'

Ayesha nods again, swallows down some wine, 'I just . . . couldn't believe it was true. So, I tucked it away, I guess.'

'Hannah and Charlie,' Chelsea repeats dully.

Ayesha's kitchen walls are crowded with framed photos and posters. Just above where Chelsea sits now, is a photo from their first year at uni, all four of them in the frame, their faces young and impossibly full, smiles wide and bright. Ayesha is wearing sunglasses and Chelsea is squinting, which makes her think it must have been taken in their final term, and she looks back at it now, as if reminding herself what Hannah looks like, as if she's ever forgotten. Her hair looked blonder in the back of the car, she thinks, but that's easy enough to do with a box of hair dye, or, much more likely, the skills of a hairdresser. But it was her, she's so sure it was her.

Hannah and Charlie? How did this happen? And when? And is she really surprised? Hannah, who had not come to visit her once while she was in prison; Hannah, who had never given her the benefit of the doubt; Hannah, whose judgment was so clouded by her love for Izzy that she hadn't ever been able to see past Chelsea's supposed guilt. It had been painful to realize it at the time, that Hannah's loyalty couldn't extend towards her in her hour of need. It had hit her full in the chest on the first day of her trial when she'd seen her friend sitting there, next to Izzy's family, eyes red, face pale. If she's honest with herself, it had felt like one of her most acute betrayals, but there was also a small part of her, even then, that wasn't surprised. Hannah had always sided with Izzy. Why would that change now? And more to the point, Hannah had always wanted what Izzy had.

Chelsea takes another sip of wine and realizes Ayesha is leaning intently over her phone, her face full of concentration. 'Oh good,' she practically murmurs, 'she's not private.'

'What?'

'Hannah. On Instagram. Oh, shit –'

'What?'

'They're engaged.' Ayesha holds up the phone for Chelsea to see, but really, Chelsea can't see anything, or doesn't know what she's looking at. So, she reaches for the phone to take a closer look at the photo in question: a close-up on their happy, smiling faces, an anonymous tropical background, and Hannah's hand held in such a way as to show off the enormous, gleaming diamond on her ring finger. 'It's from two weeks ago.'

'So, did they only recently get together?' Chelsea asks, trying to piece together this puzzle, but Ayesha just shrugs.

'Scroll back through her photos, it'll probably tell you everything you need to know.'

But Chelsea is transfixed by this particular photo, is

staring at these two faces, trying to see traces of the people she used to know. How can this be Hannah? Her Hannah. The woman staring out at her is sleek and polished, she's grinning widely and Chelsea is sure her teeth are both straighter and whiter than when she knew her, but there's something else, a glow, a shine, a sheen, whatever you want to call it, that previously, Chelsea had only ever associated with Izzy.

'Chels, you okay? You look like you've seen a ghost.'

Hasn't she? That's what it feels like anyway, staring down into the face of someone she used to know, but instead she says, 'Yeah, it's just so weird. Hannah and Izzy's brother. What the fuck?'

Ayesha nods, taking the phone from her and beginning to scroll again, 'She always had a bit of a crush on him, don't you remember?'

'Yeah, I guess.'

'Not to mention the way she was with Izzy, like she could do no wrong. Oh, look, this is from 2012. The Olympics. So, they've been together a while.'

She turns the screen to Chelsea, who takes the phone but barely sees the photograph. Once again, it's of the two of them, their faces in shot, grinning widely. Hannah looks more like Hannah here, more like how Chelsea remembers her anyway; hair a darker blonde, almost mousy in places, smile a little less self-assured, eyes wider, taking it all in. 'Those are some good seats they had,' Ayesha remarks with a raise of her eyebrows.

'Yeah?'

'Hardly surprising, I guess. We all know how rich the Dunwoodies are.'

'Right.'

'Here, give me that back and I'll order us some food. This revelation has knocked the cooking right out of me.'

'Sure,' Chelsea says, happy to pass the phone back to Ayesha. She'd been scrolling backwards through Hannah's photos. Image after image of a life she knows nothing about, square after square of achievements, memories, weddings, holidays, walks by the river, sunsets caught on camera, fleeting, unbridled joy captured and made permanent. And in amongst them, Charlie Dunwoody. There are even a few featuring Camille, and others with Ian Dunwoody's first wife Rose, as well as some other faces Chelsea recognizes from university. Feeling nauseous, she takes a long swig of water. Chelsea hadn't expected to see Hannah upon her release. Now, she thinks back to those days just after Izzy died and she was being endlessly questioned, first as a witness, then as a person of interest, and finally as a suspect. Was that when it all started, between Hannah and Charlie?

'Vietnamese okay?' Ayesha says now, breaking through Chelsea's thoughts. 'I've been craving it.'

Is it okay? Chelsea has no idea. No idea what she likes or dislikes any more, no idea who she is here, in Ayesha's kitchen. She's been trying to fool herself into thinking that this is all totally normal; that this is what normal people do. Look up old friends on the internet, drink wine in other people's kitchens, order takeaways on a weeknight. And of course, it is. The problem is that *she*'s not normal. That normal, for her, has been bent on its axis and perhaps no longer exists. 'Sure,' she says again, thinking it will be nice to find out whether or

143

not she likes Vietnamese food. It's as good a place to start as any.

Ayesha gives her some menu options, and Chelsea tells her to just order her whatever she's having, and for a while there is silence as Ayesha places and pays for their order. 'Done,' she says, putting her phone down on the table. 'Probably won't be here for at least half an hour though. I meant to ask – how was it, at the cemetery? Aside from seeing Camille?'

'Oh. Peaceful. But not what I was expecting.'

'How do you mean?'

'I thought I'd feel some . . . closure, or something, I guess, but I didn't. Maybe if Camille hadn't been there, it might have been better. Less awkward, but I don't know.'

'Something I've come to realize is that closure doesn't really exist,' Ayesha says thoughtfully, 'at least not the way we expect it to. Closure implies an ending, the closing of a door, but it's not that; it's another room you walk into, but you can still hear everything going on in the next room.'

'Yeah,' Chelsea says, playing with the stem of her wine glass, 'I guess that's true.' But it's not as simple for Chelsea. Ayesha might be right about walking into a different room, but she's in another one entirely, one with bars and a locked door, and nothing to do but sit and think and obsess over everything that's happened – and not happened – in the past sixteen years. She won't be able to get into the room Ayesha's talking about until her name is cleared, until she's no longer branded a murderer, until people can look at her without thinking she's a monster. Until she finds out what really happened to

144

Izzy. And until all of that happens, she won't be free of that room she's still in, locked away from the rest of the world.

'I've been thinking about her so much recently. Izzy. I guess, what with you getting out, and the anniversary in a couple of days, it makes sense, but I've been feeling her presence so strongly.'

'Her presence?'

'Like she's right here,' Ayesha waves her hand somewhere behind her right ear, as if Izzy were standing just to the side of her. 'I don't know, I used to think all that stuff was a little woo-woo, but it's just memories, right? And her memory's so strong . . . it's palpable.'

'She'd probably love to know she was haunting you,' Chelsea says with a rueful smile.

'Right? She'd get such a kick out of it. Well, I'm happy to let her have that, considering everything.' There is a short, heavy silence during which their eyes meet and they both reach for their wine glasses. 'Do you ever feel guilty?' Ayesha asks eventually, after a loud gulp of wine.

'Guilty?' Chelsea says, the word catching in her throat.

'I don't mean – I know you didn't kill her, Chelsea. I know that; the same way I know that *I* didn't kill her, or Hannah didn't kill her. I just mean, do you ever feel guilty for being alive, when she's not?'

'Of course,' Chelsea says, 'all the time.'

'I wish – I don't know, I know it's stupid, but I always think, what if I'd been there, you know? Not like, I could've stopped it from happening, but maybe, *maybe* just one thing different might have saved her.'

Chelsea swallows; she's finding it difficult to breathe,

'Yeah,' she says at last, practically gasping. 'I think about it all the time, just wishing I'd gone home when she did.' Ayesha nods but doesn't say anything and the silence in the room is thick, the fifteen years between that night and right now hanging heavy between them, everything said and unsaid like a fraying tapestry slowly, painfully unravelling. 'I hate the fact that we still don't know what really happened that night,' Chelsea says eventually, although her words barely cover how she truly feels. 'Hate' isn't even a loud enough word for it; it's not big enough to convey her sense of betrayal, injustice, her complete lack of control. 'I play it over and over in my mind, but I know I don't have the full picture.' And that's the most frustrating thing; it's like a memory she can't access, a many-splintered thing, a different shard held by a different person, every one unwilling or unable to put their piece down in order to attach them back together and finally see the full picture. And the only person who knows everything is long dead.

Ayesha's phone dings with a notification and she goes to check it, but it's just her delivery app, telling her their food is on its way. 'So you still think . . . you still think it was Jamie Sinclair?'

The name slices through the heavy air as though it were a knife, letting certain memories rush through, and for a second, Chelsea doesn't know what to say. Does she think Jamie Sinclair killed Izzy? At the very least, he knows something about what happened to Izzy that night, something he didn't tell the police. Chelsea is so sure of it, has been sure of it for well over a decade now. Just knowing where he is, it's like having an itch in the centre of her back she can't quite reach, can't quite scratch. But she knows it's there, present, persistent, pernicious. And she's known, for years, that the answer to what really happened to Izzy lies somewhere between her leaving the Factory and getting back to Selly Oak, and now that she's out and able to walk those roads herself, what's stopping her?

Digbeth

Izzy is regretting coming. There are so many bodies surrounding her, she keeps losing sight of Chelsea and yet also can't tell where her body ends and the next person begins, limbs sliding alongside her, slick with sweat and grime, and the floor is so sticky with alcohol the smell of it rises up to meet her as she tries to shuffle through the crowd. She closes her eyes for a second, lets herself follow along in the swell, like riding a wave, but when she opens them again all she feels is panic, her chest tight and constricting. She presses a hand down on it and feels the galloping arrhythmic beat of her heart. Is this panic or is it just the drugs? Someone grabs at her wrist and she wriggles her way out of their grip, not even bothering to look and see who it was.

God, where is Chelsea?

Tears prick at the corner of her eyes, and she feels like such an idiot, but Chelsea promised to look out for her. Promised to look after her tonight. She hates how alien all of this feels, how indescribably different she feels to everyone else here. Maybe it's not that this is alien, maybe *she*'s the alien. She laughs and then stops herself, clamping her hand over her mouth so she doesn't look like a weirdo, laughing on her own, but no one's noticed. Of course.

Suddenly, she sees her. The dancefloor parting at just the

149

right moment so that she can see Chelsea's red horns sticking out of her wild, furiously back-combed hair. She sets her eyes on her, like Chelsea is the horizon and she's a seasick passenger on a boat, and pushes her way through the crowd.

'Hey!' she shouts, pulling at one of Chelsea's waving arms, grabbing her attention.

Chelsea's eyes widen in delight, 'Hey! Where have you been?'

'Where have you been?'

But Chelsea can't hear her above the music, or doesn't want to, and makes a hand gesture to indicate this, carries on dancing. Now that she's out on the dancefloor, surrounded by even more heaving bodies, Izzy's feet feel like cement, stuck to the ground, as if she's trying to stay rooted there when all she really wants is to get away as soon as possible. She puts her mouth as close to Chelsea's ear as possible, cupping it with her hand so she can hear her better. 'I think I'm gonna leave.'

'Noooo, please don't, we only just got here! Just stay a little bit longer?'

Izzy shakes her head, feels her eyes filling with tears but blinks them away.

'Oh, come on Iz, please? Let's get another drink first, at least?'

She has no choice in this, as Chelsea swings around and leads them off towards the bar, her hand clamped around Izzy's own. Chelsea's sociology friends – Izzy can barely remember their names, although she knows she should, knows she met them at some point last year too – follow and soon they're standing locked together towards a corner of the bar, as one of the boys and the girl – Sarah, maybe? – make their way to the front.

'Are you not one for parties then, Izzy?' the boy left with them – Tim? – shouts over the music.

Izzy swallows. Why does she feel so sick? 'Normally, I am.'

'Oh, Izzy's a party animal, don't worry,' Chelsea assures him. Any other time, this wouldn't annoy her, she would maybe even feel a little proud of it, but right now she hates the fact that Chelsea can't tell how much she is hating being here, how she vibrates with it. They'd been drinking back at the house, and with enough wine in her, this had started to feel like a plausible, even good idea, but now, surrounded by all these bodies, heat pressing in and down on her, she just wants to be anywhere but here.

The other two arrive back sooner than she'd imagined, and someone is passing her a plastic glass of gin and lemonade – disgusting – and suddenly she's being carried in their slipstream back on to the dancefloor. The music is barely music, just a beat and bass, but they all seem to be loving it, eyes closed, bodies swaying and stomping. This isn't what Chelsea usually listens or dances to, and it's pretty far from what Izzy would ever choose too, but she takes a big slurp of her drink, trying to enjoy the cloying, sherbet taste, and forces herself to join in. Maybe, if she lies to herself long enough about having a good time, she'll actually start to have a good time.

I've found him on facebook. I can't believe I didn't think about doing this last term. He went to oxford and was born in 1975. How old does that make him?

32? Old.

That's not that old!

Oh god you haven't friended him have you??

That would be so weird.

No, I'm not an idiot.

He's not married!! I told you so :P

Stop. Izzy, he's ancient.

That's so rude, I'm gonna tell him you said that :P

Chelsea lets out a snort of laughter, and Ayesha looks over at her, 'What's going on?'

'It's Iz, she's found James Sinclair, our history lecturer, on Facebook.'

'Ooh, the hot one?' Hannah asks.

'Yeah, the "hot" one,' Chelsea says, putting air quotes around 'hot'.

'Is he not?'

'He just isn't in his sixties yet and has a beard.'

Ayesha laughs just as Hannah says, 'Tell her to come over.' The request comes out a bit too much like a whine for Chelsea's liking, but she texts Izzy anyway.

Han wants you to come over.

And you don't??

Ha. We're just about to watch Hollyoaks.

Tempting but I'm in my pyjamas.

That hardly matters.

Ok you convinced me.

'Okay, she's coming. Happy, Han?'

'Yeah, I can't believe we're not scintillating enough for you, Han. You've changed so much.'

Hannah blushes and looks away from the other two girls, directing her attention to the small TV, even though the ads are on.

'Have you spoken to Iz about the party?' Ayesha says to Chelsea, her voice low.

'No,' Chelsea says slowly, 'I don't know if there's any point.'

'What do you mean? You were pretty upset.'

Chelsea sighs, shrugs, meets Ayesha's eye and then looks away. 'I don't know, it just seems kind of petty?'

'Of her not to invite you, yeah.'

'I meant for me to bring it up,' Chelsea says, even though she knows Ayesha knows what she meant. 'We're fine now, so.'

'Maybe Izzy just didn't think you'd want to go,' Hannah says lightly from the floor. There's space for all of them on their university-provided sofas, but Hannah, for some reason, prefers to drag a large cushion on to the floor and sit with her back resting against the sofas instead. 'You don't exactly have a lot of nice things to say about your old school.'

'I just had a very different experience to her, that's all.'

'Exactly. She probably just thought you wouldn't enjoy yourself. She's not *mean*, guys. It's Iz.'

And then, perfectly timed, there's a knock at the door and Hannah bounds up to open it. Chelsea catches Ayesha's eye, and the other girl juts her chin at Chelsea as if to say, *come on, now's your moment*, but Chelsea just shakes her head. She can hear Hannah's laughter from the hallway, bubbling over as she pushes the door to the living room open and reveals Izzy with a home-made mask covering her face.

Ayesha lets out a small yelp, and Chelsea laughs in surprise as Izzy whips the mask away and says, 'Sorry, I just wanted to introduce you to my future husband.'

Ayesha laughs, reaching for the mask – or rather a blown-up and printed out photo of their lecturer. 'This is him?' She examines it carefully, 'I guess he might be hot. Hard to tell with all the pixelation. Isabella Dunwooooody,' she says, placing the mask in front of her face and switching to a spooky voice, 'will you marry meeee?'

'Why are you pretending to be a ghost?' Izzy laughs.

'Yeah, he's old, not dead,' Chelsea says, for which Izzy throws a cushion at her head.

'What's his name again?' Hannah says, sitting down next to Izzy.

'Jamie Sinclair.'

'Oh, *Jamie* Sinclair is it now? You two really are close.'

'That's what his Facebook says,' Izzy answers, her cheeks turning red.

'Has either of you ever actually talked to him?' Ayesha asks.

'We've emailed and we've got our first seminar with

him tomorrow,' Izzy says. 'Last term we were stuck with his TA.'

'Oh, God,' Chelsea says. 'Don't be cringe tomorrow.'

'How dare you! I'm never cringe.'

'You're already blushing and Facebook-stalking him, I can only imagine how much worse it's going to get when there's just a handful of people in the room with us.'

'I promise I'll be on my best behaviour.'

* * *

Izzy's excitement had made Chelsea think she'd be early for once this morning, but she's been waiting down in the car park for almost fifteen minutes before the other girl appears. 'Sorry, sorry, I couldn't decide what to wear,' she says breathlessly when she reaches Chelsea, who immediately starts walking in the direction of campus.

'Dressing to impress?'

'Um.'

'Oh my God, Iz, you're blushing again. Are you serious?'

'What? It's nice to make an effort.'

'Not for a seminar, you weirdo. Dude. I really thought you were kind of joking at first, but you actually fancy him, don't you?'

'Fancy who?' a voice says from behind them.

'Joe! Hey, where did you come from?' Izzy says.

Joe points in the direction of one of their neighbouring halls of residence, 'I live over there.'

'Oh, I had no idea. Hey, we didn't see you at the lecture yesterday, did you only just get back?'

'No, I was sick yesterday. Made the terrible mistake of going out on the first night of term.'

'Oh, is "sick" code for hungover now?' Chelsea says.

'It sounds a little more respectable, yeah. So, who does Izzy fancy?'

'Our lecturer. James Sinclair.'

'Oh, right, yeah. I forgot about your little crush, Izzy. You wouldn't think to look at you that you'd be into old men.'

'Ha ha.'

'Actually, now I think about it, this is one of those rare occurrences where the guy could be both a cradle snatcher *and* a gold digger. That's impressive, Iz, breaking down the gender roles,' Chelsea says.

'If he's a cradle snatcher, does that make Izzy a grave robber?'

'Oh my God, he's like, thirty, guys, he's not about to drop dead.'

'You never know.'

Izzy pushes Joe, who stumbles into the road and chuckles, 'I was kind of dreading this seminar as I haven't done the reading, but now I can't wait to see Casanova.'

'I fear you may be disappointed,' Chelsea says.

'Why didn't you get to the reading?' Izzy asks. 'Too many Christmas parties?'

'No,' Joe says with a sigh, rubbing at his face as though exhausted. 'Bit more depressing than that, I'm afraid. My dad got diagnosed with lung cancer.'

'Oh God, I'm sorry, Joe,' Izzy says, stopping in her tracks. 'Chelsea, isn't that terrible?'

'Yeah, of course,' Chelsea says, practically swallowing down her words. 'But I actually knew already.'

'Oh.' Izzy blinks at her and looks away quickly, starting

to walk in the direction of campus again at a heightened pace.

'Are you sure you're okay to be here?' Chelsea says to Joe. 'Like I said on the phone, I'm sure it'd be okay if you missed a bit of term.' At this, Izzy twists around to stare back at Chelsea, her eyebrows raised, but says nothing, her head swivelling back around to watch where she's going almost immediately.

'I know, but honestly, it's easier than being at home. Feel like a really crap person for saying that, but it's the truth.'

'Come on,' Izzy barks, 'we're going to be late if we don't hurry up.' She starts walking even faster, and Joe looks over at Chelsea, who shrugs at him. She knows Izzy is picking up on something between her and Joe and is clearly going to have something to say about it, once it's just the two of them again, but for now she tries not to let it bother her.

When they finally make it to the seminar, James Sinclair is sitting at the head of the table, rather than behind his desk.

'Nice of you to join us, ladies. Sorry, and gentleman,' he says, noticing Joe trail in behind them.

Chelsea takes a seat at the other end from Sinclair and expects Izzy to sit next to her, but instead her friend takes the seat closest to their lecturer, smiling winningly at him while apologizing profusely.

'Not to worry, these things happen. Although hopefully not habitually. I was just explaining to the others how I like to run my seminars as casual conversations, but that I still expect you all to take your reading and the work very seriously. This is where you can ask any questions you want, and we can let the discussion wander where it takes us, but that only works if we're all putting in the same amount of effort. Does that all sound okay?'

Chelsea nods as her fellow classmates mumble an uncertain 'yes'. All except Izzy, who beams and says, clear as a bell, 'Yes, absolutely, James.' And Chelsea, looking at her friend, wonders if any of this can possibly lead anywhere good.

Chelsea gets off the tube at Piccadilly Circus. It didn't take long from Balham, but she has all her stuff with her – she's heading back to Scotland this afternoon, needs to get back to her new job, to appease Nikki, who has texted her multiple times a day during this short trip, as well as Kate McClure, who has also been in touch, as if Chelsea needs any reminder that she's there, waiting for her return, watching her every move. She's thinking about all this while shouldering her rucksack as she stands on the escalator and gets caught up in a stream of people, leaving by the wrong exit, not paying close enough attention, and stumbles into the daylight, looking over, just like everyone else, apparently, at Eros as he balances precariously on just one foot. As she stands there, Chelsea sees herself, hurrying through this thoroughfare hundreds of times before, weaving through crowds, ignoring tourists taking photographs, just trying to get to wherever she was going. Someone bumps into her, swears under their breath in her direction even though it was clearly their fault, and suddenly she can't help but grin. Her heart is beating heavily, she's so nervous about seeing Camille, but the hazy autumn sunshine and the constant movement of the crowds, the feeling of being right in the very heart of a place, all make it feel like she is finally home.

That feeling lessens the closer she gets to her destination. Hotel Café Royal. Somewhere she's not sure existed – at least not in its current state – fifteen years ago. In these moments, she wishes she had someone to turn to, to check her memories and be reminded of what was then, and what is now. That person should have been her mother, of course. Or, in a completely different life, an altogether alternative dimension, Izzy. But where would she have been for fifteen years if Izzy was still alive? Nothing but duress would keep her away from London for so long. She walks through the doors of the hotel and feels immediately smaller, reduced to the state and cost of her shoes, clothes, bag, although they are all at least new thanks to Saoirse. But new or not, Chelsea knows they're not up to scratch in a place like this, for people like this.

'I'm here to see Camille Dunwoody,' she says to the immaculate-looking woman behind the desk.

'Yes, of course,' she says, the slight trace of an accent making the simple sentence sound more interesting than it really is. Behind her, a man in the uniform of the hotel minutely turns his head, gazing at Chelsea out of the corner of his eye, and she knows he has recognized Camille's last name and not only because she's a guest.

Chelsea shifts uncomfortably from foot to foot as the woman talks into the phone on her desk and nods. 'Yes, you can go up now, madam. It's suite 401.'

A suite. Of course.

Chelsea shakes her head at the memory, not daring to let it loose, although how could she not be forcibly reminded of that first time she met Camille? So the same, and yet so very, very different. Looking down at her Converse as they slap against the smooth marble floor, she sees them doing the same thing at that relatively anonymous city centre hotel all those years ago. Not that these are the same shoes, of course. Those were taken into evidence.

Outside the room, Chelsea has to take a minute, checks her clothes for dirt and fluff and touches her hair, wondering if she should pull it back into a ponytail, not that any of this will make a difference to Camille, a woman who wears Chanel and Hermès and wouldn't know a Primark T-shirt if it was staring her in the face.

'Ah, I thought it was you,' Camille says now. She has opened the door almost silently, startling Chelsea into a swallowed yelp. 'I heard the lift go and I knew you'd been checked in already. Are you all right?'

'Ye-es,' Chelsea practically stutters. 'Hello.'

'Hello, Chelsea,' Camille says with a serene smile, and then, stepping backwards, 'won't you come in?'

The suite is big, although not as big as that one in Birmingham. The Presidential Suite, the receptionist had called it then, and Chelsea can still remember the bile-tasting anxiety that had accompanied her all the way up to the top floor of the hotel. In fact, she can remember it so well because she is experiencing it again right now. 'I was about to make a coffee, would you like one? Or tea?'

'Yes, please. Coffee.'

Chelsea follows Camille into the living area of the suite, watching as the older woman stands at the marble bar where she pours two glasses of water and starts to use what Chelsea has to assume is a coffee machine. 'It's a Nespresso machine,' Camille explains, seeing Chelsea's confusion and interest. She holds something up that looks like a sweet, shimmering and brightly coloured. 'This is the coffee, can you believe it? Everything at the push of a button.' She pops the small pod-like thing into the machine and indeed, presses a button, signalling the machine to burst into gurgling life.

Camille has a corner suite, with three windows all looking over the rumble of Regent Street and the sweep of St James's down towards Westminster and the seat of power. Despite these extensive views, Chelsea is almost immediately claustrophobic. The room is decorated in light, sugar-sweet tones; walls the colour of bleached stone, candy-pink velvet cushions, a caramel parquet floor, sage-green sofas and brushed brass all designed to make the space feel tranquil and softly welcoming, but Chelsea feels anything but tranquil or welcomed. Behind her, the coffee machine stops making its noises and Camille clears her throat.

'Here you go,' she says, placing a cup on the coffee table next to a glass of water, condensation running down its sides. 'Take a seat, Chelsea.'

Chelsea does as she's told, dropping her rucksack at her feet.

'Are you going back to Scotland today?'

'Yes,' Chelsea says, indicating the bag at her feet.

Camille's gaze lands on it, 'Ah, well, at least you're able to travel light.'

'Well, I don't have too many possessions these days.'

If Chelsea expects a reaction to this, she is disappointed. Camille is as sphinx-like as ever, smooth and stoic, giving nothing away. 'Except your mother's house, of course.' She sips at her coffee, her eyes trained on Chelsea.

'Yes. That's –'

'It's being rented at the moment, I believe?'

'How did you know that?'

Camille merely smiles, but then, perhaps anticipating that Chelsea will demand more than this, says, 'These things are not difficult to ascertain.'

There is an unsaid 'for someone like me' hanging in the air, reminding Chelsea of the reach of a Dunwoody, and she has to look away from the other woman for a second. Why did she come here? Why was she even invited? It's impossible to imagine why Camille has asked her here, what her motivation could be in doing so; if she thinks Chelsea killed her daughter, why ask her into her hotel suite, alone? Why offer her coffee and make small talk? What could she possibly want from Chelsea? Already, Chelsea knows she shouldn't have come. But she couldn't help it. After seeing Hannah in that car, discovering that she's engaged to Charlie, she couldn't resist the opportunity to gain some information. Although getting it out of Camille may prove impossible.

'Why did you ask me here, Camille?' It's the first time she's addressed her by name, and it feels strange in her mouth, like it shouldn't be there, like she shouldn't be here.

'Yes, I can see why you would be confused. Do you think about Isabella much, Chelsea?'

Chelsea is taken aback by this question, and for a second it leaves her mute, her mind stuck, wheels turning in mud as she tries to imagine a world, a life, where she didn't think about Izzy. 'Yes, I think about her all the time,' she says eventually. 'Every day.'

'Yes, it is the same for me. In fact, I think we might be the only two people in the world who think about her so much, and so I thought we should meet.'

'But we saw each other yesterday.' She's stating the obvious here, but she feels like she has to, just to stay sane. She still can't wrap her head around why she's here, and Camille's answers aren't helping at all.

'Yes. Kismet.'

Chelsea fights the urge to roll her eyes and instead narrows them at the other woman. Whatever game Camille is playing, Chelsea wants no part in it, but she also knows this is an opportunity she can't waste. 'Then why invite me here today?'

'Because we have more to discuss, I believe. And I think it should be done in private.'

'Tell me what it is you think we have to discuss,' Chelsea says finally, practically gritting her teeth as she does so.

'Who killed my daughter.'

'But . . .' and here Chelsea has to ignore her confusion, to try and stare through the storm cloud of obfuscation that Camille has created and gather her courage, draw together every nerve, her muscles tensing as she sits up a little straighter in her armchair, 'but you think I killed her.'

Camille is taking a sip of coffee, and it seems to Chelsea that she really takes her time with it. Savours it. Is it possible she's enjoying this? Surely not, when they're talking about the death of her own daughter, but there is always such deliberateness to her every action, such orchestration.

'I did think that, Chelsea, I really did,' she says eventually, 'and I'm sorry. For everything you have been put through since, I really do want you to know that I thought about you too. Whenever I would think of Isabella, I would say a prayer for you too.'

'Well, your prayers didn't work. Every appeal I launched was turned down.'

'It was a turn of phrase, dear,' the older woman says with a wave of her hand. 'I do not really pray.'

Chelsea wants to scream, blood pumping loudly in her ears. How dare Camille be so flippant, so irreverent? How can she be, when there's so much at stake here, so much still in play? If she really, truly has started to believe that Chelsea might not be guilty, then that means – and surely she knows this – her daughter's killer is still unknown. Unknown and at large, walking freely out in the world, while Chelsea spent fourteen years – almost half her entire life – wasting away behind the four walls of Foston Hall. 'So, that's it?' she manages to bite out, nausea and the rising tide of anger making it difficult, almost impossible to speak, to form full sentences. 'You asked me here just to tell me you finally believe me?'

'Is that not a good enough reason to want to see you?'

'No.' Chelsea is barely holding it together, trying to wrap her head around Camille's revelation while also trying to think about what this might mean for her. Could Camille help her clear her name? Is that what she is offering her?

'Ah, you surprise me, Chelsea. I thought it would be. This isn't insignificant, you know. Because if I no longer believe you killed my daughter, then surely, I must be interested in discovering who did. Aren't you?' Chelsea can't quite bring herself to answer, and in the end, she isn't quick enough anyway, 'I think you are. I think that's why you're here, actually.'

Chelsea takes a deep breath before answering, 'Of

course I want to know who really killed her. I've wanted that for . . . for ever. If anyone had actually listened to me fifteen years ago, then we might have found out then, and we wouldn't be having this conversation now.'

'You are quite right.'

Chelsea is so surprised by this concession, it relaxes her into leaning back against the sofa. She has been so tense, so coiled up, ready to spring, that she had been sat quite literally on the edge of her seat, her posture almost as perfect and rigid as Camille's own. Then, in the silence of their stand-off, there's a knock at the door and Chelsea is once again on guard. Is it just a member of hotel staff? But Camille says, softly, 'Ah, my other guest is here,' and Chelsea can't help but stand up, head spinning, as she tries to regain her footing in this chess game Camille is playing. Whoever is at the door, Chelsea's not even sure she cares, because how could she ever trust Camille? But then, the memory of seeing Hannah sat in the back of Camille's car comes to her and she has to reach out to the arm of the sofa to steady herself. Is she about to come face-to-face with Hannah?

The suite is large enough that Chelsea can't see the door from where she is, can only hear murmurs as Camille opens and closes it, welcoming in her other guest. Annoyance roars through Chelsea as she thinks of how perfectly orchestrated, how well presented, how distinctly Camille this all is. Yesterday, at the cemetery, where Chelsea had surprised Camille – however unwittingly – all she'd felt for the other woman, for the most part, was sympathy. Yes, she's always at least partly held Camille responsible for her conviction, not because of any one particular thing Camille had said or done, but for being part of the 'other side'. Once, before the trial, Chelsea had requested to speak to Camille. All she'd wanted was a chance to talk to Izzy's mother, to try and make Camille see her as she always had done before: as Izzy's friend. But Camille had refused. Still, she'd lost her daughter to violence, just months after losing her husband to cancer, and Chelsea understood how that could tear the compassion from you, could leave you deaf to any entreaties. So, yesterday, she'd felt sympathy for that woman who'd lost so much in her life, but now, standing in her hotel suite, feeling like a silly little pawn being moved around and sacrificed, once again, she's not so sure. In fact, she's not sure of anything at all.

But it's not Hannah at the door, and Chelsea feels a small surge of relief at this, before realizing that Camille's other guest is one of the police officers who arrested her. Natalie Ajala.

'What's she doing here?' she says to Camille. 'Actually, you know what? I don't care. I'm leaving.' She reaches down for her rucksack, hands shaky with anger, but a cool hand stays her, and suddenly Camille is right in front of her.

'Chelsea, please, I know you're angry, and very likely confused, but it will all make sense soon. We all want the same thing.'

'Really?' Chelsea says, almost laughing at this statement, the audacity of it. 'I find that very hard to believe.'

'Please, just sit back down, and I'll make us all another coffee. Although, maybe tea would be best for you,' Camille says with a little smile, infuriating rather than charming Chelsea, which was surely her intent, but Chelsea, desperate to go but curious enough to stay, sits down, looking over at Ajala as she does so. The detective has already taken a seat, one leg crossed over the other, watching Chelsea and Camille intently. Chelsea remembers that attentiveness from the interview room, doesn't have to be reminded that although Detective Rob Bailey had been in charge, the most astute, observant questions had often come from Ajala instead. Sometimes, all she has to do is blink and she's back there, in the worn-out room, stuffy and overly warm, the knowledge that she's being constantly watched and listened to a persistent warning bell in her mind. On that first day she'd been sweaty and disorientated, her hangover working overtime as it combined with shock, grief and fear, but all that had been taken by the detectives and translated as guilt and even now, the memory of that, the unfairness of it, the injustice, brings tears to her eyes.

She blinks them away as Camille places a cup of tea in front of her and reminds her to drink some water. She's being almost chummy now and the false familiarity grates on Chelsea, makes her wish she really had left when she wanted to, but instead she turns to Ajala. 'What are you doing here?'

'Camille has hired me to reinvestigate Izzy's murder.'

'Hired you?' Chelsea says, looking between the two women. 'You can't just hire the police.' Although, what does she know? Camille Dunwoody probably can.

Ajala smiles at her, 'I'm not a member of the police force any more, Chelsea. Just to be clear.'

'So, you're what, a private detective?'

'Not exactly. I work as an investigator, researcher and consultant for TV, films and podcasts.'

Chelsea reaches for her tea and takes a sip, the hot water burning her tongue. She's not sure Ajala's new role makes her feel any better, or trust her any more. 'So, that's what you're doing? Making a podcast or a documentary or something?'

'Absolutely not,' Camille answers.

Ajala's eyes dart to Camille very briefly and then back to Chelsea, 'I suppose what I'm doing for Camille is more in line with being a private detective, as you said. I'm working as an investigator, but without any end product in mind.'

'"End product"?' Chelsea says, biting the words out.

'Sorry,' Ajala says with a slight grimace, 'that was a poor choice of words. Insensitive. I just mean, neither of us have any aim of making a documentary or podcast, or anything like that.'

'Absolutely not,' Camille says again.

'But I don't ... I don't understand. You put me in prison.'

'I know, and I understand why you're so mistrustful, Chelsea. But I was never fully convinced of your guilt, and I ended up just being a cog in the machine, having to follow orders I didn't really believe in. But Camille's presented me with an opportunity to right my wrongs and that's what I'm here to do.'

Ajala is speaking slowly, calmly, but her words are so explosive, they land like bombs in Chelsea's ears. Bang. Bang. Bang. She can't look at the other woman any more, nor at Camille, so she pushes the heels of her hands into her eyes and rubs them viciously. What is going on? First Camille, now Ajala? Why is it all coming now, this belief in her innocence? Far too late to make a difference, and after all this time – why now? All she wanted, in those dark days of her arrest and the months leading up towards the trial, was for a voice of note to speak up and take her side, to say she was innocent, that she couldn't have done this. She'd had her mum and aunt and Ayesha, of course, but this? A detective and the victim's own mother? That could've made all the difference. Could have changed the direction of her life, the entire course of history.

But will it even be enough now? To clear her name and find out, finally, who really killed Izzy?

Transcript of interview with Camille Dunwoody on 29 October 2007 conducted by Detective Inspector Rob Bailey and Detective Constable Natalie Ajala at Birmingham Central Police Station

Detective Inspector Rob Bailey: Thank you for coming in today, Mrs Dunwoody, and for getting here so quickly.
Camille Dunwoody: Of course.
Detective Constable Natalie Ajala: And sorry for your loss. This must be a terrible shock for you, especially so soon after losing your husband.
CD: Thank you. No one can know the pain I am in. It is too much … too much to comprehend right now.
[pause]
RB: Yes, of course. We're so sorry. We understand you saw your daughter on Saturday, Mrs Dunwoody? Was that in London?
CD: Please, call me Camille. Mrs Dunwoody is … it always felt like someone else.
RB: [cough] Camille. Thank you.
NA: How was Isabella when you last saw her, Camille?
CD: She was … she wasn't herself.
NA: How do you mean?
CD: She took the death of her father very hard. As you would expect, of course, losing him so young, but it also happened … very quickly, I suppose. It was a shock. For all of us. But Charlie is older, and I am … Ian was older than I, and it might sound callous, but I always expected to lose him first, but to Isabella … he was invincible. Her father. I don't think she ever thought about death.

NA: I don't think many teenagers do.

CD: Quite. Although, she was twenty-one. Just.

NA: Of course, sorry.

CD: No, no, it's fine. She was young. Very young. At twenty-one you may as well still be a teenager for all you know. [quietly sniffs]

RB: So, she was upset on Saturday, when you last saw her?

CD: Upset is too ... too simple a word. You are upset when you spill a drink or take a wrong turn or exchange bad words with a friend. She had lost her father. She was more than upset.

NA: Do you think she could have been depressed?

CD: Maybe, but we will never know. She was in grief. She was grieving. It covered her, completely.

RB: She was covered in grief?

CD: Yes.

RB: Weren't you worried by this?

CD: Yes, of course, no one likes to see their child in pain, but grieving is natural, it is normal, it's a process. I didn't expect her to be anything other than grieving.

NA: Were you surprised, then, when she returned to university? To Birmingham?

CD: On Saturday?

NA: On Saturday, but also in general. She could have taken more time off, I assume? Did the university tell her she had to return when she did?

CD: I don't know about that.

RB: When exactly did she come back to Birmingham? After her father's death?

[short pause]

CD: At the beginning of October, I think. Her housemates might remember better than I. The exact date, I mean. Those weeks, they're a bit of a blur, I'm afraid.

NA: Did that seem too soon to you?

CD: She said she was ready. I had to trust her. There are some that might think it wasn't soon enough. Her father had been dead a month by then already. If she had a job, they would have expected her back the day after the funeral, would they not?

NA: That's very true.

CD: I let her take as long as she needed, but I think after a while, she wanted distraction.

NA: And what about her friends, Hannah, Ayesha, Chelsea — were they supportive of Isabella after the death of her father?

CD: I believe so, yes. They all came to the funeral.

RB: Including Chelsea?

CD: Yes, of course.

RB: Are you aware that it was Chelsea who found your daughter and alerted the police?

CD: Yes, I am. Poor girl, I would not wish that on anyone.

RB: Camille, we're a little concerned with how long it took Chelsea to call the police.

CD: You are?

RB: She says she was awake from roughly eleven o'clock in the morning, and yet she didn't call nine-nine-nine until gone three o'clock, even though she knew Isabella was in the house and she hadn't seen her.

[pause]

CD: I see.

RB: Does that seem like a long time to you, Camille?

CD: Yes, I suppose it does.

NA: What was their relationship like? Their friendship?

CD: Between Isabella and Chelsea?

RB: Yes.

CD: They were close. They became quite close quite quickly, I think.

RB: Even though they weren't friends at school?

CD: They didn't know each other at school. Isabella is a year older than Chelsea ... *was*, was a year older than Chelsea.

RB: Doesn't that seem strange to you? That they didn't know each other at school but then suddenly became so close so quickly?

CD: I hadn't thought about it. Isabella never seemed to think it was strange. She invited Chelsea to spend her birthday with her – they shared a birthday – invited her to Cornwall, to Mirador.

RB: Mirador?

CD: Our home in Mallorca.

RB: Right. That was this summer just gone?

CD: August, yes.

NA: All four of them were staying with you, though, weren't they? Hannah, Ayesha and Chelsea all joined you at your house?

CD: Yes, that's right. Although Hannah stayed with us for longer. She was already there when Chelsea and Ayesha arrived.

NA: So, maybe Chelsea and Isabella had grown apart by that time? Had anything happened, that you know of?

CD: No ... not that I'm aware of.

RB: We're concerned about the fact that Isabella returned home alone on Saturday night. She went out with Chelsea, but they left the event at different times – is this normal for them, do you know?

CD: I don't know. I think you would be better off asking one of their other housemates this question.

NA: Yes, you're right, we'll make sure to do so. So, you don't think they were fighting or in a dispute over anything?

CD: I'm not sure, detective.

NA: Did Isabella confide in you much? I don't mean to imply that you weren't close, but at that kind of age … it can be difficult between mums and daughters.

CD: She confided in me about certain things. But I know there was much more she didn't like to share with me.

RB: Like what?

[pause]

CD: Well … I have been made aware that there were drugs in her system –

RB: Yes, they showed up on the toxicology report.

CD: And I wasn't aware of this. That she took drugs. But I'm not surprised by this either.

NA: What about dating and boyfriends? Did she share with you about that at all?

CD: A little.

NA: Do you know if she was seeing anybody?

CD: I don't know. If she was … where were they?

RB: Sorry?

CD: She'd been at home for a month, her father had just died. If she was seeing someone, if she had a boyfriend, I would expect them to be there for her.

RB: So, you think she wasn't in a relationship?

CD: I don't think so. But I can't say for sure.

RB: What about a secret relationship?

CD: Well, if it was secret, then I certainly wouldn't know about it.

NA: Do you think she might have kept a relationship secret, if it was with an older man?

[pause] Camille?

CD: I ... I don't know. Maybe. Was she seeing an older man?

RB: What if it was a teacher?

NA: A lecturer.

CD: Are you telling me my daughter was having a relationship with one of her lecturers?

Izzy's obsession with Jamie Sinclair lasts all the way through their second term at uni. Through the dark walks home from campus, their first, and only, dump of snow, the shivering in line for Snobs and Subway City and Oceana, the sticky floors of the student guild on a Saturday night, and of course, Sinclair's seminars and lectures. Chelsea decides to stop worrying about it – she has to, because Izzy doesn't listen, Joe just laughs, Ayesha gets bored with Chelsea complaining about it, and Hannah won't hear a bad word said against Izzy. Besides, it's only a crush. Completely one-sided, and, surely, will be over by the time they come back after Easter for summer term and final exams.

Or so she thinks.

It's one of those rare days when Chelsea is on campus early. In fact, it might be the earliest she's ever been on campus. She has a regular nine o'clock lecture, but also needs to see another lecturer during their office hours, which only last from eight until ten in the morning. She's between these two events, thinking only of the cappuccino she's going to buy before rushing to get to her lecture on time, when she spots Izzy down the hall of the History Department. She's standing on the threshold of an office, the door to which is open, although Chelsea can't quite see whose it is. Chelsea's about to call Izzy's name when the other girl stands on her tiptoes and reaches up. It's not a kiss, but it's almost as intimate as that, her fingers on the other person's face or possibly neck. Chelsea isn't breathing as she manoeuvres herself to see better, even though, really, she doesn't need to see him to know exactly who the other person is.

Jamie Sinclair.

She stands, her back against a wall, all thoughts of coffee and her next lecture forgotten, but soon Izzy is upon her, looking perplexed at first and then happy. 'Hi!' she says. 'What are you doing here?'

'Office hours,' Chelsea says, stumbling over the words a little.

'Yeah, same. I had to see Anna Fox about something,' Izzy says, naming one of their other history lecturers.

'Anna? Really?'

'Yeah.'

Chelsea looks at her and then starts walking down the stairs. They are both heading to the same lecture, but while Izzy keeps up an almost constant stream of chatter, all Chelsea can hear is that lie she just told. The lie itself isn't great, of course, but it's the reason for Izzy's lie that worries her more. Because Izzy hasn't stopped talking about Sinclair all term, so why stop now? Why, when something has clearly happened – or is happening – wouldn't she want to tell Chelsea? Izzy wouldn't be embarrassed about this development, surely, not after spending so much time detailing how much she fancies him. Wouldn't this be the moment to reveal it hadn't all been nothing?

Sinclair is a few minutes late for the start of their lecture, which neither of them remark upon, and then, when it's over, Izzy doesn't even look over to him or say, 'thank you,' or 'goodbye,' the way she has done at the end of every other lecture he's given.

'What, no love for your boyfriend this morning?' Chelsea says as they walk down the hallway with Joe.

'What? What boyfriend?'

Joe laughs at this. 'Sinclair, obviously. You barely looked at him today. Not like you, Iz.'

'Oh . . . don't be silly, he's not my boyfriend.'

'No, we know that,' Chelsea says, looking at the profile of her friend, trying to work out what she's really saying. And what she might be hiding.

'Where are we going now? Library? Mason Lounge? I could do with a coffee.'

'Yeah, me too.'

Izzy buys their coffees while Chelsea and Joe grab a table. 'What's going on with you?' Joe asks, as he sits down. 'I've never seen you frown so much.'

Chelsea looks over at the café, where Izzy is still safely standing in line, and tells Joe about what she saw in the department hallway, before their lecture.

'Wow. Izzy finally made something happen there. I'm kind of proud of her.'

'You don't think it's a little weird that she lied to me?'

Joe shrugs, his eyes going over to check on Izzy too. 'Maybe she's trying to respect his privacy.'

'Izzy?'

'Yeah, or maybe *she's* more private than we realize. We've never seen her with a boyfriend before.'

'True.'

'And it's not like we've told her everything,' Joe says,

raising his eyebrows. Underneath the table, he reaches his hand across to hers and squeezes her fingers tight.

Chelsea, who has to turn right around in her chair to see Izzy properly, says, 'What's going on, is she coming over?'

'She just paid,' Joe says, dropping her hand. 'You know, I'm starting to think you're maybe a bit embarrassed by me.'

Chelsea can feel the heat of a blush creeping up her neck, but she shakes her head. 'It's not that. I just think she'd be . . . weirded out by it.' They've been hooking up for a few weeks now. What started as drunken kisses in the hidden corners of Snobs and Subway City, has since progressed to Joe sneaking into her flat late at night, and sneaking out again early in the morning. Ayesha knows, of course, because it is impossible to get anything past her, but Chelsea can't quite put her finger on why she doesn't want Izzy to know yet. Yes, she's worried Iz will be upset about how this affects the dynamic of the three of them: her, Chelsea and Joe spend a lot of time together, thanks to their many overlapping lectures and seminars. But she also knows it runs deeper than that. Does she want something that's only hers, perhaps? Or is it more about wanting to preserve what she and Izzy have? Whichever it is, she knows she's being hypocritical, getting so heated by Izzy keeping things from her, but whatever is happening between her and Sinclair is a lot more dangerous than what Chelsea and Joe have.

'I think you cater too much to her emotions.'

'Joe.'

'What? It's true. Look at you, agonizing over seeing her

with Sinclair and whether or not you should even bring it up. Are you scared of her?'

Chelsea does turn around this time. Izzy is almost on them, her hands full of cups and chocolate, and a flare of guilt sparks through her as she stands to help. She's not scared of Izzy; Joe just doesn't understand their friendship.

But still, why lie?

'Chelsea?' Izzy says, waving her hand in front of Chelsea's face. 'Earth to Chelsea!' She looks over to Joe, making a face and laughing.

'Oh, sorry, I was miles away. Thanks for the coffee.'

'Sure. What were you thinking about?'

'Um . . .' Chelsea takes a sip of coffee, looks over at her friend, looks over to Joe who nods encouragingly. 'I was thinking about seeing you and Sinclair this morning before our lecture.' Her gaze flicks to Joe again, and she thinks, maybe, he looks disappointed. Did he think she was going to tell Izzy about them?

'Yeah, for office hours,' Izzy says blithely before taking a sip from her own coffee, 'I told you.'

'No, you told me you'd been seeing Anna.'

'Did I?'

'Why did you lie about that?'

'I didn't. I saw Anna. I went to see her before seeing Jamie.'

'So, you did see him?'

'Yes, I just said that, didn't I?' Izzy says, with a roll of her eyes. 'Joe, help me out here.'

'Can't, sorry. You sound like you're going round in circles to me.'

'I just don't understand why you wouldn't say that originally,' Chelsea continues, feeling a little dogged now, 'when I saw you up on the history floor.'

'Why does it matter? I know you're funny about Jamie, so I just mentioned Anna to keep things simple. I didn't *lie*, Chelsea. God you're so . . . puritanical sometimes. Which is funny because I was asking Anna about doing my essay on the witch trials.'

'I saw you with him, Izzy,' Chelsea says, pressing on, annoyed now. Why can't she take anything seriously? 'I know something's going on.'

'Well, I don't know that, so you better fill me in.'

'Iz, come on. Just . . . be careful.'

Izzy rolls her eyes again, drinks her coffee. 'It's not what you think it is, Chelsea, I promise,' she says after a pause, and Chelsea is surprised to hear how serious she sounds, so different to the blasé attitude of her eyeroll, her usual devil-may-care demeanour. It's a relief not to be fobbed off by Izzy, that way she has of reducing valid concerns, making you feel petty and small-minded for worrying over something, for caring at all, really. But then, Chelsea wonders if this shouldn't make her worry more.

Chelsea pushes her way out of the hotel and on to the busy pavement, breathing in the cold autumn air. It's laced with exhaust fumes and all the other familiar smells of the city, but it feels bracingly refreshing, scorching first her throat, then her lungs, after the cloying warmth of Camille's suite. She stayed too long, and if she's not careful, she's going to miss her train back to Scotland, her phone dinging with yet another reminder from Nikki that she needs to hurry. But she can't hurry, her legs are heavy with exhaustion and shock, and, if she's being honest, the reluctance to return to Nikki's cosy cottage. She knows she needs to get back, to check in with her parole officer, to pick up a shift – or several – at the veterinary surgery, but it all rings so false compared to what she could be doing were she able to stay in London for a few more days. It's all yet another reminder that, although she might finally be out of prison, she's still not free. Not really.

She starts towards Oxford Circus, walking as fast as she can, dodging shoppers with loaded bags and office workers with a phone clamped in one hand and a desultory sandwich in the other, the sight of which manages to make her stomach rumble. She checks the time again – it's hours since she had a bagel this morning in Ayesha's kitchen, and more to the point, her train is due out of King's Cross in just fifteen minutes. Shit. She picks up the pace, but she's forgotten how long Regent Street is, especially when you take account of all the pedestrians, so by the time she squeezes on to a Victoria Line carriage, breath wheezing, she already knows she's going to miss it. 'Shit, shit, shit,' she mutters to herself, staring down at her phone screen, watching the minutes disappear. She feels someone's eyes on her and for a stomach-plummeting second she thinks she's been recognized, but as her eyes flick up, the other person's eyes flick away with just the ghost of a smirk. She's not wearing her cap though, is suddenly unsure whether she packed it or not, can't believe how comfortable she got over the course of just two days in London. Maybe it's for the best she's heading back to the Highlands. She may not feel like she can hide there any better than she can here, but at least she'd be able to spot anyone coming. London is too crowded, one too many faces in the crowd to be able to figure out who's friend or who's foe. Before she knows it, though, her time is up and she's missed her train. She sighs heavily; she can already hear Nikki's disappointed voice, can imagine the text she might get back from Kate McClure if she told her. How can she have been so careless? She stayed too long listening to Ajala, had become too caught up telling her about Jamie Sinclair, how she still thinks it was him. Who else could it have been, after all? Who had the motive? Ajala had nodded sagely, told her they'd looked into him at the time, that he'd definitely been on their radar, but Chelsea had got the distinct impression she wasn't being taken seriously. Again. When she'd mentioned his name, a look of understanding had zipped between Ajala and Camille, and Camille had got up to make yet another coffee. Then, her back turned to both of them, her voice as even and serene as ever, she'd dropped a bomb: 'I have specifically asked Natalie to investigate Charlie, Chelsea.'

'Charlie? Your stepson?' Chelsea had asked, her shock causing her to need clarification, even though she already knew exactly who Camille was referring to.

'Yes. I have ... I have reason to believe he may have been involved. That he has been lying to me for quite some time.'

Chelsea is still processing this revelation when she looks up and realizes they're at King's Cross, finally. She leaves the tube, following the haphazard crocodile of fellow travellers up to the main station concourse and picking up a sandwich in Pret, chewing hungrily as her eyes scan the departure boards, searching out the next train to Aberdeen. Finished with her sandwich, she takes out her phone and calls Nikki.

'You missed it, didn't you?' she says on picking up. Chelsea has no idea how her aunt already knows this, but she swallows her nerves and admits defeat.

'Nikki, I'm so sorry. There was a delay on the Victoria Line.'

'There's never a delay on the Victoria Line.'

'Well, that's not –'

'God, Chelsea, do you have any idea how angry I am at you? This isn't for my sake, you know, I'm not doing all this to make my life any easier. This is all to make sure *you're* okay. And you're fucking it up.'

There is a pause in which all the sounds and busy-ness of King's Cross fill Chelsea's ears and head, a roaring, every-day tumult that drowns out every thought, every feeling. Nikki's right. She clamps her eyes shut, blocking out the swirling station for a moment, but her aunt's waiting for an answer.

'I know,' Chelsea says finally. 'I'm so sorry. This is all . . . it's a lot. I feel terrible. Like an idiot.'

'You are an idiot.'

'Right.'

'You have a meeting with your parole officer the day after tomorrow, you know that, right? And you've missed two days of work now. You're supposed to be working five days a week.'

'I know.'

'I feel like I'm the only one taking this seriously, out of the two of us. And that's not how it should be.'

'I am taking it all seriously, Nikki, I promise. It's just that there's so much else going on.'

'What else could possibly be going on in your life right now, Chels? You just got out of prison, you have no life, this is your life.' Her words hit Chelsea right in the chest, making her gasp, and she hears Nikki draw in a sharp breath, 'Sorry, love. I don't . . . I'm frustrated, okay?'

'Okay,' Chelsea says, her voice very small in the cathedral-like proportions of the station.

'I'm sorry, I really am. I didn't mean that to . . . I didn't mean it. I just really think, the best thing for you, right now, is to focus on the everyday. Get into a good routine, stick to your shifts, your meetings. The next part will come, I promise you, but you're effectively still serving your sentence, Chels. You're not free to do as you please yet.'

'Right.'

'You do understand that?'

'Yes, Nikki, I understand that.'

'This is no time for side quests.'

'Side quests?'

'It's something Saoirse says. So, when's the next train?'

'There isn't another train to Aberdeen today, I don't think. I can only get as far as Edinburgh.'

Nikki sighs. 'Okay, well, you may as well stay with Ayesha again tonight, if that's the case. But I want you to text me when you're on the train tomorrow.'

Chelsea assures her she will and puts her phone away before wandering over to a WHSmith's to find a book for her tube ride back to Balham and her journey tomorrow. Browsing at one of the two-for-one tables, trying to decide between historical fiction or something lighter, she gets distracted by someone standing at the table next to her. Just as on the tube, the stranger's eyes flick away as soon as Chelsea's meet them, but then they flick back. Chelsea's stomach lurches, the taste of her Pret sandwich repeating in her mouth. Does this person recognize her? She's about to stride away, head down, when the stranger moves off and she breathes a sigh of relief before realizing that the other woman had been browsing at a table full of 'True Crime' titles. True crime? Stomach still clenching, Chelsea manages to wander over to the offending table, eyes scanning the titles, trying to take it all in. Closest to her she sees the book she thinks the other woman was holding – with its black and bright pink cover, it's fairly distinctive, and designed in a mock-tabloid style, its title screams '*WOMEN WHO KILL*' at her. Jesus. She flips to the contents page, almost too scared to do so, but spurred on by a sense of curiosity that feels a lot like masochism. And there her name is.

Her vision wavers, then blurs, tears sprouting uncontrollably. Swallowing heavily, she turns to 'her' chapter, her breath short and heavy as though she's just run a marathon, and there in the second paragraph, the author writes: *including interviews from never-heard-from-before subjects, including Isabella and Chelsea's tutor, Jamie Sinclair.*

Her stomach curdles and she thinks she might be sick. He's been doing interviews? While Chelsea's been in prison, serving a sentence for a crime she didn't commit, labelled a murderer, as aberrant, abhorrent – so much so that she's been included in this book – James Sinclair has not only been safe and sound in Aberystwyth, but giving journalists interviews? She still has Nikki's words ringing in her ears, her entreaty to come home, live day-to-day, establish some kind of routine, but Chelsea can't bring herself to do that, not when Sinclair is allowed to live his day-to-day so freely, so easily. She checks her phone for the time and sees she has a text from Kate, her parole officer. Has Nikki already told her she's missed her train? Annoyance and anxiety flash through her, the one followed by the other like quicksilver. It doesn't matter, though. If she's not getting back to Aberdeen tonight, she may as well do something useful, like take a train to Aberystwyth.

They go to Snobs on their last night of term, where the drinks are cheap, the music's loud and it's always, always busy. With its soundtrack of indie hits, Chelsea, Joe, Ayesha and a couple of Joe's housemates spend most of their time on the packed dancefloor, which can at times turn into more of a moshpit – elbows everywhere, glass bottles in faces, arms waving, feet stomping – so it's a while before Chelsea realizes Izzy and Hannah have been gone for too long.

'Do you think they left?' she yells into Ayesha's ear.

Ayesha scrunches up her face, 'They'd tell us if they were leaving.'

'What if they couldn't find us?'

'We haven't left the dancefloor!'

'Well, I want a drink anyway, so let's go and see if we can find them.'

She gets Joe's attention, sliding her arm around his waist so that he leans his head towards her as she tells him where they're going. He gives her a nod, kissing her right on the temple, her hair frizzy and sweaty beneath his lips, before asking her to bring back a beer for him. Chelsea told Izzy about her and Joe a couple of weeks ago, the other girl giving her a sly smile and then a loud crow as she said, 'I knew it. I knew something was going on between the two of you!' It hadn't been the response Chelsea expected, but it was very Izzy, to claim insight where, really, Chelsea wasn't sure there was any, and besides, she'd been so relieved to come clean to her, it had felt like a weight off. Now, she joins hands with Ayesha as they weave through the crowd, going from one room to the next, ducking under sweat-drenched armpits, the soles of their shoes peeling up from the beer and Smirnoff Ice-sticky floors. The bar is heaving, several people deep, and Chelsea can't see Izzy or Hannah anywhere, so, standing on tiptoe, she scans the tops of heads, keeping an eye out for Izzy's crown of gleaming blonde hair. Finally, she spots their familiar figures in the corner by the toilets; they seem to be sitting on the floor or crouched down, Hannah leaning over Izzy, and immediately Chelsea senses something is wrong. Grabbing Ayesha's wrist without a word, she pulls the other girl through the crowd until they're on top of Hannah and Izzy.

'Han, what's happened? What's going on?'

Hannah looks up, her face tearful and red, but there is a look of relief in her eyes as she realizes who it is. 'Oh, thank God. Chelsea, I don't know what's going on, Izzy just suddenly went all weird. She can barely hold her head up and she suddenly started slurring all her words, even though we've had the same amount to drink and I didn't think she was *that* drunk, but I can't get her to get up.'

'Has she been sick?' Ayesha asks.

Hannah shakes her head, looking like she might be sick herself. 'No, but look,' she lifts Izzy up off her lap, but the other girl immediately falls back down again, a human-sized rag doll lolling against her friend. Chelsea is reminded forcibly of meeting her cousin Saoirse for the first time, when she was still in the newborn stages and her mum kept yelling at her to make sure the baby's head was supported. But Izzy is a full-sized girl – a woman, really – and seeing her lying here like this she looks even more vulnerable than a baby being cradled safely in a relative's arms. She looks like a slab of meat, fresh for the picking, and Chelsea shivers at the thought of what could happen to her without the three of them huddled over her. She looks around them; the club is still booming, throngs of students weaving around them, heading to and from the toilets, parking up at the bar. No one is paying them any notice even though they have a near-catatonic girl in their charge, but to Chelsea every person she sees is the person who did this to Izzy. Ayesha elbows her, knocking her back to the here and now, the problem right in front of them.

'Let's get her home,' Chelsea says, and Hannah nods silently as all three of them grab a part of their friend's body and guide her up the stairs and out of the club. Outside, the air is cold, and Izzy makes a sound as though she's waking up, causing Hannah to start saying, 'Iz, Iz, are you okay? Are you with us?'

Izzy only mumbles in response, but it's something at least and Ayesha leaves them to flag down a minicab. They take her back to their flat, partly because they can't find her keys in her mess of a bag and partly because they're all too worried to leave her on her own.

'Should we have taken her to A&E?' Ayesha says as they huff up their four flights of stairs. 'She must've been drugged, right?'

'I don't know,' Chelsea says, looking at her friend's almost completely limp body. Have they done the wrong thing? Should she be in hospital? 'We can keep an eye on her. If anything happens, we can call an ambulance.' She sounds much more sure than she feels, though, her head banging with worry and alcohol. Hannah says nothing, but her face says it all. 'You were with her most of the night, Han, do you think she could've been drugged? Did you see anything?'

'No!' Hannah says, affronted.

'She's not blaming you, Han. Just . . . was there anyone around you guys who seemed a bit dodge?'

'No, really,' Hannah says, shaking her head vigorously, her face still red and blotchy, 'I don't know what happened.'

Ayesha unlocks their front door and, with Izzy's arm around her neck, Chelsea walks her into their flat, just as her mobile beeps with a text message. 'It could've been anyone, I guess,' she says. 'The whole point of drink spiking is that you don't know it's happening. I'll put her in my room.'

In her room, Chelsea takes off Izzy's shoes and tries to get her under the duvet as gently as possible.

'Enngh, what's going on?' Izzy mumbles at her.

'We think you've been spiked, Iz. You're in my room.'

'Wha?'

'I'm going to get you some water and a bin in case you're sick.'

'Nuh, stay. Please. Feel sick.'

'Hence the bin.'

Izzy starts to say something else but it's indecipherable to Chelsea, so she yells for Ayesha. 'Shh,' Hannah says, following Ayesha into the room, 'we have other flatmates, Chels.'

'Sorry. Can one of you empty out my bathroom bin

and bring it here in case she voms, and get her a glass of water?'

Ayesha nods, 'You get the water, Han, I'll deal with the bin.'

With the others out of the room, Chelsea takes the moment to check her mobile. There's a text from Joe, wondering where she got to, and she messages him back, telling him they had to leave suddenly, but not why. He replies almost instantly, but before Chelsea can read it, Izzy starts to mumble again, her words slurred, and Chelsea has to concentrate in order to hear her properly.

'Shorry I lied to you, Chelshea.'

'Sorry you lied? About what?' But Chelsea thinks she knows what Izzy is referring to and is now on high alert. 'About Sinclair?' she presses when the other girl doesn't respond. Izzy's eyes are closed now, though, she's falling asleep and, despite knowing she shouldn't, Chelsea shakes her arm, trying to rouse her again. 'Iz, were you talking about Jamie?'

'Hnggh,' Izzy mumbles, shrugging her hand away, 'dunno. Sleep.'

Chelsea watches her for a while, waiting until Ayesha and Hannah come back with the water and empty bin. They huddle over their friend again, trading whispers on what should be done, who should sleep where, whether she should be left alone. She seems to be sleeping peacefully now, and eventually Chelsea sends the others to bed and goes to sleep in the living room, waking what feels like every few hours or so as her body rebels against the size, shape and comfort of the sofa. Her brain worries over Izzy, and morning light starts to inch its way through the kitchen windows and across the living room floor. It's early still when she gets up to boil the kettle for tea and take a mug through to Izzy. She doesn't really expect the other girl to be awake, but she wants to check on her, and she can already tell she's not going to be getting any more sleep herself.

The door creaks as she pushes it open using her hip but Izzy doesn't stir. Setting a mug down on the bedside table, Chelsea sits on the very edge of the bed and looks her friend over. Her hair is splayed over the pillow and there's a crust of drool – or possibly something worse – next to her mouth, reminding Chelsea to check the bin for any vomit, although it appears to still be clean. The glass of water Hannah got her is still full. In here, with the curtains drawn, morning hasn't quite yet arrived and the crepuscular light feels eerie to Chelsea, a hungover no-man's land. She's about to leave when Izzy rolls on to her back and opens her eyes.

'What's going on?' she croaks, her voice brittle and rough like sandpaper. 'Where am I?' Chelsea reaches for the water, passes it over to her, and Izzy leans up on an elbow while she drinks it, swallowing down great big gulps before handing it back to her friend. 'Ugh, feel like I'm gonna be sick.'

Chelsea points to the bin next to the bed but Izzy just shakes her head, leans back on the pillows again and closes her eyes, placing the back of her hand over her forehead like a character in an Austen novel. 'What's going on, Chels? Why am I in your room? I don't remember anything.'

'We think you were probably drugged.'

'At Snobs?'

'Yeah.' Izzy doesn't say anything to this, and Chelsea puts her hand over what she thinks is the other girl's shin, hidden under the duvet, 'You okay?'

'Did anything . . . happen?'

'No, you were with Han the whole time and then me and Ayesha found you. We brought you straight home.'

'Oh. Okay.'

'How do you feel?'

'Like my skin has been zipped up over a corpse.'

'That's . . . quite the visual.'

'Like all my blood has been replaced with bees.'

'Well, at least we know your imagination is intact.' Izzy lets out a huff of maybe-laughter that quickly turns into a sob although she doesn't let herself cry. 'You're okay, Iz,' Chelsea says, softer now, 'nothing happened, we didn't let anything happen to you.'

'Something *did* happen,' Izzy says, looking like she might be swallowing down some vomit, 'I was drugged.'

'I know, I'm sorry, I didn't mean it like that. I just mean . . . nothing *worse* happened.'

'I know, I know,' Izzy says, and Chelsea can tell by the set of her jaw and the strain in her voice that she is fighting back tears.

'Are you tired? Do you want me to leave?'

'I'm exhausted. I feel like all my blood has left my body.'

'I thought your blood was bees?'

'Yeah, exactly.' Izzy closes her eyes again, and Chelsea gets up to leave, 'No, stay, please. I'm not asleep.'

'Do you want me to get you anything? There's a cup of tea there, if you want it.'

Izzy shakes her head, and in the dim light Chelsea can see just how pale she is, 'No, I might throw up if I have anything. Thanks for looking after me, though, Chels. You're a good friend.'

'Sure.'

'I've been a bad friend.'

'What are you talking about? This isn't your fault.'

'Not this,' Izzy says, shaking her head again, looking as though she's still trying to stop herself from being sick.

'Then, what?' Chelsea asks, thinking back to last night, tucking Izzy up into her bed as she apologized to her for lying. Is this about Jamie Sinclair?

'That party I had, at Christmas, when I didn't invite you.'

'Oh, that was ages ago now, don't worry about it.'

'It was wrong though. Ayesha was so mad at me.'

'Ayesha was?'

'Yeah, she called me a thoughtless bitch. Which I suppose I can be at times. And self-involved, she also called me self-involved.' Chelsea doesn't say anything to this and Izzy smiles, still with her eyes closed, 'I'll take your silence as tacit agreement.'

'It was a bit thoughtless. But I'm not friends with your friends, it's fine, I get it.'

'*I'm* not even friends with my friends, that's the real irony here. It was such a stupid fucking shit show, that party. I felt even worse the day after that than I do now, and that's saying something.'

'What happened?' Chelsea asks, because what she can remember of the Facebook photo albums, it looked like a roaring success.

'I was trying to . . . I don't know, d'you remember our

birthday? And I told you none of my friends had texted or called me?'

'Yeah, I remember.'

'When we went home for Christmas, I hadn't spoken to any of them since August.'

'Okay. So, you were like trying to win them back?'

'I guess.'

'Why? What had they done? What had you done?'

Izzy opens her eyes just a crack, so she's squinting at Chelsea through the slowly, slowly brightening light of the room. 'Could you get me some paracetamol and a cold flannel? My head is killing me.'

'Okay, but I know you're stalling,' Chelsea says, getting up and going into her en suite. She finds the paracetamol easily enough, and hands it to Izzy along with her glass of water, and then goes back in to dampen her flannel. Once it's cold enough, she lays it over Izzy's forehead, covering her closed eyes. 'All right, princess?'

'Don't be mean to me, I've been drugged.'

'You have twenty-four hours left to use that line.'

'Harsh. I think I should get at least a full week for a drugging incident.'

'Hmm, maybe. Are you avoiding the question though? What happened with your friends from school?'

Izzy sighs so heavily, the flannel becomes slightly dislodged and she has to reach up to rearrange it. With her eyes closed and covered like this, the dim light, and the hushed quiet of the otherwise sleeping flat, there is a confessional-like quality to everything that Chelsea suspects Izzy likes and needs for this moment. 'I slept with Henry Abbott.'

'I don't know who Henry Abbott is, Izzy.'

'No, I know. You don't need to know who he is, just that he was Victoria's boyfriend. *Ex*-boyfriend at the time, but now they're back together and *I'm* the bad guy, even though we were both completely wasted when it happened, and none of them will talk to me.'

'Ah.'

'Yeah.'

'So, they didn't go to the party?'

'They did. Well, Victoria and Henry didn't, but Poppy and Soph and Emma did, but only to tell me what a disgusting slut I am and that I should be ashamed of myself, and that none of them are ever going to talk to me ever again.'

'Why didn't you tell me any of this?'

'Because it's embarrassing. Not to have any friends. To be shunned.'

'D'you want me to make you a scarlet letter?'

'It's not funny, Chels.'

'Sorry. You do have friends though, Iz.'

'I know. That's what makes this so much worse – of course, I should've invited you to my party. Or even better, I shouldn't have thrown one in the first place, and we should've just hung out at mine, because you're an actual friend.'

'Well . . . thanks.'

'So, you accept my apology?'

'Yes,' Chelsea says slowly, even though she's not sure that Izzy has really apologized. 'But what about Sinclair?'

'What about him?' Izzy says, removing the flannel from her face and looking Chelsea in the eye.

'You said last night that you lied about him.'

'Oh, that was nothing, that was silly,' she says, lying back down again, putting the flannel back in place, 'I just didn't want you to think I was losing my head over him.'

'Okay, if you're sure.'

'I'm sure. There's absolutely nothing going on there with him, seriously.'

Chelsea watches her friend carefully, but it's hard to tell if Izzy really is being serious – honest – or not. If there was ever a moment for confession, this would be it, after all, but there is still something Chelsea can't quite believe in Izzy's dismissal of the Jamie Sinclair question. But maybe Chelsea's imagining it all, maybe it really is nothing, and all she needs to do is trust her friend.

Chelsea has to change trains in Birmingham. She barely remembers putting that book down in Smith's, walking out of King's Cross and straight to Euston, where she bought a ticket to Aberystwyth, heart pounding, hands sweating, and boarded the next available train. It's taken less time than she expected to get this far, and she blinks in shock as she disembarks, worrying about how she's going to explain this to Nikki, where she's going to spend the night. She hasn't been in Birmingham since the trial and now, as she stares around herself as passengers disperse, she doesn't feel the way she expected to feel. For starters the station is changed almost beyond recognition, and anything that does feel familiar lands in her consciousness with a dull, numbing thud. She thought being here would fill her to the brim with memories — both good and bad — but instead, she feels empty, disconnected, almost as though she's never been here before.

Maybe it's because she's just passing through, moving from one platform to the next, trying to stay as anonymous and out of the way as possible. She's back to wearing her baseball cap, having dug it out of her rucksack. She won't make the mistake of not wearing a hat in public again, and even though it feels an incredibly flimsy defence against the battering ram of public scrutiny and a camera in every hand, every pocket, every bag, it at least feels like something. She can't forget the feeling of being noticed at King's Cross, the gut-pulling lurch as she picked up that book and realized what it was about. By the time she'd looked up, finally drawn from her dazed stupor, the woman was gone and her mind was made up. She has to see Sinclair. She reaches for her phone now, checks the time – she's fine, she'll make the connection – and sees she has a text from Nikki. She knows she should call Nikki, right now, and tell her where she is, where she's going, but how to explain any of this? How can she make her aunt understand that her life isn't a series of boxes to be checked, that it's a swirling vortex of a mess with Chelsea right at the centre of it, powerless to see where she is or what she's doing. She needs to make sense of it all, needs, more than anything, to feel like she has some sense of control. Nikki thinks she's spending an extra night in London with Ayesha, and that's what she'll let her think. For now. But then she realizes that she's also got a text from Kate, and she closes her eyes, trying to shore up some courage before reading it.

> Your aunt let me know you're spending an extra night in London due to trains. We can discuss at our next meeting.

Their next meeting. The day after tomorrow. Which means she absolutely has to get back to Scotland tomorrow or she will be screwed. She's all too aware that if Kate finds out about any of this, she would be well within her rights to set a curfew, or tell her 'no' the next time the opportunity or need to go to London comes up. Chelsea texts Kate back, telling her she'll see her then.

She doesn't mention Wales or Sinclair, or the fact that she's currently stood on the platform of Birmingham New Street station. Better, too, to let her think she's merely staying an extra night with Ayesha. The lie, or rather the omission of the truth, doesn't sit right, causes a snarling sense of anxiety to ride through her, but it's a necessary evil. She wants to stay on Kate's good side, of course, but there are also questions she needs to ask, answers she's been waiting fifteen years to hear.

Checking the time again, she keeps her head down as she walks to the correct platform, the train arriving as she does, and she gets on it, finding a spare window seat that will take her all the way to Aberystwyth and Jamie Sinclair.

The train takes longer than she expected, and it's evening by the time it pulls into Aberystwyth, all of Wales behind her. It's too late to explore the university now, so she heads straight to the hotel she'd asked Ayesha to book for her, so that Chelsea's name didn't come up on the reservation. It's on the front, something cheap and hopefully decent, or at the very least clean. The room is fine but small, claustrophobic, and she doesn't want to spend any more time in it than is completely necessary, so she dumps her rucksack and heads back out again. There's still some light in the sky, this far west, the sun making a song and dance of leaving the distant horizon, and she breathes in deeply as she crosses the street to stand looking down at the beach. The marine air fills her lungs, and it might be her imagination, but she thinks she can feel the salt of the sea stinging her eyes. It is a long, long time since she saw the sea, and here it is, dark, endless; black waves breaking in the distance, pulling at her memories. She can't help but think of Cornwall and Mallorca, the beaches she sat on with Izzy, the crashing waves in Cornwall, the gentle lapping at the golden sand in Mallorca, the last time she was this close to the sea. She could never access these memories in prison, as potent and alive as they feel; they were simply too much – so vastly different from her reality she didn't even let herself go there, couldn't dwell in the happy memories because when she opened her eyes, she was always right back in Foston Hall. She takes another deep breath, relishing the smell of the brine, the way the air is so fresh it almost smells green. She's tired, but she decides to walk, forcing energy back into her legs, getting a little movement in to stop her thoughts from swirling.

She hasn't been alone like this in a long time and she wonders at what point she'll get used to it again, when it will feel second nature to not be surrounded by other people all day long. It feels both extraordinarily unfettered and strangely claustrophobic. It had been different in London, where she knows the streets without a map and was staying with an old friend. She'd felt almost too safe there, too at home, but here, she knows no one, could be anyone – as long as no one recognizes her – and will go to sleep tonight in an anonymous room in a random hotel. Is this freedom? It's not the loneliness that feels strange – she's used to that – but the alone-ness. Walking here, no one by her side, no one jostling her, no constant chatter, just the sound of her shoes on the pavement, the waves, and the occasional screech of a seagull, she can sense the world around her – smell it, see it, hear it – but it's almost as if she's not really in it. When will that stop? When will all this start feeling real? When will *she* start feeling real? She sees the neon bright yellow sign of a fish and chip shop, the grease and the salt and vinegar drifting out of its open door, and walks right in without thinking. She's hungry, she'll eat this meal – scampi and chips, always her mum's order – and she'll feel more herself. More like she has a place in the world. She carries it back out to the front. It's completely dark now, any residual sunset on the horizon completely washed away, but the streetlights are on, dotting the promenade all the way down the shore, and there's still a few other people about. She huddles in a shelter, unwraps the greasy packet, cracks open her can of Coke. She dips a chip, fat, yellow and soft between her fingers, into a smear of ketchup and bites in. It's probably not actually the best chip in the world, but right now, to Chelsea, it is.

* * *

In the morning, she makes tea in her little room and sits in bed, scrolling through the Aberystwyth University website, toggling between the History Department's website and Google maps, trying to figure out exactly where Sinclair's office is, and at what time he's most likely to be in it. There's a photo of him, a small thumbnail, on his personal profile page and she's shocked to see that his hair has turned entirely white. It suits him, but he can barely even be fifty yet – isn't it a little premature? He doesn't have office hours listed, which annoys her, but she manages to figure out that he has a lecture at eleven, meaning he'll hopefully head to his office sometime after that. She has to check out at ten, so she decides to shower, pack up and go out for breakfast before heading to the university, not daring to get there too early, in case she is recognized or, even worse, in case she bumps into Sinclair accidentally. To get through this, she needs to be on steady ground, with some semblance of control, not a face in the crowd or an awkward encounter.

After talking to Ajala about Sinclair yesterday in Camille's hotel room, Chelsea had debated over whether or not to let the detective know where she was going. She's still not completely sure she trusts her, but she does have experience in these things, so she'd texted her last night – Ajala had forced her mobile number on her yesterday – and Ajala had messaged back almost immediately, telling Chelsea she wished she'd leave this part of the investigation to her. But Chelsea can't leave this to her; she already tried that fifteen years ago, and nothing came of it. Eventually, Ajala had messaged again, presumably realizing that there was nothing she could do to stop Chelsea going ahead with her plan, and advised her to remain as calm as possible when talking to Sinclair, to leave emotion at the door, but not to warn him she was coming; a shock could often lead to honesty.

So, Chelsea waits for him in the History Department, and in the end, she hears him before she sees him. She's been sat for almost forty minutes and there are no chairs, so she's slumped with her back against the wall, baseball cap pulled down low. No one has said anything to her, despite a number of students, lecturers and admin staff wandering down the hall while she's been here, so, much to her relief, she must just look like a loitering student waiting to get an extension or complain about a mark on an essay. It's a different university, a very different building to the one they were housed in at Birmingham, but it still brings it all back. She wonders if these memories are so easy to draw to the surface because of the blank space that came after them. If she'd gone on and out into the real world, as she'd been supposed to, would these university memories be so strong, so vibrant, so vital? Because despite all its differences, it smells the same, feels the same. She can hear the whirr of a photocopier somewhere, the distant chat and laughter of students as they file down the staircase, the low, consistent murmur of the staff in the department office who make everything happen. She's wishing she had a book to read – that she hadn't been so distracted in Smith's yesterday that she'd walked out, practically in a trance, empty-handed – when she hears him. He's on the phone, she thinks, because there's no discernible voice in reply and she's trying to listen to what he's saying while she scrambles to stand up and suddenly, suddenly, he's there in front of her, eyes empty, skating over her until there – yes, there it is – the flash of realization, fear locking into place, jaw slack with shock and then tight with anger.

'Hello, Jamie.'

'Chelsea Keough.'

It comes out as a croak and Chelsea can't help it, she feels a little thrill of victory to have surprised him like this, to have scared him really. But then he's opening the door to his office, ushering her in, and she's in his space now, his domain, his world. She swallows heavily and it tastes a little like vomit and she realizes it's not just Sinclair who's afraid; she is too. But that's okay, that makes sense, because fear brings everything into focus, and she has to remain focused now. Sinclair sits down at his desk and Chelsea takes a seat on the other side of it without waiting to be offered. The room reminds her of his office at Birmingham although she realizes she can't remember any details from it, so maybe it's just the mere fact of being in a room with him that has it feeling so familiar.

'Well, this is a surprise,' he says after a while, 'a bit of a shock, actually.'

'You probably thought you'd never see me again, I imagine.'

'Well, yeah.' Despite the white hair, he looks exactly the same, and she wonders if he thinks the same about her too. 'It's been a long time, Chelsea.'

Chelsea nods, 'Fifteen years.'

'Is it really that long? Well.'

'I need to ask you a few questions.'

'Uh huh?' Sinclair has started sorting out papers, looking through his things, trying to demonstrate his importance, and how busy he is, how little time he has for all this.

'About Izzy.'

'Right.'

He's still searching, searching, looking for anything that will keep him from meeting her gaze and looking her in the eye, but it's all fake, this couldn't-care-less ruse, and Chelsea's anger rises up inside her, coming untethered and, forgetting Ajala's advice entirely, she smacks her hands down on to his desk, disturbing his papers, stopping him in his tracks. The air in the room seems to vibrate and Sinclair finally stops moving, looks her in the eye. He leans back in his chair, that faux insouciance again, but his breath hitches as he does so and Chelsea knows he's nowhere near as calm as he wants to seem. Good. She's not calm either, and she wants them to be on an even playing field, she wants this to be a fair fight.

'It's just a few questions, Jamie, you can give me that, can't you? After all this time?'

His gaze narrows, his face becoming pinched, and suddenly he looks his age. Fifteen years older. There's that shock of white hair, of course, but he wears it well, just as he did in the photo on the university's website. But here, now, looking at Chelsea with anger and annoyance, he looks as middle-aged as he really is.

'I just don't know what it is I could tell you, Chelsea. Haven't all the questions already been asked and answered?'

'I've got a few left over.'

He raises his eyebrows, 'Left over? From your own trial, you mean?'

'I didn't get to ask a lot of questions then; it's sadly not really how that works when you're the one on trial.'

Sinclair's mouth quirks into a smirk which he appears to immediately regret, before saying, 'Right.'

'I know something was going on with you and Izzy.' Sinclair shifts in his seat, a pulse starts up in his jaw and Chelsea raises a hand. 'I'm not saying anything . . . romantic or . . . untoward, but I know she confided in you.' Chelsea doesn't really believe this, of course, but she wants him to think she does, to ease him in by offering up an olive branch, no matter how fake it is.

And it seems to work because Sinclair straightens up, sitting up a little taller, his brow furrowing as he's forced to remember. 'Well . . . yes. I was her personal tutor during your second year, so, yes, we were in discussion about numerous issues. Mostly to do with her father's death. As I'm sure you remember, she was, well . . . deeply depressed. She was grieving. I arranged for extensions on several of her essays, catch-up sessions with her other lecturers, recommended her to the university counsellor. But you know all that already, surely?'

'I don't remember her going to a counsellor.'

'Well, sadly, I don't believe she ever saw them. Her first session was due to be the week after reading week.'

'So, the week after she died?'

'Yes.'

'Can you remember the name of that counsellor?' Chelsea asks. She can't remember even being aware such a service was available at the university, let alone that Izzy may have been in contact with a counsellor.

'Oh, I don't know, Chelsea, it was so long ago. I think it was Lisa or Linda something. But they never actually met, so it's all beside the point, isn't it?'

'I suppose so,' Chelsea says, although she disagrees with him. It's not beside the point – it kind of *is* the point, because here she is, all these many years later, finding out something new about her friend. 'I thought she was seeing someone. Right before, I mean. Before she died.'

'Seeing someone like a therapist?' Sinclair asks, looking puzzled.

'No, romantically.'

'Ah. And you think that person was me?'

'It's crossed my mind.'

Sinclair shakes his head, lets out a small, disbelieving

laugh. 'I don't . . . I don't know what to say to that accusation, Chelsea. If she was seeing someone, it certainly wasn't me, but honestly, I doubt she was. She was very broken up about her dad's death. I don't think she had the emotional capacity to deal with anything more than what was already on her plate.'

'So, nothing ever happened between the two of you?'

Sinclair sighs, runs a hand through his silver-white hair, 'No.'

'She said something did.'

'Well, then she was lying. Or you're lying right now, trying to get a reaction from me.' He stares at Chelsea for a second, jaw pulsing, before starting to tidy his desk again. 'I think we're done here. I'd like you to leave.'

'Why did you leave Birmingham?'

'Because . . . because it was very difficult to lose a student in that way. As hard as that might be for you to believe or understand, it's the truth. I never expected to have to deal with something so . . . so violent and tragic in this line of work, and I needed to get away from it all.' Chelsea doesn't say anything, but she doesn't make a move to leave either. She can hear the accusation implicit in Sinclair's words, that it was her, her actions, her violence that pushed him away from Birmingham and out of a job. She can hear her blood in her ears as she watches him, so safe and protected behind his desk, still not taking any responsibility, still not telling her the truth. Finally, Sinclair says, 'Is that everything? I really do have things to be getting on with.'

'Where were you that night?' Her voice cuts through the room like razor wire.

'What night?' he says, sighing and reaching, unnecessarily, for a pen on his desk.

'Oh, for fuck's sake, the night she was killed, obviously.'

'I was at home, Chelsea, with my wife and child.'

'Your wife and child.'

He scratches at his neck, just beneath his collar line, 'Yes. Just as I told the police back in 2007.'

'And just as you told the author of *Women Who Kill*?'

Sinclair finally meets her eye, stares at her, 'I, um – I'd almost forgotten I did that interview.'

'Well, I only just read it, so it's fresh in my mind. You said, and I quote, "it's always the ones you least expect". Not very original that, Jamie.'

'Look,' he says, swallowing heavily, 'I do regret doing that interview, it was much more . . . sensationalist than I was imagining it would be. But I was in a bad place –'

'You were in a bad place?'

Sinclair continues, as if she hasn't said anything, 'My marriage was breaking down, all sorts of things were happening. I don't think I was thinking entirely . . . well. Is that why you're here? Because you're angry with me for taking that interview?'

'I'm angry at you because I think you know more than you're letting on.'

'I don't, Chelsea, I really don't.'

'I don't believe you.'

Sinclair raises his hands, palms up, to the sky. 'Well, there's not a whole lot I can do about that, right? I imagine you're the expert in not being believed.'

Chelsea stares at him for a second, hatred and disgust rising to a crescendo, so much so that she can almost taste it in her mouth. She doesn't need to be here, there's no point. He's never going to tell her anything; he's kept his secrets for way too long, protecting them, even if they have pushed him to the very edge of the country. She picks up her rucksack, trying to get up so quickly that she trips over a trailing strap. Sinclair stands up just as quickly, reaching over his desk to stop her from falling, but before his hand can touch her arm, she swats it away. 'Don't,' she says, almost growling.

Sinclair's eyes widen and he holds his hands up again, 'Okay, okay,' he says softly. He looks as though he's about to say something else, but thinks better of it, and Chelsea takes the opportunity to stride out of his office, letting the door swing shut behind her, swallowing down any other questions she may have had.

Out in the hallway she stops for half a second to take a breath and pull her rucksack on to her back. She can't think clearly, not here, with the sound of his voice still ringing in her ears, and the distant echoes of her life before all around her. Her rucksack bumps against her back as she rushes down the stairs, the chatter of students trailing her, and she could be back there, all those years ago, hurrying to her next lecture. But she's not. It's fifteen years later, she's fifteen years older and Izzy is long gone. Was she right to come here? The truth of the matter is she has no idea. She walks quickly to the train station, arriving in a cold sweat with just enough time to buy herself a coffee before the next train. She is two stations away from Aberystwyth when she gets a text from Natalie Ajala.

Looked into Sinclair. Very unofficial but he was let go from
Birmingham due to 'inappropriate relations' with a student.
Unconfirmed whether this was Isabella or not, but timing makes it
seem like it could be.

The train rumbles on, green and brown countryside
flashing by the window unseen as Chelsea takes this in.
How could we find out for sure? she texts back.

Honestly, this is where office gossip would come in most handy. Any
former colleagues would be most likely to have heard the rumours, if
there were any. I used an old police contact for this, but they couldn't
give me any more details. Leave with me though, and I'll look into it.

But Chelsea can't leave it with Ajala, not now she's
started down this path. She has to change trains again in
Birmingham, and she's still got plenty of the day ahead of
her, plenty of time to take a quick little detour to campus
and maybe get some answers.

Digbeth

She's lost Chelsea again. She went to the loo and the queue took so long that by the time she got back to where she left the others, they were gone. She's starting to feel really wasted now. The room churns around her, not just spinning but going back and forth beneath her feet, like she's on a travelator inside a washing machine set to spin. She puts her hand out against a wall, to touch something solid and catch her breath. Where the fuck is Chelsea? Maybe they went outside. It's hot in here, sweat dripping down the wall she's leaning against, and outside there's a courtyard open to the night air, the night sky. Izzy takes a deep breath. Even if they're not there, it'll be good to get some fresh air, to feel the cold against her skin.

She keeps looking for the red horns as she pushes through the crowd, but Chelsea's not the only devil here tonight, so she keeps spotting her, only to be immediately disappointed. She keeps an eye out for the tall guy too – Ravi? Yes, Ravi, but she can't see him anywhere. Finally, she gets out into the courtyard, breathes in the cold October air, but all she can smell is the tang of weed and the spluttering whiff of cigarette smoke. She keeps going. There's as many people out here as there are inside, so she has to keep weaving and lurching through them, but eventually she reaches the edge of the pond. It's been drained, probably for safety, and there are people dancing in it, some people even lying in it, but Izzy finds herself a spot to sit down on the cement rim and takes out her phone.

Where are you????? she texts Chelsea.

She checks her own messages and sees one from Charlie.

Can you answer your phone please?

Ugh, not this still. He'd been banging on about signing those papers all morning, why can't he just let her have some time to think? Some breathing space. Dad wouldn't want him hounding her like this … but no, she can't think about Dad. Tears immediately spring to her eyes and she sniffs, loudly enough for the girl crammed in next to her to turn around and shout, 'Are you okay?'

Izzy nods, but the girl just squints at her, and then starts rummaging in her bag. She hands Izzy a slightly ragged looking tissue, 'There you go, babe. Your mascara's starting to run a bit.'

'Thanks,' Izzy gasps, and the girl just shrugs in response and turns back to her friends. Her phone starts to vibrate in her hands and she goes to answer it, assuming it'll be Chelsea, trying to track her down, but when she sees Charlie's name on the screen instead, she slams it shut. She wants to go home. She's wanted to go home since she got here, and she's given it a good try, hasn't she? Biting down on her bottom lip, she checks her phone again to make sure Charlie has given up, and texts Chelsea:

Going home, sorry. Have a great night xx

She gets up, gives tissue girl a little wave and heads out through the courtyard gates into Digbeth. Out on the street, there are people milling about all over the place, some dressed up for Halloween, some not. It's a main road and cars fly by, beeping loudly any time a drunken partygoer gets too close to the edge of the kerb. There's an ad hoc waiting area for minicabs, and Izzy joins the queue, praying it will move quickly. She checks her phone again, and Chelsea has finally replied:

Nooooo, plz don't go! We're in the orange room, come find us?

Then a few seconds later:

Sry Iz I thought u'd enjoy it. Let me know when ur home xx

Izzy is close to the front of the queue by now, shivering in her short white macramé dress – Chelsea and Sarah had threaded through toilet roll back at the house, to make her look more like a mummy, but it's almost all gone now, just a few shreds here and there, and she picks one out to blow her nose. When will she stop crying? She's so tired of it, so tired of feeling so much and yet also feeling so numb. None of it makes sense. Maybe nothing will make sense now, for the rest of her life. Finally, it's her turn, and she slides into the minicab's back seat, that familiar, cloying scent of air freshener almost immediately making her feel sick and as she gives the driver the address, she has to stop herself from heaving. She cracks the window a tiny bit, hoping the smell will dissipate, and leans back in the corner of the cab, huddling around her bag. She senses the driver's eyes flick to the rear-view mirror, keeping an eye on her just as she takes a deep, shuddering breath that rolls through her entire body and tears begin to leak, once again, out of her eyes. She thinks of the girl earlier, telling her that her mascara was beginning to run, and wonders what a state she must look. She pulls another piece of loo roll from her dress, wipes under her nose and tries to hold her breath, to stop herself from crying.

'You okay?' the driver barks at her.

She nods, too scared to say anything or else she'll just start sobbing uncontrollably. She thinks of her bed and closes her eyes. She'll be home soon.

They get a month off at Easter and Chelsea goes down to the Dunwoody Cornwall estate for the last week of the holiday. Izzy has been there since the beginning because, apparently, they always spend Easter there, anyway, but Chelsea's sure this retreat to the countryside has more than a little to do with what happened at Snobs. While Izzy hasn't told her so, Chelsea is sure she would have confided in her mum, and whisking her traumatized daughter away to a coastal haven sounds exactly like something Camille Dunwoody would do. At first the weather is terrible. Grey, cloudy and cool, it rains constantly, until finally, three days into Chelsea's visit, the weather breaks and the sun appears, the surprisingly hot sun of April that has both Izzy and Chelsea burning their noses, shoulders and knees after a morning spent on the beach.

'We're not that far from Frenchman's Creek here, did you know that? It always makes me think of rum running and smugglers. Damsels in distress.'

'I just assumed that was fictional,' Chelsea says, squinting over at Izzy.

'Nope, it's a real place. Have you read the book?'

'No, just *Rebecca*, but maybe we could go and have a look?' Chelsea says, turning lazily on to her front.

'Yeah. Tomorrow? We could a little du Maurier tour, I had no idea you were such a fan.'

'Well, I've only read the one book, but it would be cool to see the house. We can visit it, right?'

'You mean real-life Manderley? No, sadly not – oh shit, isn't Joe coming tomorrow?'

Izzy had texted Chelsea the previous week, telling her that she could invite Joe to Cornwall too, if she wanted. The proposition had taken her by surprise a little, because, despite Izzy's claims that she'd seen their relationship coming a mile off, she hadn't mentioned it much since. 'Yeah, he is,' Chelsea says with a shrug, 'but that doesn't matter, does it? He'll want to see the sights.'

Chelsea reaches for her can of Coke and takes a sip, but the can has warmed up in the sun and all its original refreshment has long gone.

'Have you told him, by the way? About what happened at Snobs?' Izzy says, picking at one of the tassels of the wool rug they're lying on. It's laid over pebbles and shingle, so it's not exactly the most comfortable spot in the world, but the beach is only accessible from Izzy's house, which means there's no one else there, the quiet scene only broken by the softly lapping waves on the shore.

Joe had asked her, of course, why they had left so suddenly that night, but Chelsea had just told him that Iz had been unwell and left it at that. It hadn't been hers to tell, so she didn't. Now, squinting into the sun at this peaceful view, the occasional call of a seagull, the high sides of the cliffs, the almost-turquoise colour of the water, she can't think of anywhere further from Snobs, from their student halls in Birmingham, from her own home in London. 'No, of course not. You haven't, have you?'

'No.'

'I don't think it'll come up . . . unless you want to talk about it?' As Chelsea says this, Izzy looks away, down at the ancient orange-spined Penguin paperback she brought down to the beach with her, sliding it off one of the many over-stuffed bookcases in the house, the pages tea-stain coloured and crinkled with saltwater and age, something by Evelyn Waugh – Chelsea can't remember the title, and so far, it's gone unread and unremarked upon. Izzy hasn't talked about Snobs at all since Chelsea arrived. They texted about it a bit in the days following, mainly Chelsea checking up on how she was feeling, but then the conversation moved on to different matters and Chelsea decided to just wait and see if Izzy brought it up again. Nothing had actually happened to Izzy, nothing truly bad, but Chelsea can tell she's been rocked by the experience, her usual bullet-proof confidence gone.

'We should go to the pub tonight,' Izzy says suddenly, stoutly. 'What time does Joe arrive tomorrow?'

'Um,' Chelsea says, retrieving her mobile phone from her pocket. 'He says he gets into Falmouth at one fifteen.'

'Okay, perfect, we can pick him up, get lunch and then do some Daphne du Maurier sightseeing. Plus, that gives us enough time to get over our hangovers if we go to the pub.'

'Yeah, but we don't need to make it a big one,' Chelsea says. She's not sure why she's so worried, but she's noticed Izzy drinking a lot so far this week. They're on holiday, sure, but there is something about Izzy's perpetual reach for a bottle of beer, a glass of wine, a cocktail that has Chelsea on edge and wondering. Camille doesn't seem to have noticed, or if she has, hasn't said anything about it – at least within Chelsea's earshot – but Izzy is always the first to suggest a drink, and always the last to stop drinking, waking up every morning with a fuzzy head and slightly bleary eyes which always clear before noon. The day after the Snobs incident had not been pretty. Izzy hadn't been able to keep anything down until the following morning, taking only the smallest sips of water before feeling nauseous enough to stop trying. She'd described it simply as, *the worst hangover of my life*, but it seemed like more than that. She'd had a poison in her body, and they just had to wait until it finally leeched out. When it did, she called her mum, who sent a car to pick her up and bring her straight to Cornwall while Chelsea, Ayesha and Hannah headed back to their family homes for the break.

'Yeah, yeah, just a couple of pints,' Izzy says sleepily, resting her head on her crossed arms and closing her eyes. 'We should get the fish and chips though, they're sooo good there. I dream about them all year.'

* * *

They pick Joe up the next day. His train is running late, so Izzy and Chelsea sit on a wall outside the station, swinging their legs like children, faces to the sun while drinking mediocre lattes. When he arrives, to much fanfare from Izzy and a hug from Chelsea, they drive into the centre of Falmouth, where they have gooey paninis for lunch before setting out on a DIY Daphne du Maurier walking tour that Izzy spent most of the morning devising herself. There is an ever so slightly manic edge to Izzy all afternoon, which Chelsea puts down to her excitement over hosting, but when they're in a pub towards the end of the day, Joe says, 'What's going on with her?' inclining his head towards where Izzy is disappearing in the direction of the ladies' loos. 'She seems a bit off.'

'Yeah, I don't know, she's been a bit like this all week, but it's definitely amped up this afternoon.'

'Is she on something?'

'No,' Chelsea says, hiding her disquiet over Joe's line of questioning with a sip of her Doom Bar. 'She's not "on something" . . . she's excited.'

'Hmm, that's the fifth time she's gone to the toilet since I arrived. I've been once.'

'Women pee a lot, Joe.'

'You've been three times. And I consider you someone who goes to the toilet a lot.'

'What?' Chelsea says, but she can't help but laugh. 'You've been counting? You take note of when and how often we wee?'

Joe shrugs, 'These are the types of things I notice. I'm highly observant.'

'About women's toilette.'

'Actually, I think *toilette* in that sense refers more to like, putting on make-up.'

'Which is sometimes what we're doing.'

'Sometimes.'

'What are we talking about?' Izzy says, suddenly appearing again and sitting down.

'Women's toilet habits.'

'Oh, fascinating stuff, guys, so sorry to have missed out on such high-level conversation. Do we need another round?'

'No, I'm good,' Chelsea says. 'You've got half a pint left there, Iz.'

'Oh yeah,' Izzy says, looking down into her glass as if she's forgotten all about it. 'Did I really order a pint? I'm way more in the mood for wine.'

'I can get you a wine, if you want,' Joe offers.

'No, it's fine.' Izzy smiles at him. 'I'll finish this.'

'So, what did you get up to before Chelsea arrived?'

'Oh, this and that, not a whole lot. We had everyone here for Easter weekend, including Charlie's new absolute bore of a girlfriend, but Dad and I just laughed at them the whole time, so that was fun at least.'

'Your dad's back in London now, though?' Joe asks.

'Yeah, they all left on Easter Monday. I'm not sure where Dad is at the moment, actually.' Izzy takes a sip of her beer and puts it back down on the table with a slosh. 'He's being courted by a giant American conglomerate, I think he might actually be in Chicago.'

'Wow, that's kind of a big deal, right?'

'Yeah, but he won't sell. His whole thing is family business, family business, family business. He tries to pretend it's about legacy, but really it's all about being a control freak,' she says with a smile. 'How's your dad though, Joe? Is he any better?'

'Uh, he's not great,' Joe is spinning his pint glass around in one hand, staring down into the near-black liquid of his Guinness. 'We've actually had to put him in a hospice.'

'Is that like, a private hospital?' Izzy asks, two lines forming between her eyebrows.

Chelsea can't quite believe Izzy doesn't know what hospice care is. Chelsea's gran had been a hospice nurse for most of her career before retiring and moving back to Ireland, but if that wasn't the case, maybe she wouldn't know either, unless she'd had a relative die from a slow disease. Joe's face is pained as he clears his throat and shakes his head, 'No, it's um, it's end of life care.'

'Oh.'

'Yeah.'

'Oh my God, Joe, I'm so sorry. Shouldn't you . . .'

'Shouldn't I be there?' he says with a hollow laugh. 'Yeah, I probably should. But Mum convinced me to come. It's only two nights.'

'But we're going back to uni so soon, don't you want to spend as much time with him as possible?' Chelsea can tell Izzy is coming from a good place, a place of compassion and wanting to understand, but it doesn't make Joe look any less uncomfortable or awkward.

'We don't have to talk about this if you don't want to, Joe. If you came here to be distracted, we can do that,' Chelsea says in a low voice, her hand reaching for his.

'Oh, yeah, we can definitely do that,' Izzy says, eyes wide. 'I mean, Cornwall is your oyster, or at least this pub is . . . what about that?' she says, pointing in the direction of what looks like it could be a freestanding cash machine, but is actually a QuizBox.

'Sure,' Joe says with a laugh, taking a sip of his Guinness. 'It wouldn't hurt to beat you two at some trivia.'

'Fighting words, Joe Hemsley.'

'Yeah, you're gonna regret that over-confidence,' Izzy says, standing up and leading the way. 'Chelsea has the uncanny ability to remember *everything*.'

Chelsea is nervous as she sits on the train to the University of Birmingham campus. It's only two stops from New Street, but the ride is long enough to make her think this might have been a bad idea. Because she finally feels like she's back in the Birmingham she knows and remembers, the one she inhabited and learned to love, the one she sees when she thinks of Izzy and Ayesha and Hannah, and sometimes even Joe, the one she was expelled from. She takes a shaky breath as the train pulls in at the station. It's started to rain, the sky purple and portentous with clouds, and as she pulls her cap even lower over her face – she doesn't have an umbrella – she thinks about all that rain during their first weeks. She remembers the feeling of those first few days of uni, the expectation and excitement coupled with the nerves and worry that she wouldn't fit in, that she wouldn't find friends, that she'd never find her way around the campus, that she'd be unable to keep up with the work. But then she'd quickly found her footing, and everything had fallen into place. Until, that is, it all fell apart.

Walking across campus to the arts building, she sees the ghosts of those first weeks everywhere. Campus has changed, of course, in that fun-house mirror way that London has – the same, but different – but just as now, the rain had been unremitting that year: it sloshed into Izzy's ballet flats, soaked Chelsea's Converse, trickled down their backs, made their clothes stink like wet sheep. But it hadn't mattered, or at least, it hadn't mattered much. There are students everywhere, scurrying to their next lecture or seminar in groups of two, three, five, looking miserable beneath their hoods and umbrellas, shouting to one another, shouting *at* one another, laughing and chatting about the previous night's events, tonight's prospects. She'd give anything to feel like one of them again, but she couldn't feel more different; she's just an observer, watching a scene, or multiple scenes play out in front of her. She doesn't get to take part, not any more. The walk's longer than she remembered, and she is momentarily startled by the loss of the old library, the gaping space where it used to stand now open and free, but soon the arts building is coming into view, looking just the same with its tired redbrick almost completely hidden by clinging ivy. She stands in front of it, getting steadily damper, and takes a deep breath. There is something both comforting and disconcerting about it looking so exactly as it did, so many years ago. Has everything that happened, really happened? She almost feels as though she could push her way through those doors, walk into the Mason Lounge and find Izzy there eating a Twix, enjoying her third coffee of the day. But that's not going to happen, so she follows someone much, much younger than her into the building and heads up the staircase to Anna Fox's office.

'Chelsea,' Anna says, on opening the door, 'welcome.'

'Thank you.' Chelsea had emailed ahead, from the train, and to her surprise, Anna had not only replied promptly, but been receptive. They had actually stayed in touch a little during Chelsea's time in prison, and Anna had even acted as a reference when Chelsea had started her Open

227

University degree, but still, providing a reference from the safe distance of an email is a different matter to talking face-to-face with someone convicted of murder. Chelsea knows Anna didn't have to agree to do this, and she feels a rush of relief when Anna smiles and ushers her inside, directing her towards a chair. 'You look exactly the same,' Anna says as she sits down behind her desk.

'People keep saying that, but I don't see it.'

'Really? Honestly, I felt like I was opening the door to the past just then.'

Chelsea grimaces a little, squirms in her seat to get comfortable. 'I look in the mirror and I don't know who it is looking back at me.'

Anna's eyes widen, almost imperceptibly, and then she blinks rapidly three times, taking in what Chelsea has just said. 'Well. There's a lot to unpack there, I'd say. Have you . . . have you spoken to anyone about it?'

Chelsea wonders what Anna means exactly by 'it'. There are so many 'its' in her life – she could be referring to getting out of prison, *going* to prison, Izzy's death, the trial, losing her mother. The list goes on and on. 'You mean, therapy? See a therapist?'

Anna nods, but she is also tapping insistently at her desk, betraying her nerves and possible misgivings. Is she regretting agreeing to talk to Chelsea, now that she's sat in front of her? 'Mmm. It could be very helpful. You've been through a lot.'

'I've thought about it.'

'Good.' She coughs, awkwardly clearing her throat. 'Keep thinking. Now. You wanted to ask me some questions about after you left the university?'

This is such a delicate way of referring to how and why Chelsea was forced to leave university, she almost laughs. But she doesn't, because she really does appreciate Anna seeing her today, and doesn't want to make her feel any more ill at ease than she already is. 'Yeah, I want to know a bit about when and why Jamie Sinclair left the department.'

'Jamie,' Anna says, her forehead scrunching up, eyebrows drawing together, 'gosh, that's a long time ago.'

'Well,' Chelsea says, holding up her hands, 'I was here a long time ago.'

'That's true. I don't know where it's all gone, to be honest with you,' Anna says on a nervous trill of laughter.

Chelsea, who knows exactly where her time has gone says nothing. 'Um,' Anna continues, leaning back in her chair and looking up at her popcorn ceiling, 'Jamie Sinclair, yes, he left in 2008.'

'At the end of that academic year – 2007 to 2008?'

'I would think so.'

'Is there a way you can check?'

Anna is staring at Chelsea, rapidly blinking again. 'Jamie Sinclair left because the department received multiple student complaints regarding his conduct during one-on-one interactions.' She says this so fast it comes out breathlessly, but also, almost robotically, and for a second Chelsea can't quite take the information in. Given up so quickly and so easily. 'That's what you were really asking about, wasn't it?'

Chelsea swallows, her mouth suddenly incredibly dry. 'Yes.'

Anna nods, just once, as if to say *there, that's that done*, and then her face softens as she takes in Chelsea's response. 'Are you okay? Do you want something to drink? I should've offered you tea or coffee when you arrived, sorry. Terrible host.'

'No, no,' Chelsea says, waving her offer and her apology away, not really concentrating. But Anna is already up and out of her seat, leaning over a makeshift tea and coffee station that sits on top of a glossy black mini fridge. She has one of those pod coffee machines, and she's popping a pod in and pressing a button, despite Chelsea's protestations.

'Do you know who the complaints were from?' Chelsea asks over the noise of the coffee machine. Anna is still standing, leaning back against a bookcase with her arms crossed against her chest, and at first she pretends not to have heard, so Chelsea is forced to ask again.

'No,' Anna says, finally, as the machine stops, and the coffee is made. She hands Chelsea a small earthenware mug, and begins the process of making another one for herself.

'Anna,' Chelsea says, holding her cup stupidly, looking down into the coffee she hadn't even asked for or wanted, 'please. This is important.'

Anna has her back to Chelsea now, but she nods slowly, indicating that she's heard her, and Chelsea watches as the older woman's shoulders rise and then slowly fall as though she has taken a deep, steadying breath.

Finally, she sits back down at her desk, with her coffee. 'What you have to understand, Chelsea, is that was a very difficult time in the department. For all of us. I had never had to deal with the death of a student before. Let alone a murder.'

'Do you think I don't understand that? Me?' Anna just stares at Chelsea, worrying at her bottom lip. She's biting down so hard on it, Chelsea wouldn't be surprised if she drew blood. 'It sounds like you're making excuses. For Jamie's behaviour.'

'No, no,' Anna says, waving her hands as though they were two white flags, and looking, to her credit, aghast at the accusation. 'No. Not at all. But maybe for the way it was dealt with. I'm head of department now, but I wasn't then, and honestly, I had no idea about the complaints until the rumours started to trickle out and we were all talking about it.'

'Were there rumours before he was fired?'

'Um,' Anna swallows, and reaches for a pen on her desk, twitching it into place, 'he wasn't fired, exactly. He was asked to leave.'

'Which is why he's teaching somewhere else now,' Chelsea says, 'right?'

'Yes.'

'Where he may be doing the exact same thing.'

Anna winces, 'We can't be sure about that.'

'Can't we?' Chelsea asks with a laugh.

'I do feel very badly about all this, Chelsea, really. If it happened now, I know I would handle it differently, but it wasn't up to me. And there's nothing I can do about it now.'

'Now that he's someone else's problem?'

Anna sighs heavily, finally meeting Chelsea's gaze, 'Yes.'

'But these rumours, before he was let go or asked to leave, or whatever. Were any of them about Izzy?'

'I . . . I can't say. I don't know.'

'You don't know?'

'I . . . there was a lot going on at the time. A lot being said. We were in crisis mode.'

'So, you don't remember if Izzy's name was ever

mentioned alongside these accusations against Jamie from other students?' Chelsea asks, surprised at how cleanly the words come out considering she is vibrating with frustration and anger. She had walked in here thinking Anna was going to help, that Anna actually *wanted* to help, but instead it seems the tutor she remembers – the one, in fact, who opened the door to her – has turned into some sort of politician, forever dodging the question, dancing around the real answer.

'Yes, of course, she was,' Anna finally answers, the words coming out in a flat rush.

'And what did you make of that?'

'I thought . . . I *think* there was a lot of confusion, a lot of conflating going on. I think they were two different issues that happened around the same time, but we couldn't quite wrap our heads around it all. Not all at once, anyway.'

'What are you saying, Anna?'

'I'm saying there were definitely some people who thought Jamie had been involved with Izzy. Not necessarily with her . . . her murder, but who thought something might have happened there. But I'm no longer sure what I think about all that. It's . . . it's difficult to unravel everything that happened and make any sense from it. And, to be clear, the rumours were circulating after her death. After the investigation. A student – a different student – came forward just before Easter in 2008 and that's where everything regarding Jamie stemmed from.'

'So there was nothing before then? No whispers on the grapevine?' Chelsea says, unable to keep the scepticism out of her voice.

'Not that I'm aware of.'

A silence drops over them, like a thin blanket, as they stare at one another. Anna has her back to a large window, and outside, rain picks at it. The day is dark, but even so, Chelsea can see the almost bare trees, and the outline of the new library, practically glistening in the rain.

'We're close to the anniversary, aren't we? Was it this week?'

'This Thursday,' Chelsea says shortly.

Anna nods, 'I was remembering it all just a few days ago. Saw the date, and couldn't believe it. Fifteen years. It seems almost unbelievable. Is that what this is all about? The anniversary?'

Chelsea doesn't answer immediately, lets the silence hang over them again. Finally, she says, 'It's about being able to ask the questions I wasn't able to before. Did they talk to you at the time? The police?'

'Um, yes, they did. They came here and interviewed any of us who had a class with Izzy in it.'

'And that included Jamie?'

'Well, yes. Of course.'

'What sort of questions did they ask?'

'Oh, Chelsea, it was a long time ago, I couldn't possibly –'

'How many times have you been interviewed by the police in an active murder investigation?'

Anna blinks at her again, 'Only the once.'

'And it hasn't stuck in your mind? Hasn't become a distinct memory you replay over and over again on a loop? Lucky you.'

'No, no, you're right,' she says after a pause, her voice soft again, her eyes downcast, 'I do remember. Not exact questions, but it was all about her last few weeks, how she'd seemed to us, whether she'd missed classes, who she spent the most time with, that kind of thing.'

'Did the rumours about her and Jamie come up at all?'

'No,' Anna says slowly. 'Like I said, the rumours came after. Nearer to when Jamie eventually left.'

'So, it wasn't mentioned to the police?'

'I don't know, Chelsea,' she says with a sigh and a small shrug, 'the interviews were private. I can only speak for myself. I do remember they spent a lot of time with him, though.'

'With Jamie?'

'Yes. But I didn't think much of it in the moment. He was her personal tutor, after all. He knew her best, out of all of us.'

'Too well, perhaps.'

Anna opens her mouth to reply, but Chelsea isn't sure she wants to hear it, so she thanks the other woman for her time and heads out of the door. Walking along the corridors she used to know so well, she thinks back on Anna's words. It's clear that Sinclair made a habit of inappropriate behaviour with some of his female students; if it happened with Izzy and it happened with the student who came forward, then it probably happened to other girls too. Why couldn't the police have taken her seriously when she first mentioned him? Her phone vibrates and she takes it out of her pocket, but she's too angry at first to see the screen properly. If they'd only done their jobs, then not only might her life have been changed – saved, even – but Izzy's real killer might have been caught, and that other girl might never have had to have gone through whatever it is she went through. But now, she's starting to feel like she'll never know the truth of what Sinclair did and where he was that night. She doesn't believe for a second that he spent the entire night tucked up at home with his wife. She has no evidence to prove otherwise, of course, but it's just a feeling, an instinct. And she's had to learn to trust her instincts very well. Finally, she looks properly at her phone and sees that she actually has a ton of notifications, all of which seem to be alerting her to two separate online articles. She doesn't want to, but she opens the first message, which is from Ayesha earlier today. Someone just sent this to me, so sorry Chels. Let me know if there's anything I can do?

The link sends Chelsea's phone to a *Daily Mail* article from yesterday, the headline sending a spike of fear through her.

A KILLER IN THE CEMETERY: MURDERER OF SLAIN PARTY-GIRL CAUGHT ON CAMERA BY TIKTOKER IN SOUTH LONDON

Killer Keough, renowned murderer of Pennington's heiress Isabella Dunwoody in 2007, has been released from prison early and is now living free in South London. An astounded passer-by caught 36-year-old Chelsea looking gaunt in West Norwood Cemetery in South London. One of the city's 'Magnificent Seven' cemeteries originally built in the 1830s, it is home to the Dunwoody family mausoleum.

Pictured here with Isabella's mother, Camille Dunwoody, Chelsea was released from HMP Foston Hall just a few days ago. A women's and young offenders' prison, Keough had been held there since her conviction in 2008 and released early on good behaviour. Made infamous for having bludgeoned her housemate to death, it's unclear whether this meeting between her and Isabella's mother is intentional or not. We reached out to Dunwoody's representatives, but they declined to comment.

Keough, who proclaimed her innocence throughout the trial, grew up in South London and had known Isabella since their schooldays. Taken in by the wealthy family – even joining them on holiday in Mallorca the summer before Isabella's murder – Keough and Dunwoody were believed to have drifted apart in the autumn of 2007, with some reports saying they were in dispute over a paramour.

What's not in dispute is the interest in this case. Since 2007, there have been several documentaries, and a podcast series based on these notorious events and the original TikTok capturing the moment Keough met with her victim's mother has gone viral.

A paramour? She has to roll her eyes at the word, even though this is no eye-rolling matter. She scrolls through Ayesha's other messages, and types a reply back, explaining where she's been, what she's been doing, and why she hasn't been able to respond until now.

Ayesha texts back her shock almost immediately, wanting to know more about Sinclair, but then she writes:

BTW, Joe DM'd me today. He saw the Daily Mail article but didn't know how to reach out to you. Should I send him your number?

Joe?

Yeah. Joe Hemsley.

Sunday, 28th October 2007, 1:11 a.m.

Somewhere on the Bristol Road

The cab is speeding along the Bristol Road. Not literally speeding, but the road is fairly empty and as the shopfronts and lights whizz past, Izzy leans her forehead against the cool surface of the window to try and stop herself from feeling nauseous.

'Are you going to be sick?' the driver demands.

She shakes her head, whispers, 'No.'

'I've had too many people be sick in my car this month. Don't want to clean up any more sick.'

'I'm not going to be sick,' she says, but she has to swallow heavily to stop her voice from cracking and she can see the driver frown at this. He doesn't believe her.

Suddenly, the cab pulls to a stop. 'Get out.'

'What?'

'Sorry. No charge for this, but you have to get out. I don't want sick in here. Again.'

'I'm not going to be sick, I promise.'

'I don't believe you. You look like you're about to vomit. Get out, please.'

Izzy starts to argue with him, but the driver stares resolutely out through his windscreen, his hands tight at the steering wheel as he shakes his head, and she knows it's a lost cause. She's been on the edge of tears the whole journey so far, and now she feels like she's about to burst. She doesn't want the driver to see it, so she hurries out of the car, making sure she has her bag before she slams the door shut behind her and watches as the cab practically squeals away. She lets out a sob, drawing in a deep, shaking breath to try and steady herself, but it does the complete opposite, letting something loose that she's been trying to hold back for hours.

'Shit,' she says to herself, looking around through bleary eyes. She's barely out of town yet, it would probably take an hour to walk home from here, and she just doesn't have the energy for that. She can barely even contemplate it. She staggers back towards the shelter of a building and pulls her mobile from her bag. Who can she call? Chelsea? She doesn't want to force her to leave before she's ready though. And, more to the point, how likely is she to even pick up her phone? Ayesha and Han are both out of town, Han back tomorrow morning, but that doesn't help her now. Shit. She scrolls through her address book and stops at the one person she can think of who might be able to help her right now, and, cringing inside as she does so, presses 'call'.

It takes over half an hour, but finally a dark blue very old-looking Volvo pulls up next to her, and Izzy gets in.

'Are you okay?' Jamie asks, as he checks his rear-view and flicks on an indicator.

'I'm fine. Thanks for coming. I couldn't think of anyone else, sorry.'

'It's okay. I'd rather you call me than risk ... well, whatever. No need to worry about that now. What are you meant to be?' he indicates Izzy's dress with his hand.

'A mummy.'

'Right. I'm not sure it quite –'

'It's been a long night. It looked better earlier.'

'I'm sure. So, what happened? How did you end up on the side of the road?'

Izzy had tried to explain the situation on the phone, but Jamie had just shushed her, told her to tell him where she was and hurried her off the call. Now, she explains that the cab driver was convinced she was going to be sick and feels Jamie look over at her, 'Were you?'

'No. I just … no, I wasn't.'

'Well, you've had a rough couple of months, I wouldn't blame you if you'd had a bit too much to drink.'

Izzy stares out her window, as the dark world whips by, and says nothing. She hates this feeling of everyone watching her as she falls apart. Waiting for the moment she breaks down, nodding their heads, and saying, *Well sure, she just lost her dad*. She squeezes her eyes closed, once again feeling tears threaten, and sighs heavily.

'Maybe it'll be good, to get back to normal life a bit next week?' Jamie says. Reading week is almost over, and lectures start back up on Monday, which suddenly seems all too close, all too soon. Izzy nods in response, even though she can't really bear the thought of being in a lecture or seminar, just wants to be in bed, maybe for the rest of her life.

'Maybe.'

'There's a few things we need to go over,' he says, looking her way again, 'maybe Chelsea mentioned it? We need to make sure you're on track to pass your exams next term, or –'

'Not right now, please.'

'Right, sorry, okay.' He starts to tap out a rhythm on the steering wheel and Izzy digs her fingernails into the palm of her curled-in hands, to stop her from saying anything. They're just coming into Selly Oak now, the road narrowing by the Tesco Metro, and Izzy has to remind Jamie which road she lives on.

'Thank you for doing this. It's so late, and I know you didn't have to.'

Jamie nods, glances at her, 'Well. I've been worried about you, to be honest. I was relieved to hear your voice, despite how late it was.' Izzy doesn't say anything, and Jamie has to turn his attention back to the road, indicating and turning left up Tiverton. 'I'm sorry about everything that happened last year, Izzy. I know it must be strange for you to have had me assigned as your personal tutor, but I really do have your best interests at heart.'

'Oh, really?'

'Yes, I promise. I wasn't … I got carried away last year, I wasn't thinking straight. About anything. About you, about my job, the department. My wife.'

'Your wife,' Izzy repeats dully. 'Your wife I didn't know about.'

Jamie clears his throat. He's inching up the road, waiting for further directions from Izzy, but when none come, he says, 'I didn't realize how inappropriate I was being, not until I stopped … stopped and thought about how I'd feel if I found out something similar had happened to my daughter.'

'Right. How gracious of you to start considering the full repercussions of your actions now your daughter has shown you that girls are also real people.' Jamie is silent, the only sounds those of the car creeping up the hill, until Izzy impatiently continues, 'We're up past Exeter Road, so you may as well speed up a bit.'

Jamie obliges, slowing down ever so slightly to make sure

there aren't any cars coming from either direction as he crosses Exeter. Izzy points out the house, and he pulls into a free space a few houses short of it.

'It wasn't just me, you know,' Jamie says, turning towards her in the dark. 'You made your feelings very clear too.'

'Well, this is awkward,' Joe whispers to Chelsea as he leans forward to grab his drink from the coffee table. They're in the room Izzy refers to as a 'games room', which is long and wide and full of low, squishy sofas, slightly worn-out armchairs, a pool table, ancient table tennis table, and lined with bookcases. It's the kind of room designed to be cosy, but instead, on a windswept April afternoon, is cold and damp. It's the first full day of Joe's visit, and after a sunny morning down on the beach, they have retreated here, wet and cold once a storm broke, soaking them to the skin as they ran back through the rain.

Ten minutes ago, the general peace was shattered by the arrival of Izzy's brother, Charlie. He had crashed through the front door with a shout, his loud, braying voice boring a hole through the tranquil haze of the house, and Izzy's eyes had widened, her head whipping around to where his voice was coming from with a muttered, 'What the fuck?' the only explanation as she left the room to see what was going on. Now, Chelsea and Joe sit on the sofa closest to the fire, waiting for her to return, unable to stop themselves listening to the raised voices out in the hall.

'Have you met him before?' Joe asks Chelsea.

'No,' she says, shaking her head, 'but I've heard enough from Iz to not exactly be surprised by this entrance.'

'Why's he here, though? Didn't he just leave?'

Chelsea shrugs. She's managed to determine some of the Dunwoody family dynamics from Izzy's complaints and stories, but for the most part, they remain a mystery. She has still only met her dad once, just after Christmas, and even though Camille has been with them the entirety of Chelsea's stay in Cornwall, Izzy's mother remains enigmatic, unknowable. She talks easily, and seemingly happily, with both girls at mealtimes, but otherwise they hardly see her and Chelsea has no idea what she does all day. Chelsea gets the sense that there are many layers to peel back, but Camille is resolute in only showing the outermost layer to anyone but her family. Maybe she doesn't even reveal much to them.

The door creaks on its hinges and in comes Izzy, stony eyed and rigid, a tall, dusty-blond-haired man on her heels. Charlie.

'You're not meant to be here this weekend, Izzy,' he's hissing at her and Chelsea is taken aback by his bared teeth and narrow eyes. She turns to Joe and catches his eye, just as he stands up, brushing something invisible from his lap.

'Mum told you we were staying for the whole Easter holiday. I've not been well.'

'Oh, yeah, you look like you're having a terrible time with your friends practically moving in,' he says scathingly, his gaze straying to Chelsea and Joe just as his top lip curls back. They haven't even been introduced and already they've been dismissed. Joe coughs awkwardly, red creeping up his neck from the collar of his jumper, and Chelsea's stomach churns with embarrassment.

'Oh my God, you're such a drama queen,' Izzy says with an eyeroll, picking up a snooker ball from the pool table and pushing it idly into the centre of the table.

'I have the house every year, Iz. This weekend, every year, it's been the same for six fucking years, so can you stop being such a fucking little bitch about it.'

'*I'm* being a little bitch?' Izzy says.

'Fuck you, Isabella.'

'Look, I just don't get the problem. Mum told you we were here until I go back to uni.'

'Stop calling her that. She's not my mum.'

'Fine, *my mum*. Jesus.'

'Camille didn't let me know the dates, did she? Evi-fucking-dently sending a text is too much to ask when you do nothing all day.'

'Now, now, the house is big enough for all of us, isn't it?' Camille's voice comes calmly from the doorway. If she heard Charlie's words – which, surely, she must've done – she gives no indication of it.

'I have six friends on their way down here now. As we speak,' Charlie huffs.

'Yes, and we have plenty of space.'

'That's . . . that's not the point,' Charlie says, looking like he's talking through gritted teeth. 'I'm not hosting a summer camp, Camille, I don't want my little sister and her little friends getting in the way. Not to mention their chaperone,' he waves his arm towards her and Camille smiles through pursed lips.

'No need to worry about that, big brother,' Izzy says acidly. 'You'd have to pay me to spend time with you and your Bullingdon crew.'

'Ha, no one's buying your disdain, Isabella, not when dear old Daddy couldn't even pay your way into Oxford.'

Izzy's face reddens, and Chelsea watches as her jaw

tightens in annoyance and her eyes flash. Chelsea hasn't ever seen Izzy like this, but it looks as though she's about to explode, so Chelsea stands, suddenly and unsteadily, and bursts out, 'Why don't we just go to the pub, Iz? Get out of your brother's hair for a bit.'

Izzy's face is surly at this suggestion, but Camille, still standing in the doorway, calmly murmurs, 'That's an excellent idea. Charles, your friends can take the rooms in the stables and the north wing, I'll leave you to set all of that up.'

With that, Camille departs silently and Charlie rounds on Chelsea.

'Which one are you, then?' he practically barks.

'Chelsea. And this is Joe,' she says, indicating him beside her.

'Well, you lot just better stay out of our way. This is a fucking nightmare, if you ask me, but no one ever bloody does.'

'Because we'd rather not hear the sound of your voice, dear brother. Or what you have to say.'

Charlie laughs and shakes his head, suddenly looking like a different person as he stalks from the room, his laughter echoing down the hallway as he goes.

* * *

They miss the arrival of Charlie's friends, but by the time they return from the pub the driveway is full of cars, old, new and expensive, and the house is lit up, every window with a light burning so it glows against the black night. Chelsea can't help but imagine Camille hiding out in one of those rooms, a prisoner in her own home.

'God, Mum told him to stick to the stables, but look at this,' Izzy says, stopping suddenly to stare up at the house. Even through the dark, Chelsea can see her scowl. The pub, and more specifically the booze, had lightened all their spirits after the run-in with Charlie, but now they're back Chelsea squirms with discomfort as she thinks of Charlie, and his six identical friends, taking over the house which has, for the last few days, felt entirely theirs. She'd felt a little awkward when she first arrived, moving through a house so unlike her own, opening kitchen cupboards, making cups of tea for her and Izzy as though she owned the place. But she'd felt at home soon enough – sooner than she'd anticipated, really, never expecting to feel so at ease there – and now that aura of comfort has been broken by Charlie and this caravan of cars in the driveway. She can feel Joe's discomfort next to her too as he scuffs at the ground with the toe of his Adidas. 'They've taken over the whole bloody place.'

'Maybe we should just grab some wine and go up to your room, Iz?' Chelsea suggests.

'Yeah, yeah,' she says, still scowling. 'It's so annoying though. We were here first.'

Once they're in the house, it's clear Charlie and his friends have taken over the games room. Braying laughter assaults them from down the hallway, interspersed with harsh words thrown at one another in jest, prompting yet more gales of laughter. The large, rambling house, which had once felt welcoming in an old-fashioned way that Chelsea only recognizes from films, books and TV shows, suddenly feels cramped, the walls closing in on her and Joe and Izzy, whose scowl has deepened so much that if

Chelsea's gran were to see her now, she'd warn the girl that if she wasn't careful, her face might stay that way.

'God, he's such a dick,' she mutters. 'Mum must be livid.'

'Why don't you go and check on her, and we'll meet you upstairs,' Chelsea says. She's not sure why exactly, but she's keen to keep Izzy and Charlie as far away from one another as possible tonight. Charlie's entrance earlier this afternoon hadn't been pretty, and at that point, he hadn't even been drinking. Throw hours of alcohol into the mix, and God knows what the result would be. Izzy nods and heads up the staircase, leaving Chelsea and Joe to head to the kitchen. It's along the same corridor as the games room, and as they get closer the shouts and the laughter get louder and clearer. From here, they can discern words and sentences, punctuated all too often with that stream of obnoxious, insistent laughter.

'God, do you think they have any idea how they sound?' Joe says quietly as Chelsea opens the door to the kitchen. In here, all is quiet and dark with only the light of a single table lamp still on. The windows don't have any blinds or curtains and beyond them, the chilly Cornish countryside they've just come in from glowers in the dark, trees shivering in the wind. Joe turns the main light on and the spell is broken, the dark night banished by their own reflections.

'I think they like the way they sound, Joe, that's part of the problem.'

'It's like nails down a chalkboard. Have to admit, I didn't realize quite how posh Iz is until I got here. I can't believe this isn't even their main house,' Joe says, leaning against the counter while Chelsea gets out three wine glasses. 'What's her London house like?'

'Nice,' Chelsea says with a shrug. 'Big.'

'You're really painting a picture for me.'

Chelsea pauses, concentrating on removing the cork from a bottle of white wine she found in the fridge before saying, 'It's more polished than here, I guess. Fancier. I didn't feel like I should touch anything there. It's more homely here.'

'Until the lord of the manor turned up.'

'Right.' Chelsea eyes the kitchen door, as if one of them might barge through it at any moment, and then turns back, pouring out the wine carefully. When they leave the kitchen they do so as quietly as possible, both understanding, without having to say it to each other, that they do not want to bump into Charlie or any of his friends. They pad silently down the hall and up the stairs, both moving as though they're in an action movie. When they get to Izzy's room, Chelsea lets out a long breath of relief before pushing the door open.

Izzy is sat on her bed, taking off her make-up with a wipe. 'Mum's fast asleep,' she greets them. 'I think she must've taken something. Literally, she's dead to the world.'

'Well, that's good at least,' Chelsea says, joining her on the bed and passing her one of the wine glasses.

'Did you bring the bottle up?' Izzy says, eyeing both Chelsea and Joe so she can see that they clearly didn't.

'I'll go and get it when we're done with these,' Chelsea says. 'I didn't want it to get warm.'

'Ah, I've taught you so well,' Izzy says, and Chelsea

answers with a roll of her eyes. But they finish their glasses quickly, and soon Chelsea is heading back down to the kitchen with instructions to 'just bring a couple more bottles back with you'.

Downstairs, the party is still going, and walking down the stone-flagged hallway, Chelsea feels like she's somewhere she shouldn't be, like an invading species, small and unremarkable, but for some reason – the wine, probably – this makes her feel powerful rather than weak and overlooked, and as she nears the kitchen, she decides to keep walking a little further to where the games room door stands ajar, whorls of music, chatter and laughter escaping from it. She's drunk now, there's no doubt about it, and she steadies herself against the wall, pressing her back against it as she stands there, listening.

'It just makes me sick to think about her living here. Even owning the whole bloody place whenever Dad eventually kicks the bucket.' Charlie sounds as though he's talking through a mouth full of marbles, the words careering around his tongue, but clear enough to understand, even to Chelsea, standing outside the room. 'It's disgusting,' he continues, practically sobbing out the words, 'that whore living in this house, like it's her own, when I grew up here, it's –'

'Shhh,' someone interrupts, and Chelsea is startled to realize it's a girl's voice – or rather, a woman's. 'Charlie, come on, there's no need for all this. We're here now, let's just enjoy it.'

'Yeah, and the old man's not dying any time soon, is he?' a braying voice asks, although it's not really a question.

There's a short pause, almost infinitesimal, where

Chelsea is sure she can hear Charlie issue a sniff, as if stopping himself from crying. 'No, he'll live 'til he's a hundred if he has anything to say about it,' he says robustly, suddenly sounding a lot less drunk.

'So, this is all just hypothetical whingeing,' comes the woman's voice again.

'Whingeing? Fuck you, Florence.'

'Shh, all right, all right, someone can't take a joke when they're drunk, Jesus. Noted.'

'I'm not drunk.'

'Okay.'

'I'm not.'

'Whatever you say, boss,' this is the same guy as before, 'but you might want to pay attention, because I'm about to thrash you.'

'Fuck off, no you're not, mate.'

Chelsea hears the sounds of pool being played, and she's about to take off, thinking the argument is over and she should really get back to Izzy and Joe anyway, when Charlie starts up again. 'It's just not fair, y'know? Being made to feel like I'm the one who's not supposed to be here when it's my house and I'm older . . . I was coming here before Izzy was even fucking born, before Dad had even met little miss French model wife and now I'm the unwanted guest? No fucking thank you, no fucking way. Mum was so depressed when he left, it was disgusting how he treated her, and now I'm just expected to smile and nod and be nice even when they're in MY HOUSE?' He bellows the last two words, and Chelsea takes a step back towards the kitchen, her heart pounding in her chest.

'Charlie mate, no need for all that. Wasn't this all like, twenty years ago? What's brought all this on?'

But Charlie's friend is reasoning with a drunk man who continues to talk as if he hasn't been interrupted. 'And now this house is going to be left to that bitch, and then her little bitch will inherit it and then God knows what little bitches she'll bring into the world –'

'Charlie, stop,' Florence's voice cuts in, 'there's no need to bring Izzy into this, she's done nothing wrong.'

'Ha, that's a joke . . .'

Chelsea leans towards the door again, trying to hear because the voices surrounding Charlie have dropped to a murmur and Charlie himself has started to mumble. Suddenly the door is pulled open and Chelsea stumbles backwards, her eyes wide as a woman – Florence, presumably – leaves the games room, shutting the door firmly behind her.

'Shit,' she says on noticing Chelsea, 'how much of that did you hear?'

'Uh . . .'

'Don't worry about it, I won't tell him you were there,' she says smoothly, passing Chelsea and leading the way to the kitchen. 'Which one are you, anyway?' she continues, echoing Charlie's question from earlier.

'Um, I'm Chelsea.'

'Florence,' she says, turning to look at her as they walk into the kitchen. 'You won't tell Izzy about any of that, will you? It'll only make things worse. He can sort of fake the pleasantries most of the time, it's only when he gets drunk that he gets like this.'

'He hates them so much.'

'It's complicated,' Florence says with a sigh as she fills a coffee pot with water and transfers it to the reservoir of the filter machine. 'Do you know anything about how Izzy's mum and dad got together?' Florence's gaze is on Chelsea as she speaks, and Chelsea shakes her head in response. 'She was the other woman for five years or something. Already pregnant with Izzy by the time he finally got round to leaving Charlie's mother. All very painful and traumatic for little Charlie, but of course instead of doing the sensible thing like paying a professional to help him get over it, he just drinks, and vents to us instead. He's not all bad. Although I don't blame you for thinking so.'

'What was all that about the house, though?' Chelsea says after a beat.

Florence shrugs, 'Who knows? Charlie's obsessed with who gets what, it's a bit of a well-worn path with him. But Daddy Dunwoody did have a big meeting with the board yesterday, so it could have something to do with that.'

'Isn't Izzy a board member now? Shouldn't she have been there, too?'

Florence shrugs again. She's added a filter and several heaped tablespoons of coffee to the machine and turned it on, and now she's leaning against the kitchen counter with her arms folded, looking at Chelsea. 'God knows, probably. Could be that that's what this is all about. Charlie's convinced Izzy's just going to waltz into the business after she graduates and walk off with the keys to the kingdom.'

'She doesn't even care about any of that stuff,' Chelsea says.

'That's almost worse. Charlie cares so much, it just riles

him up. Doesn't help that Izzy's clearly Daddy's favourite. Almost makes me glad to be an only child.'

'Same,' Chelsea says with a smile, not adding that not only does she not have any siblings *or* a father, but she doesn't have anything to inherit either.

The coffee machine begins to gurgle and Florence turns to it, grabbing a mug from the cupboard directly above and filling it to the brim. 'Well, nice talking to you, Chelsea,' she says, 'and remember, none of this happened, right?' At this, she holds a finger to her lips and gives a little wink, not bothering to hear Chelsea's response before leaving the kitchen.

Transcript of interview with Charles Dunwoody on 29 October 2007 conducted by Detective Inspector Rob Bailey and Detective Constable Natalie Ajala at Birmingham Central Police Station

Detective Inspector Rob Bailey: Right, Mr Dunwoody –

Charles Dunwoody: Call me Charlie.

RB: Charlie. Can you talk me through when you last saw or spoke to your half-sister, Isabella Dunwoody?

CD: Izzy. Only Camille ever calls her Isabella. And I consider her my sister, no 'half' necessary.

RB: Of course, my apologies.

CD: None needed. Erm, when did I last see or speak to her? Well, those are two different occurrences.

Detective Constable Natalie Ajala: Talk us through both of them, please, Charlie.

CD: Of course. Well. I last saw her Saturday morning, that must be ... the twenty-seventh?

NA: That's right.

CD: Right. Sorry, yeah, it's all been such an awful blur. So, yes, I saw her Saturday morning at ... at the house in London. Sorry, I was about to call it my dad's place but well, it's not any more.

[sighs]

RB: Had you stayed the night there?

CD: No, no, I've never lived there, that was – is – Dad and Camille's place. And Izzy's. I have a flat in Kensington.

RB: So, what were you doing there that morning?

CD: I was there for breakfast. We'd had a meeting the day before about some of my father's last requests, and it had

been quite intense, a lot to take in, for everyone. Just, very ...
final. So, I went over to spend a bit of time with Izzy away
from all that.

RB: Was your stepmother there too?

CD: Yes, she was.

NA: Anyone else?

CD: Erm, I don't think so, although, I suppose – the
housekeeper. She was there.

RB: What sort of time was this?

CD: I suppose it was about ten, ten thirty. Izzy was never an
early riser so there was no point going any earlier than that. I
probably left about midday, around the time she headed back
to Birmingham.

RB: But you spoke to her again? Later that day?

CD: Yes, mostly I was just checking in on her. She'd taken it
all ... well, it's been very hard, on all of us. First Dad and now
this ...

[pause]

RB: Take your time, Charlie. Can we get you any water?

[short pause]

CD: No, no, I'm fine. She wasn't herself, but then that's
hardly ...

NA: It's completely understandable.

CD: Yes. Right. Well. So, I was checking up on her, but then I
realized she'd forgotten to sign something, so I had to call her
about that.

RB: And this was all phone calls? Or did you text her too?

CD: Both. But surely ... surely, you've got her mobile phone?
You can see her phone and text history?

RB: We haven't been able to locate her mobile actually,
Charlie.

CD: Oh, you mean ... what do you mean?

RB: We don't have her mobile phone, and we've so far been unable to locate it.

CD: Oh.

RB: Changing track here a little bit, are you surprised she went out that night, on Saturday? Considering you say she wasn't in the best frame of mind.

CD: Erm, well. To be honest, I went out that night too, ha [cough]. Wanted to get obliterated, frankly, as bad as that sounds. I imagine Izzy might've felt the same way.

RB: You went out too, you say?

CD: Yes, to Annabel's.

RB: Is that your girlfriend?

CD: No, no. No ... that's, ah, a private member's club. In Mayfair.

RB: Right, okay. Not your girlfriend, then.

CD: No.

NA: Were you with anyone at the club, Charlie? Friends?

CD: Yes, plenty of friends. It was a friend's birthday, in fact.

RB: And can you remember what time it was when you last actually spoke to Izzy?

CD: Not precisely, no. Maybe around eleven?

NA: That's quite late. Can you remember what you spoke about?

CD: She was a little drunk, if I remember correctly. Maybe we both were. But she was upset about something, certainly.

RB: Did you call her or did she call you?

CD: I believe I called her. I was trying to get hold of her for this signature, to try and arrange a time for her to come back down to London, or I was thinking I could have it couriered to her house in Birmingham.

NA: You were doing this when you were at the party?

CD: I don't know, it seemed incredibly important at the time, although obviously it doesn't now. The logic of the drunk. And the grieving.

RB: So, you called her about this document you needed her to sign, but she was upset, you say?

CD: Yes, I remember her being very upset.

RB: About your dad?

CD: Well, I'm sure that was part of it. Why everything felt so upsetting to her at the time, but no, it was about something one of her housemates had done or said, I can't remember.

RB: Which housemate?

CD: Chelsea. Chelsea Keough.

After Chelsea has told Nikki exactly where she was last night and what she'd been doing, who she'd been to see, Nikki refuses to talk or look at her the whole drive home from Aberdeen train station, but as she pulls up in front of the cottage and cuts off the engine, she turns to Chelsea and says, 'We really need to talk about this.'

Chelsea nods, unbuckling herself, and as her feet meet the gravelled driveway, she feels leaden, as though she could sink right through the earth, down to its molten core. The last thing she wants to do right now is talk all this through with her aunt, but she knows she has to. Knows she owes Nikki that much. So, she pulls her rucksack from the back seat, slams the car door shut, the sound whistling through the clear air, and follows her aunt into the soft warmth of the cottage.

The dogs are curled up by the wood burner, as usual, the embers from Nikki's earlier fire still glowing. They both raise their heads as the two women walk in, and Shandy gives a soft bark in welcome, happy to have the whole pack home. Chelsea bends to stroke both their heads, whispering hello. What she wouldn't give, to be curled up and taken care of like they are.

'You hungry?' Nikki asks shortly. 'There's some soup I could heat up.'

Chelsea pulls a chair out from the table, its legs

scraping loudly at the flagstone floor, causing Guinness to stare at her balefully. It's almost eleven o'clock at night but she is starving, having had nothing since she picked up a woeful salad in Birmingham. So she says yes, and Nikki nods, turning the flame back on under a saucepan on the stove. 'It's leek and potato. I made it earlier.'

'Smells delicious.'

Nikki turns, resting back against the stove, arms crossed. 'You can tell me everything, while that heats up.'

So, Chelsea tells her everything, from bumping into Camille at the cemetery, to the meeting with Ajala at Hotel Café Royal, to her trip to Aberystwyth and her alma mater. Nikki has already seen the original *Daily Mail* article – Saoirse sent it to her, panicked – as well as the other piece published yesterday that had her spotted in the WHSmith's in King's Cross. As soon as Chelsea had seen it, she'd known that other woman browsing the True Crime table was the culprit, had kicked herself for not being more careful, for not having turned tail and run as soon as she saw her eyes move over to her.

'You've been so reckless, Chelsea. So reckless. I just can't wrap my head around it. Going to London was one thing, but meeting with Camille? Going off to Wales and Birmingham, talking to Sinclair? Do you not care at all about your rehabilitation? Did you not stop to think for a second about the ramifications? You're going to have to explain all this to Kate, and I'm sorry, love, but it's not going to look good. It's going to look like you're trying to settle some scores.'

'Settle scores?' Chelsea says, the words almost getting stuck in her throat. 'I'm not trying to settle scores. I'm trying to . . . to clear my name. To find out what actually happened to Izzy.'

The soup has started to boil, the saucepan lid rattling noisily, and Nikki turns to switch off the burner, before looking back at Chelsea. 'That's not – that's not your job, Chelsea. According to the law, and everybody else, you killed Izzy and you have paid your dues for doing so. Now you have to be reintegrated back into society, and I'm very afraid that the parole board aren't going to see any of this as an attempt to do so.'

'I can't . . . I can't not do anything, Nikki. Don't you see how I'm treated, talked about? "Killer Keough"? It makes me feel physically ill –'

'I know, I know, it does –'

'No, you don't. Because it's not you. It's me, my life, my name being dragged through the mud.'

'That's my name too,' Nikki says quietly, eyes cast down, her arms still stoically crossed against her chest.

'It's not the same,' Chelsea practically spits. 'And it's not just for me. Izzy's killer, the person who did this to her, they've been out there for fifteen years, while I paid for their crimes. I've had to sit on my hands, stare at the same four walls, have my entire life dictated to me, for fourteen years, while they've been free to do as they please. And I can't do it any more. I know I'm still on licence, I know there's still people watching my every move, but I just can't stay still and do nothing any more.'

'Couldn't it wait, just a little while longer? You've got all this attention on you, people taking photos and videos, that fucking article, not to mention your parole officer. Couldn't you just wait until everything calms down a bit?

None of this is going anywhere, after all – you've got all the time in the world to figure out what happened to Izzy, if that's really what you feel you need to do.'

Everything Nikki is saying might be true, but Chelsea still can't agree with her, can't heed her warning. She knows her aunt is just trying to keep her safe, but there's so much she can't understand. She can't know what it feels like to have had time ripped from your hands and then given back to you, misshapen and truncated. Chelsea certainly doesn't feel as though she has all the time in the world, to solve this or to do anything; instead she feels as if time is her enemy, working against her, slowing her down while everything and everybody else speeds up, and she's left, breathless and spinning her wheels in the dust. But she doesn't know how to convey this to her aunt, doesn't know if she'd even be heard, so she just shakes her head, tears brimming in her eyes. She is so fucking exhausted, she's barely able to form a sentence anyway; words come to her and then disappear like distant figures through a dense fog.

Nikki seems to sense this at least, as she sighs heavily before serving Chelsea her soup, telling her they can talk more in the morning. Chelsea nods, taking a spoon from her aunt and gratefully digging in, hoping, more than anything, that Nikki might forget the need to discuss all this further tomorrow, but knowing full well that she won't.

***

Even worse than facing Nikki, is facing Kate. Unlike Nikki, she still doesn't know that she's been to Aberystwyth and Birmingham, as well as London, but she's texted Chelsea a few times, checking in with her and making sure she'd arrived safely back in Scotland. Waking to a freezing morning shrouded in thick fog, Chelsea and Nikki talk through breakfast, and on the drive to Kate's office. By the time they get there, the fog has mostly lifted, but Chelsea still feels it all around her, feels as though she's fumbling, searching for answers to a question she isn't even supposed to be asking. Kate's face is set in hard lines when Chelsea walks in, barely even looking up from her computer screen for the first thirty seconds.

'Sorry,' she says, finally meeting Chelsea's eye, 'fielding a ton of emails today. You've caused a bit of a stir.'

Chelsea takes a deep breath, nods, 'I'm so sorry. Obviously I didn't want this to happen.'

'Right,' Kate says, her shoulders set rigidly, eyes narrowed. 'But it did. I know I gave permission for you to travel to London, but this is one of the worst things that could've happened. Why did you have to go to that cemetery? You were supposed to be meeting with your solicitor and the estate agent. Did you even do either of those things?'

'Yes, of course,' Chelsea says, proceeding to describe both of those meetings, relieved to have some truth to fall back on. Despite Nikki's reservations, they had both agreed that it was best not to mention Chelsea's trip to Wales and Birmingham to Kate, and although keeping this information from her makes her nauseous with nerves, Chelsea is relieved not to have to disappoint her parole officer even further. It's dangerous to lie like this, she knows that, but for whatever reason, she's sure that holding this back is the best thing to do. For now, at least. Of course, if any photos of Chelsea in Aberystwyth or Birmingham surface online, she'll be screwed, but if they existed, they'd be out there by now, wouldn't they?

'Mmm,' Kate responds, twirling a pen between deft fingers. 'And you met up with the mother of Isabella? Izzy?'

'We bumped into each other. At the cemetery. It was a coincidence.'

'Right. And have you been in touch since?'

Chelsea swallows, wishing she had some water with her, 'No.'

Chelsea can't tell her about the hotel meeting either. It's one thing to accidentally run into the relative of a victim, but quite another to knowingly meet up with them, not to mention Ajala. She wonders what Kate would actually say to all this, if she knew. Probably something along the same lines as Nikki, but harsher, less understanding. She could also punish her, of course. Kate is the person standing between Chelsea and prison. If Kate wanted to – or felt she needed to – she could very easily recommend that Chelsea be taken back into custody. Is the lie worth that risk? Chelsea's not sure, but she's too worried by how much Kate might limit her current circumstances if she knows the full truth. What if she needs to go to London again? If Kate knew she'd met with Camille and Ajala, even worse if she knew she'd seen Jamie Sinclair, there's no way she'd let her leave the area again.

'I want to remind you that there are certain conditions attached to your licence agreement – which you have signed – but that I can recommend extra conditions, if

I believe them to be necessary to your ongoing rehabilitation and the safety of the public. Do you understand that?'

'Yes.'

'Not making contact with the Dunwoodies is not an explicit part of your agreement – yet – so at this moment, you haven't broken any agreement, but I can make it one. Do you plan on making contact with Mrs Dunwoody again?'

Chelsea thinks of her conversation with Camille, that hotel suite with its clean, glamorous lines and subtly sweet décor, the smell of coffee suffusing the room. It couldn't be more different to where she sits now, the only similarity being the coffee smell, although here it smells more stale than fresh. 'No. I have no plans to get in touch with her.'

'Good. The photo and video were unfortunate, but I know there's not much you can do about the public's interest in you. Except keep a low profile, of course.'

'I plan to. I thought I was, but . . .'

'You don't have any more plans to visit London?'

Chelsea hesitates, but then says, 'No.'

'Good. Best to stay close to home for now, I think. I don't have to tell you how lucky you are to have your aunt, and your aunt's home to live in at this time, do I? Really, not all offenders leaving prison have this kind of opportunity and support, Chelsea.'

'I know. I really do.'

Kate's eyebrows raise, and she leans back in her chair. 'Okay. Good. Well, less about the past, and more about the here and now. How has your work at the vet surgery been going?'

Chelsea shrugs, 'Fine. It's mostly administration, plus cleaning up at the end of the day. It's nice to see the animals.'

'What did you think you might end up doing, for work, when you were at university?'

Chelsea blinks at her, the question taking her back to another life, where she actually had options, and questions like 'What do you want to do with your life?' didn't lead to a dead end. She'd felt like she had so many options – too many, really – so she hadn't ever settled on what she wanted to do or be. Hannah and Ayesha had set ideas about what they wanted, theatre and publishing respectively, but neither Chelsea nor Izzy had come up with anything, at least not by the time Izzy died. And by then, neither of them had any choices left. 'I don't know,' Chelsea says finally. 'It hardly matters now, does it?'

Kate sighs. She's back to twirling her pen around again, 'Chelsea, I want you to think and focus a little more on the present and the future, spend less time in the past. Start preparing for what's to come. You need to make the most of all this and only you can do that.'

Chelsea blinks at her. She hasn't even told Kate everything, and the other woman is still warning her to stay away from her past. She can't imagine what Kate would say if she knew the truth. She shifts in her seat, suddenly unbearably uncomfortable, and Kate seems to notice because she starts talking about something else completely – time sheets and check-ins. And then, a little later, when everything has been gone through and Chelsea is picking up her bag to leave, Kate says, 'We don't currently have a curfew in place, or any restrictions in spending the night away from your official place of residence, but I can do that, you know.'

She says this in an informative rather than threatening way, but Chelsea, bag in hand, hears the threat anyway – the promise of tighter controls, a closer watch. She can feel Kate's disappointment in her, it fills the room, colours the air between them, and she knows that, were it to come to it, Kate wouldn't hesitate to make Chelsea's life harder, in order to make her own easier. Chelsea nods in response, tells her she understands, her heart thumping furiously as she leaves the cold, windowless office, the door barely making a sound as she closes it behind her.

'God, he sounds awful,' Ayesha says, 'was he there the rest of the time you were there?'

'Yeah,' Chelsea says.

They're sitting in the garden of Gunnies on the first day of summer term. Both of them are wearing cheap plastic sunglasses; Ayesha's are red and heart-shaped and are so at odds with her usual nature that Chelsea wants to laugh every time she looks at them, although she has now acclimatized to the visual. They're waiting for Hannah and Izzy, who are at the bar, and Chelsea has taken the opportunity to fill Ayesha in on her stay in Cornwall, including Izzy's brother Charlie. 'We sort of got used to him after a while,' Chelsea concedes, 'we even ended up partying together on the last night.'

Ayesha grimaces, as if she can't think of anything worse, and Chelsea shrugs. 'It was all right.'

'What was all right?' Izzy says, coming up from behind, clutching three pint glasses in her hands. 'Look at me,' she says, dumping them unceremoniously on their picnic table, 'I'm practically a barmaid.'

'What did you do with Hannah?' Ayesha asks.

'Loo,' Izzy says simply and Chelsea reaches for the pint nearest her, condensation running down the sides of the glass. 'I really need to stop drinking beer,' Izzy says after taking a long pull from her own glass, 'I've put on so much weight.'

Ayesha makes a face just as Chelsea says, 'No, you haven't.'

'Oh, I think I have,' Izzy says blithely, before continuing, 'anyway, what were you talking about? What was all right?'

'Our last night in Cornwall.'

'Oh, you would have hated it, Ayesha. *Hated* it. My brother and his friends are like, the anti-Ayeshas.'

'Chels says you all managed to get along all right in the end.'

Izzy rolls her eyes, 'Chels was too drunk to know what was going on.'

'I wasn't that bad. We had a good time.'

'Where?' Hannah says, sitting down.

'We were just talking about Cornwall, Han,' Ayesha explains. 'Sounds like we missed quite a party.'

'Oh,' Hannah says, taking a sip of her bright pink rosé. 'I'm so sad I missed it.'

'Oh, you didn't miss anything, Han. Chelsea was off with her boyfriend all night, abandoning me to Charlie's Bullingdon buffoons.'

'Florence was all right,' Chelsea says.

'Yeah, yeah, Florence is okay . . . and Charlie's not all bad, I suppose.'

'You don't get on?' Hannah asks.

'He's just so . . .' Izzy waves a hand around, trying to find the words to describe her brother, 'He's just got a bit of a stick stuck up his arse. Can't take a joke.'

Chelsea looks sideways at Izzy, remembering Charlie's drunken vitriol and Florence's words in the kitchen the night they'd all arrived. Is she downplaying the complexities of her relationship with her stepbrother, or is Florence right, and she actually doesn't realize how differently Charlie views things? It's hard to tell. Izzy is so unflappable and so rarely gets upset, but it's certainly true that she can also be pretty oblivious. Not that it matters. They're a long way from Charlie now.

'I suppose you've got quite a big age difference,' Hannah says. 'Maybe you'll get on better when you're both a bit older?'

'Yeah, maybe. That's a nice way of looking at it. Although honestly it's more of a not-being-a-dick-all-the-time difference, than an age difference.'

'I'm sure he's not a dick *all* the time.'

'Eighty percent, maybe. He has his moments. Oh, hey, is that Joe?'

Chelsea twists in her seat to see Joe walking out of the dark doors of the pub, into the beer garden. He raises his hand that isn't holding a pint and she waves back, but when he gets to their table, it's Izzy he addresses first, 'I didn't just see your brother up on campus, did I, Iz?'

'What?'

'Yeah, I could've sworn it was him, but why would he be here?'

'He wouldn't.'

'Yeah, right, that's what I thought. Must've been his doppelgänger.' Joe meets Chelsea's gaze at last and smiles, 'Hey.'

'Hey.'

'Oh, shit,' Izzy says. She's poring over her mobile with a look of concentration on her face, 'It is him. What the fuck? What is he doing here? Guys, I better go, I don't want him coming here, I better go meet him on campus.'

'Okay,' Chelsea says, watching as Izzy gulps down some of her beer and shovels her possessions into her bag.

'I can come with you if you want?' Hannah says to Izzy, leaning across the picnic table to gently touch the other girl's bare arm.

'No, no, don't worry, I'll be fine.'

'But I'd like to meet him?'

'Why?' Izzy snorts. 'Seriously, Han, you're better off where you are. I'm doing you a favour, really.' She gets up to leave, fondly ruffling Hannah's hair, who looks more than a little dejected to be left behind. Chelsea knows how much Hannah had wanted to come to Cornwall too, but her parents already had a holiday booked by the time Izzy asked them to stay, and hadn't been too keen on the idea of Hannah missing it. They'd fielded a lot of text messages from Hannah, all about how much she was missing them, but honestly it had been hard to feel sorry for her, knowing she was sunning herself in Sicily at the time. Hannah sips on her wine now, watching Izzy's hurried retreat with ever so slightly narrowed eyes. She must feel Chelsea watching her though, because just as Joe takes the space vacated by Izzy, Hannah turns to her, eyes suddenly bright, and her trademark smile back in place.

'That was weird,' Joe says, sitting down. 'Right? Why would Charlie come up here unannounced like that?'

'Maybe he just wants to hang out with his sister,' Hannah says.

'I don't think their relationship is really like that,' Chelsea points out. Did Hannah not hear a word Izzy just said about her half-brother?

'Well, maybe he wants to smooth things over.'

'Maybe.' Hannah isn't the best at putting herself in other people's positions, which, Chelsea has to admit to herself, is strange for someone wanting to act for a living, but she's noticed over the months they've known each other, that although Hannah can be deeply sympathetic and compassionate, she also has a tendency to only see things from her point of view. So, because Hannah has such a good relationship with her siblings, she naturally assumes Izzy can and will too.

'Did you think Charlie was a big fat Bullingdon buffoon too, Joe?' Ayesha says.

'A little bit, yeah,' Joe says, looking from Ayesha to Chelsea as if for confirmation. 'He didn't make the best first impression, did he?'

'Guys?' Hannah says, colour rising in her cheeks. 'Please don't think I'm stupid, but what the hell is Bullingdon?'

Ayesha laughs and pats her on the back as Joe says, 'It's just a stupid drinking society at Oxford. Half our prime ministers were a part of it.'

'A drinking *society*?' Hannah says, incredulous. 'But isn't that just like all of university?'

* * *

Later, walking back through the twilight from Joe's flat, Chelsea bumps into Izzy in front of their residence halls. A large dark car is on its way out of the car park, and Izzy

272

is staring so intently at it as it leaves, that she doesn't even see Chelsea walking towards her.

'Iz?' Chelsea says, watching as her friend snaps back into herself, almost as if all the lights have been turned back on. 'Was that Charlie just leaving?'

'Yeah.'

'He's been here this whole time?'

Izzy nods, 'Yep. A fun afternoon for the Dunwoody siblings.'

'What's going on? Why was he here?'

'Oh, it doesn't matter,' Izzy says, waving an arm in the direction of the car, 'he's gone now.' But she looks so defeated, Chelsea doesn't want to let it drop and asks her again. 'It's fine,' Izzy says with a shake of her head, 'nothing to worry about. He was just trying to convince me to come to London for a meeting of the board on Friday. There's a big vote, and he doesn't think I should just let Dad be my proxy.'

'Oh. Okay.'

'He's voting against Dad, and he's trying to shore up his own votes.'

'He wanted you to vote against your dad?'

'Yeah. As if.'

'But don't Charlie and your dad get on?'

They've wandered over to the bottom of the steps to Izzy's block and here she pauses, tilting her head. 'They do and they don't.'

'But why would he vote against him?'

Izzy shrugs, 'Money, I guess.' She turns to look at Chelsea, her face half in shadow, and Chelsea suddenly realizes how tired she looks, how defeated. 'This isn't really about who likes who, or who gets on with who best, it's . . . well, it's business.'

'It's also your family.'

'Yeah, I never said it wasn't complicated,' she says with a harsh laugh.

'What do you think your dad will do? Does he know Charlie is going to vote against him?'

'Oh, he'll know. He always knows. He'll ice Charlie out for a while, let him stew in his mistake, and then he'll let him back in again, roll out the red carpet. It's how it's always been with them.'

Izzy yawns then, her whole face and mouth stretching with exhaustion, and Chelsea tells her to get up to her flat and go to bed, but when they hug goodnight she's sure Izzy holds on just a little bit longer, a little tighter than usual, her whole body clinging on to something that might hold her still and root her to the spot, if only for a little while.

Chelsea is sitting on her bed in Nikki's cottage having showered after her shift at the veterinary surgery, when she finally has time to call Ayesha back. 'So, Joe Hemsley messaged you?'

'Yeah, can you believe it? Has he been in contact with you at all since Izzy died?'

'No.' And why would he have been? They didn't end on a good note, and Chelsea had always suspected Joe had believed she killed Izzy. It had been a hard pill to swallow, that someone she felt she knew so well could think that of her, but could she really blame him? Even if he'd thought she was innocent, Chelsea was still, at best, merely a blip on his university experience, maybe even a story to be told in some dark bar somewhere, sharing intimacies with new friends and colleagues, *oh you'll never believe who I went to uni with*. 'I'm surprised he'd get in touch now, to be honest.'

'I'm not. He said he'd seen the *Daily Mail* article. I bet it piqued his interest.' Ayesha's voice is acid-tinged here and Chelsea shifts on the bed, getting more comfortable, and in doing so, disturbs her towel turban. She'd forgotten that Ayesha hadn't been much of a Joe fan, at least not by the end, but it was at least pretty astute of him to contact her first; he must've figured out that Ayesha was the only person still in contact with Chelsea, that she was the best route to her.

'What do you think, should I message him back?' Chelsea asks her now.

'Well, I took the liberty of doing a little light Instagram stalking, and it seems he's married with a child now.'

'He's a dad? A husband? God, that's . . . surreal. Did he say why he wanted to get in touch?'

'No, he was a little vague. The message in full was: "Saw that Chelsea's been released. Wow. I've thought about her a lot over the past few years, wondering how she's coped. If you could pass along my details – assuming you're still in contact with her – I'd appreciate it. Just want to say hi. Also how are you?"'

'Ah, snuck the pleasantries in right at the end there, I see.'

Ayesha laughs, 'Lest I think him impertinent.'

'Do you think it's genuine?'

'Hard to tell in a DM. I think the more important question is, do *you*? My opinion hardly matters here.'

'Yeah, it does. I trust your judgment – maybe more than I trust mine.'

'Well, I think you should leave it, to be honest. It might be completely innocent and genuine, but why take the risk? It's not like you were great friends by the end.'

'No,' Chelsea says quietly, thinking about that last term she had at Birmingham, everything that went wrong. There's only one lamp on in her room and the dark seems to seep into her, makes her feel like she could melt into it, into the bed, and disappear completely, but she doesn't want to do that, has spent too much of her life invisible, behind walls. Everyone wants her to continue hiding a little longer, and as much as she hates the articles and intrusion from the press, as much as it makes her feel wary and unsafe, she can't live like this either. Can't hide for ever. 'He did know Sinclair, though. So, he might have some thoughts there, might know something useful.'

'What could he know?'

'Well, he was still at uni when Sinclair was made to leave – maybe he'll be able to tell me more about what it was like, the rumours and everything else. Anna was only able to give me the teacher's side of things. As a student, there might have been more rumours going around.'

'True, I guess he might know a bit more.'

'Did anyone ever approach you? For an interview, I mean?'

'Oh, like that book? I was approached by a couple of outlets, but I always said no. I assumed that's what you would have wanted me to do. And, I don't know, it never felt right, raking over Izzy's memory like that.'

'Right. Of course.' Seeing Sinclair quoted in that book at King's Cross had taken Chelsea by surprise, but not because she didn't know about the interest in her and her case. She'd been approached plenty of times since going to prison, by journalists writing one-off pieces for newspapers or magazines, documentary filmmakers and later, podcasters, and always, always refused. She knows her mum had been approached too, and had also steadfastly turned them away. But seeing Sinclair's words in the pages of that book had made her wonder if they hadn't chosen the wrong route. If someone had been there, answering questions in her favour, would the public perception of her changed at all? And is it all too late now?

'Chels, are you there? What do you want me to do about Joe?'

'Oh, yeah, maybe it could be useful to talk to him.'

Ayesha is quiet at the other end of the phone until finally she says, 'Okay. I'll DM him your phone number. But I'm still not sure this is the right idea.'

Chelsea knows she shouldn't, but after talking to Ayesha, she gets Nikki's ancient laptop and signs in to Facebook again. Talking about Sinclair and Joe's out-of-the-blue Instagram message has got her thinking about getting in touch with Sinclair again in order to ask him more about the circumstances around his leaving Birmingham University. It just doesn't seem fair, that he's been able to elude all these questions for so long, while she's been made to be guilty for something she didn't even do. Even if Jamie didn't kill Izzy, he still caused a lot of trouble and trauma by the sound of it, and how has he been punished? With another nice, safe job and a new life by the sea. When she signs in, though, she is surprised to see how many notifications she has, that tiny red flag in the top right corner causing her heart to hammer at her chest. Her profile is private, but that doesn't stop people from messaging her, thinking they have every right to call her any name they want because she's been in the news. Swallowing, she clicks on the notifications icon and sees that she's correct in her assumptions; it's a barrage of swear words and name-calling, some going as far as to say she should be dead herself. She takes a deep breath, lets it out, and navigates the cursor to the search box, to look up Sinclair again. But then she sees something that stops her. In amongst these virtual insults, there's one message that looks different. Instead of an insult, it's a warning, written in stark capital letters: WHATEVER IT IS YOU THINK YOU'RE DOING, STOP.

She clicks on the profile of the sender, but not only are they, of course, set to private, but it appears to be a burner account. The name is Jane Smith, as innocuous and anonymous as you can get, and doesn't even have any friends. Who is this? It feels so different from the other messages, the stream of insults and online cruelty, that a shiver runs right through her. This seems less like someone throwing stones for the sake of it, for the small thrill it might provide them with after a long day, and more like someone keeping tabs. More like someone who might actually know her. She peers at the timestamp of when it was sent and sees it was the day after the *Daily Mail* article with the photo of her and Camille at the cemetery was posted online. Could this be Sinclair, trying to keep her away? If the message was sent the day after the article, then that means she'd already been to seen Jamie in Aberystwyth. What if he'd decided he hadn't quite done enough to scare her away? What if he was trying, desperately, to get her off the scent? If that's the case, and it is Sinclair, then all he's done is ignite Chelsea's suspicions. Because why try to scare her off if there's nothing for him to be afraid of?

* * *

Joe calls her the next day, but she misses it, and has to call back during her lunch break at the vet surgery. Nikki has packed her a homemade sandwich, and although the day is cold, it's also bright and blustery, so she takes it outside, clouds skimming the light blue sky, the autumn-weakened sun doing its best to warm her skin as she sits on a wooden bench around the back of the surgery building. Joe picks up on the third ring.

'Chelsea,' he says, sounding pleasantly surprised, and his voice takes her almost instantly back, decades falling away as he says, 'I'm so glad you called back.'

'Hi, Joe.'

'Wow, it's amazing to hear your voice. And a bit weird, to be honest. You sound exactly the same.'

'You too.'

'I really wasn't sure Ayesha was going to put me in touch with you when I messaged her, but I'm glad she did.' Chelsea shivers – she pulled on her coat as she walked out of the surgery, but she's only wearing the required scrubs underneath, so despite the sunshine, she can feel the chill. She's so tired she feels practically hungover. She'd been unable to sleep last night, her brain running around in circles, unable to slow down enough to rest, constantly thinking about Sinclair and that message. After all that, she wasn't so sure about talking to Joe, but he called her, so now she's here, calling him back, hoping the cold air will help keep her awake for the rest of the afternoon. 'I want to ask you how you've been, but that seems . . . redundant,' Joe continues.

Chelsea lets out a huff of laughter, 'Maybe a little. I can ask how you've been, though.'

'Well,' Joe says with a little laugh, 'where to start? I'm a lawyer now, can you believe that?'

'Really?'

'Yeah, did a conversion course after uni. Wills and

estate planning mostly. It's pretty boring, but it can get exciting at times.'

'Wow, that's – and Ayesha tells me you're married.'

'Oh,' Joe says, with a trace of surprise.

'Yeah, I think she had a peruse of your Instagram.'

'Ha, right. Well, I can hardly blame her, I did the same to her. You're not tempted to join?'

'I don't think so,' Chelsea says. She can't think of anything worse, in fact, especially after last night, but she doesn't feel the need to tell Joe that.

'Listen, Chelsea, I don't have loads of time – I'm meeting a client in a minute – but I just wanted to say how sorry I am. I'm sorry I didn't stay in touch at all. It's no excuse, but I don't know, life just really got in the way. And then I saw all this stuff in the news this week, and I just – I realized this will never go away for you. You're still living it.'

Somewhere far off, a crow squawks, and Chelsea looks up, trying to catch sight of it, surprised when she notices, high above her, not the crow in question but a wheeling bird of prey, wings open to the wind, surfing the cold November air. 'Right,' she says finally, 'I am.'

'Yeah, so I know this probably means very little to you, but I just wanted to reach out. I can't imagine what the last few years have been like for you.'

Chelsea bristles at his condensing of fifteen whole years to just 'a few', but says nothing; it's not worth it. Maybe it does only feel like a 'few' to Joe, who has been able to go on and live a full life, who doesn't have to pick up the pieces and start again aged thirty-six, who isn't walking through life as though he's spent a decade at sea and he's still trying to find his land-legs. 'Thanks, Joe,' she says shortly. 'Actually I did want to ask you something. It's about Jamie Sinclair, do you remember him?'

'Our lecturer? Sure.'

'Do you remember him getting fired from the department? This would have been after Izzy died.'

Joe is quiet for a beat before he says, 'Yeah, yeah, I do. God, I'd forgotten all about that, but yeah, he left that year.'

'You mean 2007?'

'No, sorry, I meant that academic year. So, he left in 2008, but didn't come back that September.'

'Right. But do you remember why?'

'I can't remember if we ever knew the so-called official reason, but there were definitely rumours about something to do with a student. It wasn't anyone we knew, though. I think it was a master's student, maybe final year. Older than us.'

'So it wasn't Izzy?'

'Izzy? No. No . . . she was dead by then, Chelsea.'

'No, I know, but there weren't any rumours that they'd been involved at all?'

'Oh, actually. Maybe, yes. But it was more like people were just stirring the pot at that point. I don't know if it stemmed from anything . . . real.'

'But you remember they had a thing, right?'

'Did they?' Chelsea hears the change in Joe's voice, the words stiffened with harder edges.

'Yeah, you must remember her crush on him, she talked about it all the time.'

'But nothing ever *happened*.'

'I always thought it might've done, and she just didn't

282

want me to know. She never mentioned anything to you, then?'

'No. Izzy fancying him is a bit different from them being in a relationship, Chelsea.'

'Yeah, but after the rumours surfaced, you really never thought it might've been a possibility?'

'Um,' there's a waver in Joe's voice that Chelsea wants to interrogate, but almost immediately, he says, 'shit, sorry, this meeting's about to start,' and says his goodbyes.

Even as he hangs up on her, Chelsea can hear Kate, her parole officer, telling her to stop living in the past and focus on the future, but she's glad she called Joe, because even though he wasn't able to give her anything concrete, he did give something away; he didn't want Chelsea to think he remembered Izzy's feelings for Sinclair. Why perform such a charade for her? Was he protecting Sinclair? That didn't seem likely, but was it possible he still knew more than he was letting on? She looks towards the sky again; the wind has picked up, raising the hair at the back of her neck. The bird of prey is nowhere to be seen now, perhaps diving down for an innocent field mouse or in the woods, perched on a branch. She checks her phone again – break time's over – and heads back towards the vet surgery. As she approaches the entrance, a woman is getting out of her car and so Chelsea holds the front door open for her, the woman's cairn terrier leading the way, pulling against its lead. Chelsea crouches down, keeping the door open with her back, to give the dog a ruffle, but it's quickly tugged away by its owner, and as she stands and meets the owner's narrowed eye, sees her clamped together mouth, her squared off shoulders, she realizes why.

'Welcome,' Chelsea says, as breezily as possible, but the woman walks silently and stiffly past her, as if she wasn't there at all. Chelsea tries to ignore the burn of shame but it lands anyway, much to her chagrin. Why should she have to feel this sting of guilt when it's second-hand? When, really, it belongs to someone else? She heads to the reception desk, ignoring the woman, and logs back into the surgery's computer. There's nothing for her to do though, so she pulls her phone out of her pocket and sees she has a new message. From Joe, perhaps? But no, it's a number she doesn't recognize, and just like last night, the message is written in stark capital letters: BACK OFF OR YOU'LL BE BACK IN PRISON.

Her eyes flick up involuntarily, and the woman and her dog are staring right at her, the woman's eyes cold and assessing, as if she knows exactly what the message says. But it can't be her, of course it's not; that's just silly. This is someone who knows who she is, who knows what she's doing. Who knows this phone number, which she's only had for a month. And if that's the case, that means it can only be Camille, Nikki, Ayesha, Joe or Ajala. And surely, *surely*, it's not any of them, is it?

Detective Inspector Rob Bailey: What was it Chelsea had said to Izzy, Charlie?

[pause]

Charlie?

Charles Dunwoody: I'm sorry, I'm trying to remember. It's a bit embarrassing, but honestly I was so drunk, it's all a bit of a blur. I just remember speaking to her – I can't remember if I called her or she called me, to be honest – and she was very upset. Crying, the whole thing.

RB: About Chelsea?

CD: I think so. Things had been a bit ... up and down with them.

Detective Constable Natalie Ajala: How so?

CD: Well, Chelsea could be a little ... clingy. Needy.

NA: And that upset Izzy? She was crying over Chelsea being clingy?

CD: No, God, sorry, I'm not explaining this very well. She was jealous. Chelsea was very jealous. And then, she'd ... I don't know, lash out?

NA: At Izzy?

CD: Well, Izzy hadn't been spending much time with her, of course. Not recently, what with our dad dying. And Chelsea was constantly sort of checking in, imposing. I think she thought she was almost part of the family, and that got on Izzy's nerves, so that set her off. I don't want to imply that my sister was some sort of saint or anything, she could … give as good as she got, as they say.

RB: So, you think the girls had a fight on Saturday night?

CD: Yes.

NA: And that's why Izzy would've left the party early? The club?

CD: I think so … yes. There was also something going on with some Joe person.

NA: Joe?

RB: Do you have a last name for this Joe?

CD: God, I don't, sorry. I met him once. Well, more than more once, I suppose, technically, as he was staying at the place in Cornwall at Easter, but I can't for the life of me remember a last name. I can barely remember what he looks like, to be honest – one of those faces, you know? That look like everyone.

RB: Right.

NA: Can you remember how Izzy and Chelsea knew him? Was he in their halls last year, or something?

CD: No, I think they met him on their course. History.

NA: Great, thanks, that might narrow it down a bit. What was the issue with him, Charlie? Had he had a fight with either Chelsea or Izzy?

CD: Well, as far as I could tell – and I really wasn't in on any secrets here – but as far as I could tell, Chelsea and Joe had been an item but broke up over the summer, and I think, I *think* Izzy may now have been seeing him. And obviously that would have upset Chelsea somewhat.

RB: Right. So, they could have been arguing over this Joe character on Saturday night?

CD: I do believe that could have been part of it, yes. A big part of it.

[pause]

RB: Okay. So, Izzy was seeing Joe, we think?

CD: I believe so, yes.

RB: And Chelsea found out about this on Saturday?

CD: Ah, well, I don't know about the whens and hows of all that. But quite possibly, yes.

NA: Is that what Izzy said she was upset about when you spoke to her?

CD: Yes, that's what had made her so upset. Obviously there was alcohol involved, and I think our meeting about our father's will had also had an effect, but it was Chelsea she was focused on when we spoke that last time.

NA: Wouldn't Chelsea have more cause to be upset over this, though?

CD: Well, exactly.

RB: Ah.

NA: Have you ever witnessed Chelsea and Izzy having a fight before?

CD: A physical fight?

NA: I meant more of an argument, but if you've witnessed anything physical obviously that would be relevant.

CD: No, no, I've never seen anything escalate to anything physical.

RB: Escalate? So, you have seen or heard them fighting or arguing before?

[pause]

CD: It's a bit more ... it's not as simple as that. It's a bit more complex.

RB: How do you mean?

CD: I don't think I'd go as far as to say I'd seen or overheard an argument, per se. But there was always something rather controlling about Chelsea. It's the clinginess, like I say. She didn't want anyone else to have Izzy's attention, or at least not as much of it as she had. She spent so much time with us, the family, it was a bit weird, I thought. Doesn't she have her own family she wants to spend Easter with?

NA: We were under the impression Chelsea came to stay after the Easter bank holiday.

CD: Oh, maybe, I can't remember exactly. Terrible with dates. She was there though. And again in the summer. She even stayed after Dad was admitted to the hospital. It was all a bit grim, really. Creepy. Let us deal with everything as a family, you know? I don't know, that's my opinion, I suppose. Others may have felt differently.

NA: Weren't Ayesha and Hannah there in the summer too?

[short pause]

CD: Yes, you're right, they were there. I don't know, I just didn't get the same feeling from the two of them. Chelsea was the ring leader.

RB: Was this Joe there too?

CD: No, no. Just the girls.

NA: Did Izzy confide in you at all, about Joe?

CD: We spoke about him on Friday.

RB: This Friday?

CD: Yes. That's how I know that they'd started seeing each other.

RB: And do you know if they saw each other on Saturday at all? Izzy and Joe?

CD: I don't know that, no, I'm sorry.

[pause]

But I do know he wrote her a letter.

RB: A letter?

CD: Yes, she said he'd written her a letter. I haven't seen it, but I assume it's here in Birmingham, at their house, somewhere. She didn't have it with her on Friday.

Exam season is upon them before they know it, and as long, and arduous, and never-ending as it feels, it also goes by in a blink of an eye, the days of cramming in the library, late nights poring over books they should've read months previously, testing each other from lined notecards suddenly over, and summer, suddenly, upon them too. Chelsea has felt a distance form between her and Izzy; just when she thought the other girl would pull closer, she has instead, drawn away. Maybe she feels more like a third wheel, now that Chelsea and Joe are together, but really, nothing has changed between the three of them when they're all together, at least not to Chelsea's mind. This distance is hard to determine from the outside – they all still do everything together, after all – and sometimes, Chelsea wonders if it's all in her head. But then, on a lazy, sunny afternoon, all their essays handed in, and only one last exam to go, Hannah plops down next to Ayesha and Chelsea on the grass in the main quad, a vanilla Mini Milk in hand, and says, 'God, I can't wait for Mallorca.'

'Mallorca?' Ayesha says, looking over at her.

'Yeah. Izzy's house. Mallorca.' She licks the side of her Mini Milk.

Ayesha turns her gaze slowly to meet Chelsea's, peering over her sunglasses, 'Am I missing something here, are we all going to Mallorca?'

'Aren't we? Oh my God, I thought she'd invited us all,' Hannah says, red creeping up from the base of her throat, all the way up her neck, until finally it reaches her cheeks.

'Nope,' Chelsea says, 'just you, Han.'

'No, that can't be right. She'd never invite me and not you, Chelsea.'

'Thanks,' Ayesha says drily.

'No, I don't mean ... oh, you know what I mean. They're just so close, she'd never leave Chelsea out of something.'

'Wouldn't she?' Ayesha asks, clearly thinking of Izzy's Christmas party.

Chelsea rolls her eyes at her, but she's glad she's wearing sunglasses as she blinks down at the green, green grass, and starts to not-so-idly pull at it with her fists. 'There must be some mistake,' Hannah says, shaking her head in absolute disbelief that Izzy would do something like this, while also looking, if Chelsea's not mistaken, a tiny bit pleased with herself. Or, maybe, simply relieved, that she's not the one to have been left out. 'There's no way you're not invited.'

'Who's not invited where?' It's Izzy, hovering above them, holding an iced coffee and chewing at the straw. She sits next to Hannah, folding her legs neatly to one side.

'To your house in Mallorca,' Ayesha says bluntly.

'What?' Izzy says. 'Oh, but you guys are going Interrailing, aren't you? That's what I thought.'

'I thought *we* were going Interrailing,' Ayesha says, making a circular motion with her hand that takes in all four of them.

'Oh, no,' Izzy says, 'no, I'm planning on spending the whole summer at Mirador. I've already booked my flights.' She says this as though it were a known fact, as if she's already apprised them all of her plans, even though it is very much news to Chelsea.

'What about you, Han?' Chelsea asks, turning her attention from Izzy. 'You don't wanna come Interrailing?'

'Um, well,' Hannah says, the blush on her cheeks deepening even further, 'I've already said yes to Iz.'

'Of course you have,' Ayesha says.

'Guys, this is stupid,' Izzy says with a clap of her hands. 'Why don't you join us, while Han's out there? You can get the ferry from Barcelona or something. That would be fun, right? Then we all get to do exactly what we want for the summer.'

Chelsea feels rather than sees all three of their gazes land on her. She rips up another handful of grass and lets the stems fall through her fingers, before meeting Ayesha's eyes and shrugging, 'Sure, why not? We wanted to go to Barcelona anyway, right?'

'Yeah. Right. Sounds fun, Iz,' Ayesha says and although this receives grins from both Izzy and Hannah, Chelsea isn't sure Ayesha sounds all that convinced.

'Oh, we'll have *so* much fun,' Izzy promises. 'Mirador is just like . . . heaven. It'll blow your minds.'

* * *

The next morning, Chelsea and Izzy are walking to their final exam. It's early, before the heat has had a chance to settle over the day, a gauzy haze of summer light filtering through the trees of the vale as Izzy idly eats a banana – her only concession towards breakfast, claiming to be too nervous to eat anything more substantial.

'Are you pissed off at me?' she asks, seemingly out of nowhere, although Chelsea had been able to feel her build up to this question for quite some time.

'No. I'm nervous.'

'Me too, but we're almost done. It's almost over. If Han was here, she'd probably say how sad it is. Last exam, last walk to campus this year.'

'Yeah, probably.'

'Where's Joe?'

'He's already there. He probably slept there.'

'Such an overachiever.'

'Maybe.'

'You *are* mad at me. Is it because I invited Hannah before I invited you? To Mirador?'

Chelsea stops herself from rolling her eyes at the word 'Mirador'. Why can't she just say 'Mallorca' like a normal person? She knows Izzy's family has several houses, but do they have to have such pretentious names? 'I'm not mad about that,' she says. 'It's your house, you can invite whoever you want. Whenever you want.'

'It's not because I didn't want you and Ayesha to come too. Hannah had just been talking to me about how nervous she was about Interrailing, so I thought this was a good way around that.'

'What?'

'Yeah, I don't know if you noticed this, Chelsea, but Han's a bit of a scaredy cat,' Izzy says with raised eyebrows.

Chelsea laughs, feels a knot untie in her stomach, across her shoulders, 'Yeah, no kidding. She was really worried about Interrailing?'

'Not just that, but she's worried about you guys doing it. She's convinced you're gonna get raped and murdered.'

'Don't say that.'

'I didn't! Her words.'

'Jesus. Why didn't she just tell us?'

Izzy shrugs, 'I guess she thought you and Ayesha wouldn't understand.'

'Hmm. So, why don't you want to come? You can't be scared.'

'No, duh, obviously not. I'm just lazy, like staying in one place. I think, once you see it, you'll understand.'

'Okay, okay.'

'So, you'll definitely come?'

'Yeah, of course.'

'Are you gonna stay with Joe?' Izzy asks, and this time, this seemingly out-of-nowhere question really does come from nowhere for Chelsea.

'Stay where?'

'Stay together, Chels, come on, keep up.'

'Um, yeah,' she says slowly, 'why? Why'd you ask?'

'I don't know . . . summer, travel . . . you guys haven't been together all that long. He's not going with you, is he?'

'No, Ayesha would never allow that.' Chelsea laughs.

'Well, won't that be hard? Being away from each other?'

'Sure, but we can keep in touch.'

'What, by sending long, loving emails? Oh, I bet you'll be great at that, Chels.'

Chelsea looks at Izzy out of the corner of her eye,

almost stops walking. She's too hot in what she's wearing and her feet are sweating in her Converse. Why didn't she just wear flip flops? 'What's that supposed to mean?'

Izzy shrugs, 'Just that you don't really seem like the love letter type.'

'Well, they won't be *love letters*.'

'Exactly. Look, all I'm saying is, aren't you a bit worried? It's still pretty new between the two of you, and now you're jetting off for over a month.'

'I think we'll be fine,' Chelsea says, even though Izzy has made some good points. She and Ayesha have been planning this trip for weeks now, and even though she's talked about it constantly, Joe hasn't asked her one question about it. She knows he's had a lot on his mind – not just their exams, but his dad's condition has got steadily worse, and he's been torn between revision and home, never knowing where to put his efforts. But is it possible he doesn't want her to go? Maybe even thinks she shouldn't go? It really feels too soon in their relationship for Chelsea to be changing her plans, but she does care about him.

'Okay, if you're sure,' Izzy says, looking at her over the top of her sunglasses, 'but just remember, if you guys do break up then next year's gonna be super awkward.'

'Izzy, stop,' Chelsea says with a short laugh, 'we're fine. And it wouldn't have to be awkward. It's a big class.'

'The seminars aren't big. And I was thinking more about me.'

'Of course you were.'

'Would you be mad if I stayed friends with him? If you broke up?'

'Would I be hypothetically mad at you if you hypothetically stayed friends with a guy I'd hypothetically broken up with?'

'That word has lost all meaning, I hope you realize that.'

'We'd be fine, Iz. We'd all be fine.'

As they approach the Aston Webb building, Chelsea spots Joe slouched on the top steps, leaning over a folder that's resting in his lap, the red brick and domed roof rising up behind him. 'Why's he taking this so seriously?' Izzy asks. 'He knows first year marks don't count, right?'

Chelsea doesn't answer. She knows Izzy is technically correct, and that the marks they get on these exams will have no bearing on the final grade they achieve at university, but her attitude grates on her. Is it really so impossible for her to take anything seriously? Suddenly, she is glad Izzy's not joining her and Ayesha on their month-long Interrail trip, that they'll only spend a week – if that – at the oh-so-magical Mirador. She realizes, quite by surprise, that she's ready for a break from Izzy. She gives the other girl a sidelong glance, relieved to see that Izzy clearly has no idea what she's thinking, as Izzy lets out a tinkling laugh and trips up the steps headed straight for Joe, flipping his folder up towards him as his face turns red in surprise and embarrassment. Chelsea hears Joe mutter 'What the fuck' as he glares up at Izzy, his eyes hard with annoyance.

'Take it easy, Joseph. Jesus,' Izzy says with a roll of her eyes, 'we all know you're gonna be top of the class anyway.'

'Yeah, because I actually work, Iz. Revise, study, ever heard of it?'

'Yeah, but I thought it was just a nasty rumour.'

'Izzy . . .'

'Chill *out*, Jesus. We're almost done, breathe a little.'

'Fine,' Joe says, taking a theatrically deep breath in and turning to Chelsea, 'hey.'

'Hi.' They share a kiss, just as the doors to the building open, and Izzy turns to give them both a wounded look before sauntering in, telling Chelsea that she's just going to pop to the loo. 'Just ignore her,' Chelsea says to Joe, watching Izzy's back disappear around a corridor, 'she's right after all; it's all over in a couple of hours.'

'Yeah,' Joe says, but he doesn't look any more convinced.

'You okay?'

'I have to go home right after this, Chels.'

'Oh, shit.'

Joe swallows and nods, everything about him tense and held in, 'I think this is it. I almost sacked off the exam completely, but Mum told me not to.'

'Maybe you should've done? It's not like this actually matters. I'm sure the department would just give you the pass anyway.'

Joe's face is pained, 'Don't say that, it just makes me feel worse.'

'Sorry,' Chelsea breathes. She wants to comfort him, to be able to help, but she has no idea what to say or do, and just as she's about to reach for him, the doors to the exam hall swing open and the crowd of waiting students begins to move. Their final exam is about to begin.

Chelsea and Nikki are just getting back from work when Ajala calls, Chelsea's phone vibrating violently as they walk through the door.

'I'll pop the kettle on,' Nikki says, shucking off her boots in the tiny entryway and heading into the kitchen, followed closely by the two dogs, who spend every work day at the surgery, mostly tucked up behind the reception desk, sleeping at Chelsea's feet.

Chelsea nods and answers the call as she heads up the stairs to her room, 'Hi, Natalie.'

'Hi, how're you doing?'

'Okay.'

It's now a week since Chelsea's visit to London and her wild pursuit of Sinclair through the West Midlands and Wales. The Facebook message and text message have shaken her up, of course, but she does feel calm here, safe. Can see why Nikki was so drawn to this place, loves the act of coming home at the end of every day, the comfort of Shandy and Guinness, how fresh the air is, how the cold slices through you, reminding you you're alive. But that doesn't mean she's forgotten about Sinclair or that message. She'd texted Ajala, telling her about the Facebook message and her suspicions, asking her to help her out with trying to find out a little more about her former lecturer, and she's hoping, now, she might finally get some useful information from her. Sinclair can't have sent the text though, and that still weighs on her, the possibility that someone she knows and even trusts, is doing this to her. She hasn't mention the text to Ajala, because, although it wouldn't make much sense for her to have sent it, she is still on Chelsea's list of suspects.

'So, I've got the transcripts of our interviews, and like I told you, he did have an alibi for that night. I always thought he was worth pursuing, but after his alibi was confirmed, it just seemed like a dead end. We even checked ANPR for that night and his car wasn't on the road, so that seemed to corroborate what he and his wife said.'

'His wife.'

'Yes, his wife. Or his former wife, to be precise, and to whom I have just spoken. Do you want to know what she said?'

'Of course.'

'Well, I didn't remember this, but after not being able to find the transcript from her interview, I'd got suspicious, and it turns out her interview was conducted by Bailey alone. I wasn't there. But she remembers Bailey interviewing her at the time, and she said she told him that she couldn't be one hundred percent sure Jamie didn't leave the house that night.'

'Wait, you weren't at the interview too?'

'No.'

'Is that unusual?'

'Pretty unusual, yes.'

'And why wasn't she sure about whether or not Jamie left the house? What was it that made her think he might've been gone?'

'She was a light sleeper at the time, she said. Their daughter wasn't yet two, and not a great sleeper, so Michelle – that's her name – didn't sleep well either, as she was constantly listening out for her, I guess. And she thinks she heard Jamie get up and out of bed at one point, but she wasn't ever sure how long he was gone for, or if he was really gone at all. He might just have been getting up to go to the loo or check on the kid, she wasn't properly awake, so she doesn't know.'

'But the ANPR? You know he didn't take his car out that night?'

'Right, but she confirmed she also had a car.'

'And he might've used that.'

'Exactly. Especially if he was leaving to do something clandestine, or potentially even criminal.'

'Is there any way you could check for her licence plate number?'

'Nope, sadly not. All that footage and data will be long gone.'

'Shit. Did you ask her about anything else? About whether or not she thought he might have been involved with Izzy?'

'So, she said she'd had her suspicions at the time, that he was having an affair. And later, when he was asked to leave Birmingham University and she found out about the students, she wondered about Izzy, because of all the coverage her murder had got.'

'So, it had crossed her mind that he could've been involved with Izzy's death?'

'She said yes, but obviously not enough to alert anyone at the time, so it's hard to tell how serious she was.'

'Well, I was already on trial by then. She probably assumed the police had actually done their job.'

Ajala is silent and then Chelsea hears her draw in a deep breath. 'Right.'

'I didn't mean that to sound so . . . look, I am grateful for you looking into this, I know you don't need to.'

'No, I do. For my own peace of mind as much as anything. This case . . . it's always loomed over me. I did try, you know, to keep all avenues open during the investigation, but once certain things came to light . . .'

'You mean the table lamp.'

'The lamp, yes. But also the missing mobile phone –'

'You really never thought it was strange, that I'd supposedly only bothered to walk down the road to get rid of the murder weapon in a neighbour's bin, but had managed to bury Izzy's phone so thoroughly it still hasn't been found?' The words come out in a rush, so long held in and bitten back, but now allowed to pull free. Chelsea can feel her anger and frustration rising like a tide through her body, all of it directed at Ajala, who is now trying to help her.

Ajala sighs, 'Of course I thought it was strange.'

'And my fingerprints, on the lamp – it was a lamp from our living room, of course it had my fingerprints all over it.'

'I know that, Chelsea.'

'Do you? Because it didn't seem like anyone considered that at the time.'

'I know, I kept pressing, I really did, but there were just certain things that were beyond my control. I was only a DC at the time, Bailey and I didn't really get on, it was a pretty tough place to work. For me, at least.'

302

Chelsea takes a deep breath, tries to listen what Ajala is saying rather than give in to her anger. 'The interview Bailey did with Sinclair's wife . . . you didn't know about it?'

'I knew he'd confirmed Sinclair's alibi, but if I'd been there, and knew what she said about not being able to be sure if he was in bed the whole night, I definitely would have pressed even harder to ensure Sinclair was investigated more intensively.'

'So, why wasn't he?'

'One answer is because we weren't ever able to place him at the scene.'

'And I was right there.'

'Right, the time you said you got home, it coincided closely enough with Izzy's time of death, whereas, as far as we were aware, Sinclair was over in King's Heath the entire night, nowhere near Izzy or Tiverton Road.'

'But the affair, or her suspicions about Jamie being involved with someone else, did she mention that to Bailey at the time? Did you ask her?'

'Yes, and she thinks she would have done. Although . . .'

'What?'

'Well, she had a very clear memory of the interview, was very clear about the fact that she told Bailey she couldn't be sure Jamie had been at home all night, but when I asked about whether or not she'd mentioned her suspicions to Bailey, she wasn't *as* clear. She said she thought she had, but she couldn't be sure. That makes me think she didn't but wishes she had done, so was dissembling with me a bit. Trying to make herself feel better, maybe.'

Chelsea takes all this in. She hasn't sat down since entering her room, instead has paced up and down, from the doorway to the window and back again, occasionally looking out at the thick, black night, the only light coming from the stars dancing above them. A few nights ago, Nikki had dragged her outside into the frozen air after dinner, just to show her the Milky Way, the whole galaxy showing off, just for them. 'Have you mentioned this to Camille?' Chelsea asks.

'I have, but as you know, she's asked me to concentrate my attentions on Charlie.'

'What was it, though, that caused her to become suspicious of Charlie? I know they had a ... difficult relationship, before Izzy died, but it seemed her death had brought them closer together.'

'I think it did, initially. They were both grieving the same two people at the same time, and Camille told me that this seemed to soften Charlie a bit, especially towards her.'

'So, then what? Did he do something recently to annoy her, and she got in touch with you? I just don't get it. What could have caused such a change in her thinking?'

'All she told me, was that she found something that made her think Charlie might have been more involved than she or anyone else realized, and this made her reach out to me.'

'Found something?' Chelsea asks. 'Do you have any idea what?'

'She hasn't told me.'

'You're kidding me. And you're okay with that? That just seems ridiculous, like asking you to do a job with your hands tied behind your back. Why can't she tell you?'

'I'm not sure. I think she wants to have all her ducks in a row first. As much as she has her suspicions, he's still her stepson, after all.' That, at least, sounds like Camille. Because she's not someone whose curiosity would get the better of her, and send her off down a million rabbit holes. She's someone who would see or hear something new, ruminate on it for weeks or possibly months, and then slowly and steadily build her case. Which is exactly what Chelsea thinks she is doing, only she and Ajala are now only working with half the story. They've come in at the middle, when what they really need is the inciting incident.

'Well, thanks for telling me about Sinclair at least. Is there anything we can actually do with this information?'

'*We* shouldn't do anything, Chelsea,' Ajala says with a sharp laugh.

'What about the Facebook message? Don't you think there's a chance it's Sinclair? Is there any way for us to find out?'

'I don't know about that. If you want my advice, really, it's to carry on ignoring it as you have been. Your only job right now, is to stay right where you are, doing what you're doing. You can leave this to me.'

But Chelsea isn't so sure about that. She appreciates Ajala sharing all this information with her and finally taking her suspicions seriously, but she clearly remembers what happened last time she left the investigating to the professionals.

'So, I have good news and I have bad news,' Izzy says. She's picked them up from the ferry port in a bright yellow, open-top Jeep, and now she's having to shout over the sound of the wind as she drives back to Mirador. Her hair is flying in her face, streaming back towards where Chelsea sits amid their backpacks, crowded into the surprisingly small quarters of this four-by-four. When they'd spotted her, trailing off the ferry, legs tired, heads aching, Chelsea's stomach still roiling from the movement of the boat, Ayesha had taken one look at the car and muttered, 'Jesus Christ.'

'What's the good news?' shouts Ayesha now.

'We went to the vineyard yesterday and there's now enough cava at the house to fill the swimming pool. Two swimming pools. The bad news is that we're sharing said cava – and the swimming pool for that matter – with my dear brother and Florence.' She turns back in her seat to make a sad face at Chelsea, but all Chelsea can see is her own reflection in Izzy's mirrored aviators.

'Oh, that's not so bad,' Ayesha says. 'We've been staying in *dorms*, Iz. I'm assuming there's enough space for all of us at this palace of yours?'

'Oh yeah, that's not the problem. Just that Charlie can be a bit of a dick sometimes.'

'And this vineyard you just mentioned . . .' Chelsea says, 'is this a family vineyard?'

'Yeah, we own it.'

'Right. Wow.'

'We can go and visit it while you're here if you're interested?'

'Yeah, cool, sounds amazing.'

'What else d'you guys wanna do while you're here?'

'God, I'm so tired, I could sleep for about a week,' Ayesha says.

'Well, that's no fun,' Izzy pouts.

'Sorry, Iz, we've just been moving about so much, we're exhausted. Ten countries in four weeks, can you believe it?' Chelsea says.

'Very impressive. Especially considering the most I've done is walk from bed, to pool, to beach, to bar.'

'Has Han arrived?' Ayesha asks.

'Yeah, she's been here just over a week already. She would've come with me, but we didn't think we'd fit in the Jeep with all your stuff.'

The drive to Mirador from Alcúdia isn't all that long, but the roads are steeper and more winding than Chelsea could have imagined. The road seems to play tricks on them, curling and unfurling like a gymnast's ribbon, the pristine turquoise of the sea on one side, sheer rock face on the other. The view is mesmerizing, but Chelsea almost can't look at it, her stomach plummeting every time the car makes a turn and the drop down to the ocean is laid bare. Izzy seems to know where she's going, but she's not the steadiest of drivers, and more than once Chelsea has the feeling that the car might simply keep on going, on, on, on and right down over a precipice, diving into the blue of the Mediterranean. But it doesn't happen and eventually, they reach a set of iron gates that open automatically – if Izzy has had to press something to make them do this, Chelsea has completely missed it – and a tiny, inconspicuous sign just off to the side that announces this as 'MIRADOR'. From here, the road is unmetalled, and suddenly the Jeep makes sense as Chelsea, Ayesha and all their luggage bump up and down over the dirt. With trees thick on both sides, they are suddenly lurched into the gloom and shade of the woods, the scent of pine mingling with the hot earth, and just for a second, Chelsea wonders where the hell they're going. This wasn't what she was expecting, but then all she'd really been able to imagine was something approximating a vast, and vastly expensive, hotel, and Mirador apparently isn't that.

She needn't have worried though, because soon they are leaving the woods behind and driving into a painting. Or at least it feels like it because there, right in front of them, is a perfect and perfectly private cove. Cradled by sandy cliffs, the water is even bluer and clearer than the sea they'd marvelled at from the road. The view is so overwhelming that at first, Chelsea doesn't even see the house, until Izzy pulls up to a stop, hops out and says, 'We have to walk this bit, I'm afraid. Good thing you've got rucksacks; you wouldn't believe what a nightmare it can be with a wheelie bag.' She sets off, Chelsea and Ayesha hauling their bags on to their backs once again, the grit and gravel of the dirt road getting into the footbed of Chelsea's sandals. She stops to take one off and shake it out, leaning against the hot metal of the car for a second, and then has to jog a little to catch up, breathless and suddenly annoyed in the burning heat of the sun. Ayesha is telling Izzy how starving they are – all they had to eat on the ferry was stale pastries – but then they turn a corner and Ayesha falls silent, struck dumb by the sight of the house. It seems to be born from the rockface, precarious and precipitously positioned on the side of the earth, shimmering over the clear water of the cove, presiding over it all in secretive, unassuming glamour. Chelsea never could've imagined this, not in her wildest dreams. The closest she can come to describing it – she's already drafting the email to her mum in her head – is something from a James Bond film, but it's not quite bombastic enough for that. The more she looks, the more she realizes there is to take in; different terraces and levels peering out from the cliff's edge, pathways leading to other buildings, hidden in the trees or further along the turning of the cove, gardens of citrus trees, sage, rosemary and lavender, their heady scents mingling with the pine and earth, the marine salt of the sea. No wonder Izzy wanted to spend her whole summer here. It is a world in and of itself.

'Here she is,' Izzy smiles back at them, 'the happiest place on earth.'

She's about to say something else when they all hear an ear-piercing shriek, and suddenly, Hannah is barrelling down the terraced pathway, in an all-white prairie-style skirt and top, bare feet slapping at the golden paving stones.

'You're here,' she calls to them all, 'you're finally here!'

She runs straight for Ayesha, who gives her a fierce, tight hug before gently pushing her away and giving her a once-over. 'Jesus Christ, Han, who knew you could get this tanned? Wait, are those teeny, tiny little braids in your hair?' she says, reaching her hand out to Hannah's blonder-than-ever hair, and giving one of the braids a flick.

Hannah bats her hand away, 'Stop, there are no rules on holiday, everyone knows that.'

Ayesha gives her a sceptical hmm as Hannah hugs Chelsea. 'I'm so glad you guys are here.'

'Yeah, she was really starting to get bored of me.'

'Not true,' Hannah says, with one of her trademark blushes, 'I'm just so excited for all of us to be together. Plus now we might actually stand a chance of beating Charlie and Florence at Trivial Pursuit.'

'Wow, sounds like you guys have been having a really wild time,' Ayesha says drily.

'We've had some fun nights out too!' Hannah promises.

'Honestly, it's a bit of a bitch going anywhere at night here, so I do become a bit of a hermit, it has to be said,' Izzy says.

By now they've reached the villa's front door, which, just as with the iron gates, appears to open completely unbidden, although once they step through into the cool, tiled hallway Chelsea realizes it wasn't magic or mechanics, but a maid or housekeeper. The uniformed woman hovers just inside the door, nodding at each of them as they slide their rucksacks from their backs to leave them slumped on the floor.

'Welcome,' she says to them both in slightly accented English.

Next to her, Chelsea feels Ayesha stiffen in surprise and hopes she is the only one to hear her mutter, '*There's staff?*'

'This is Valencia,' Izzy explains, 'she knows everything there is to know about Mirador, including where you're both sleeping, so you can just leave your bags there and we can go have a drink out on the terrace.'

'Surely we're not leaving that tiny woman to carry our rucksacks up to our rooms?' Ayesha asks as they troop along behind Izzy.

'Don't worry about it, Ayesha,' Hannah says in a low voice, *there are others.*

'Okay, but why did you make that sound like a horror movie?' Chelsea says.

Out on the terrace, the only sound comes from the ever-present crickets and the gentle lap of the waves down at the beach below. They're greeted by an enormously long table, protected from the afternoon sun by a canopy of heavy vines and spindly wisteria. At the end, slouched in a chair reading an English newspaper and with only an espresso cup for company, is an older man with a deep tan and a balding head, wearing a faded orange polo shirt. Ian Dunwoody.

'Ah, hello Piz, your guests have arrived?' he says, putting the newspaper down and staring down the long table at them all.

'Yeah, you remember Chelsea,' Izzy says, pointing towards her, 'and this is Ayesha.'

'Hello, hello. I promise not to cramp your style too much while you're here. And welcome, of course. You're all very welcome.'

There is the briefest of pauses until Chelsea and Ayesha rush to say *hello* and *thank you* and *nice to meet you* at once, and Ian just smiles back at them, the serene, equanimous smile of a very generous host. 'Well, I can see my presence isn't necessary here, but I'm sure we'll all meet again at dinner,' and with a nod, he gets up from his seat and disappears off up another hidden pathway.

'I didn't know your dad was going to be here,' Chelsea says, as his peachy-orange shirt disappears completely.

'Yeah, I mean he's working all the time, but he likes to be here as much as possible in the summer. You'll barely notice him, I promise.'

'That's not what I –'

'Shall I go get us some drinks?'

Everyone answers in the affirmative and Chelsea offers to help, following Izzy back into house. 'Your dad looks like he's lost weight,' she says as they walk into the enormous kitchen.

'I know, I think Mum's had him on a diet or something.'

'Has he been here all summer with you?'

'No, just for the last ten days.'

'And how's it been with Charlie?'

Izzy is reaching for some champagne flutes from a cupboard, and looks back at Chelsea for a second, answering with a shrug, 'It's been fine. He only got here a few days ago and he seems to firmly be in holiday mode. Can you grab a couple of bottles from the fridge?' Chelsea goes to the fridge – it's one of those ones with double doors and a built-in ice maker – and pulls two bottles of cava from the wine shelf. There are dozens more nestled in there, a whole shelf dedicated just to beers, another to tonic and soda water, and, somewhat strangely, a whole shelf full of yoghurt. She picks one up to inspect it, wondering if there's anything special about this Mallorcan yoghurt, as Izzy says, quietly, 'I heard from Joe. Are you okay?'

'Oh,' Chelsea says, putting the yoghurt back in its place as though the packaging has burned her fingers. 'Yes. I'm fine. It wasn't anything dramatic.'

'Still. A break-up by email, that's pretty savage.'

'Mmm.'

'Why didn't you tell me?' Izzy asks, expertly twisting the cork out of one of the cava bottles.

'We've just been moving around so much, I only get to check my email like every few days.'

'He said you seemed totally fine with it.'

Chelsea rolls her eyes, 'I haven't spoken to him in a month, so I don't know how he thinks he can possibly know that.'

'Well, maybe that was his point. You didn't try to keep in touch, so he assumed you didn't care any more.'

'Whose side are you on?'

'I'm friends with both of you, Chelsea. It's a little awkward for me, to be honest. Just like I told you it would be.'

'Look, this really isn't a big deal.'

'To you, maybe. He's pretty upset.'

Izzy has poured out three glasses by now and Chelsea reaches for one, taking a long sip and letting the bubbles fizz and cool in her mouth, slip down her throat. It's dry and reminds her of toasted almonds, delicately sweet and nutty, with just a hint of something a little more bitter. 'That's weird, considering it was his idea.'

'Right, but only after you started pulling away.'

Chelsea sighs, 'I told him I wasn't going to be able to keep in touch all that much . . . and then, suddenly, I'm reading an email that's just like, "Sorry, but I need more from you and I might have feelings for someone else."'

'He has feelings for someone else?'

'Yeah, did he skip past that part with you, then?'

'Mmm, yeah. Do you know who?'

'I don't know, I think someone from his old school maybe. He gave the impression it was someone he already knew,' Chelsea shrugs.

'Right. Shit, sorry, Chels,' Izzy says, pulling her face into a comical grimace, 'I feel bad now.'

'You should,' Chelsea says, poking her in the ribs, 'you bitch.'

Izzy laughs, 'Drink your cava and shut up. Let's just try to have fun.'

'Yeah, let's, thank you. That's what I've been trying to say all along.'

'Yeah, yeah, you're always right. Come on, top these up and help me take them out to everyone,' Izzy says before draining the glass that's in her hand and gathering up the rest.

Later, they all head down to the beach. They've unpacked and settled into their rooms, marvelling at the size of the beds, the en-suite bathrooms, the sea views. Chelsea and Ayesha are sharing, but after weeks of loud dormitories, keeping everything in lockers and living out of their rucksacks, it really does feel like luxury. It *is* luxury. It's almost four by the time they're padding down the carved steps to the beach, flip-flops slapping on the stone, but there's still so much heat in the sun that once they reach the sand Chelsea immediately slips hers off and walks into the water. It's like moving through silk, and as the sand shelf slips away, she dunks her head beneath a wave and pushes off into a breaststroke. Bobbing back up she takes a deep breath, getting air back into her lungs, and smiles at the sound of shouts and shrieks from the beach. No one else has followed her in, and as she treads water, she watches her friends set up their towels and books and drinks. Hannah is shaking her head at something and she laughs to herself, watching her hair catch the Mallorcan sunlight. With its seclusion and privacy, high cliffs and stony path, the beach reminds her of the one in Cornwall and lying there with Izzy in the washed-out April sunshine, making plans for Joe's visit. She hasn't yet responded to Joe's break-up email, which at least in part might be why he reached out to Izzy, trying to find out where she is and what's going on. She wasn't ignoring him on purpose – hadn't in fact, been ignoring him at all – but when she'd read the email, it was the last one she opened before they left the internet café in Marseille and her credit was running out. She'd blinked at the screen, surprised at the tears that were springing to her eyes, as the words swam before her, not making sense. Because he had told her who he's developed feelings for, and that person is Izzy.

Chelsea watches her now as she flips her head upside down to put her hair into a perfect messy bun. She's in a turquoise bikini and, just like her dad, is very, very tanned. She grins at something Ayesha has just said, white teeth flashing in the sun, and then throws her head back in laughter. Has Joe told Izzy too? It's hard to know. Chelsea had been cagey with her in the kitchen, and could feel Izzy's response to that was to be cagey too, but did that mean she knew how Joe really felt about her? Chelsea takes a deep breath, suddenly tired of treading water and staying still, and pushes further out into the sea, swimming until she's past the safe boundary of the cove and in open water. From here, her friends on the beach look like tiny moving dots, their shouts barely audible, blending with the sound of the sea, creating a watery harmony. It's rougher out here though, and as she continues to bob, she realizes that one of them – she can't tell who – is waving their arms at her in alarm. It's probably Hannah, ever the worrier. Chelsea smiles to herself and dives beneath the surface, propelling herself back towards the shoreline. Without goggles the salt stings her eyes, but she keeps them open, because the water is so clear she can see almost to the bottom and she doesn't want to miss out on the sight, doesn't want to miss out on a single thing.

* * *

Dinner is served late – they're in Spain, after all – and by the time they all sit down, Chelsea is starving and more than a little drunk. They had all got ready together in Izzy and Hannah's room and all of them, except Ayesha, have chosen to wear items from Izzy's wardrobe, so Chelsea is in a black prom-style dress that she'd never normally wear and is regretting immensely. The netting material is scratchy, irritating some sunburn she hadn't realized she had, and the puffball skirt is almost impossible to sit down in. It's also the first time the whole household is sitting down together, and the awkwardness of it is palpable, filling the air and mingling with the scent of pine and rosemary and trailing jasmine. As Chelsea pulls her chair in, everyone is silent, waiting for someone to break it. She locks eyes with Ayesha, who is sitting right next to her, and the look her friend gives her is so desperate, she can't help but laugh.

This seems to break the spell, and suddenly almost everyone starts talking at once, just as three people dressed almost identically to Valencia earlier, come out of the house bearing armfuls of dishes. Sitting directly across the table from her, Florence catches Chelsea's eye and smiles, 'Nice to see you again, Chelsea.'

'Um, thanks, yeah, you too. How long have you been here?'

'About a week. Your boyfriend's not with you this time?'

'No,' Chelsea says slowly, watching as one of the waitresses places a dish of patatas bravas and another of padron peppers, their green skins slick with oil and dotted with huge fat salt crystals, in front of her. She reaches for one almost immediately, her stomach giving a low growl that makes Ayesha chuckle. 'No, we actually broke up.'

Florence's eyebrows raise above her glass of white wine, 'Sorry to hear that. You seemed very sweet together.'

'Thanks,' Chelsea says, trying to give her the benefit of the doubt and not to read too much into her condescending tone. It could just be how she talks.

'How long have you and Charlie been together?' Ayesha asks.

'Oh,' Florence says, laughing, 'we're not together. No, no, we're practically brother and sister.'

'Oh, sorry, I just assumed –'

'It's fine, it happens quite a bit. Although Charlie isn't exactly my type, considering I like women.'

'Oh,' Chelsea says, her response eliciting a serene smile from Florence that reminds Chelsea forcibly of Camille. 'So how long have you known each other?'

'Oh, for ever. For ever and ever. His mum and my mum are old friends, so we've grown up together. I've been coming here since I was eighteen months old.'

Chelsea, who is thinking of the conversation she and Florence had back in Cornwall, nods. This explains why Florence was so defensive, and yet also able to explain Charlie's behaviour to her – acting as a kind of translator. Chelsea looks down the table now at where Charlie is sitting. It seems significant to her that he has chosen a chair as far away as possible from his stepmother, and is sitting instead by Ian, who is at the head of the table, and Hannah. Chelsea is surprised to see Hannah chatting so easily with him, but then again, she's already been here for quite a while, and must have spent many meals getting to know Izzy's family. There's something about the way she's turned towards Charlie, though, that gives her away, not to mention the deep flush at her collarbone, neck and cheeks. Chelsea nudges Ayesha, tilting her head in Hannah's direction, 'What's going on there?'

'Looks like Han might have a crush,' Ayesha says.

'Oh, Hannah definitely has a crush,' Florence confirms, 'it's been interesting to witness.'

'Really?' Ayesha says. 'What have we missed?'

Florence laughs, 'Oh, not a lot. I don't think it's going to go anywhere,'

Izzy, who is sitting next to her mum, rolls her eyes. 'All you've missed is Han embarrassing herself. I don't know what she sees in him, honestly.'

Chelsea glances down at them again, wanting to make sure none of them can hear the conversation happening at her end of the table. They're both laughing at something and Hannah's face is tipped up towards Charlie's in a way that makes Chelsea's stomach drop. There is far too much adoration in that look, especially as Charlie doesn't really seem to have noticed. It's Ian who is holding court, telling a story, and Charlie's eyes are on his dad, just as Hannah's eyes are on him. What does it matter though? Hannah can have a holiday crush; it won't go anywhere or harm anyone. Hopefully. She reaches for a serving spoon, helping herself to more food – as well as the patatas bravas and padron peppers, there are prawns swimming in garlicky oil, crispy fried calamari, a tomato salad doused in red wine vinegar, but as she tucks into her meal, clumsily peeling off the shell of a prawn, there's a metallic clatter from the head of the table and a strangled yell that sounds almost like a growl, followed by complete silence as everyone stops what they're doing or saying for half a second, if that, and turns as one to see Ian Dunwoody fall from his chair to the tiled floor of the terrace.

Then, suddenly, everyone is on their feet, shouting, crying. Over everything, Chelsea clearly hears Camille call her husband's name as she rushes up from her chair and down to the other end of the long table. But Charlie is already on his feet, leaning down over his father, who is prone on the ground, as he shakes his shoulder and bleats the word 'Dad' over and over. Camille pushes him aside, crouching down by her husband, murmuring in French, but before she can do anything, Charlie reaches for her arm and drags her up to standing, forcing her back from Ian. She whirls towards him, and even in the twinkling lights of the terrace, Chelsea can see her dark eyes flash, 'You have no idea what is going on here, Charlie, please let me see to my husband.'

'He's having a heart attack!'

319

'He is not,' she says, before turning around to seek out the housekeeper, '*Valencia, por favor, llame una ambulancia.*'

'*Si, señora.*'

'Mum? What's going on?'

'Sweetheart, he's going to be fine, it's all okay,' Camille says, but her face has lost all colour and she looks as worried as her daughter.

'How do you know?' Izzy cries as Florence goes to put an arm around her, issuing a calming *shhh*, which Chelsea can see annoys rather than comforts Izzy, as she shrugs the older girl's arm away.

'Everything's okay.'

'Stop saying that, Camille, my father just collapsed at the dinner table,' Charlie practically growls.

But Camille is already on her knees again, crouched over her husband, 'We need to get him inside. Chelsea, Ayesha, can you help me?'

Ayesha, eyes wide and face as drained as Camille's own, just nods and looks at Chelsea, who joins her next to Ian – dazed, but thankfully now awake – helping to lift him from the ground. Before they can even get to the house, a man Chelsea has never seen before is rushing out, taking over from both of them and escorting Ian through the doors, leaving Chelsea and Ayesha empty-handed, as Camille, Izzy and Charlie follow in pursuit.

'What the fuck?' Ayesha says quietly, turning to Chelsea with a furrowed brow. 'What the hell just happened?'

'It looked like he fainted.'

'I hope that's all it was.'

'Yeah, right. Do you really think it could have been a

heart attack? Han, you were sitting closer to him, what happened?'

But all Hannah can do is stare back at Chelsea, mute. Her formerly blushing face has gone puce, and she looks as nonplussed as everyone else. 'Right,' Florence says, with a clap of her hands, 'I don't think there's anything the rest of us can do, so why don't we all sit down and let the family deal with it?'

Slowly, they all return to their seats and although Chelsea immediately reaches for her wine glass, she doesn't feel like drinking. 'Do you know what that was all about?' she asks Florence.

Florence shakes her head, 'Nope. But I'm sure he'll be okay.' She's trying to sound firm, sure of herself, but her voice gives her away, cracking a little halfway through. She swallows heavily, nodding, as if to herself, and picks up her glass of wine to take a couple of big gulps. Izzy returns, sooner than Chelsea expected, ashen-faced and on the verge of tears, but with good news: Ian has been taken to the hospital for observation, but the paramedics were able to assure them that he had merely fainted. Possibly as a result of low glucose levels. Charlie and Camille have gone with him. So, the girls sit around the table until the candles gutter and smoke out, the air as hot and sultry as ever, crickets the only soundtrack to their worried talk. Izzy is quiet throughout, and when Florence softly suggests it's time for them all to go to bed, she only nods, getting up in a daze and making her way up to her room in a trance. There is a hushed pall to the house now, the hallway dim and silent, as though it too is holding its breath for news. Chelsea wants to go with Izzy into her room, make sure she's okay, but when Hannah follows her in, she closes the door firmly behind her as though that's that. Chelsea and Ayesha are left standing on the airy landing, the only light coming from the soft glow of hidden bulbs beneath the skirting, and the star-streaked sky that continues to show off through the large picture window.

* * *

Chelsea finds it almost impossible to fall asleep, so she hears the crack of the door opening even before the sliver of light and the sound of her whispered name encourages her to open her eyes. She gets up and glances towards Ayesha, who has her back to her and is emitting the telltale rhythmic rise and fall of someone fast asleep. Izzy is on the other side of the door, shaking in her pyjamas, despite the warmth of the night.

'What's wrong?' Chelsea whispers. 'Is everything okay?'

In the half light of the landing, Izzy's face is washed out and blotchy with tears as she shakes her head, 'Dad's sick, really sick.'

'What? What did the hospital say? I thought he just fainted?' But Izzy can barely get the words out, her mouth gaping open and closed like a goldfish. Chelsea takes her arm and starts to lead her down the stairs, 'Come on, let's go outside.'

Out on the terrace, the warm air seeps in through her pyjamas, and Chelsea hears Izzy take a deep, steadying breath as they walk over to the patio sofas and curl up together in a corner. 'What's going on?' Chelsea says in a low voice.

'He's got cancer,' Izzy gasps, 'pancreatic cancer.'

Chelsea doesn't say anything at first, the sound of the night-time crickets and waves down below on the beach filling her ears. Eventually, she says, 'What do you mean, did he just get diagnosed?'

'No.' Izzy shakes her head. 'They've known for about a month, but didn't tell us.'

'Why?'

'I don't know,' Izzy says, her eyes beginning to fill with tears.

Chelsea reaches for her hand, squeezes hard, 'Shhh, it's okay.'

'It's not, Chelsea, he's going to die.'

'You don't know that.'

'I do. It's inoperable, Mum said. Incurable.'

'Oh.'

'It's spread to his liver.'

'I can't believe it, he doesn't look . . .'

'It's why he's lost so much weight, and he fainted because it affects his glucose levels or something, I don't really know.'

'But he's not able to get any treatment at all?'

'I don't know,' Izzy says, wiping at her eyes. 'I think it's just . . . just making him comfortable.'

'Palliative?'

'Yes.'

'Izzy, I'm so sorry,' Chelsea whispers. Even through the dark, she sees Izzy's face crumble as she says this, the realization of what is happening to her father hitting her as she hears and accepts her friend's sympathy. Her shoulders shake as she begins to cry, properly, and Chelsea doesn't know what to do, except squeeze her hand even harder, hold on even tighter. They stay out there for the rest of the night, until the sky starts to turn various shades of violet and purple, and then pink and orange, and then, finally, blue and with the rising of the sun, Izzy finally asleep next to her, Chelsea wonders what on earth will happen now.

'It's good to see you making so much progress, Chelsea. It really seems like you're settling in now.'

Chelsea is back in Kate's office, is getting used to her frequent visits here and was even offered a cup of tea this time, a sure sign Kate is pleased with her. She nods back at the other woman, 'Yeah, things are going okay. I feel on a pretty even keel.' This is a lie, of course. She checked her Facebook again last night, and made the sickening discovery that 'Jane Smith' had messaged her again. This time they'd written: I SEE YOU'VE TAKEN MY ADVICE. GOOD. KEEP IT THAT WAY. But instead of feeling reassured, as apparently her anonymous messenger did, she'd felt not just fear, but a strange mix of being both frustrated and galvanized. She's become too complacent, up here in Nikki's cosy cottage, in her new routine. As much as Kate and Nikki would like her to stay where she is, doing exactly as she's been doing, she can't. She has to clear her name and she has to find out who killed Izzy, because if she doesn't, then her whole life is going to be a series of anonymized messages, taunting and torturing her, never allowing her to be truly free, never allowing her to be herself. Whoever that may be.

'That's so good to hear. Now, I don't know if this is something you're going to be interested in, but Camille

Dunwoody has requested restorative contact with you. Do you know what this means?'

'She – she what?'

'It basically means she has requested contact with you, as a way for her to move forward as a victim. Or relative of a victim, in this case.'

'So . . . she wants a meeting with me?'

'Essentially, yes. I have asked if this can be done online, but she seems quite keen to see you in person, which would be in London.'

'Oh.'

'Normally, I'd push back harder on this, but she seems fairly . . .'

'Insistent?'

'Yes. Are you comfortable meeting her in person?'

Chelsea is so taken aback by this development that it takes her a second to answer. 'Yes. I mean, obviously we've seen each other already, but it might be easier for both of us if it's not so . . . accidental.'

'Right. She's requested that it take place at her hotel, which, again, isn't exactly orthodox, but there'll be someone from victim support present the entire time.'

'Oh, okay,' Chelsea says, nodding.

'Are you sure?'

'Yeah, I'm just surprised. It didn't seem like she wanted to see me again.' This isn't strictly speaking true, of course, but Chelsea is surprised nonetheless. Why is Camille doing this so officially, when she could simply contact Chelsea through Ajala, or text her herself? Is something else going on here? Does Camille have an ulterior motive? It's a very un-Camille thing to do and doesn't make any sense, considering she too is looking into who really killed Izzy, but Chelsea's list of suspects is so short, she has to suspect everyone.

'Does it say anything about Charlie? Has he requested the visit too?'

'No, just Camille Dunwoody,' Kate says, turning to her computer screen to double-check. 'Are you surprised it's Camille rather than Charlie?'

Kate's forehead has creased in curiosity and confusion, and Chelsea knows she has to tread lightly here. 'No, it's not that, I was just wondering, that's all.' She's about to mention Charlie's recent engagement to Hannah but thinks better of it – she doesn't want Kate worrying that she won't stick to the rules and keep her head down this time.

'And you're okay going to London?'

'Sure, yeah. I can probably stay with Ayesha again.'

'Great,' Kate says, checking her screen and reading out Ayesha's address to confirm where Chelsea will be spending the night.

'Yep, that's it.'

'Just one night should do it, right? It's a bit far to go for a day trip, I understand that, but like I keep saying, it's best for you to stay in your routine up here, keep settling in.'

Chelsea nods, 'Yeah, one night. That should be fine.'

* * *

'Of course you can stay with me,' Ayesha says on the phone to her that evening, her voice so full of pent-up excitement, what she says next comes out in a rush. 'I know this is going to sound a bit mad, but it's Hannah and

327

Charlie's engagement party this weekend too, and well, Hannah's invited me.'

'What?' Chelsea is sat at the bottom of the stairs. She'd been on her way from her room to the kitchen when Ayesha rang, so she took a seat where she was. 'How? When?'

Why?

'I started following her on Instagram, after that time we were looking at her page, and well, I just decided to DM her, to get a feel of the waters with her.'

'And she messaged you back?'

'Yeah, and we've just been chatting a lot, going back and forth, and then she just . . . invited me.' All of Chelsea and Nikki's shoes and boots are piled up in the hallway, and she stares at the mud on the bottom of a particularly hard-working pair of Nikki's boots. She reaches for it, flicking some off from the edge of the sole so it skitters across the flagstones, making a tiny percussive sound in the otherwise silent hallway. 'Chels, you there?'

The signal at the cottage isn't great, and it's not unusual for calls to be cut off or interrupted by static, but that's not the problem right now. 'Yeah, I just . . . I don't know what to say.'

'It's mad, I know.'

'I mean, you probably shouldn't go.'

'What? Why? This is such a great opportunity; I'd get to see Hannah and Charlie in the wild.'

'It could be dangerous, Ayesha. Camille thinks he might've been involved in Izzy's murder, it just seems a bit risky.' And another possibility has just come to Chelsea: what if, all along, it's Charlie who's been messaging her on

Facebook? Or could it even be Hannah? She's not sure why she would, but messaging with Ayesha after so long in silence, right after Chelsea's been released from prison and spotted talking with her fiancé's stepmother, isn't that a bit too much of a coincidence?

'But you don't even think he killed her. You think Sinclair did, and you still went to the bloody end of Wales, on your own, to confront him.'

Chelsea is quiet at first, before finally saying, 'Yeah, you're right. But that was risky too. Will you just, at least, think about it before you tell Hannah yes or no?'

'Fine, yeah.'

The end to the call is a little awkward. This is the first time Chelsea and Ayesha have had a disagreement since Chelsea got out, but Ayesha acting so rashly, jumping at the opportunity to spend time with the Dunwoodies, just isn't like her at all. It's set Chelsea on edge. Maybe Ayesha simply misses Hannah, and that's all this is. Ayesha didn't just lose Izzy when she died; she lost Hannah too, simply for standing by Chelsea, believing her. And then, when Chelsea went to prison, she lost her too. Chelsea remembers sitting in Ayesha's kitchen last month, realizing that not only were there photos of all them, all over the walls, but there was also a poster, framed, of the university production of *The Glass Menagerie* they all went to in that last term of their first year. Hannah's name was right at the top, in capital letters. She'd played Laura. Chelsea sighs and goes into the kitchen, where Nikki is feeding the dogs and boiling water for pasta.

'Shit, sorry, Nikki, I said I'd cook tonight.'

'It's all right, love, I don't mind.'

'No, please, sit down. I can take over.'

Nikki raises her eyebrows at her, but shrugs and takes a seat. 'I could do with a glass of wine too, if you're in a serving mood. Was that Ayesha on the phone?'

'Yeah,' Chelsea says, grabbing the half-full bottle of red that's on the kitchen counter and pouring them both a glass.

'She excited about you going back down to stay?' There's something in Nikki's voice, a hesitance maybe, that lets Chelsea know her aunt isn't fully on board with this, but she chooses to ignore it, for now at least.

'Yeah, yeah, it'll be nice to see her again.'

'What did she think about this set-up? Camille requesting to see you?'

Chelsea passes Nikki a glass and takes a sip from her own, 'Um, she thought it was a little weird too. I guess I won't know what's going on until I see her, though.'

'But you could refuse the meeting if you wanted to?'

There's already an onion, cut in half, lying on a chopping board, and Chelsea starts to peel and slice it, her back to Nikki as she says, 'I actually don't know. Kate didn't say.'

Nikki is silent, the only sound in the kitchen the slice of Chelsea's knife, the snuffling of the dogs and the slurp of Nikki drinking her wine. 'I don't like this, love. I really don't,' she says eventually. 'I just can't see what Camille wants from you. It's one thing to bump into you at the cemetery, and then you saw her and Ajala, but . . . haven't you thought, for a second, what she's getting at in all this? What she gets from it?'

'She wants to know who killed her daughter. She no

longer thinks it was me. That's huge, Nikki. I . . . I don't know how to explain to you what that means to me. Someone else thinks I'm innocent, and it's Izzy's mum? I know she's difficult and . . . very particular –'

'And very powerful.'

'Right. But that's a good thing, now that she thinks I'm not guilty. We could finally clear my name. She could help us do that.'

Chelsea finishes with the onion and moves on to the garlic, but by the time she's finely chopped two cloves, Nikki still hasn't responded. When Chelsea turns to look at her, she's staring into the garnet glow of her wine as though hypnotized. Chelsea says her name and she looks up, shakes her head from her reverie and says, 'I'm just worried she could be using you. To get what she really wants.'

'What she really wants? What do you mean? She wants to find out who killed Izzy,' Chelsea repeats.

'Yes. But couldn't there be something else?'

'Like what?'

'Like money, Chels.'

'She already has money. Tons of it.'

'Her husband died fifteen years ago, we have no idea how good with money she is. Maybe she's running out.'

'Okay,' Chelsea says slowly, 'but what does *that* have to do with *this*?' She waves her knife in front of her chest, and Nikki winces.

'Well, Pennington's ended up being sold for almost a billion pounds and because she wasn't a shareholder, I'm not sure Camille would have seen any of that money.'

'And you think she's after it now? That's why she's investigating Charlie?'

'Honestly, I don't know. But there's a lot a person might do for that kind of money. I just think you need to be careful.'

* * *

Chelsea goes to bed with Nikki's words of warning ringing in her ears. The concern she's voicing isn't anything Chelsea hasn't also felt herself. Of course, she's worried about any ulterior motive Camille may have, but even if clearing Chelsea's name is just a by-product of Camille's investigation, it's still worth the risk. She knows Camille isn't doing this for her, isn't doing it because she feels guilty for how long Chelsea spent behind bars, doing time for a crime she didn't commit. She's doing this for her own selfish reasons. But that's okay, because if there's one thing Chelsea knows, it's that grief can make you selfish, and as wary as she is of Camille, the fact is that Chelsea is using her too: for her resources, her power, her position. And she may have been surprised by the other woman's official request to meet with her, but she's determined to use this opportunity to her advantage.

Detective Inspector Rob Bailey: Thanks for coming back in again, Chelsea, we know it's late.

Chelsea Keough: Sure.

RB: We wanted to ask you few questions about Joe.

CK: Joe?

RB: Joe Hemsley?

CK: Right. Yeah, sure.

Detective Constable Natalie Ajala: He's your ex-boyfriend?

CK: Um, yeah, that's right.

NA: When did the two of you break up?

CK: It was sometime in August.

NA: You can't remember?

CK: Ayesha and I were Interrailing, the days and dates are all a bit blurry. I remember we were in Marseille, though. I have a very clear memory of sitting in an internet café at six o'clock in the morning reading a break-up email.

NA: He broke up with you?

CK: Yes.

NA: Did he explain why?

CK: He — his dad died at the beginning of the summer holidays. Close to the beginning of them anyway, and that was obviously really tough on him ... I already had the Interrail trip planned and booked with Ayesha. I asked him if he wanted me to stay, but he said no, and then in the email he said he felt like I hadn't really been there for him. The way a girlfriend should be.

NA: How did you feel about that?

CK: Well, I felt pretty shit, obviously. I felt bad for him already and I already knew I hadn't really handled things very well. I've never really lost anyone like that. My grandad, but I was only five and I barely remember him. So, I dunno, I already felt guilty about how … I didn't know how to help him? So, I sort of felt like he wasn't really being fair at first, but I dunno, he was probably right.

RB: Was Joe meant to go on the Interrail trip with you and Ayesha, Chelsea?

CK: No, he wasn't ever going to come.

RB: So, he wasn't meant to join you at Isabella's family home in Mallorca?

CK: No.

RB: But, as far as you're aware, he and Izzy remained friends?

CK: Yeah, I guess so.

NA: Chelsea, were you aware they'd started seeing each other?

CK: What? No – no, they weren't seeing each other. Where did you hear that?

RB: We have a letter here, from Joe to Izzy. We thought you might have seen it?

CK: No.

[sound of paper rustling]

RB: You've never seen this? We found it in one of Izzy's history course files. On the Napoleonic wars.

CK: No, I've not seen it. I wasn't taking that course.

NA: Was Joe?

CK: Um, maybe, I don't know. But … Izzy hadn't been to many lectures this term.

RB: Right, of course.

NA: So, maybe Joe had been taking notes for her?

CK: Yeah, maybe. That would make sense, I guess. You'd have to ask him.

NA: We will.

RB: Chelsea, the letter – from Joe – says he's in love with Izzy. He's proposing starting a relationship.

CK: Proposing?

NA: Not proposing, proposing. He's asking her out, basically. When she's ready.

[pause]

CK: Right.

RB: Maybe you could read it out for us, DC Ajala? So, we're all on the same page. As it were.

NA: [clears throat] 'Dear Izzy …'

They offer to leave early, but neither Izzy nor Camille will hear of it, although Chelsea is sure Charlie thinks they have more than overstayed their welcome. So, they stay and keep Izzy company as she and the rest of the family go back and forth from the hospital, and Chelsea can't help but feel like what they are really doing is keeping vigil. Ian's prognosis is bad, so bad that Charlie writes up an NDA for all of them to sign, ensuring they won't leak the news of his fatal illness to the press, which could in turn scare shareholders and cause Pennington's share price to tank. It's a ghoulish request, one that makes Izzy scream and call him names, but Charlie has no reaction to this, clearly thinks he is doing the right thing, and really, by the end of their five days, although Chelsea wishes one of them was staying behind to watch over Izzy, she is glad to be going. This was their last stop of their Interrail tour, and Hannah is booked on the same flight out of Palma, so they all return to England together.

But they don't return to Birmingham together.

'It's so weird being here without her,' Hannah says. It's their first night in Selly Oak and they've ordered a celebratory Domino's, but without Izzy and knowing that she's still in Mallorca, sitting by her father's hospital bed, it doesn't feel like much of a celebration. Hannah has lit a crowd of tea lights on the coffee table, though, and hung a strand of fairy lights over the obligatory Klimt poster, and with the rain pattering at the window, it does at least feel cosy.

'Yeah, it's all wrong,' Ayesha says, biting into a slice of pizza, oozing cheese and grease. 'Did she say when she might head back?'

Chelsea shakes her head. She spoke to Izzy that morning after her mum dropped her off at the house. She'd been the first to arrive, and the stale, un-lived in air of the house had felt even more unwelcoming knowing that Izzy wouldn't be joining them. 'No, she doesn't know. I think she just wants to . . . to stay until the end.'

Hannah's chin wobbles at this, and Ayesha wordlessly pushes her glass of vinegary red wine towards her. 'I just can't believe he's going to die,' she whispers after taking a large gulp.

'It's pretty shit,' Ayesha concedes.

'That's a bit of an understatement,' Hannah says, blinking at her through unshed tears.

'Sorry. I'm just not very good at the tea and sympathy thing.'

'Well, we're going to have to get good, because Iz *is* coming back eventually, and we'll all have to support her.'

'I know, you're right, Han.'

'Chelsea, have you heard from Joe?' Hannah asks.

'No, we haven't been in touch.'

'Well, that's gonna be awkward on Monday.'

'I know.'

'He'll probably want to know about Izzy's dad, don't you think?' Hannah says through a sniffle. 'Considering he lost his dad too this year.'

Chelsea nods, and her stomach suddenly feels heavy as she thinks of Joe and the way she left things with him. The way he left things, too. She feels terrible that their break-up came so close his dad dying, but he just hadn't let her in. And then he'd delivered the news about his feelings for Izzy.

Later, when they've all gone to bed and Chelsea is trying to settle in her new single bed – she offered to take the smallest room in the house on the grounds she'd have the cheapest rent – she tries calling Joe, but he doesn't pick up. She can't blame him for that – they haven't spoken in almost two months now after all, not to mention it's late – but she's already texted him a few times and got no response. She flips her phone closed angrily and puts it on her already crowded bedside table. She hasn't drawn the curtains yet, and the rain is still falling slickly down the tiny window that overlooks their back garden, weeds waving in the cracks between paving stones. She watches it for a while, the wind and the rain, her bedside lamp still on, the warm glow creating a womblike feeling. Even though she'd opted for the smallest room, she'd been annoyed at first, knowing how much more space the others all had in their much larger bedrooms, but now, tucked up and safe, it doesn't feel so bad. Her phone beeps next to her, and she reaches for it immediately, thinking it might be Joe finally messaging her back. But it's not, it's Izzy, texting her from Mallorca, her message just two words long:

He's gone.

Chelsea immediately tries calling her, but just like Joe, there's no reply and so she texts Izzy back and then puts the phone down and tries to settle down to sleep, her mind rushing with thoughts of Izzy and Joe and Izzy's dad. She wonders where Izzy is now – are they still at the hospital? Is she back at Mirador, or did they stay the night in a Palma hotel? She also can't help but wonder about where Ian is now, but she pulls back from these morbid thoughts and visions as soon as they rear their ugly heads. Eventually, she sleeps, the pitter-patter of the rain getting heavier as a storm thunders through the neighbourhood, and dreams eventually drown out her waking thoughts.

* * *

On Monday, she heads to her first history lecture alone, and walking the unfamiliar route from Selly Oak to campus, she can't help but think of her first lecture last year, when she and Izzy spoke for the first time before bunking off for the rest of the day in favour of Gunnies. Just a year ago, and yet already so much has changed. She checks her phone, but Izzy hasn't texted since her last message earlier that morning, but she still dashes one out to her friend, wanting her to still feel connected to this moment, no matter how far away she is. Pushing open the lecture hall door, she sees that she's one of the last to arrive and Joe is already seated, sitting with a group of other guys who Chelsea doesn't really know. Joe barely acknowledges her, just raises his eyebrows as their gazes lock, and Chelsea takes a deep breath and walks up the steps to a free seat somewhere in a centre row. She's already forgotten which tutor is leading this class, so she pulls out her schedule and rolls her eyes when she sees the name. James Sinclair. Of course. Sitting there without Izzy, Chelsea feels like she's starting all over again, like this could be her first day of uni, instead of just the first day of their second year, but then Sinclair walks through the door and she takes out her notebook and pen and starts taking notes.

* * *

'Chelsea?' Sinclair says, as she's trying to leave the lecture hall. Someone she barely recognizes looks back at her and raises an eyebrow and Chelsea wonders what that is supposed to mean. 'Chelsea? Can I have a word for a minute?'

She steps out of the stream of students and nods, walking over to the lectern where Sinclair still stands. 'Is everything okay? Where's Izzy?' he asks.

Chelsea frowns; she's sure Izzy told her that she'd already been in touch with the department to let them know about her late start to the term. Maybe this simply hasn't been communicated to individual lecturers yet. 'Her dad died. Two days ago. So, she's not back yet. I thought you knew, sorry.'

'Oh,' Sinclair says, capping his pen and placing it purposefully back on the lectern, 'I'm very sorry to hear that. Is she okay?'

Chelsea shrugs, 'I don't think so, no.'

At this, Sinclair winces, 'Right, of course she's not. That was a stupid question. Do you know when she might be getting back?'

'I don't know, it's so recent still. They're in Mallorca so they have to fly . . . fly the body home and then there's the funeral. I'm really not sure, sorry.'

'No, that's okay. I'll talk to the head of department

about it, I'm sure we'll be able to work something out so she can catch up with everything once she's back.'

'Right.'

'Not that she needs to worry about any of that right now, of course. Will you – will you let her know . . . that I'm thinking of her? That we're all thinking of her.'

'Sure,' Chelsea says. Sinclair has lowered his gaze and is focused on that pen that he just put down. He picks it up, twiddling it between his fingers until it clatters back to the surface, and he looks up to find Chelsea still staring at him.

He smiles, a little grimly, 'Are you okay, Chelsea? This must be a strange time for you too.' He picks up the pen again, along with the papers he was reading from during the lecture and packs them away.

'Yeah. I just feel bad I can't do more.'

Sinclair nods, shouldering his messenger bag, and finally walking out from behind the lectern, he nods in the direction of the doors, signalling it's time for them to leave. 'I'm sure she's glad to have you here. Or at least, she will be, once she's back. Did you meet him at all? Her dad?' He opens the door for her, and as Chelsea walks past him, he places his hand at her lower back, not heavily, just hovering there, as if guiding her through.

'Yeah,' she says, trying to ignore the moment, 'we stayed with them in the summer. In Mallorca.'

'Ah, so you'll probably want to go to the funeral then.'

'Yes.'

'Well, let me know if you need anything – a little extra time for that first essay, perhaps. We're all here to help you. Both. You and Izzy.'

When she gets back to the house, Chelsea opens the door to the ground-floor bedroom that should be Izzy's bedroom but is still, currently, just an empty room. Dust motes dance in the late afternoon sunshine, and the sight of the bare mattress and empty desk pushed into the bay of the window makes her absence all the more obvious. Sighing, she closes the door again and goes into the living room, where Ayesha is sitting on one of the sofas. 'What's all this?' she says, standing over the coffee table, which is littered with newspapers. Picking them up, she realizes that the headline – or at least one of the front-page stories – of each one is about Ian Dunwoody's death. 'Oh. Did you buy these?'

'Hannah did,' Ayesha says, as Chelsea joins her on the sofa with a copy of the *Sun*. 'I'd never pay money for that old rag.'

'How many did she buy? She must've spent a fortune.'

'I don't know, she was in a kind of hallucinatory state, to be honest. It was like she went into a trance when she saw them.'

'This is so weird.'

'I know. How was your lecture?'

'Fine. Strange being there without Iz, and Joe barely looked at me, and then Sinclair was asking where Izzy was. All a bit weird, I guess.'

'It'll be weird for a while, I suppose. Until she gets back. You do think she'll come back, right?'

Chelsea glances at Ayesha, 'Yeah, of course,' she says, although the truth is, this is the first time she's even contemplated the idea that Izzy might not want to come back to uni. Would she really leave? The empty bedroom on

343

the other side of the wall seems to be taunting her now, and so, for distraction, she starts to read the article in the *Sun*. 'This is all a bit ghoulish, isn't it? Hannah buying all these papers about it? Are they for her scrapbook or something?'

'I don't know, she didn't seem to know why she was buying them herself. But she was very adamant.'

'Where is she?'

'In her room.'

Hannah's door is closed, and Chelsea knocks before going in but doesn't wait to hear her answer – a habit she hates in other people but has yet to give up herself. As the door swings open, she realizes Hannah is on the phone, talking to someone in a low voice. Sat at her desk, she has one leg pulled up on her chair and is resting her cheek against her knee as she pulls at her lower lip in worry. She doesn't hear Chelsea at first, and Chelsea has to whisper her name for her to spin slightly towards her, her eyes widening in realization.

'I have to go,' she says to whoever is on the other end of her phone call. 'I'll talk to you later?'

'Was that Izzy?' Chelsea asks, sitting down at the foot of Hannah's bed. Where Izzy's room is still completely barren, Hannah's is the opposite. She hasn't unpacked completely yet – there is still a suitcase vomiting clothes lying open on the floor, but she has decorated in her usual manner. The bed is covered in a floral duvet and five or six throw pillows, there are three posters already taped up on the wall – another Klimt, Audrey Hepburn in *Breakfast at Tiffany's*, her sunglasses just tipped forward off her face, and *An American in Paris* – while next to her desk, she's covered a pinboard with overlapping post-cards, mostly landscapes and cityscapes by Old Masters, and quotes cut out of newspapers and magazines. Looking a little closer, Chelsea thinks one of them might be a Brontë.

Hannah shakes her head, still biting down on her lower lip, 'Charlie.'

'Charlie? Charlie Dunwoody? What are you doing talking to him?'

'I couldn't get through to Izzy, so I called him.'

'What were you calling him about?'

'I wanted to let them know about all the papers . . . Remember they made us sign that NDA when we were at Mirador? I just thought they should know what was being reported.'

'They made a statement to the press, Han, you don't need to worry about that NDA any more,' Chelsea says, her eyebrows pulling together in a frown, 'and "they" didn't make us sign anything, it was only Charlie.'

'I know,' Hannah says, colour rising in her cheeks, 'he explained all that.'

'Well. What else did he say? Are they doing okay?'

'They're flying home on Thursday and the funeral's going to be on Monday.'

'In a week?'

'Yes.'

'That seems so soon. It's all happened so quickly.'

'I know,' Hannah says. 'Charlie said they hadn't even had a chance to arrange an interim CEO.'

'That's hardly what matters right now, though, is it?'

'Well, I don't know. It matters to Charlie.'

'That's just weird to me, that his dad just died and that's what he's worrying about.'

'It's important, Chels,' Hannah says, her blush deepening even more as she starts to push herself off from the desk, so that her chair swivels back and forth, back and forth. 'Just because you don't understand something, doesn't make it wrong.'

'Right,' Chelsea says, standing up, 'noted.'

'Chelsea,' Hannah whines, her voice following Chelsea out of the room. Chelsea isn't quite sure why this has annoyed her so much, but she ignores Hannah's entreaties and goes into her own room, firmly closing the door behind her. Why does it matter that Hannah was talking to Charlie on the phone, and what's it to Chelsea if Charlie is worrying over interim CEOs rather than the death of his father? None of this affects her. But it does affect Izzy. She pulls her phone from her jeans pocket and flips it open. Nothing from Izzy. Still. Lying down on her bed, she goes to their text messages and realizes there is actually a new one. She must've sent it when Chelsea was in a lecture, with her phone on silent.

Call me when you get this. Please?
Chelsea?

She presses call immediately, listening as the ringtone makes that weird sound that indicates she's calling someone in another country, and briefly wonders how much this is going to cost her on her next mobile phone bill, when Izzy picks up.

'God, finally. Where have you been?'

'Sorry, I didn't see your text for ages, I don't know what happened. What's going on?'

Even down the phone, Chelsea can sense Izzy's nervous energy, can imagine her pacing across the wide space of her bedroom, limbs jangling.

'I just needed to talk to someone . . .' she says, trailing off.

'Okay.' Chelsea wants to say something more, something that would let Izzy know she's here for her, but she just doesn't have the words, is choked by the way Izzy's voice is so wrapped in grief. The sound of her breath comes quick and staccato down the line, and Chelsea can tell Izzy's crying, but she senses that there's something else going on too. Is she angry?

'I overheard Charlie on the phone this morning.'

'Right,' Chelsea says slowly, unable to guess where this might be going.

'I don't know who he was talking to, but it was about Dad's will. He was saying something about making sure he hadn't made a new one, or that there *was* a new one, I couldn't quite work it out. I don't know, it just seemed a little off, and I couldn't quite hear everything but it just felt so *icky*, you know? Why is he worrying about wills and new wills, and whatever else right now? I mean, Dad literally *just* died, can't we leave all that alone for even a second?'

'Have you spoken to your mum about it?'

'No,' Izzy says with a sigh, 'she's barely speaking. Hasn't really said a word since he died.'

'I'm sorry, Izzy. About everything.'

'I know. I wish you were all still here. I feel like I'm

going mad, like I'm in a film or something. It's horrible. I just keep feeling like I'll wake up and everything will be normal again, but it won't be, will it?'

'I don't know. Maybe things will start to feel a bit more normal once you're home? You're coming back on Thursday, right?'

'Yeah, how did you know that?'

'Hannah spoke to Charlie.'

'What? Why?'

'I don't know, she said she'd tried calling you first. It's a bit weird, but she also bought every newspaper with a story about your dad on the front page.'

Izzy is quiet at the other end of the phone, and Chelsea thinks she can hear the insistent sound of crickets in the background, but maybe she's just imagining things. 'That is weird,' Izzy says finally, 'but I guess it might be nice to read them all eventually. Once I'm up to it.'

'That's true.'

They say their goodbyes, but Chelsea stays lying on her bed looking at the magnolia ceiling for a long time afterwards, thinking about her friend pacing the rooms of her palatial home on a far-off island, her mother silent and unyielding, her brother scheming, and her father dead. Chelsea has had her moments of envying Izzy. Not so much for her clothes, or homes, or credit card and credit-card bill that gets paid off by someone else, but for the way she can glide through life, safe in the knowledge of her comfort, security, and what's to come. But now that's gone. Chelsea has no doubt that Izzy will still be taken care of for the rest of her life, but she'll also now know that anything can happen, at any time, that a bump in the road can lead to a detour you never saw coming, or even worse, to an overturned car bursting into flames and changing your life for ever. Maybe this realization has come late in life, maybe it's come early; either way, it's there and will leave an indelible mark on her, change her entire worldview, and Chelsea starts to wonder who the Izzy who eventually returns to them will actually be.

'I have taken the liberty of ordering us some tea,' Camille says, once she has welcomed Chelsea into her suite. It's the same one as before, its sugary tones softened even further by the late afternoon sunlight.

'Fine,' Chelsea says shortly. She's tired and thirsty, having come straight from the train, but Camille's dedication to her hostess role is grating, and in front of the victim-support representative, who is sitting on one of the pristine couches, it feels strange and unnatural. Is she going to be here the whole time? Camille introduced her as Monica, and as Chelsea sits down on the sofa opposite her, she can't help but wonder how Camille is going to talk openly and honestly about her investigation into Charlie in front of her.

Still, that's for Camille to worry about and for now she's busy with room service, the tea tray being expertly carried in by a neat and discreet member of staff. Once it's all been set up, Chelsea's question is answered, as Monica rises, nods at Camille and walks silently into another room adjacent to the sitting room.

Chelsea stares at her retreating back as she says, 'What's going on? Where is she going?'

'Monica has agreed to let us talk alone for a while.'

Camille leans forward to lift the heavy lid on the silver teapot, its sides delicately etched with flowers and branches, and checks how steeped the tea is. Apparently deeming it strong enough, she begins to pour into the cup closest to Chelsea, amber liquid falling from the pot's ornate spout.

'That – that can't be allowed?'

Camille raises her eyes to meet Chelsea's, 'That hardly matters, does it? She is here to support me, not you, and we both agree you are not a threat, so why such worry?'

She is now dripping milk into the teacup, the action bordering on mesmerizing. 'I'm not worried, Camille,' Chelsea says finally, 'I'm confused.'

'That is understandable. I have come to realize that I have been less than transparent with you, and that hasn't been fair. This is what this meeting is all about, Chelsea.' She passes the cup of tea to Chelsea, like a peace offering, and Chelsea takes it.

'Why couldn't we have done this over the phone, though? Or through Ajala?'

'Natalie doesn't know you're here. Although she is the reason I called you here today. She told me about your continued suspicions regarding James Sinclair and that she'd spent time re-investigating his alibi. So I decided it was necessary to let you know that this is a waste of time.'

As ever with Camille, everything feels very formal, set up, as if they're sitting on a film set and Camille is reading lines fed to her by a script. Chelsea wants to take her and shake her by the shoulders, tell her to spit it out, get to the point, to act like a normal person for once, and less like a beautiful wind-up doll. All this luxury leaves her cold, annoyance rattling through her as Camille plays around with an antique tea-set, brushes invisible crumbs from her cashmere cardigan. Her rings flash in the hotel's subtle lighting: gold, platinum, ruby. A giant diamond. A billion pounds – or as close as – that's what Nikki had told her Pennington's had sold for. Of course, she'd Googled it afterwards, read so many articles she felt sick seeing Charlie's name in print so many times. But Nikki was right, Camille hadn't got a penny of that, victim to something someone online had called 'The Second Wife Clause'. Still, could this really all be about money?

'How could you possibly know it's a waste of time, Camille? What is it you know, that makes you so sure it can't be Sinclair?'

Camille's demeanour doesn't change, her face doesn't soften and her rigid posture doesn't relax, but Chelsea is sure she sees something flit through her eyes; a decision made. She doesn't say anything for a long time, for so long, in fact, that if it was anyone else, Chelsea would wonder what on earth they were doing. But as closed a book as Camille is, Chelsea has at least learned enough to let her lead the conversation. Eventually, she places her cup back on the table and reaches into the depths of the handbag that sits at her feet. When she straightens up, her hand is closed in a tight fist, but her eyes are locked on Chelsea. Without saying anything, she unfurls her fist and holds it out to Chelsea, nodding towards it as if to say, *Here, here it is.* And there it is, bright and hot pink, a relic from the past. Chelsea doesn't even have to ask, she knows immediately, knows instinctively, and as she reaches out to take hold of Izzy's Motorola RAZR, fear races through her, but it's quickly followed by anticipation, that feeling of rushing through the pages at the end of a book, desperate to know all the answers. She flips it open and is surprised to see it is turned on and working, the screen blinking up at her.

'Where did you find this?' she asks, and suddenly she is desperately thirsty, her mouth bone-dry.

'In Cornwall,' Camille says quietly.

'When?'

'A few months ago. It was turned off, of course. I had some trouble finding a charger that would allow me to turn it back on, but eventually I did so.'

'I . . . no one ever knew how or where she lost it that night. How did it get to Cornwall?'

'She did not lose it, Chelsea. Someone took it.'

'Charlie?'

Camille nods at the phone again, 'Open up her text messages.'

Chelsea does so, and there, right at the top, right above her own name, in fact, is Charlie's. Anger thunders through Chelsea's veins, throbbing at her temples, and despite sitting right in front of her, Camille's image seems to waver as her vision blurs and she realizes her eyes are filling with tears. 'How long have you had this?'

'As I said, a month or two. I found it towards the end of September. It is, what, November now?'

'A month or two? A month or two? Do you realize how much this changes? How much this could impact my life?'

Camille nods. Chelsea wipes impatiently at her eyes, and her vision clears. She wants to get a hold of herself, to calm her breath, lower her heart rate, but she can't believe the audacity of this woman, calmly sitting here, in her thousands-of-pounds-a-night hotel room, with evidence that could help clear Chelsea's name, and answer the question of who actually killed Izzy. She takes a deep, shuddering breath and turns her face away from Camille, the sight of her smooth glossiness simply too much to bear. She stands up, goes to the window and looks down at the street, the pedestrians like Sims characters, all just doing exactly what they do every day, never veering off course or finding themselves at a precipice, unsure whether they want to throw themselves off it, or run away as fast as humanly possible.

'I'm very sorry, Chelsea, perhaps I should have told you from the beginning. But I just wasn't sure what it all meant, and Charlie . . . He's a difficult person, I can't lie about that, and his relationship with Isabella was always a little . . . fraught, but until this, I never thought he was capable of hurting her.'

'Talk me through it. How did you find it? Where did you find it?'

'It was in the back of a cupboard in the games room at Appledore, the house in Cornwall.'

'The games room?'

'Yes. I have finally decided to sell the house and have been going through some things. I haven't spent much time there since Isabella and her father died, and I wanted to be sure I went through everything myself, so that I didn't accidentally throw or give away something of theirs that I wanted to keep.'

'I didn't realize you still had that house.'

'Yes, I inherited all of Ian's properties. I sold the Dulwich house, as I live mostly in Paris now, but I kept the others. Until now.'

'Does Charlie know?'

'That I'm selling Appledore? Of course. He is the buyer.'

Chelsea has been resolutely looking out of the window, but now she turns to stare at Camille, 'And does he know you've been going through everything there, or does he think he's buying it as is?'

'I am unsure,' Camille says slowly. 'I haven't discussed it with him, so there's no reason he would know.'

'Okay. That's good. He probably assumes the phone is exactly where he left it.'

'Unless Charlie has forgotten he left it there.'

'There's no way he's forgotten where he left this.' Chelsea leaves her position by the window and takes a seat on the sofa opposite Camille. 'You do realize this proves he was in Birmingham that night?'

'The text messages don't prove that, do they?'

The messages are damning but not incriminating, it's true. There are many, many texts from Charlie to Izzy from that night. And the later it got, the more persistent and aggravated Charlie became, his annoyance palpable, even through the tiny phone screen. Was this someone on the edge, the edge of doing something terrible? It's fair to say that, like Izzy, Charlie had been going through a lot at that time – had something tipped him over, making him capable of killing his own sister? Whatever the answer to that question, the phone does at least prove one thing to Chelsea: he was in Birmingham. And he lied about it.

'No, but the fact he has had the phone all this time does. The only way he can have got hold of it is if he saw her the night she died, and then took it before getting out of Birmingham. Because she definitely had it earlier in the night, I saw her with it; she was texting me when we got separated at the Factory.' Camille nods her head at this, seemingly in agreement. 'Not that it helps me now, as we have no way to prove you found it in Cornwall, and that it's been there the whole time. Why didn't you tell Ajala about this when you found it? She could have made sure the right people got involved, so it could be taken into evidence.'

'I'm sorry, Chelsea. But it's as I said – I couldn't quite bring myself to believe Charlie could have hurt Isabella. And, well, I'm sorry, but I'd never had any reason to believe that you weren't guilty. As awful as that must be for you to hear, it's the truth. So I had to be sure.'

'Are you sure now?' The words are hard to get out. Chelsea can barely stand to look at Camille, let alone continue polite conversation, when all she wants is to bellow and scream, but she has to remain as calm as possible. Camille now holds the key to her freedom. She hasn't done everything correctly, that's true, but Chelsea knows her position as Izzy's mother, her social standing, her wealth will help now. Chelsea could be about to clear her name. She can't afford to annoy or anger Camille.

'I don't know,' Camille says on a sigh. She has been sitting, as ever, rigid and straight, her posture perfect, but now she leans forwards, her elbows on her knees, and rubs at her face with her hands. It takes a while for her to sit back up again and look Chelsea in the eye. 'In my own strange way, I love him, even though I know how little he liked or approved of me when I first married Ian – for most of our marriage, in fact. But he is Ian's son, and for that, I've always been able to forgive anything, because when I see him . . . I see Ian. And since Isabella . . . he's taken care of me, Chelsea, softened his attitude, I would say. Maybe it is simply that he finally has almost everything he wanted – CEO, head of the family. Or I think Hannah may have helped adjust his mind towards me. She's always been very kind. But now, I wonder . . . if he has been keeping me close so that I would never begin to suspect. And if he could do that, for all this time? Well, he would be capable of anything,' she says, her eyes wide as a shiver rolls through her body. 'I'm not afraid to admit that I'm afraid of him, Chelsea. If all this is true.'

A silence settles over the two of them as Chelsea takes this in. She thinks of Hannah, about to marry Charlie, of Ayesha, who is getting ready for their engagement party right now, who will be seeing Charlie in just a few hours. 'But why?' she says eventually. 'Why would he do this?'

'You know Pennington's was sold just over six months after Isabella's death?' Camille says quietly.

'Yes.'

'And you know, I think, that Isabella did not want that? That she wanted to respect her father's wishes and ensure Pennington's remained a family company?'

'Yes, I remember all that.'

Camille nods once, 'And you know why she came to London that weekend? Or not that weekend, that Friday?'

'It was for a reading of Ian's will, wasn't it?'

'Not quite. The will was fairly straightforward in terms of my husband's assets – everything had been decided on a long time ago – but towards the end of his illness, Ian changed his decision on who should inherit his shares in the company. Originally, they were to be split fifty–fifty between his children, Isabella and Charlie, until he realized just how strongly Charlie felt about selling the company. They'd had an offer Charlie thought it was stupidity to refuse. Ian did not agree. So, Ian left the majority of his shares – eighty percent, in fact – to Isabella.'

'Oh,' Chelsea says, thinking back to Izzy on the last day of her life, the weight she had so clearly been carrying. She had just been delivered a huge responsibility, and not only that, but it had caused an impassable rift between her and her brother, at a time when they should have been drawn together, leaning on one another.

'Those texts that my stepson sent that night, some of them are quite nonsensical, if you do not know the whole story. But he wanted Isabella to refuse the shares, essentially, to pass them on to him.'

'And when Izzy died, the shares – they went to Charlie?'

'Of course. She did not have a will, which was an oversight, I think, so everything – her trust fund, et cetera – passed to her nearest next of kin, which was me. But I am unable to own any shares in Pennington's – this was part of my prenuptial agreement with Ian, at his first wife's behest – and so, they went to her next, next of kin.'

'Charlie.'

'Yes.'

'We need to call Ajala,' Chelsea says, finally putting the hot-pink phone down on the coffee table between them. It seems to glow there like an ember, throbbing with latent power, just waiting to cause a spark.

'Yes,' Camille says, her usual formality returning to her posture, her calm armour fully in place once more, 'I'll call her now.'

The next few weeks are both a blur and incredibly slow moving. They go to London for the funeral, of course; Chelsea, Ayesha and Hannah all travel down, returning on the train after the service. Chelsea had texted Joe, asking if he wanted to go with them, but he never responded with a yes or no, nor addressed her when they saw each other on campus, so she was surprised when she spotted him towards the back of the church as they were taking their seats. It seemed petty of him, to come without letting any of them know, but it was the right thing, she supposed, to show support for Izzy. Although, when she saw them hug later, on the steps, she couldn't help but wonder what his intentions really were, considering the contents of the email he'd sent her in the summer.

Izzy had told them that day that she wanted to get back to Birmingham as soon as possible, but it's another week before she returns, and just as Chelsea suspected, it is not the Izzy they know, not really. She sometimes leaves the house for lectures and seminars, and they manage to drag her out to the pub once or twice, but it's as if she's not there, not quite. Chelsea knows she isn't doing the work required, because she doesn't say anything in seminars, and doesn't take any notes in lectures, and whenever she checks on her, she's in bed sleeping or trying to sleep. Soon, it's the last week before reading week and Chelsea has attended another of Sinclair's lectures alone, when he asks her to stay behind after class again.

'I'm worried about Izzy,' he says, leaning against the lectern. 'She's getting so behind, it's going to be hard for her to catch up.'

'I know, but I can't force her to come to lectures. Or to do the reading.'

'I understand that, Chelsea, and I'm not asking you to, but you have exams after Christmas this year, and the way things are going, Izzy won't be able to answer a single question.'

'Isn't there such a thing as, like, bereavement or compassionate leave?'

'Yes,' Sinclair says slowly, 'but she still has to actually do the work. And at this rate, she'll have to take this entire term again in order to be able to do the resits in the summer.'

'If she does the reading, it'll be okay though, right? She wouldn't be penalized for not coming to lectures if she manages to catch up and then take the exams?'

'That would probably be okay,' Sinclair says, nodding. 'But –'

'I'll talk to her, okay? I'll make sure she does the reading.'

Chelsea buys a bag full of junk food on the way back from campus – Haribo Tangfastics, Dairy Milk fruit and nut, two packets of Doritos – and several mindless magazines, and dumps them on Izzy's bed, before crawling underneath the duvet with her. She immediately reaches for the Doritos while Izzy opens the Haribo and listens as Chelsea explains Sinclair's worries.

'Have you been in touch with him recently?' she asks.

360

'He's sent me a bunch of emails, but I haven't replied,' Izzy says.

'About the work?'

Izzy shrugs, 'I guess so.'

'Everyone just wants you to keep up, so you don't fall behind so much you have to repeat the term, or worse, the whole year.'

'Yeah, I know.'

'If you stay here for reading week, we could get through it together.'

'I'll never catch up in a week, Chels,' Izzy says, ripping open the bar of Dairy Milk and breaking off a big chunk.

'Maybe. But you might feel more on top of things, less overwhelmed.'

There's a pause while Izzy chews through her chocolate, before reaching for the open packet of Doritos and pulling out a handful. Finally, she says through a mouthful of crisps, 'No offence, Chelsea, but it's not the workload that's overwhelming me.'

'I know, but still. You want to pass this year, don't you?'

'I honestly don't know if I care.'

'You might do, though. In a couple of months.'

'Then maybe I'll think about it in a couple of months.'

'Okay.'

Chelsea does manage to convince her to stay for reading week, and with campus a little quieter than usual, they even spend a few days in the library together, although Chelsea often looks over to see that Izzy has fallen asleep to the sound of pens on paper and turning pages. With Ayesha and Hannah both gone for the week, it's just the two of them in the house, and although the silences are long and the energy low, it also feels homey and comfortable. Chelsea goes to the pub a few times with some friends she's made on her sociology course, and even though she extends the offer to Izzy, she always declines. Closing the door behind her, Chelsea feels guilty at the weight that lifts off her as she turns out of their garden gate and down the street towards the Bristol Road. It is fully autumn now, leaves crunching underfoot, mingling with the occasional black sack full of rubbish that her student neighbours invariably leave out on the wrong days, attracting rats and foxes. As she walks to the pub to meet Ravi, Sarah and Tim, she thinks how different this year feels to the last. A year ago, she never would have been going out to meet up with anyone other than Izzy, Hannah or Ayesha. They were joined at the hip. Now, she can feel them splintering, and even as they should be pulling together, it feels like she's the only one holding on by her fingertips, while at the same time she's at a total loss as to how to help Izzy. She checks her mobile now, and dashes off a text telling her to come and join them if she changes her mind. But she knows she won't.

'Your housemate didn't want to come?' Sarah asks as Chelsea joins them with a pint.

'No, she's not up for it just yet.'

'That's a shame.'

'Yeah. She's going through a lot, though . . . it's hard to know exactly what to do.'

'I'm sure she appreciates you just being there,' Sarah says, eliciting nods from Ravi and Tim, 'not right now, of course . . . but in general.'

'Ha, thanks Sarah.'

'Hey, you guys should come to the Halloween night at the Factory this weekend. D'you think she might be up for it by then?' Ravi says.

'I'm not sure. I've only just got her back in the library; a rave might be a bit of a push.'

'I mean, it's not quite a rave, but it could be good, you know? Let loose, dance, remind yourself you're alive.'

'You should come even if Izzy doesn't, Chelsea. We went last year, and it was so good. Everyone's outfits are insane,' Sarah says.

Chelsea smiles at this. She does love Halloween. But she'd been planning on renting some scary movies for her and Izzy to enjoy, maybe trying her hand at baking some brownies although that's definitely more Hannah's area of expertise. 'I'll think about it,' she says finally, and this seems to be enough. She'd like to go, of course; she can't remember the last time they all went out properly. They attempted a few nights out before Izzy came back to Birmingham, but they'd always ended up coming home early, the night winding down before it had even begun as they thought about their friend and why she wasn't with them. It had almost felt like a betrayal, and she's sure it would feel the same now, if she went out without Izzy on Saturday. But still, she's glad for the invite. On the way home – she is the first to leave, and it's not yet late – she runs into Joe at the bottom of her road. She's fully expecting him to blank her, just as he's done every time they've crossed paths on campus, so she's taken aback when he starts to remove his headphones from his ears at the sight of her.

'Chelsea. Hi.'

Chelsea blinks at him. *Hi*, is that really all he's got to say?

After months of silence? 'Are you coming from seeing Izzy?'

'Oh,' he says, looking over his shoulder at the darkened street, as if checking to see if he's been followed. 'No, no. Just headed to a friend's. How is she?'

Chelsea shrugs, 'Coping, just about. It's a bit touch and go sometimes. What about you, though? Your dad . . . I've thought about you, since Izzy's dad died. I'm sorry –'

'Don't, Chelsea.' His voice is a hard line in the night air.

'I just wanted to say I'm sorry. I know I should have tried harder, to be there for you.'

Joe has been staring down at the ground, and his head flips up at this, eyes flashing in the amber light of the streetlamp that towers over them. He looks as if he wants to say something, but then, suddenly, his shoulders slump and he seems to deflate. 'Don't. Chelsea, it's . . . it's fine. I handled everything really badly. After he died, I kind of . . . expected you to drop everything and that's really not fair. I mean, you clearly haven't even done that for Izzy, and she's supposedly your best friend.'

Chelsea's cheeks start to burn, and she's momentarily silenced by this accusation. 'What the fuck is that supposed to mean?' she finally croaks out.

'Well, you're here, coming back from the pub, where I'm sure you had a lovely time, while your friend's at home on her own . . . you're just not the sharing and caring type, Chelsea, and that's fine.'

'You don't know what you're talking about.'

'Don't I?'

'Have you told her?' Chelsea spits out. 'Have you told Izzy how you feel about her?'

Joe sighs, rubs a hand down over his face, 'So, that's what this is about. I knew I shouldn't have mentioned it. Is that why you never emailed me back?'

'Do you even care that I didn't?'

Joe looks momentarily stunned. He opens his mouth to say something, then closes it again.

'Well?'

'Yeah, of course I do. Look, I'm sorry about that. I guess I just wanted to hurt you.'

'So, you didn't have feelings for her? Or don't?' But the way Joe looks down at his feet again, tells Chelsea everything she needs to know. 'So, have you told her?'

'I – I can't talk about this with you, Chelsea.'

'Fine.' It's started to rain, and Chelsea flips the hood of her sweater up, covering herself over as she stalks past Joe, leaving him there to put his headphones back in. By the time she gets to her front door, she's shivering, her hoodie poor protection from the rain. But when she gets into the house, slipping off her coat and shoes, she's still shaking and she has to admit to herself that Joe's words, his entire attitude, have hurt her. She knocks on Izzy's door and pushes it open to see her friend rolled up in her duvet, watching a DVD on her laptop, just as she was when Chelsea left her. The curtains are pulled, and she only has her desk lamp burning, so the room has a cosy glow, warm and welcoming.

'I just saw Joe,' Chelsea says, getting into the bed.

'Really?'

'It was really weird.'

'Mmm,' Izzy says. Chelsea looks at her friend, but it's hard to see her face from here, she's concentrating so hard on her computer screen, a *Dawson's Creek* episode flickering across it. Was Joe actually coming from here? And if so, what did he say to Izzy? What happened between them?

'You okay, Iz? Everything all right while I was gone?' Her voice is sharper than she intended, and Chelsea coughs to clear her throat, trying to get herself under control.

'Yep,' Izzy says, rolling towards her a little, so she can rest her head on Chelsea's shoulder, 'just glad you're back.'

'Have you heard from him?'

'Who?'

'Joe.'

'Nope.'

'He wasn't here?'

'Here at the house?' Izzy says, reaching towards her laptop. 'No, Chelsea, he has not been here. This episode is terrible, let's skip it.'

But much later, when Chelsea leaves Izzy's room, the other girl finally fast asleep, Chelsea turns on the hallway light and notices something crumpled up among the mess of shoes underneath the coat pegs. Reaching down to pick it up, she knows what it is before she even touches it: Joe's grey beanie. She looks back towards Izzy's closed door and then to the locked front door, as if either of these portals could give her a definitive answer to this riddle, when she already knows the truth. Joe was here. But then, why did they both lie?

Transcript of interview with Chelsea Keough on 30 October 2007 conducted by Detective Inspector Rob Bailey and Detective Constable Natalie Ajala at Birmingham Central Police Station

Detective Inspector Rob Bailey: Hello, Chelsea.

Detective Constable Natalie Ajala: Thanks for coming in again, Chelsea.

Chelsea Keough: Yeah. Of course.

RB: Anything to help?

CK: Well. Yeah.

RB: That's interesting. You think you've been helping us, do you?

CK: Yes. Haven't I?

RB: You tell us, Chelsea.

CK: I'm … I'm here. I've been here every time you've asked me to be. I'd do anything to help find out who did this to Izzy.

RB: Anything? Except tell the truth, perhaps.

[pause]

CK: What?

NA: We've seen your emails, Chelsea.

CK: Right … what? How?

NA: The warrant covered all your technological devices.

[pause]

CK: Okay.

NA: So, we've seen the email Joe sent you, when you were in Marseille.

RB: The break-up email. If you will.

CK: Okay.

NA: We know he told you about his feelings for Izzy.
[pause]
CK: Yeah ... yeah, he did. I remember now.
RB: So, you misremembered the email?
CK: Um ...
RB: You forgot that Joe, your boyfriend at the time, had told you in an email that he had feelings for your best friend? Your best friend who is now dead?
[pause]
NA: Chelsea, you have to hear how that sounds to us. You didn't forget, did you?
CK: No.
RB: No. You deliberately lied to us.
CK: I just ... this has nothing to do with ... with Izzy's death.
RB: Why don't you let us decide what is and isn't related to Izzy's murder?
CK: I'm sorry. I should have told you.
NA: You see how all this looks now, don't you, Chelsea? You're a smart girl.
RB: Jealousy.
CK: I wasn't jealous.
NA: Oh, you weren't? You weren't jealous of your best friend – who already has everything – also getting your boyfriend?
CK: But she didn't like him that way. Joe. Izzy didn't fancy him. She was obsessed with Jamie, for one thing.
NA: She'd been through a lot recently, though. And Joe could relate to what she was going through ... they both lost their fathers in the space of a few months. That could really pull two people together, don't you think?
[pause]

CK: Maybe.

RB: And you've already told us you weren't sure how to help, how to be there for Joe when his dad died. So, maybe you felt the same when Izzy's dad died?

NA: And maybe Joe knew how to be there for Izzy, and maybe Izzy appreciated that, and maybe feelings developed from there. Isn't that possible?

CK: Yes ... That's ... I suppose that's possible.

RB: Yes, I think that's very possible. Because then we have Izzy's phone.

CK: You found it?

RB: No, we haven't been able to locate it, but we have been able to determine that it was last used in Selly Oak and that it was turned off at around three thirty in the morning. Isn't that right around the time you got home?

CK: I ... I told you, I'm not one hundred percent sure what time I got home. But I haven't seen Izzy's phone since ... since the night she died.

RB: When you turned it off and disposed of it?

CK: No, no, that's not what I mean. I mean, I know she had it at the Factory, and that she texted me when she was leaving, but I ... I've already told you all this. I haven't seen it, I don't know where it is.

NA: You didn't get rid of it?

CK: No! Why would I do that? If I knew where it was, I would tell you.

RB: Like you told us about the coffee table that was missing from the living room?

[short pause]

CK: Yes, exactly ...

RB: And what about the table lamp?

CK: What?

RB: It seems there was a table lamp missing too, Chelsea.

CK: It … there was?

RB: There was. It was eventually found by a neighbour of yours, deposited in their outside bin.

CK: I … I'm sorry, I don't understand.

NA: It was what was used to kill Izzy, Chelsea. Blunt force trauma to the head.

CK: What?

RB: And it has your fingerprints on it.

CK: No … I … I don't know what you're talking about. If there was a lamp missing, I just didn't realize. I promise, I had no idea there was anything missing. I didn't kill her, I'm telling you I didn't kill her.

RB: Chelsea Keough, I am arresting you on suspicion of murder. You do not have to say anything …

Chelsea wakes up with a dry mouth and a thumping head. She didn't pull the curtain properly last night and there's light coming in at the edge where it's been pulled too far over, and she blinks into the brightness. She pushes the duvet away from her, sitting up slowly before swinging her legs out of bed, which was a bad idea because nausea swoops through her belly and she swallows hard, the taste of bile travelling down her throat. Was she sick earlier, when she first woke up? She doesn't think so. She stands up gingerly now, cold air slamming into her bare legs, and then sinks back down on to the bed again, reaching for a pair of tracksuit bottoms that are crumpled up next to her bedside table and pulling them on. She notes the tea standing on the table there, a scum of age on it, and she tries to remember if she made that earlier this morning or when she got in last night. Not that it matters, she'll need to make a fresh mug, regardless. Outside in the hallway, the air feels lifeless, hollow. She's so used to the muffled sounds and movements of Ayesha and Hannah that staying up here without them feels wrong, like the house is missing something crucial, the thing that makes it tick. Although it hasn't ever felt as homely as their flat in halls did; they've tried their hardest to make it cosy and welcoming, but they haven't really got over the false start of having Izzy missing for so long.

She calls Izzy's name as soon as she gets to the bottom of the stairs, assuming she's awake already, probably watching something on her laptop in bed. But there's no answer, so she heads to the kitchen to put the kettle on, thinking that she might be in the downstairs bathroom, but she's not. The living room is in an absolute state, and Chelsea tidies it up a little, picking cushions up off the floor, throwing away empty packets of crisps and chucking empty bottles in the recycling while waiting for the kettle to boil. None of it helps her headache, her brain pushing at her skull every time she reaches down for something. She makes her tea, eyeing the things in the sink that she really should wash up, but she still can't shake that feeling, that empty house feeling, like something's missing, something's wrong. Did Izzy go out somewhere? Chelsea would've thought she'd come out of her room to say hello once she heard Chelsea downstairs, but she hasn't yet. Maybe she's asleep still. She has been sleeping a lot recently, and even though she came home much earlier than Chelsea last night, it's a more likely explanation than her having gone anywhere.

Back in the living room, she looks down the hallway, noting that Izzy's coat is still hanging on one of the hooks, and that her door is shut. So, she must be here. As she turns to go back into the kitchen, she realizes why the house feels so strange: the coffee table that usually sits in the centre of the living room is gone. She looks down at the empty space, trying to pick apart the night. Did something happen to it when they were all here for pre-drinks? She has a clearer memory of that part of the night, but can't remember anything in particular happening to or with the coffee table. She shakes her head – this is a problem for another time, when she's less hungover – and goes back to the kitchen to make a cup of tea for Izzy. But when she knocks at Izzy's door there's no answer. She knocks again and even though she wouldn't normally do this, something tells her she should, and she pushes the door open regardless.

Izzy has the duvet pulled up, covering her face, but her hair is spread out over the pillow, the blonde standing out brightly against the turquoise cotton.

'Iz?'

But there's no movement from Izzy, no sign that she's awake or has heard Chelsea. Chelsea takes a step further into the room and the door bangs shut behind her, making her jump. 'Izzy?' she says again, sure that this time she'll stir and turn around – how can that bang not have woken her up? But when she still doesn't stir or make a sound, Chelsea puts the cup of tea down on the bedside table and reaches across to the other girl. Unlike Chelsea, she has a double bed, and she's sleeping on the far side of it, face turned towards the wall, so Chelsea has to kneel on the edge of the bed in order to grasp her shoulder. She's not quite sure why she has a sudden need to wake her up, but there's something twisting and turning in her gut that makes her grab Izzy's shoulder and say her name again, this time louder, sharper.

But as soon as she touches her, she knows something's really wrong. She's still. Too still. And there is a depth to the silence in the room, a silence so thick you could cut it. Chelsea starts to shake Izzy even as she realizes, in that moment, what the silence is: Izzy isn't breathing. She

373

turns her over, and the girl lolls on to her back, her closed eyes facing up to the ceiling, and that's when Chelsea notices the blood. Her heart is pumping in her chest, banging, banging, banging as she gently moves some of Izzy's long blonde hair, and retching, feels blood encrusted in it, sees blood soaking through the turquoise cotton of the pillowcase. There's bile in her throat again and this time she can't hold it back. She springs away from Izzy, holding her hand over her mouth, and rushes to the front door. She wrenches it open and steps outside, just as the vomit falls from her mouth on to the cement slabs of the paving stones in the front garden. She's bent over, hands on her thighs, and she stays there for what feels like a long time, for too long, but she can't unbend herself, can't move from that position and go back into the house, back into Izzy's bedroom, back to Izzy's body. She closes her eyes. This can't be happening.

She squeezes her eyes even tighter, wishing someone else was here with her, wishing Ayesha was upstairs. She swallows down another wave of vomit as it rises up her throat, but it's not enough. She throws up again, the smell of it full in her nose, the residue sticking to the corners of her mouth. She straightens up, finally, wipes the back of her hand across her mouth, stands for a second, making sure it's not about to happen again, and takes a step back into the house. She doesn't close the door behind her, though. For some reason, she can't bring herself to seal herself up inside the house. Just her and Izzy. She goes back to the door of Izzy's bedroom, stands on the threshold looking in on her friend. How has this happened? Chelsea's blood is thrumming through her body so loudly, she swears she can hear it as she tries to think back to last night, to Izzy leaving the Factory, to Chelsea getting home. The memories are blurry, barely there, full of flashing lights and loud voices. She remembers losing Izzy early on, she thinks she'd gone to the toilet or something, but they met up soon after, didn't they? And then Izzy had texted, to say she wanted to go home already, and Chelsea knows she should've gone with her, but she'd been having such a good time, had wanted to stay loose and having fun, laughing and dancing, and so she'd let her friend go home on her own and now here she was. She can't bring herself to think the word *dead*, even as Izzy lies there, lifeless, but she knows, standing there, that this is all her fault. If she'd just come home with her, none of this, whatever *this* is, whatever happened here, would've happened. She chokes down a sob, which turns into another wave of nausea she has to swallow down again. She has to do something. She moves into the room, and then immediately takes a step back again. She can't do it, she can't do it; she can't touch her again.

Her eyes fill, and the room goes misty, wavy, Izzy disappearing against the force of her tears. She takes a deep breath and it shakes all the way through her body. She has to call the police. She draws her mobile from the pocket of her tracksuit bottoms, her hands shaky, her limbs feeling as if they're no longer really a part of her body, and dials 999.

Mayfair

'For fuck's sake, Izzy, pick up,' Charlie mutters to himself. He's standing in the corridor for the men's bathroom, and there's been a steady stream of men coming in and out, as he's tried and failed to place a call with Izzy. 'Fuck,' he says again, as it rings out.

He slips the phone in his jacket pocket as someone he vaguely recognizes stops in front of him, slapping him on the shoulder. 'Dunwoody, good to see you, sir. Terrible news about your old man – how're you holding up?'

Charlie tries to focus on this other man, but his image slides in front of him, refusing to coalesce, 'Been better,' he grunts, hoping this will suffice.

'Well, if there's anything I can do, you know where to find me,' the other says, ironically, considering Charlie has no notion of who this man is, or where he might normally find him. 'Can I interest you in a little ...' he tilts his head towards the bathroom and subtly passes a finger underneath his nose, but Charlie shakes his head. He's had too much already. 'Righto,' the interlocutor says, finally moving on.

Charlie heaves in a breath and dashes off a text message to Izzy. He's not angry at her for forgetting to sign the papers, he just needs her to respond, so he knows what to do about it. It took him all morning to get her to agree to sell three-quarters of her shares to him, but she'd left the house before doing the one thing that would make it official, and with the board meeting on Monday, he needs this done now. Okay, maybe he is a little bit angry. He's starting to wonder if she might back out, or if she just agreed to sell them to shut him up, her refusal to sign a clear *fuck you*.

He heads off in the direction of the bar, hoping to find Doyle, whose party this is, but instead stumbling into many more maybe-acquaintances, some with a word for his dad, others not mentioning it at all. He doesn't know which he hates more. At the bar, he gets a whisky and finishes it in two big gulps, before asking for another, and checking his phone again. Nothing from Izzy. He clenches his jaw. How hard is it to check your phone every once in a while, to call or text back? He needs to get these papers to her, as soon as possible. Across the room, he spots Doyle's distinctive dark curls, and lurches towards him. It's a packed room, so it's pretty difficult, and he can feel eyes on him, but he doesn't care.

'All right, old boy?' Doyle says as he approaches.

'Fine,' Charlie barks.

'Bit early for this kind of showing, isn't it?'

Charlie swallows down some more whisky. 'It's your birthday.'

'Right, still. Listen, I know I encouraged you to come, but if it's all a bit too much, then say that. Didn't you have the will reading yesterday? Must've been tough.'

'Didn't go great,' Charlie huffs. 'Dad left all his shares to Izzy.'

'Ah.'

'Can you believe it? The controlling stake left to a child, Doyle. A *child*.'

'He must have had his reasons. Your father wasn't one to do anything lightly.'

Charlie makes a noise like a snort and takes another gulp of whisky. 'He also might not have been in his right mind when he made that decision,' he says, tipping his glass towards Doyle, whisky sloshing out of it and on to Doyle's lapel, 'ever think of that?'

'Well,' Doyle says, dabbing at the spill with a handkerchief, 'was he? In his right mind?'

'Painkillers, Doyle, so many painkillers, you wouldn't believe. He could've been doolally on them.'

'Yes, but *was* he?'

Charlie shrugs, 'Maybe.'

'Listen, old man, I think you might need to go home.'

'What? No, the night is young.'

'You're practically slurring already. You can take my car, I'll let the driver know.' Charlie starts to shake his head, but the action sets something loose inside his brain and suddenly the room begins to blur and Doyle has his arm clamped around his shoulders, his voice in his ear, 'Come on, man, this isn't a good look. Let's get you home, okay?'

And Charlie nods. He stops at the bathroom on his way out, though, and when someone offers him a bump, this time he accepts. He could do with a clearer head. Doyle has his car waiting, clapping his shoulder as he says goodbye, clearly relieved to be cleaning up a mess before it happens, and Charlie crawls into the back seat, suddenly feeling a little bit clearer.

'Where to, sir?' the driver asks, and Charlie gives him his address.

But then, as they're driving down Hyde Park Place, he leans

379

forward and asks the driver if he'd be willing to take him to Birmingham.

The other man meets his eye in the rear-view mirror. 'For a price, of course,' Charlie assures him, 'just name it,' and the driver nods, heading west out of London and towards the Midlands.

As soon as Ajala arrives, Chelsea can tell she's annoyed.

'That's it?' she asks, standing over the coffee table, staring down at the hot-pink phone as though it's a bomb about to go off. Chelsea isn't sure what Camille said to get her to leave, but Monica from victim support has been dispatched elsewhere and so it is just the three of them in the quiet hotel suite.

'Yes, that's it,' Camille says.

'And how long have you had it in your possession, Camille?'

'Well, I found it just over a month ago. But I believe it's been in the house much longer than that.'

'Your house in Cornwall?'

'Yes.'

'Did Charlie have access to the house in Cornwall?'

'Yes.'

'He had a key?'

'He still has a key.'

'And you've both touched it?' Ajala asks, looking between Camille and Chelsea, both of whom nod in confirmation. 'Christ. Well, this is a monumental fuck-up.'

'I should have told you sooner, Natalie. I apologize.'

'You should have told me immediately, Camille. This is tarnished evidence now. Even if it could prove Charlie's involvement, we're unlikely to be able to submit it. It wouldn't stand up in court.'

Chelsea, who knew Ajala was likely to say something like this, turns her back on both women and looks out of the window. Dusk is beginning to settle over the city, the streetlights have been turned on, and the rain from earlier in the day has partly swept away to reveal a sky striated pink and turquoise as the sun sets. The windows are too well glazed for her to hear any noise from the traffic below, but she lets the sound of Ajala and Camille blur and become a murmur to her as she watches the world go by and the sky change colour. It wasn't all that long ago that this – simply standing here, with the world at her feet – had been impossible, and as she tunes back into their conversation, she remembers what it was like to have every decision made for her, every move dictated by someone else, a force so much bigger than her. She'd told herself that she never wanted to feel that way again, but here it is, that feeling, rising to the surface, taking hold. Helpless and waiting to be saved, while knowing full well that no one is coming to save her. She sits down on the sofa, and while Ajala and Camille are still busy talking, slides Izzy's long-lost phone towards her.

What would happen if she used this to text Charlie back? She's not even sure it can send messages any more – it won't be connected to the internet, and Izzy's contract must have run out years ago – but the thought of the scare it would give Charlie almost makes her smile. But when she opens up the messages, it's not Charlie's name that catches her eye this time – it's Joe's.

She can't imagine how she missed it earlier, hovering just below her own, and she's not quite sure why seeing it there bothers her so much, but some ringing bell makes her open it. It's the last text Joe sent Izzy at 00:37 on Sunday, 28 October:

Can you reply to me plz? I just want to talk to you.

Chelsea tries to think back to that night, and the days just before it. She'd bumped into Joe in Selly Oak during reading week, but both he and Izzy had told her they hadn't seen each other. She'd found his hat in the hallway, though, had suspected he might have paid Izzy a visit. But when she'd asked her again the next day, she'd once again denied it. And Chelsea, with everything else going on, had decided to believe her and forgotten all about it amid everything else that had happened in the following few days. She navigates back to Izzy's inbox and scrolls down, the flip phone slow and staccato in a way she's no longer used to, but luckily, she doesn't have to look for long before finding Joe's previous message, sent earlier that night:

Iz? Are u there? I can meet you whnevr.

And, just before it:

I just want to talk to you about Thursday night.

Blinking down at the screen, Chelsea tries to piece this all together, but she can't see Izzy's replies to any of these messages, she only has half the story, and she's about to try and find her sent messages when Ajala says sharply, 'Chelsea, what are you doing?'

'Sorry, sorry,' Chelsea says, looking up at her and Camille as if breaking free of a hypnotic daze, 'I know I shouldn't be touching it.'

'So, put it down,' Ajala says.

'What are you looking at, Chelsea?' Camille asks, her voice sounding even more serene than usual, despite the situation.

'Oh, erm, nothing. Sorry.' But the question has galvanized her and she stands up suddenly, as though electrocuted, and says, 'I think I have to go.'

'Okay,' Ajala says on a sigh, 'but you have to leave that here,' she nods at the phone still in Chelsea's hand. Chelsea nods back at her and places it on the coffee table before getting out her own phone. Joe has texted her a few times since their phone call, 'checking in', as he called it, but now, those check-ins seem like something else. Was he actually checking up on her? Had he been the anonymous Facebook messenger this whole time, warning her off? And what about the texts from an unknown number? They'd only started up once Ayesha had given Joe Chelsea's mobile number. Without stopping to really think about it, and knowing full well it's a long shot, she sends him a text:

Hey, I'm in town and at a bit of a loose end. Any chance you're around for a drink and a catch-up?

Soon after, he replies:

Thought you were in Scotland! I'm actually at a pub with some friends right now. You want to stop by?

Chelsea doesn't want to do this in front of an audience, but she says yes, and Joe sends his location; he's less than a fifteen-minute walk away at the Blue Posts on Newman Street. She says goodbye to Camille and Ajala, both of whom appear more than a little confused by her sudden rush to leave, and hurries from the suite and out of the hotel. She wishes she'd had more time with Izzy's phone before Ajala had taken it from her, so she could see what Izzy's replies to Joe had been, so that she had a clearer picture of what was going on, but the picture she has is just enough to convince her something was, and is, very, very wrong.

The streets are crowded with pedestrians, so she has to dodge and weave if she wants to move with any speed, occasionally dipping down off the kerb to avoid a particularly large group of people insisting on walking four abreast, or someone else particularly slow-moving. Dusk is turning to night, and this kind of light always makes this part of London seem particularly Dickensian to Chelsea, the glow of streetlights, the twisty alleyways looming out of the gloom, surrounded by people but all alone. She's almost at the pub before she knows it and has to stop and lean against the wall of a building to gather her breath and her thoughts, which have been scrambled ever since she left the hotel. As she pushes off from the wall and starts to walk again, one thought rears in her mind: Joe's feelings for Izzy.

Izzy's feelings for Joe.

What the police – and everyone else – thought, was that Izzy had told Chelsea that she and Joe had started, or were going to start, a relationship, and she, Chelsea, had killed her for it. And even though she'd ultimately gone to prison for it, she'd never known whether anything had ever actually happened between Izzy and Joe; that was how in the dark she was about that night. As she nears the pub, the door swings open and Joe walks out. There's a bit of a sway to him and she wonders how long he's been drinking. Through the murky evening light, his figure is weak, wavering, but then he takes a swig from his pint glass and the action solidifies him, makes him real. Clouds have swooped back over London as she's been walking and it's started to rain again, but lightly, that insistent, spitting rain, and Joe is hunched over a little, to protect his face from it, but even so, Chelsea can see worry and something more, something darker, in the lines of his face.

She says his name and he looks up, his face clearing, 'Hey! That was quick. You want to come inside? We're right at the back, so I didn't want you to miss us.'

Her heart is banging at her chest. Why did he get in touch with her? Things hadn't been good between them when Izzy died, and he hadn't made contact during her entire sentence, so why now, when she's out? 'Actually, could we talk out here?' Chelsea says, motioning over to one of the pub's outdoor tables.

'Out here? It's fucking freezing, Chels. Look at you, you're practically shaking.'

It's true that her faux-leather jacket is no match for the November cold, but they can't have the conversation Chelsea wants to have with an audience, so she tells him she's fine and sits down, the damp of the wooden bench immediately beginning to seep into her jeans. Joe follows suit, but then he jumps up again, telling her he'll get her a drink. Chelsea huddles into her jacket as he disappears through the pub's door. He didn't even give her time to tell him she didn't need or want a drink, but despite the cold, she's glad for this moment so she can gather her thoughts. The story she'd been told – and she always thought of it as that, a story – was that Izzy and Joe had grown closer, Izzy turning to him when she lost her dad, just as he had done earlier in the year. But what if only half of that was true? What if, instead of Izzy telling Chelsea she had feelings for Joe, and Chelsea taking her shock and anger out on Izzy, Izzy told Joe she didn't feel the same way as him and it was Joe who killed her? He has always been protected by the alibi of his friends – he'd been at a party elsewhere in Selly Oak and they had vouched for him. But how easy is it to slip out of a party with no one noticing? To convince drunk friends that, no, actually you were there all night, remember? Because, looking at those texts he sent Izzy on the night she died, that's exactly what Chelsea thinks might have happened.

The pub door bangs open and Joe comes out with two pints of Guinness and a packet of crisps clutched in his hands.

'So, what was it you wanted to talk about?' he says, sitting down. 'I get the feeling this isn't just a social call.'

'I wanted to talk to you about the night Izzy died. There's just so much I don't know still, and I've only ever known what I've been told, and so much that I've been told has been a lie, or just plain wrong.'

'Okay,' Joe says, a crease between his eyebrows, 'I don't know how I can help with that, though.' He opens the packet of crisps and pops one into his mouth.

'I've seen Izzy's phone, Joe.'

'Izzy's phone?' he says, shifting in his seat, sitting up a little straighter. There is a bleariness to his eyes from all the beer he's clearly had already today, but he is suddenly very focused on her. 'But they never found Izzy's phone.'

'I know. Camille found it recently. She showed it to me earlier.'

'Camille?'

'Yes.'

'Has she had it this whole time?'

'No, that's – that's beside the point. I've seen your texts from that night, Joe. You wanted to see her, you were trying to get her to come to that party you were at, or to meet up. And you did, didn't you? You did see her.'

Joe shakes his head. His right hand is gripping his pint glass, knuckles white in the twilight grey. 'No, I didn't, I –'

'Joe, please. Please don't lie to me, I can't take it any more.'

'I didn't see her, Chelsea, I promise. I –'

'Did you kill her?' Chelsea asks, because she can't think what else might make him continue to lie to her like this. She has never thought Joe might be guilty; as rocky as their break-up was, and as aware as she was of his feelings for Izzy, she's never considered him a possible suspect. It was partly the alibi, yes, but it was also her belief that it had to have been Jamie Sinclair. Even walking over here, she wasn't sure of it, but here he is, steadfastly lying.

'No, God, no, I didn't kill her,' Joe gasps out.

'What did you do, Joe? What happened?'

But Joe doesn't say anything, seemingly unable to speak. Chelsea watches as he turns his face to the street, pedestrians passing by, umbrellas up, a car whooshing past them, but his eyes are unseeing, taking him back somewhere else. She knows he's there, back in Birmingham, back, even to that very night. If he did kill Izzy, then she has to know, and if he didn't, then she has to know what he knows. Because he does know something.

Finally, after a long time, he turns back to her, his face washed clear of any colour, his eyes still haunted by those long-gone memories. 'Okay, okay. I'll tell you.'

Selly Oak

'Yes. And you should have told me to fuck off,' Izzy says, as she unbuckles her seatbelt and goes to open the door. Jamie blinks, his face blanching, and for a second Izzy feels sorry for him although it soon passes. She sighs, 'It doesn't matter any more, just go home to your wife. And thank you. Really.'

As she gets out of the car, back into the night-time cold, she feels very sober all of a sudden. Maybe all she'd needed was a difficult conversation to clear her head. But then she stumbles over something lying on the pavement, just as Jamie pulls out of his parking space and races off up the road, and nausea swoops through her as she swears out loud. Shaking it off, she walks up to her house, but stops in surprise when she hears someone call her name. Squinting, she tries to see who it is, a figure outlined in the dark, stepping from the shadow and out into the pool of the streetlamp's light.

'What are you doing here?' Izzy says, stopping just short of the garden gate.

'You weren't answering my texts,' Joe says, stepping towards her. 'I just want to talk, Iz.'

'Now?' Exhaustion runs through Izzy like water down a drainpipe and she can't think of anything worse than having yet another conversation with someone she'd rather not see or talk to. She drags herself up the path and unlocks the front door.

'We need to talk about Thursday night.'

'Now?' she says again, turning to look at him. She's unlocked the door, and as it stands ajar behind her, Joe peers through and past her, looking down the darkened hallway.

'Is Chelsea in?' he asks.

'No, she's still at the Factory.'

'Can we please just go inside and have a chat? It's freezing.' Joe isn't dressed up for Halloween, which doesn't surprise Izzy at all, and instead is in his usual uniform of Adidas, jeans and a Fred Perry jacket, the collar turned up against the cold.

'Fine. Come on, then.'

She turns on the hallway lights and slips off her heels as Joe shuts the door behind him with a crash. She doesn't look at him as she pulls on her slippers and walks into the living room, before heading into the kitchen beyond it. The living room is still littered with empty wine bottles and used glasses, open packets of Doritos, and a chopping board with a cut-open lime and kitchen knife abandoned on top of it. The kitchen is freezing, as it almost always is now that autumn has descended, and the overhead light gives it a clinical feel, making it feel even colder. She flicks on the kettle, and turns to see that Joe has followed her in there.

'I'm just gonna grab a jumper. Will you make the tea?'

He nods, and she heads to her bedroom, picking up the jumper she'd been wearing earlier and left curled up in her duvet like a cat. She pulls it on and sits down on the edge of the bed, daring herself to lie back on it. But if she does that, she may never get up again. And if she does that, Joe may take it as an invitation. Sighing, she gets up and goes into the living room, where Joe has collected up some bottles and glasses, taking things into the kitchen and lining them up next to the sink.

'Hey,' he says, walking in, 'I made tea, but I also poured some wine.'

He puts two glasses, filled with some leftover red wine from earlier, on the coffee table, and goes back into the kitchen for the tea. She doesn't want it, but Izzy unthinkingly reaches for the glass nearest her, settles down on one of the sofas and takes a sip. After all the sweet drinks earlier, it tastes a little sour in comparison, but she takes another sip anyway and closes her eyes, so she feels rather than sees Joe join her on the sofa.

'Who was that dropping you off earlier?' he asks, after a second or two of silence. 'Was it Sinclair?'

Izzy opens one eye and then the other, and decides to take the path of least resistance, 'It was a minicab.'

'Why were you in the front seat, then?'

She takes another sip of wine, looks over at where her cup of tea sits on the coffee table but decides it's too far away, and drinks some more wine instead. She feels sluggish and slow, all the adrenaline and alcohol and anxiety of the night coming to an abrupt end, and she feels pressed up against a brick wall, any energy she had left slammed out of her. 'Fine. It was Jamie. I got kicked out of my cab, so I called him.'

'Why didn't you call me?'

Calling Joe hadn't even crossed her mind, and the thought of this makes her laugh, but when she sees Joe's face, she stops. 'Sorry,' she says, realizing that in her exhaustion, she's sort of begun to slur, 'not laughing at you. Just tired.'

'Are you back together with him?' he asks, but the words come out wrong and circular, like the sentence is walking around and around in a maze. Is he speaking out of order? Why would he do that?

'Back together?' she says eventually. 'We weren't ever together.'

'I know you were.'

'No,' she says, shaking her head and leaning it up against the back of the sofa. She wants to be enveloped by it, pulled into its very fabric. She takes another sip of wine, and then stops and looks down into the glass.

'I just want to know where we stand, Iz.'

This makes her laugh again, because the last thing she could do right now is stand. 'No standing,' she says.

'What?'

'No standing, just lying.'

'Okay,' Joe says, peering at her. 'Are you okay?'

'Feel weird,' she says, and before she can remember not to, she takes another gulp of wine. 'Did you put something in this?' she asks.

But she must really be slurring now, or maybe she didn't say anything at all, because Joe doesn't reply, just leans forward so that his face swims in front of her eyes, like he's checking her for something. She feels him take the glass of wine from her and then his hands are on her face, but she can't really feel them there, just knows they're there because he's there, right in front of her. He leans in further, and she wants to pull back but she can't, and then there's a sound – a big sound, something crashing to the floor maybe, and he's away, he's off her.

'Is there someone here?' he demands.

394

But she can't answer. Is there someone here? There shouldn't be.

And then – yes, there is someone here – because the door to the stairway opens and there's someone standing there, there in her home which was supposed to be empty.

But thank God, it's only Hannah.

'Hannah? Hannah was there?' Chelsea manages to croak out.

Joe nods, his face wan. He reaches for his pint, swallowing down a large gulp before saying, 'I don't know what happened after I left, but Hannah was there, and Izzy was alive. I didn't kill her, Chelsea. I promise.'

'But you did put something in her drink?' Chelsea says.

Joe swallows, folds his lips into a thin line and shakes his head, 'I . . . I'm not that same person any more, I need you to know that.'

'You drugged her?' Chelsea says, the words shooting out of her on the force of her rising heart rate. Joe nods his answer, still unable to look at her. 'I don't understand, wouldn't that have come up when they did the drug tests?'

Joe is still hiding his face from her, every line in his posture telling her he's defeated as he gives a shrug, 'I don't know about that. I kept expecting . . . expecting something to come up, but it never did. I can't explain that.'

'Oh, that you can't explain.' Chelsea has to bite back her rage, stop herself from forcing him to stare her in the face. 'Did you rape her, Joe?'

He shakes his head, 'No.' The word comes out whisper-soft and for some reason this whispered denial makes the anger scream in Chelsea's veins, fill her body to the brim.

'Were you going to?'

'I, I . . .' he stutters in response, the perfect answer from a person who has always put himself first, no matter the cost to anyone else.

'Is the only reason you didn't because Hannah walked in and caught you?'

It takes a while but eventually he nods, the coward's confession. 'I don't know . . . I don't know if I would've gone through with it.'

Chelsea wants to stand up, to walk away from this table, this pub, this street and never see Joe again, but she has to ask, 'Did you ever do that to me?' He shakes his head, his face white and pink and strained.

'I . . . I . . .'

'Did you ever do it to anyone else?'

'Chelsea – I . . . you can't tell anyone? Please, I have family, a wife, a child now. I can't –'

'You can't what? Be arrested? Go to prison?'

Colour finally returns to Joe's cheeks as he blushes with realization. 'I'm so sorry, Chels, so sorry for everything that's happened to you. But I didn't kill her. Izzy was alive when I left that house. If you want to find out what really happened to her, you'll have to ask Hannah. But please, for the love of God, please could you leave me out of it?'

There's roaring in Chelsea's ears, and for a second, she thinks it might be her, roaring out loud, but no, 'That's enough,' she manages to bite out, 'I've heard enough.'

* * *

Chelsea isn't sure how she makes it back on to Oxford Street with Joe's words ringing in her ears, his confession, his revelation, his plea, but eventually, on shaking, foal-like legs, she finds herself standing in front of a gleaming Zara, crowds of shoppers weaving around her as she gets her bearings. She can't quite deal with his confession yet, has to leave it here for now, so she can concentrate on the matter in hand.

Hannah? All this time, and it's Hannah, of all people? Surely, that can't be right. For a second, she wishes she'd stayed longer, asked Joe more questions, but she couldn't, not for one second longer. With shaking hands, she takes her phone from her pocket to check the time. Will Ayesha be there by now? She knows where the engagement party is taking place – at Hannah and Charlie's penthouse apartment overlooking the Thames. She's not sure of the exact address but Ayesha showed her a photo of the building, and she's pretty sure she'll recognize it once she gets there. She knows Ayesha would tell her this is a bad idea, but Ayesha doesn't know what she knows, doesn't know that Charlie has had Izzy's phone, hidden for all these years, and that Hannah lied to them and the police even as Chelsea was being questioned and arrested for their best friend's murder. And none of them know that Chelsea is on her way.

The building is easy to spot, even from Blackfriars Bridge. Slightly tucked away from the river, it's sharp and angular, with its knife blade edges and soaring windows, but coupled with primary-colour accents and giant steel braces, Chelsea can't help thinking it looks a little like the toy of an overgrown child. Nearing the entrance, she is relieved to see other people coming and going. She'd been worried about getting into the building; there's no way Hannah or Charlie would buzz her in, after all, but with so many guests arriving for their party, she can slip in, uninvited and unseen. She follows a pair of beautifully dressed women through the entrance and stands with them in the entryway, waiting for the lift to arrive. Still shivering in her jacket, with rain-dampened jeans on, she couldn't look more different to these invited guests, but if anyone asks, she can say she's part of the catering staff, simply running late. But they don't even look at her, don't give her a second glance as she follows them into the lift. One of them is almost immediately distracted by the mirrored back wall, using it to expertly reapply some lipstick as her friend complains about the rain. Chelsea huddles in the opposite corner, trying not to look conspicuously inconspicuous. The doors ding open at the penthouse and she lets her fellow travellers get out first, hoping she can scoot into the apartment in their wake without anyone noticing. But she doesn't even have to worry about that; the door to Hannah and Charlie's home is wide open, the party in full swing. Ahead of her, the two women melt into the melee, almost immediately enveloped in welcoming embraces and happy hellos. There are servers passing with silver trays laden with champagne glasses, but Chelsea resists taking one, and instead skirts to the edges of the crowd, trying to lay eyes on Hannah and Charlie. She is keeping an eye out for Ayesha as well, but knowing what her friend would say to her appearing here like this, it wouldn't be terrible if she didn't see her.

Scanning the room, Chelsea tries to take everything in: floor-to-ceiling views of London at her night-time best, even in the rain, mid-century modern furniture, antiques, original paintings and prints. She turns her back on the windows; the view, pretty as it is, makes her feel dizzy, makes her think about how far they are from the ground, how long that fall would be. She inhales deeply, trying to regain her sense of control, and the noise causes a suited man standing nearby to glance at her out of the corner of his eye. She turns quickly, not wanting to give him the chance to recognize her, and almost immediately sees Hannah. She's standing talking to someone, her head tilted slightly, nodding intermittently, listening intently. Her hair is blonder than it ever was when they were at university, and styled in sleek, glossy waves. She's wearing a long, champagne-coloured dress; the square neck almost reaches her collar bones, but the straps are thin, creating a criss-cross against her back, which, like the rest of her, is subtly tanned despite summer being so long gone. Looking at her, Chelsea can't help but think of Izzy, something about Hannah's poise, her shininess; she looks beautiful, that fact is undeniable, but Chelsea isn't sure she looks like Hannah any more, can't help but think that she preferred Hannah when she was less polished, less glossy, a little soft and fuzzy around the edges.

Hannah turns her head, as if she can hear Chelsea's thoughts, but her eyes glide right over her. She's looking for someone, Charlie presumably, and Chelsea follows her gaze, trying to seek him out too. But suddenly, there's a hand clamped on her arm, someone at her elbow saying, 'What the fuck are you doing here?'

Ayesha pulls her through the crowded room, away from Hannah, sliding open a door that leads out to a terrace, where potted plants are being battered by rain, pools of water forming on the tarpaulin covers of the patio furniture. 'Chelsea,' Ayesha practically hisses, 'what the fuck are you thinking, coming here?'

'I need to speak to Hannah.'

Ayesha stares at her. They are standing underneath part of the building's overhang, so neither of them is getting wet, but the wind sluices through Chelsea's clothing and she crosses her arms against her chest, trying to make herself feel just a little bit warmer.

'You can't talk to Hannah. Not here, not now. Look inside there, Chels,' Ayesha says with a tilt of her head towards the window, 'this is not the time.'

'You don't understand, I need to talk to her. Right now.'

Ayesha shakes her head, 'Chelsea, what is going on?'

'She was there. That night. Hannah was there.'

Something crosses Ayesha's face, something like understanding, but then she shakes her head again, shakes it away, a fact she can't compute. 'What are you talking about? No, she wasn't.'

'She was. Joe told me.'

'Joe?' Ayesha lets out a puff of laughter. 'What does he know?'

Chelsea wants to explain it all to her, but Camille has just walked into the apartment, dressed head to toe in black. Usually she's clad in creams, camels and expensive neutrals; Chelsea can't help but think there is something pointedly funereal about this choice. 'Please, Ayesha, just trust me on this. I need to talk to Hannah.'

Ayesha blinks at her, clearly trying to take it all in. 'Okay,' she says at last, 'but you stay here. I'll go and grab her.' Chelsea, who has just spotted Charlie greeting his stepmother, nods. She has no desire to be caught here by either one of them.

By the time Ayesha returns, Chelsea is shivering, huddled beneath the overhang, forcing herself to think warm thoughts. The rain has eased off a little, but it's still spitting, and Hannah stops in the open doorway, not wanting to come any further, 'Chelsea?'

Her voice wavers a little, and she sounds so much like herself, so much like the Hannah Chelsea knows and remembers, that tears come to her eyes. 'Hannah.'

'What are you doing here?' She looks behind her, clearly searching for her fiancé once again, and then, deciding that being cold and wet is better than being caught here with the accused killer of her fiancé's sister, she steps out on to the balcony, Ayesha following, and closes the door behind her.

'I need – I need to ask you a question.' It's hard for Chelsea to get this out. With Hannah right in front of her, gleaming in the greyscale of a wet London night, Chelsea feels less sure of herself. Could Hannah – her Hannah – really have kept this a secret for so long? Could she really have known what happened to Izzy all this time and not only kept that from everyone, but watched, and done nothing, as Chelsea went to prison? Could she really have *killed* her?

'You were there, at the house that night.'

Hannah shakes her head, 'That's not a question.'

'That's hardly the point here, Han,' Ayesha says quietly.

'I don't know where you've got that idea from, Chelsea, but you know I wasn't there.' Hannah crosses her arms against herself, and Chelsea can see, even from where she's standing, that her skin has started to goosebump.

'Joe told me.' Hannah blinks, swallows, looks back through her apartment's floor-to-ceiling windows, still searching for her husband-to-be. 'Charlie was there too, wasn't he?'

'No . . . no, I don't know what you're talking about, Chelsea, this all sounds a bit mad.'

'Hannah –'

'You know I wasn't there that night, I don't understand where any of this is coming from. We all know what happened to Izzy. I don't know if this is just residual guilt or something, but I really think you need to move on with your life, now that you're out of prison.'

Something clicks for Chelsea as she realizes it was Hannah, all along, sending those Facebook messages, warning her off. The realization makes it hard for her to stand still, to not pick up one of the rain-soaked plant pots and throw it over the side of the terrace, just to hear the smash of the terracotta on the concrete below, just to get Hannah to stop talking, to admit to everything. She even sounds more like Izzy now, if that's possible. Her tell-tale whine is gone, and in its place is something smoother, rounder, long vowels filling the space between them. 'Hannah, Joe saw you. He saw you there, in our living room.'

Hannah shakes her head, eyes glistening, 'No. Joe? Of course he didn't see me, why would he even say that?'

'Exactly, why would he say that if it wasn't true? He told me what he did to her – he drugged her, did you know that?'

Hannah's face pales, even beneath her perfectly applied make-up and November tan, and she shakes her head again, 'No, that would've come up in the toxicology report. I don't know why he's told you any of this, Chelsea, but I'm sorry, it's not true. You're going to have to find some other way to make yourself feel better.'

'Feel better?' She spits the words out and takes a step towards Hannah. 'Feel *better*? Do you have any idea, any idea at all, what I've been through for the past fifteen years? This isn't about feeling better,' she practically snarls at Hannah, 'this is about clearing my name, so I can actually start my life, and finding out once and for all what happened to Izzy.'

Hannah has nothing to say to this, her eyes wide as she stares at Chelsea. She opens her mouth and closes it again, with nothing to say, when finally, Ayesha saves her from having to do so.

'But, Chels, she has a point. The toxicology report didn't say anything about Izzy having been roofied. All it showed was the pills you guys took at the Factory.'

'I know, I can't explain that, but there must be a reason. Maybe it just didn't show up because of everything else she'd taken?'

Ayesha's eyebrows pull together. 'But . . . it would have been in her system more recently and therefore more likely to show up, wouldn't it? Look, I just think . . . can we really trust Joe?'

'Why would he lie about drugging Izzy, Ayesha? That makes no sense. It doesn't serve him at all. And besides, Camille has the phone.'

'What phone?'

'Izzy's phone. She has Izzy's phone. Charlie's had it, been hiding it this whole time.'

Ayesha emits a noise of surprise and looks towards Hannah, who is shaking her head, but her eyes are now trained on the windows, looking for someone to come and save her, to come and take the wheel of her sinking ship. Chelsea takes another step towards her, sees her stiffen and turn back to her. 'Hannah, this is important, you have to tell the truth now. It's all going to come out soon anyway, Camille's not going to let this stay covered up. Don't you think I deserve to know the truth? Don't you think Izzy deserves better?'

'It's not – that's not – you don't understand. We'll lose everything. Everything will get taken away.'

Chelsea takes another step closer to her. Blood seethes in her ears, her eyes narrowed, 'I've already lost everything, I've already had everything taken away. For what, Hannah? For a lie – for *your* lies.' She reaches for Hannah's bare arm, wanting to shake the truth out of her, wanting her to feel just an ounce of the fear Chelsea's had to live with for the past fifteen years.

Hannah's hand flies up to her face, cowering from Chelsea's grip as she grabs hold of her upper arm, pulls her closer. 'No, please, don't. I don't . . . please don't hurt me.'

'I'm not going to hurt you. Just tell me what happened that night.'

'I can't.'

'Hannah, you have to. I know you were there, I know Charlie went up there. What happened?'

'I wasn't there, you know that, you know I wasn't there.'

Hannah's tell-tale whine is back now, as Chelsea pulls back the layers, forces her back to that house in Birmingham fifteen years ago, and she can't help but feel a little bit triumphant that she's managed to peel away the Dunwoody sheen to reveal the real Hannah. 'Joe was there, Han. He saw you.'

'No, no, I didn't see him –'

The words fly out of her, a Freudian slip perhaps, but it doesn't matter; Chelsea launches herself upon them, catching them before they disappear, '*You* didn't see *him*?'

Hannah swallows deeply, her eyes wider than ever and filling with tears as she realizes what she's done, what she's said. Chelsea tightens her grip on her arm and the other woman gasps.

'Hannah,' Chelsea says through gritted teeth.

'It was an accident,' Hannah says finally, practically in a whisper, 'you don't understand, it was just an accident.'

Sunday, 28 October 2007, 2:43 a.m.

Selly Oak

'Hello?' Hannah says, her mouth feeling like cotton wool. The living room is almost dark, the only light coming indirectly from the kitchen and the hallway, and she's not wearing her glasses or contact lenses, so has to squint just to see anything. 'Iz, is that you? Chelsea? What's going on?'

She steps off the bottom stair and into the living room. Someone has stood up from the sofa but hasn't moved or said anything, like whoever they are is playing musical statues and the music's just stopped. Hannah's heart is beating at her chest now, all tiredness gone. That isn't Izzy. And it's not Chelsea. She wants to scream for help but when she opens her mouth again, no sound comes out and she watches, desperate, as the figure turns, leaps over the coffee table, down the hallway and crashes open the front door. Her heart is beating so fast she can barely think, and she follows them to the front door, limbs and hands shaking as she stands on the threshold and watches whoever it was pelt down the street in the direction of the Bristol Road.

Should she call the police? She looks back down the hallway and realizes that there's still someone on the sofa, but there's something about their hair, or the way they're lying, that makes her think it's Izzy. But before she can go and check on her – she looks completely out of it, she might have to carry her to her bed – someone steps out of the shadows of the street and Hannah yelps.

'Who was that?' they ask, and Hannah peers a little closer, heart starting to slow down as she realizes who it is. Charlie.

'Charlie. Thank God you're here. I think someone was about to rob us.'

'Who was that?' Charlie asks again.

'I don't know, I didn't get a good look. But I think they might've done something to Izzy.'

'To Izzy?'

Hannah doesn't know how to explain, so she motions into the house, and Charlie follows her, shutting the front door behind him.

Once she gets to the sofa, she crouches down next to her friend and shakes her shoulder, but Izzy feels like solid jelly in her hand, like a dead fish. She remembers that night at Snobs just before the Easter holidays. 'I think she might have been drugged.'

'Why aren't there any bloody lights on in here?' Charlie asks, coming into the room, 'I can't see a thing. What's going on with Izzy?'

'There's something wrong with her, I think she's drugged.'

'Drugged?' Charlie says. 'What do you mean, what did you guys take?'

'No, I mean I don't know. But I think someone has drugged her.' Hannah looks at Izzy again. There's no way she got home from the Factory in this state, is there?

Even in the half-light of the unlit living room, Hannah can see Charlie roll his eyes, 'Really?'

'Yes, look at her, Charlie,' Hannah gestures towards where his half-sister is collapsed on the sofa, completely unaware of her surroundings, 'she's practically catatonic.'

'Right. Well, what do we do about it? Shall we call an ambulance?'

'I don't know,' Hannah chews on her bottom lip. 'The last time she was drugged, Chelsea just stayed up with her all night and made sure she was okay.'

'The last time? Christ, what's been going on up here?'

Hannah's cheeks warm and she turns back towards her friend, 'Could you help me get her to bed? I don't want her to wake up on the sofa and wonder what's going on and where she is.'

'Sure. Fine,' Charlie says.

'I'm going to get her a bucket and some water,' Hannah says, remembering Chelsea's orders after Snobs. She has no idea if this is the right thing to do, but it seemed to work last time, and it's all she can think of.

In the kitchen, she looks under the sink for a bucket, but it turns out they don't have one, so she gets the bin from the bathroom and empties it into the larger one in the kitchen, before rinsing it out and filling a glass up with water. Back in the living room, Charlie has his arm around Izzy and is leading her towards the stairs, limp as a ragdoll and just as unanimated.

'No,' Hannah cries, going towards them, 'not up there, her bedroom's down here.'

'Down here?' Charlie grunts, stepping backwards, the deadweight of Izzy's body making him stumble as he does so. He tries to correct himself, but the smooth leather soles of his shoes slip on the rug and slide across the laminate, and with the weight of Izzy in his arms, he begins to fall precipitously backwards. Hannah drops the plastic bin and it clatters to the floor, but she keeps hold of the glass of water in her right hand, not knowing what else to do with it, and immediately

411

grabs on to Charlie's back to try and steady him, but he's already let go of Izzy and as Hannah helps him to stand upright, the other girl drops through the air like a stone falling through water. Izzy doesn't make a sound as it happens, doesn't appear to be cognizant at all, but Hannah swears she can hear her body falling through the air, a slow, juddering sound like a misfiring motor that she's surely imagining, but which only gets worse when Izzy's head strikes the corner of the coffee table with a sickening, stomach-plummeting *thunk*.

'What happened then, Hannah?' Chelsea asks.

But Hannah has gone silent, shakes her head, 'I don't know,' she whispers.

'You don't know?'

'I . . . I don't know.'

'What did Charlie do?'

'I can't tell you, it's not my story to tell.'

'Not your story to tell?' Chelsea roars. 'You forced me to live a story that wasn't mine for fifteen years, and now you don't even have the decency to tell me how it ends? Look at me, Hannah. Look at me!' Chelsea had dropped Hannah's arm as she spoke, but she grabs her again now, pulling her closer, close enough to see that her face is red and blotchy, all her finely applied make-up wiped away, streaked with tears. But all Chelsea sees is someone with no idea of what she's done, who cannot even fathom the extent of the consequences of her actions.

'I'm sorry, Chelsea,' Hannah says, still whispering, 'it all got so out of control so quickly. When I got into that car, I still thought she might be alive, I really did.'

'What car?'

'Charlie . . . he got me a car, and a hotel room –'

'A hotel room?'

'Yes,' she says, still whispering, her voice a waver in the

roar of the wind, 'it was . . . it was somewhere in town, I can't remember.'

'But your parents, they corroborated your alibi, didn't they? They knew you weren't with them that night.'

Hannah is silent, lip and chin trembling, tears tracking down her face. 'I . . . they . . . I asked them to lie for me.'

'*What?*'

'I . . .' she takes a deep breath, looks away from Chelsea for a second, 'I told them I'd been at the house but hadn't heard anything, and then in the morning I went to the library and didn't know anything until you called me, telling me what had happened.'

'And they offered to lie for you?'

'I . . . my dad, he knew it would look bad, that I was there during the night and didn't see or do anything –'

'Because that's so clearly impossible and untrue.'

Hannah blanches even further, swallows, 'So, he came to Birmingham and we decided he'd just say I'd been at home with them.'

'So your whole family knows?'

'Chelsea, please don't be angry at them –'

'Oh, believe me, they're pretty far down the list.'

'You have to understand, I was so scared, I had no idea what was going on. I just trusted my dad and trusted Charlie. I didn't know what was going on until it was too late. I never, ever thought you'd get convicted.'

'Hannah, you've had fifteen years to tell the truth. You could have ended the nightmare I was living with just a single sentence. Why the fuck didn't you do anything or say anything?'

'I don't know, Chelsea, I don't know,' her face is pleading

now, still turned up towards Chelsea, a supplicant begging for mercy, 'it all just felt so out of my control. I just ... I allowed myself to go along with whatever Charlie did or said, because I ... I didn't know what else to do. I was scared.'

'Were you scared when you started sleeping with him? Living with him? Got engaged to him?' Chelsea snarls.

'Chels,' Ayesha says warningly, but Chelsea doesn't care; she can't stand to hear Hannah talk about not having any control when she's the one who's known the whole story all along.

'It wasn't on purpose,' Hannah says, tears crawling down her cheeks, 'it was an accident. He never would have hurt her on purpose.'

'Maybe not. But everything else he did afterwards was.'

'That's enough,' a voice suddenly cuts in, 'you can stop torturing my fiancée now.'

Charlie is standing, champagne glass in hand, in the open doorway, sliding it shut behind him as he steps out on to the terrace. At some point in the evening he must have removed his suit jacket, and as he comes towards them, watery dots begin to appear on the white material of his shirt as the rain starts up again in earnest.

'Please take your hands off my fiancée.' He takes a sip of his champagne, his smooth, unthinking confidence and constant use of the word 'fiancée', rather than calling Hannah by her name, pushing Chelsea to the brink. She takes a step towards him, and he holds a hand up as if to say *stop*. 'Think for a second, Chelsea. I could have you packed off back to prison in a heartbeat. Do you really think I don't have the name and number of your parole officer? What do you think she'd have to say about you making an appearance at my engagement party?'

Chelsea hasn't given a second thought to Kate, or indeed to Nikki, since she met Camille at the hotel and saw that hot-pink phone in her hand. And she can't stop to worry about her now, either. Who cares about probation and protocol when the truth is finally, at long last, about to come out? Rain is pouring down her face and neck, dripping down the back of her collar, plastering her hair to her head, but she couldn't care less. She reaches for Charlie's champagne glass, the move surprising him enough to disarm him, and smashes it to the floor. It shatters immediately, splinters of glass and a puddle of champagne glittering in the light that pours through the apartment windows. Hannah yelps and Ayesha says Chelsea's name, the plea to stop written in her voice. But Charlie doesn't make a sound.

'Camille found the phone, Charlie,' Chelsea says, 'Izzy's phone. And I know Hannah was there; she's told us you were, too. You don't get to hide behind all this,' she raises her arms to take in his penthouse, his rooftop terrace, all of London, 'any more. It's over.'

There is a beat, filled with the pounding sound of a train passing by and pulling into Blackfriars. 'That all may be true, Chelsea, but who's going to believe you? Wasn't that always the problem you came up against, after all? That no one ever believed you?'

'Charlie,' Hannah says, his name coming out almost as a whimper, 'please.' His eyes meet hers and something passes between them, his mask slipping just a little as something real gets in and something real slips out.

But then, 'No. As far as the world is concerned, you killed my sister, Chelsea, and you paid for that crime, and that's the way it's going to stay. There's nothing you can do. It's done.'

'It's done? It's *done*?' Chelsea takes a step towards him. Her mouth is bone-dry, blood thrumming in her ears so loudly she can't hear anything else. She opens her mouth to continue, but no words come out. Instead, she swoops down to the ground and picks up the stem of Charlie's broken champagne glass, its end jagged, sharp as a knife. Lethal. It's slippery from the rain, but she grips it tight, raises it towards Charlie.

'Chelsea, no,' Ayesha says from behind her. But Chelsea can't hear her. Can't hear Hannah scream. She is deaf to everything but Charlie's claim that it's over. Done. It will never be over, not for Chelsea. She may be out, but every time she closes her eyes, she is back in prison. Every time she contemplates the future, she is forced to think about the past. All that time she's lost, everything and everyone she's had taken away from her.

She steps towards him again, raindrops hitting the jagged stem like tiny jewels. From this close, she can hear his hitched breathing. 'Very good, Chelsea. Keep going,' he practically whispers, 'we'll have you back in prison in no time.'

She wants to scream but doesn't. She swings her arm, directing the stem towards Charlie's neck, but he towers over her and is far too fast. His hand grabs her wrist, clenching around her as he drives her arm up and behind her, twisting in its socket. She lets out a strangled yell and his jaw clenches, his eyes narrowing as he pushes her back,

417

back, back towards the roof terrace's balustrade until she is up against it, her spine curving over it, her head hanging over the side.

Around them, Ayesha and Hannah are screaming, shouting, rain still pounding down, but Chelsea can't hear anything but Charlie's ragged breath, can't see anything but his face, red and taut, his eyes dark. His right hand is still holding on to her wrist, her arm straight up in the air with the champagne glass stem still gleaming, like a flesh and blood statue of liberty, but with Chelsea hanging over the side, going nowhere. Charlie uses his other hand to pull the broken stem from her grip, tiny red drops of blood popping up immediately as it pierces her skin. He throws it over her head to the ground far, far beneath them. She doesn't hear it land, but in her mind's eye she sees it shatter and break, just as Charlie wants her to. She pushes back, grunting as she tries to heave him off her. There's movement just behind him, Ayesha and Hannah both pulling at his shirt sleeves, but Charlie is six foot three, could hold them off all day.

There's a wail in the distance, the pitch of a siren, but Chelsea doesn't stop to hope it might have anything to do with them. This is London, there's always an emergency somewhere. She has forgotten about the apartment full of people behind them, has forgotten that they are on a stage, so when someone shouts 'Enough!', their voice piercing the air, puncturing the scene, Chelsea's heart stutters in surprise. There is Camille, suddenly, standing on the terrace, rain battering her black dress. In her monochrome outfit, she's barely even an outline in the sooty air, but there's a spot of bright, Barbie pink in her hand, a beacon in the dark. Chelsea feels Charlie notice it, react to it; he loosens his grip, pulls away from her and Chelsea breathes out, thinks she might be able to slip free of him, but in a flash his hand flexes around her wrist again, holding tighter than before, and his other goes to her neck, shoves her back into position, her head dangling over the precipice.

'Charlie!' Camille's voice comes almost as a command. 'Charlie! The police are on their way. You should let her go.'

But Charlie doesn't. Won't. His face leers over Chelsea's, lips pulled back in a grimace, eyes narrow and focused. In the freezing air, his breath is hot against her face, smells as sweet as toasted almonds. She closes her eyes, hears his juddering breathing, feels his chest move in and out, up and down. She thinks of Izzy, drugged and falling to the floor. She sees the blood in her matted hair, on her turquoise pillowcase, feels her skin cold beneath her fingertips, smells that copper, old penny tang, tastes it on her tongue, in her mouth. Charlie's hand tightens on her neck. Is she still breathing?

There's shouting but it's distant, so distant.

There are sirens but who is coming to save her now, when no one has ever come to save her before?

She tries to take a breath. It's now or never.

Sunday, 28 October 2007, 3:06 a.m.

Selly Oak

Hannah lets out a short scream, but Charlie barely hears it as he stands over the motionless body of his little sister. Her legs are collapsed at odd angles beneath her and her head – which is bleeding – lolls on the rug, eyes closed as if asleep. For a second, he thinks he might throw up, but instead he suddenly tunes into Hannah, as if he's been searching through static on a radio but the right station is now coming through. She moans Izzy's name and steps towards her, but when she's about to lean down and reach out to touch her neck, Charlie snaps into action, pulling her back with such force that Hannah cries out, 'What are you doing?'

'You can't touch her.'

'What are you talking about? We need to make sure she's okay. Izzy, Iz,' she calls, crouching down over Izzy's body, 'Izzy, can you wake up?'

But Charlie can already tell Izzy's not going to wake up. 'Hannah,' he says sharply, wrenching at her arm to drag her back up to standing, 'Hannah, I need you to stand back and be quiet so I can think.'

'No, we have to call an ambulance … Charlie, she needs help.'

Charlie shakes his head. He needs to engage his brain, slot into management mode, but his mind teems and surges with panic, thoughts and worries pinging from neuron to neuron, never finding quite the right resting place, not helping him at all. Goddammit, why can't it just stop, for once, this incessant, going-nowhere panic. He takes a huge, deep breath, closes his eyes and tries to pretend there's no one else in the room with him. Not Hannah, and certainly not Izzy.

He has to get rid of Hannah.

'Hannah,' he says, opening his eyes, 'I think you should go and stay somewhere else for the rest of the night. Can you go home?'

'I am home.'

Charlies shuts his eyes for half a second again, 'To your parents' house.'

'I – I can't, it's miles away.'

'Okay. Where's Ayesha? Is Ayesha with Chelsea?' Hannah shakes her head. 'What about another friend? A boyfriend?' but Hannah just stares blankly back at him. That wouldn't work, anyway; she needs to be out of the way, but turning up somewhere in the middle of the night like this – any friend or boyfriend would start asking questions.

'Okay, here's what we're going to do. I'm going to get you a room in a hotel, and you're not going to tell anyone you were here tonight, okay?'

'Why?' Hannah whispers.

'Because I don't want you to go to prison, and I certainly don't want to go to prison.'

'But she – she's not –'

'I'm afraid she is, Hannah.'

'No ... no, no, no –'

Charlie grabs Hannah's shoulders and then loosens his grip as soon as he sees her flinch, 'Hannah, I'm sorry, I'm very, very sorry, this is a horrific accident, but I have to clean it up, and you have to help me by doing exactly what I say, okay? I know it's not fair, and I know you're in shock right now, but do as I tell you and everything will be all right.'

'But Izzy ...'

'I know,' Charlie says, swallowing deeply. He has almost forgotten what lies at his feet, but not quite, and as he blinks into Hannah's pale, strained face, tears fill his eyes. 'I know, but we have to stay strong and be smart right now. Can you do that for me?'

Hannah's lip and chin tremble but she nods and Charlie nods back at her, pulling her into a swift, tight hug before letting her go. 'Okay, now are you absolutely sure you don't know who that was, running out of here earlier?'

'No,' she says softly, 'I didn't see his face.'

'Dammit.'

'Why?' Hannah has started to shiver and Charlie wants to put his coat around her shoulders, but he can't risk mislaying anything, not tonight.

'It doesn't matter, it would just be helpful to know.' What he doesn't say is that it would be helpful to know so that they could pin all this on him. 'Just go into the hallway. I have to make a call, okay?'

Hannah does as she's told, and he pulls out his BlackBerry, searching for hotels in Birmingham on the web browser before calling the DoubleTree. Next, he goes into the hallway and asks Hannah to lend him her house keys. If she questions this, she doesn't say so, just digs into the pocket of a coat hanging on a wall hook and passes them to him silently. 'Okay, let's go,' he says, opening the front door to the bitter night, and pulling it closed behind him.

Up the hill a little, he finds his car and driver and opens the back door for Hannah to get in. He tells the driver to take her to the hotel, and then to come back here and wait for him. The driver nods, but when Charlie looks at Hannah, he can see every fear, worry and question she has written all over her face.

'Just try and get some sleep, okay?' he says as gently as possible. 'I'll call you in the morning.'

Back in the house, he pulls on his leather gloves, closes the front door as quietly as possible and leans against it, trying to think. He doesn't know where Chelsea is, but he surely doesn't have much time before she gets home – she could arrive at any moment, could, in fact, be on her way home right now. He takes a deep breath, and walks back into the living room, pushing the door to Izzy's room as he goes, so that it's open, waiting for him. Standing over her, Charlie breathes in and out very slowly, trying to calm his mind, to think all this through. His heart is pounding at his chest and his brain is going a mile a minute, telling him he can use this to his advantage, just as long as he's absolutely nowhere near it. He swallows down the taste of vomit that has just launched itself up his throat and tries to look down at the body as though it weren't his sister. Izzy is no more. He blinks, and a tear leaks out of the side of one of his eyes. Izzy is no more, but there are ways he can make her legacy last for ever. Ways he can make that legacy work for him. With Izzy out of the way – and he never wanted this, he never would've wished for it to happen this way, all he wanted was a signature, just one fucking signature and look what's happened – with Izzy out of the way, all her shares will naturally become his, and in due course, he can sell the company for a price that is right.

He takes another big breath. He's feeling steadier, his breath is steady once more, he's shed a tear, but if anyone were to see him now, they wouldn't know he'd been crying. But he needs to move fast. As he leans down to pick up his sister, he tries to forget what or who she is, tries to empty his mind of everything so that as he lifts her up and carries her like a baby, she could be anyone, be anything. She is remarkably heavy, though, and he has to be careful not to allow her head or feet to sway and hit any part of the walls or doors. He doesn't want to leave any unnecessary marks. In her room, he pulls back the duvet and places her as carefully as possible in the bed, taking off her slippers and rolling her to the other side of the bed, so that she's as far away from the door as possible. Then, he arranges her so her back is to the door, goes into the living room, picks up a marble table lamp that sits on a side table, returns to his sister's bedroom and cracks one of its sharp corners into her already caved in skull. He tries not to notice how it sinks beneath his gloved hands or the way it sounds like someone trying to breathe through blood, or that the word 'bludgeon' is almost onomatopoeic. He tries not to think of anything. He has to make sure he is as far away from this as possible; Camille knows about the shares, of course, and now he's mentioned it to Doyle too and what is that but motive? He strikes her head a few more times, breathing heavily, bile rising in his mouth, and then stops, panting at the effort. Outside, he walks quickly down the road for a while and throws the lamp into a bin in someone's front garden before running back towards the house and closing the door behind him again. Walking past Izzy's room, he closes that door without looking in at her, and goes into the living room, where he has to decide what to do with the coffee table and

425

rug. Under the sink he finds a roll of black bin bags and some-how manages to wrestle the table into two of them, rolling the rug up and dropping it in with the table, and taping it up like a giant present.

He takes a deep breath and seems to return to his body. His eyes pull towards where Izzy previously lay and he feels his body begin to shake and weaken. No. He can't fall apart just yet. Everything will be okay. Everything is slotting into place. At the front door, he leans out to see if the driver has returned, the flash of the Mercedes' rear lights indicating yes, so he picks up the cumbersome black bag and edges out of the house, pulling the door closed and locking it behind him. The driver must see the bulk of the black bag in his arms because the boot silently pops open for him and he shoves it inside, closing it with a bang. In the back seat of the car, he breathes a sigh of relief, leaning his head back in exhaustion as the driver asks, 'Back to London?'

'No – ah, fuck. Sorry, mate, I need to go back for something.'

He runs back to the house, unlocks the front door and goes into Izzy's room, trying not to look at her. He needs her phone. Where is it? Then he remembers seeing a handbag in the living room, slumped against the bottom of one of the sofas, and, yes, there it is, Izzy's Barbie-pink Motorola RAZR. He turns it off, slipping it into his coat pocket, and leaves the house, he hopes for the last time. In the car he asks the driver to take him back to the DoubleTree, where he'll leave Han-nah's keys at the front desk, just as another car turns up the road from the bottom of the hill. He watches as it stops by the house and someone gets out. As she turns back briefly to shut the door behind her, Charlie immediately recognizes Chelsea. Perfect timing. He may not be able to pin this on whoever that running man was, but something tells him Chelsea could well be the perfect fall girl. There was always something a little off about her anyway. He tells the driver to go and the man nods silently back at him. He'll have to give him an almighty tip, but Charlie's good for it. So, DoubleTree, then Cornwall, then London. It'll be a long time 'til he gets home, but he tells himself he's almost there.

Epilogue

'Welcome to the first episode of *Everything But the Truth*, hosted by me, Natalie Ajala. In this season, we'll be diving deep into the newly reopened case of murdered heiress Isabella Dunwoody, who died in October 2007 at the age of twenty-one. As one of the investigating officers in the original case, which saw Chelsea Keough wrongfully convicted of her murder and imprisoned for fourteen years, this story is a personal one for me, and goes to the heart of police corruption, family dysfunction, and what happens when everyone's looking for the easiest answer.

'During this season, we'll interview members of Isabella's – or Izzy as she was more commonly known – family, her friends, university lecturers, and yes, even Chelsea Keough, as we try to find out just how one rich and powerful figure was able to manipulate a police force, in order to cover up a tragic accident, and get everything he wanted in the process.'

Chelsea presses pause and pulls out her earphones. She knows how the rest of this episode goes; hell, she knows how the rest of the entire season goes. She's out of breath and her thighs are screaming in agony, but she's finally made it up the mountain behind her aunt's house. She's looked out at it almost every day since Charlie confessed, and told herself she needs to get up it, to see the world from a new perspective, and now, finally, almost six months later, she's made it. This still doesn't feel like her world, her home, her view. But looking around her, spinning in place, so she can get the full 360-degree view, she is happy to be here. And to be happy about anything feels like an important step. She's not sure how much longer she'll stay in Scotland; it has been good to retreat here, to try and stay out of the media glare as much as possible, and spend time with Nikki, but she can feel her time coming to an end. She's anxious about what moving back to London might look like, but she can't imagine living anywhere else, and what she wants, more than anything, is to finally go home.

She's still out of breath, so she perches on a well-placed boulder and tries to get her heart rate down. At least she doesn't have vertigo any more. She's faced harder things than heights, after all. She takes a photo of the view with her phone, sends it to Ayesha, smiling at her response. She switches over to Spotify, thinks about pressing play on the episode again – she knows how much work Ajala has put into it, and is grateful that the public will finally be able to hear her side of the story, and get the full truth of what happened that night. But she also lived it, and maybe that's enough. Maybe she doesn't have to re-live it.

Ajala has even interviewed Hannah, which Chelsea is interested to hear, but that won't come until later in the season. She still can't believe everything Hannah did and agreed to. She may not have killed Izzy, but her lies ever since then mean that she may as well have. When she was standing, tear-stained, in front of Chelsea on her rooftop terrace, Chelsea could believe that Hannah felt bad for what she'd done, that she felt guilty, but to never have done anything about it made that guilt worthless. There was a part of Chelsea that hoped that guilt ate away at Hannah, that it left its mark, but the fact that she had waited for Chelsea's sentence to end, for her to figure it out and confront her, to admit to her part in Izzy's death and everything that followed, meant that, at the very least, Chelsea could never forgive her. Ajala had even managed to get out of her that she was the one sending Chelsea all those messages on Facebook. She told Natalie that she'd been trying to warn Chelsea away, to try and keep her from getting too close to Camille and Charlie, because she had been worried about the lengths Charlie would potentially go to in order to protect their secret, but Chelsea can't see the supposed altruism in this fact. Only the self-protection. Charlie, meanwhile, has yet to admit to sending Chelsea the text messages, but she's sure it was him. Who else would it be, after all? It wouldn't have been all that difficult for him to get Chelsea's number from Camille's own phone, and there was something about the way he'd threatened Chelsea with going back to prison when they were out on that rain-soaked roof terrace that was an echo of those threatening texts. She doesn't need his confirmation to know it was him – as far as Chelsea's concerned, he's already given himself away.

Nikki has tried to counsel forgiveness, as has her new therapist, and even Kate McClure, her parole officer, all saying that she'll need to let go of all this, in order to finally move on. But Hannah and Charlie have so far only spent six months in custody, compared to her fourteen years, so she can't move on quite yet. Both have been charged with perjury and perverting the course of justice, while Charlie has also been charged with falsifying evidence, bribery and manslaughter. Chelsea had been furious when she first heard Charlie was being charged with manslaughter rather than murder, but because both he and Hannah now claimed that Izzy's death was accidental, Ajala explained that manslaughter was a more likely conviction than murder. Even a manslaughter charge will be tricky and might not stick when it comes to the eventual trial because the evidence had been so tampered with and corrupted, a jury might be hesitant to convict, and the Crown Prosecution Service will be fighting against their previous conviction of Chelsea. So no, they're not even close to being forgiven.

The sun is watery, and she closes her eyes against it as it warms her face and arms, allows herself to appreciate this, just being out here, in all this land on her own. Charlie has told the police that he'd paid off the driver and then had interfered in the investigation, bribing both Detective Rob Bailey and the head of the Scene of Crime unit to look the other way, should they find any evidence that placed him there, as well as the medical examiner, whom he paid off for excluding the Rohypnol in Izzy's system from the toxicology report, thinking it might muddy the waters and confuse jurors if it was reported. In every situation, he had steered them towards Chelsea, but in her mind, he still hasn't really explained why. Was all this really just a case of wrong place, wrong time? If Ayesha had showed up that night, would he have pinned it all on her instead? What about Hannah? If she'd been dropped off by her dad just a few hours later, would Charlie have seen her and decided his future wife was the ideal scapegoat?

Chelsea can't let herself chase down these other possibilities; she's spent her life wandering down avenues of 'what if?' and all she wants now is a semblance of certainty. But it's so hard not to get distracted by how differently everything could have gone, if only, if only, if only.

At her trial, the piece of evidence that had secured her conviction was, of course, the table lamp. Deposited in a neighbour's front garden, it had been found fairly quickly after Izzy's death, and, having lived in their sitting room, had Chelsea's fingerprints all over it. Of course, it also had plenty of other people's fingerprints on it, but because she'd overlooked it being missing when Bailey and Ajala asked her if anything was out of place that day she found Izzy, it only served to make her appear even more guilty. She takes a deep breath now, filling her lungs, and opens her eyes to the scene. It is nice here, she'll give her aunt that.

She wonders if she'll ever stop thinking about what Charlie and Hannah did, how they twisted everything to work in their favour, sentencing her to a life that wasn't hers. Charlie had seen her arrive back at the house, and decided then and there that he could use this to his advantage, discarding her and throwing her to the wolves like a Roman emperor. Thumb up, thumb down, who lives and who dies? He'd decided in that moment that his reputation, and his controlling share of his company, not to mention close to a billion pounds, was more important than her freedom. And Hannah, sweet, yielding Hannah. What had she done? Absolutely nothing as one of her best friends was wrongly accused of and then convicted for murder. The view starts to waver in front of Chelsea and she has to take another deep breath, to steady herself. Then she opens her mouth and lets out a body-deep yell that roars down the mountain and soars through the valley below. Maybe no one can hear her, but it's the most alive she's felt in fifteen years.

Acknowledgements

I wouldn't have written this book if it wasn't for my time spent at the University of Birmingham. I've attended four universities, and Birmingham is still the one I look back on with the fondest memories and which has had the longest lasting impact on me as a person, but also as a student and a writer – it was, in fact, the first time I realised I really could write.

In writing this book, I also realised that I have no idea what the uni experience looks like for undergrads these days, and I have the saddest feeling that it doesn't look much like the one I had, one that was as much about finding your feet as a person, having a great time, rotting in front of the TV, and spending nights out – and the hangovers that followed – with friends, as it was about getting a decent mark at the end of the year. I have my suspicions that that kind of uni might not even exist anymore – that the double whammy of increased tuition fees and the legacy of Covid means students barely get to enjoy themselves while they're studying. And that's before we even get to lack of funding, a shrinking of the arts, and accessibility. So, this was my way of trying to enshrine a moment in time and pay homage to an experience that helped to make me who I am. And it might seem strange to write an homage to a place and time that I loved so much with a murder at the heart of it, but hey, that's just how my mind works.

So, thank you to Birmingham, and everyone I met there, but most importantly Alicia, Isabel, James, Zoe, Alice, Sophie and Corinne. Thank you also to my dear sister, Ruthie, who was the reason I went there in the first place, and to all your friends from there who became my friends, but most especially JJ. Thank you, Katie, Betty, Shaks, Emily and Fi, and thank you to Caroline in far-off Kansas City.

Thanks, as always, to my parents for their continued and very great support.

And thank you to my agent Emily, editor Grace, and the whole team at MJ who have helped to make this book a book, especially Philippa, my copy-editor Sarah Bance, and everyone else who worked so hard on it.